THE
UNDOING

UNDOING

SHELLY LAURENSTON

𝓀

KENSINGTON BOOKS
www.kensingtonbooks.com

THE
UNDOING

PROLOGUE

He packed more dirt on her body.

She felt it now. Felt the dirt falling against her face, her arms and legs. He was trying to wipe away all evidence of her. Pretend she didn't exist. Pretend she'd never existed.

He'd like that.

She breathed and dirt went up her nose. She began to panic. Then she remembered the words.

The words the veiled woman had spoken to her. Her voice had been strong, confident. She'd called herself Skuld and she'd offered her something no one ever had before.

"You'll be my vengeance. You'll be my rage. It's in you and now . . . now you can let it out. Release it. Revel in it. Drown yourself in it."

Could she? She'd allowed her rage to come out once before . . . and now she was in her grave. Her husband piling dirt on her. Burying her. Burying the truth.

Her truth.

No. She wouldn't let him do that. She'd never let him get away with that. She'd told him to back off just once and this was what he did. He killed her.

But Skuld was giving her more than just a second chance. She knew that as the rage flowed through her like wine. Through her bloodstream, into her muscles.

She pulsated with life and hatred.

So. Much. Hatred.

She couldn't wait to unleash it upon the world.

But first . . . him.

The dirt was packed tight, but she was stronger now. No longer the weak thing he kept weaker with bizarre diets and restrictions on when she could eat. Strength pounded throughout her body and she used that strength to force her fists through the dirt he'd packed on top of her. As she moved up, pushing her way through, she could hear voices. He was no longer alone.

Orders were given. "Drop the shovel! Hands above your head! Do it now!"

The police.

She didn't care.

Her hands broke through the dirt, and she took a moment to stretch her fingers before she pressed them against the ground and pulled the rest of her body out.

As she cleared the earth, one of the officers, gun held out in front of him, leaned over and with wide eyes watched.

So shocked, he didn't say a word, even as she launched herself out of her grave and at her husband's back, wrapping her arms around his shoulders, legs, and around his waist.

Opening her mouth wide, she bit down on the side of his neck, tearing through flesh and muscle into the veins below.

He screamed, spinning in circles, hands reaching back, trying desperately to pry her off. But she wouldn't let go. Not until he was dead. She wanted him dead.

"Get her off me!" he begged the officers. "Dear God! Get her off!"

Some of the police began to laugh, until they saw the blood stream down her husband's shoulder and chest.

More hands reached for her, trying to pull her off. They could do nothing. She was too strong.

At least she was until the officers were pushed away by one man and big hands grabbed her around the waist, yanking her away.

"Jesus!" someone screamed when a good chunk of her husband's neck went with her. She spit it out, along with blood and saliva, snarling like a wild animal as she struggled to get back to him. To finish him off.

Her husband dropped to the ground, hand over his wound, eyes locked on her. They both knew that he'd killed her . . . and yet she lived. *Despite him* she lived.

"*I'll kill you for what you did!*" she screamed. "*I'll kill you! I'll kill you! I'll kill you!*"

She just kept screaming that last phrase over and over again. She couldn't stop herself.

The big hands around her waist quickly carried her out, around the house, and over to a black SUV. He shifted her into one arm and used his free hand to open the back door. He put her inside, hand on her chest to keep her pinned to the seat.

Then he spoke to her. Not in English but in a language that sounded distantly familiar. He just kept saying the same thing over and over. She still didn't understand him, but the voice and the sound of the words moved through her until the rage dissipated.

When she finally calmed down, he stared at her for a long moment, studying her. And she studied him right back. Blond hair. Blue eyes. Big. Nordic.

He glanced back at the other officers coming toward them.

"Just be calm," he ordered her. "I'll get you where you need to go, but you need to calm down."

He stood straight, releasing her, watched her a second more until he finally shook his big head.

"I fucking hate dealing with new Crows," he complained. "Hate it."

CHAPTER ONE

When he touched her knee again, Jace Berisha gritted her teeth and forced a smile.

Keep it together, she told herself. *You can do this.*

Although she really didn't *want* to do this. She didn't want to be in this temporarily closed Santa Monica club haggling over gods-blessed trinkets. She wanted to be back at the Bird House, reading . . . something. Anything. But, sadly, she was the one among the Los Angeles Crow Clan who could speak Russian as well as a whole host of other Slavic and romance languages and some that were neither of those. A skill that had one time served a very different purpose. But it had been her key. The key to getting her out of her First Life and—happily—into her Second. True, she'd had to die for that to happen. At the hands of her bastard ex-husband.

But it was a price she'd pay again to be here.

So although undercover work was not really her forte, she'd do it for the women she called sisters and the goddess who'd given her so much. Because she chose. Something she was told never to do.

She'd just have to find a way to keep her now-infamous temper in check.

Because she wasn't just a Crow. She was a Berserker Crow. A Crow whose rage was used during battles to terrify and destroy, not necessarily in that order.

Jace wished she saw her role as Berserker Crow as some sort of curse, but she didn't. She enjoyed her rage the way some people enjoyed babies or a gorgeous new sports car.

Still, if only . . . if only she had more control over it. She had a little, but once her rage was really sprung, there was no pulling back until she'd spent it on whoever had set it off in the first place.

A tendency that worked well in the heat of battle but not so much when the Crows were trying something a little different from their usual "get in, kill everybody, get out" work scenarios.

Tonight the Crows were trying negotiating, a skill most of them were only known for in the downtown LA jewelry district.

Usually, when the Crows were called in, it was so they could get back what had been stolen from the gods and kill everyone who'd had anything to do with the theft. And if the blood of an innocent had been spilt . . . let's just say, some of what the Crows had done over the years to avenge that had become legendary.

This time, however, they knew for a fact that those who currently had the Rhine bracelet that belonged to one of the Fates had absolutely no clue what they held. They hadn't used it. Hadn't spilled blood over it. They were simply some club owners who were trying to sell the pretty bracelet to the highest bidder. So it was decided that killing these men would be unnecessary.

Of course, none of the gentlemen they were dealing with were innocent in the big scheme of things, but they weren't pure evil, either.

At least that had been their leader Chloe's belief. Jace, however, knew better. Before she'd been taken away by her mother all those years ago, Jace had grown up around men like this. But she couldn't think about that now. If she did . . .

"So," Tessa tried again, working hard to ignore the male beside her who'd sniffed her neck, "how much for the bracelet?"

"It is expensive," the big Russian said in strained English. His name was Vadim Ekimov, and he ran the docks in San Pedro. The bit of research they'd done on Vadim before heading over here showed that he was a medium-sized gangster, but no better or worse than any of the others. He definitely hadn't earned a Crow attack that neither he, nor his men, would ever recover from. Because if the Crows started going after every minor scumbag who lived in Los Angeles . . . Yeah, well. That would just be a bad idea. "We can't just give it away, my pretty."

Knowing that these idiots had no idea what they were haggling over was beginning to wear on Jace. The man sitting between her and Tessa in the booth, whose hand was steadily moving up Jace's thigh, was wearing on her even more.

"We have money," Tessa promised. "And it's just so gorgeous, Vadim. I must have it."

The hand on Jace's thigh inched up a bit more, and she was seconds from breaking the man's fingers.

"And what will Vadim get for such pretty bracelet?" he asked, leaning forward across the round table, eyes on Tessa.

"My fist up your ass if you don't give us a goddamn price."

The men all looked at Jace. And that's when she realized that she'd not only said that out loud . . . she'd said it in flawless Russian in the men's Southern Russian dialect.

She couldn't have given away her secret any more obviously if she'd put it on a billboard on the I-10 Freeway.

"Ahhh, a sneak, Vadim," one of the men joked, still not taking any of the women seriously. "They brought in a pretty little spy."

Tessa leaned back in her seat. "What's going on?" Tessa, an African American born and raised in San Diego, knew Spanish and a little Korean from her time as a nursing student in a hospital in Koreatown, but that was about it. She now had no idea what was being said.

Realizing she'd blown any chance of being subtle here, Jace simply replied, "Just give us the bracelet, Vadim. We'll pay you. Well."

"And how will you pay us, little girl?" Vadim suddenly grabbed her chin and held her.

Tessa was nearly out of her seat when one of the men pressed a gun to the side of her head. She silently sat back down, but her face said everything that was needed. At least to Jace.

These men had just lost their one chance not to end up as "bird feed," as the other clans called it.

"I don't like to be touched, Vadim Ekimov," Jace warned. "So get your hand off me."

"Or what, little girl? What will you and your brown friend do to me?"

"The question," a voice from the dark corners of the closed club explained, "isn't what she will do." A blade slipped around Vadim's neck and pressed against his jugular. "But what will the rest of us do?"

Vadim immediately released Jace's face and raised his hands.

Jace wiped the spot where he'd touched her. Not because she had a problem with him in particular, just . . . again, she didn't like to be touched.

From the darkness they emerged, easing into the few lights that were still on in the mostly deserted club. Jace's strike team. The girls she fought with, lived for, would die for if it ever became necessary. Her sisters. All Crows were her sisters, but these women . . . they meant everything to her. Always would. She adored them in a way she never said but felt deep down in her bones. In her blood. In the soul that now belonged to Skuld until Ragnarok came. Because she chose. A choice she'd happily make again and again.

Kera Watson, the last to join their team, but the most naturally protective of any of the Crows, reached over the booth back, slipped her hands under Jace's arms, and lifted her up, out, and away from Vadim and his hands-y friends.

"You all right?" Kera asked, quickly releasing Jace.

Kera was a former Marine and she knew people. Understood them in a way the rest of the Crows didn't really bother to do. One of the first things she'd learned about her team was their personal foibles. She knew Jace didn't like to be touched and she knew she didn't like to sit close to people. So Kera had made sure to get her friend out of that situation as soon as she could. That was Kera. The full-time "fixer" of the group.

Jace nodded her thanks before addressing Vadim again.

"Give us the bracelet," she said in English so that everyone could understand. "This can all be over if you hand over the bracelet."

Vadim turned a bit to look at her, shrewd eyes sizing her and the others up. "Why is bracelet so important to you? Why do you need it?"

Jace shook her head. "Don't haggle, Vadim. Not anymore. You lost that right when you pulled guns on us. Just give us the bracelet."

"Fine. We want a million for it. In Euros."

Jace let out a sigh. Men. Always so difficult.

The Crows laughed at that, which the Russians didn't seem to appreciate. But Vadim was being ridiculous.

"No," Tessa finally said. "You can have fifty grand. In American dollars. And you'll be damn happy with that."

"Fifty grand?"

"Fifty grand," she said again. "And we all go away. Wouldn't that be nice? Everyone getting out of this unscathed? Because trust me," Tessa promised, grinning, "you *will be* scathed if you don't let this go."

"I have better idea—" he began, but Jace let out a loud sigh that had Vadim looking at her again.

"Problem?"

Jace nodded. She didn't want to talk anymore. She was tired of talking.

"You see," Erin explained for her, "you're probably about to say something really sexual and disgusting, and she's going to get really pissed and you won't like that. We will," she added. "But you won't. So just give us the fucking bracelet."

Vadim glanced at his men and, finally, he agreed. "We will give you bracelet. If you have money now."

"We have the money," Alessandra Esparza promised, slapping a briefcase on the table and opening it. One of the men quickly looked through the stacks of bills before nodding at Vadim.

"Come." He stood, and Erin pulled back the blade she'd had against his neck. The standard Crow weapon given to each of them almost from their first day. Made of the finest steel, it was a thin blade that could tear through either major arteries or hard bone without much effort. The Crows were taught to fight with one in each hand, but if they ever lost one during a fight that was not a problem. They also had talons that could tear through flesh and bone just as easily. Why they had both, Jace didn't know, but she also didn't mind. Sometimes she wasn't in the mood to have blood under her nails.

Together, as one large group, the men with their guns, the women with their blades, all walked to the back of the club and down a long flight of stairs to the basement. All the liquor was down here. They moved through the cases until they reached a back office, where, using a key, Vadim unlocked the door and pushed it open.

And that's where they found them. The door to the walk-in closet–sized safe blasted open. The six men standing around it froze, staring at the Crows as the Crows stared back.

It was the Protectors, a powerful Clan created by the god Tyr after the Crows and Odin's Ravens had wiped out one too many villages for Tyr's very moral tastes.

Tyr had given his human warriors a powerful sense of justice and a "no enemies shall survive!" sense of battle. Just a few Protectors, with their owl-like wings, could silently swoop in and take out entire battalions of Crows and Ravens. In the beginning, they'd had no other purpose, but that had changed when the other Clans began to realize that the Ravens *and* Crows were needed to keep Ragnarok at bay.

At the time, it was easy to accept the Ravens as one of the Official Nine. Chosen by Odin himself, they were all of the finest Viking stock. The Crows however . . .

They were slaves brought to their Scandinavian shores and turned into vengeful warriors with black wings and dark souls by the Fate Skuld herself. She took these women as they were breathing their last, giving them a chance at a second life and to finally have an outlet for their anger after being ripped from their homes and dragged to a foreign land. For centuries, they were not allowed to be part of the Official Nine because everyone assumed that when the raiding and slavery faded away, the Crows would, too.

But they never did. The Crows were as strong now—if not stronger—than they had been "back in the day." Skuld still chose from the dying, and like their small but brilliant avian namesakes, the Crows existed all over the world. Some groups smaller than others. Some in infinitely more danger than others. But they still all worked together to protect the world from it-self. Not an easy job but one they all loved.

They were still human, though. None of the Crows was im-mortal. They were faster, stronger, and more powerful than they had been in their first lives, but they could still die when hit with a well-placed bullet or a knife to an artery. At least now they were promised a place at Odin or Freyja's tables in Asgard. They would fight with all the other warriors when Ragnarok came. That was more than most people had to look forward to in their afterlives.

Still . . . even though the Crows and Protectors were no longer the hard-core enemies they once had been—immediately trying to kill each other without question or consequence—the Crows and Protectors didn't actually trust each other, either. At all.

"What the fuck are you doing here?" Tessa demanded of the men.

"Well, if you must know—" one of the Protectors began, but the Russian snapped in rage.

"Treacherous *bitches*," Vadim snarled.

"Wait," Jace told him quickly, going back to Russian in the hopes of keeping Vadim calm. "We had nothing to do with this. We still have a deal."

"Fuck you and your deals," he growled before jerking back, slamming into Erin, who'd still been behind him with her blade out.

Erin hit the door, momentarily stunned by the large man ramming her.

He reached for the gun he had under his jacket and Jace made a mad grab, pushing the hand and weapon toward the ground. That's when she felt the fingers of Vadim's free hand dig into the back of her head, and before she could stop him, he smashed her face-first into the wall.

Danski "Ski" Eriksen cringed when he saw Jacinda Berisha hit that wall. Watched as the other Crows fell silent, hands dropping to their sides, the expressions on their faces one of hopelessness.

"Why?" the Crows' strike team leader asked. "Why did you do that?"

"What?" the big Russian asked, smirking. "Was she a favorite of yours? Did you take turns licking each other's pussy?"

"Well, this won't end well," Gundo muttered behind Ski. Followed by a sighed, "What an idiot."

"Get the books," Marbjörn Ingolfsson—they mostly just called him "Bear"—ordered his team. "She"—and they all knew who he meant—"is going to burn this place down!"

Before they could follow Bear's orders, they all heard that growl. They'd heard it before. In battles or during particularly nasty Trials, and once at a party when a drunk Valkyrie went to punch the Crow leader and, instead, punched Jace Berisha.

It was a sound that they'd all learned to fear over the last couple of years.

And Bear was right. She would burn this building down and everyone in it.

The Russian stepped back, eyes narrowing as Jace slowly turned to face them all. Blood poured from an open cut on her forehead and her nose appeared a bit . . . smashed. But it was her eyes. They'd gone from a pretty dark blue to a dark blood red. Her talons tore out of her fingers, curling at the tips, and her wings exploded from her back.

The humans backed away; some started to run.

"*What the fuck are you?*" the big Russian screamed.

They'd never get an answer from Jace. Not when she was like this. She could speak. But she never answered questions. Right now, she was trapped in whatever rage-filled vortex slamming her into the wall had set off.

Jace locked on to the Russian, grabbing his tailored jacket with both hands, and yanking him close. She did begin to speak to him, but it was in what Ski guessed was Russian.

Yet even though he couldn't really understand exactly what Jace was saying, Ski knew it wasn't good. The words torn from the back of her throat had her victim's face blanching, his eyes wide in desperate fear.

He tried to pull away from her but she wouldn't let go. Instead, she held on tighter, lifting her legs until they wrapped around his waist. And still those Russian words spewed out of her, her voice getting louder and louder, more and more rough and raw. Her face was now red with rage, her muscles bulging, the veins in her neck and arms throbbing and pulsing.

Then it began. The screaming. That gods-awful screaming.

Jace released the Russian's jacket and slapped her talons against his face, digging them into the flesh and holding him tight. Then, still screaming, she grabbed his nose with her teeth and . . . bit it off.

"Jesus Christ!" Borgsten barked, forgetting his own gods as they all watched her spit the Russian's nose out so she could go for the veins in his neck . . . while still screaming.

That's when the new girl, Kera—who probably still didn't know better—tried to pull Jace away from her victim. Jace held on to the Russian's face with her talons, elbowing her friend, who was desperately trying to get her to let go.

Finally, the one Ski's brothers referred to as the "vicious little redhead"—Erin Amsel—joined in. Together they were able to pull Jace off, and then Kera kept her grip on the berserker while Jace panted like a wild animal, blowing her blood-filled breath out past grinding teeth.

Skuld had turned that quiet, tall, pretty woman with long curly brown hair, deep set blue eyes, and sharp cheekbones into a true berserker. They'd never had any in Ski's bloodline, but he'd heard tales of them at family get-togethers. Especially when they'd traveled to Iceland to see his mother's family or Sweden to see his father's.

Ski wondered what that was like. Having absolutely no control. Allowing your rage to rule your impulses.

Curious, Ski patiently watched Tessa gaze down at the Russian. Most of the man's nose was gone and his face was shredded from Jace's talons. But he wasn't dead. He was screaming and cursing. Both in Russian and English.

After a few seconds, Tessa lifted her gaze and saw that all of the Russian's men had pulled their weapons on her team. One had his gun aimed directly at her forehead. While Tessa stared the man in the eyes, she slowly unfurled her wings. They emerged from her back big, black, and shiny, stretching out nearly five feet.

Shocked, the men stepped away, looking at each other. Making sure they weren't going insane. They didn't understand. They'd never understand.

"So," Tessa softly asked the men. "What are you going to do?"

That's when the shooting began. Bear immediately did a full-body dive toward the boxes they had out while screaming, *"Protect the books!"*

Ski laughed, a few shots whizzing past him and the others, but the Russians weren't aiming for him or his brothers. Or the damn books.

The firing from semi- and not-so-semiautomatic weapons went on for a good two minutes until the men stopped, smoke still rising from the barrels.

They looked around the room until their eyes settled on Ski. He smiled, waved, then pointed and said, "Behind you."

They all spun, shocked to find the Crows behind them, unharmed, and seemingly unconcerned.

Then, grinning, Kera Watson released the still blood-foaming Jace to the ground. She landed in a crouch, head down, but her eyes lifting so she could see her prey. And, with a scream that would rival any Viking of old, she ran at them.

A few got off shots, but she dodged the bullets—not with skill, but with pure adrenaline-based animal instinct—and ripped into the first male she ran into, taking him to the ground as her talons tore him open from bowel to diaphragm and she pulled out his heart.

Horrified, a few of the men gawked down at her, while some just dropped their weapons and tried to make a desperate run for it.

But Annalisa Dinapoli was there to slam the open door closed with a toss of her hand.

"Kill them all," Tessa calmly ordered.

Bear tapped Ski's shoulder. "Books," he reminded Ski. The big man was calmer now. Probably a little embarrassed, too. But they had promised Ormi, the leader of the Southern California Protectors, to retrieve these books and bring them back to their library. How these men had gotten their hands on such important artifacts, Ski didn't know. And he didn't care. Ormi had tried to negotiate with them, but the Russian had played games and, unlike the Crows, Ormi had no patience for that sort of thing.

So he'd sent Bear and his team to retrieve the books and ordered Ski to go along with them.

Ski was second in command. Ormi reported directly to their god, Tyr, himself. Ski reported to Ormi, and everyone else reported to Ski. He'd come along to ensure the books were safe, but Bear was more OCD about the books and their care than Ski could even dream.

Ormi, also knowing about the gold torc the Russians possessed, had worried that something like this would happen. That the Crows would come, and in the ensuing slaughter, the books would be lost forever. So Ormi had attempted to get the books before the Crows came for the bracelet. A gold torc filled with so much magic it could destroy half the continent. If one knew what he or she was doing, of course. Thankfully, the Russians knew nothing about what they really held, but the word was spreading among those who did know. The Crows had no choice but to secure the stupid thing.

Ski would never understand why the gods insisted on imbuing weapons and jewelry with magical powers and then proceeding to *lose* said items. Honestly, how many times had Thor lost that idiotic hammer? How many times had Freyja's ridiculous necklace gone missing? Or Idun's fucking apples been stolen?

And then it was up to one of the clans to go in and retrieve these missing items from the humans who had them . . . only for the damn things to end up lost or stolen again in a few months or years.

Did the gods do that on purpose? He wouldn't put it past any of them. Apparently immortality could get boring.

Ski stepped aside as an arm flew by. An *arm*. Why was the arm separated from the body at all? Why was that necessary? True, it was holding a gun, but that still seemed excessive.

Then again, the Crows were known to be excessive in a lot of ways.

Thankfully Odin's Ravens were not also in attendance. Dumb oxen with no sense of restraint, they would have killed the Russians long ago and torn the entire club apart until they got what they wanted.

But the Crows . . . at least they'd *tried* to keep things low-key. It wasn't their fault the Russians hadn't listened to their instincts. Those instincts must have told them *something*.

Speaking of which . . . the big Russian was trying his best to crawl away as his men dropped all around him. But Jace had not forgotten him. She never would.

She caught hold of his ankle and dragged him back, flipping him over and ignoring what now sounded like begging in Russian. She straddled the man's hips.

Before he might see more, Ski turned away. He'd already seen what Jace Berisha could do when her sanity snapped; he didn't need to watch it again. Yet seconds after he took a step to help the others with the books, his body jerked forward, a burning pain in his left shoulder.

Gundo and Borgsten—two of the brothers he also called friends—leaned over to study the area. Blood poured from the wound, and the three men turned and stared at the one who'd shot him. The man made a small choking sound and they tilted their heads to the side the way an owl might, trying to catch the sound better, but the movement seemed to terrify the man even more, and he yelled to his comrades in Russian. Several ran over, guns raised.

Gundo turned his head until his nose aligned with his spine and called out to his team leader. "Bear?"

"Yeah, yeah," Bear replied, only half-interested as he and the rest of the team carefully packed the books into the wooden crates and began to carry them out the back exit. "But be quick about it."

When Gundo's head swiveled back around, the man and his comrades screamed in panic and began firing . . .

The Russian stopped moving. She hit him a few more times. She needed to be sure he was dead.

She needed him dead. She hadn't done her job if he wasn't dead.

He didn't move so she sat up straight. She still straddled his waist, but his breathing had stopped.

Good. Good. Yes. Good.

She sensed someone behind her and jerked to the side. Bullets raced past. More shots came and she jerked the other way.

She looked over her shoulder so she could target the one who'd tried to kill her, the dead Russian's blood still pouring down her chin.

She couldn't believe someone had shot at her. At her! More rage poured through her and she stood.

Bringing her hands down, she again unleashed her blood-soaked talons, watching with great satisfaction the utter fear in the man's eyes.

Nothing gave her greater joy than seeing the fear in her enemy's eyes. She loved it. She loved it so much that—

Eyes narrowed, her rage now increasing, she watched as the male of another clan silently walked up behind *her* prey. His hand whipped out and he caught hold of the man's neck in the same way an owl would catch its prey with its mighty talons.

Twisting his hands the neck snapped, bones breaking like so much kindling. The Protector made it look easy, but those blunt fingers were as powerful as any edge weapon. As any mallet or hammer.

What did this male think he was doing? That had been *her* prey. Hers and hers alone!

And this . . . *man* thought he could just take it away from her?

Talons still out, she charged the man. Even as she heard the voices of her sister-Crows begging her to stop, screaming, "No, Jace! No!" she kept charging. For him. For vengeance!

She barreled into him like a linebacker, managing to take Ski down. He couldn't believe the power behind that hit. But as they landed on the ground, he lifted his legs, placed them against her hips, and tossed her up and over his head.

He flipped onto his belly at the same time Jace did. They faced each other, both getting to their hands and knees. Jace growling at him. Ski smiled. He couldn't help it. She was so cute when she was drenched in the blood of their mutual enemies. But his smile just seemed to piss her off more.

She started toward him, but that big foot came down on Jace's back, shoving her to the ground and pinning her there. Screaming, she tried to get out from under it, but Bear held her in place with the strength of that one leg and glared at Ski.

"Are you done fooling around?" Bear asked him.

"I didn't know I was."

After finishing off the last of their victims, the Crows abruptly turned at the sound of Jace's screams of rage. They stared down at their friend, then up at Bear.

And then they came at him.

Not to fight. Unlike a still-raging Jace, their bloodlust had been satiated with the human men they'd killed.

Nope. They came at Bear to yell at him. All at once. Like a bunch of squawking birds, their wings bristling, talons pointing.

Ski couldn't even understand what any of them were saying. It was just a big cacophony of female squawking.

"Shut up!" Bear barked, covering the sensitive ears he'd been given by Tyr, and very briefly silencing the women.

"Shut *up*?" Tessa snapped. Then they all started again. Yelling at him. Calling Bear all sorts of names. Alessandra yelled at the poor man in Spanish. Leigh in Japanese. Maeve in Mandarin, which was kind of fascinating since her entire family came from India.

Ski got to his feet, thoroughly entertained by it all.

Due to a very old peace treaty between their Clans, Ski knew the Crows would not physically attack Bear unless he struck first. And he would never strike first when precious books were at risk.

Because if the Crows thought for a second that those books were important to the Protectors, they'd take great pleasure in using their talons to tear each one apart while poor Bear cried over the loss.

Of course, there was some pushing from the Crows, but Bear was six-seven and about three hundred pounds, so their pushing didn't mean much.

But the yelling . . . the poor guy couldn't tolerate all the yelling.

All those Crows screeching at poor Bear at one time . . .

Ears still covered, Bear roared and the Crows immediately backed up, their fighting blades held tight in their hands, ready to strike. Although Ski never understood why they needed the fighting blades when their talons did as much damage. Seemed redundant, in his estimation.

With everyone at a standstill, Ski realized it was the best time to move. Crouching down, he gently gripped Jace by her chin and lifted her head. Her eyes closed, her mouth hanging open, the woman snored.

She'd just run out of rage, and that meant one of two things would follow. Sobbing or sleeping.

He was glad it was sleeping. He'd hate to see her cry again. It had broken his heart a little the last time he'd witnessed it.

"Lift your foot, Bear," Ski ordered.

"But—"

"Do it."

Without a choice—Ski outranked him—Bear lifted that massive foot and Ski carefully pulled Jace out and up until he held her tight in his arms. She snuggled in close, her bloody chin resting against his neck, turning the front of his sleeveless white hoodie a very dark red.

Getting to his feet, Ski carried Jace over to Kera Watson. She was the physically strongest of the Crows—an extra blessing from Skuld, like Jace's apocalyptic rage and Erin Amsel's power over fire—and she easily took the woman from him and placed her friend over her shoulder in a fireman's carry.

Thank you, she mouthed to him. He'd found that the last thing Kera Watson seemed to want to do—ever—was fight. And he appreciated that. It made things much easier.

"The books are stowed," Gundo announced from the back door.

Ski nodded and tapped Bear's arm. "Go."

"Yeah, but—"

"Books aren't safe until they're in the library," he quickly reminded the obsessive Bear.

Immediately forgetting the Crows, Bear dashed out the door, shoving Gundo aside and disappearing into the dark.

Ski faced the women again and tipped a nonexistent hat. "Ladies, as always . . . it's been an amazing pleasure."

"You made me wait." She stood in front of Hel's table in her hall, *Éljúðnir*. "Weeks."

"So?" Hel asked, not even glancing up from her plate filled with food but still called "Hunger." The knife in her hand was called "Famine." Her luxurious bed with all the furs and silk sheets was called "Sickbed."

"I make everyone wait. Do you know why?"

The goddess tossed her blond hair off her face with a flick of her head. "Because you ca—"

"Because I can. Exactly." Hel leaned back in her throne, arms spread wide.

She wore black armor that covered her from neck to torso,

but left her head, arms, and legs bare. Those were the parts of her body that appeared normal. What was under that armor? Rot.

A rotting body that would rot for eternity. Or until Ragnarok came.

"So what do you want, Vanir?" Hel asked, making sure to make lines clear. The Aesir gods ruled this world. The Vanir gods did not. "What do you come to me for?"

"You know why."

"Because you're still pissed at that sister of yours?" Hel smirked. "I see you wear her necklace."

"On occasion. When it goes with the outfit. But it's mine now. It'll all be mine."

"But you need my help. Yes?"

"Don't you want them to suffer? They've condemned you to remain here. They've—"

"Shuh-shuh-shuh-shuh," Hel said, waving her knife. "Please don't bore me with tales of what my Aesir kin have done to me. I don't care. This is my domain, and I like it here. So find another direction if you want to interest me."

"You're the daughter of Loki. Think of it as just one more way to fuck with everyone since that seems to be your family's thing."

"We do get bored. Must be our vast intelligence."

"Will you help me or not?"

"I don't like you. But I don't loathe you, either. For me, that almost makes us friends." Hel grinned at the blond goddess in the Hervé Leger dress, gold and diamonds on her neck, wrists, waist, and dangling from her ears. "And I always try to help friends."

CHAPTER TWO

Ski was sound asleep. Comfortable. Happy. But that wasn't to last. He heard his cat, Salka, hiss seconds before a hand tapped his shoulder.

"What?" he asked without lifting his head from the pillow or opening his eyes. His shoulder still hurt from the gunshot wound he'd received the night before. But the bullet had been removed, and he'd be completely healed in another day or two. One of the many benefits of being blessed by the gods. But as the Holde's Maid who'd treated him—Ormi's unpleasant but surprisingly lovable wife—had told him, "Get as much sleep as you can. If these big idiots will let you."

Sadly, though, the big idiots didn't let him.

"We have an issue," Bear told him.

"What issue?"

"It's the books we got last night."

Sighing, realizing Bear wasn't going to go away any time soon, Ski turned his head to look at the man but ended up laughing.

"You don't have to let her do that, you know."

Bear sighed, as always tolerating that Ski's easily annoyed cat had attached her claws to his jaw and hung from him like a scratching post.

Salka didn't like anyone interrupting her sleep.

"At least this time she didn't go for my eyes. I've learned to appreciate the little things."

Sitting up, Ski unhooked his feral cat from Bear's face, wincing when he saw the blood.

"Sorry." He carefully placed Salka in her space on the pillow beside him. "So, what's the problem?"

"The books."

"What about them?"

"They're in Russian."

"Seriously? This is considered an issue worth waking me up over?" An issue worth risking the wrath of Salka?

"Well . . . none of us speaks or reads Russian. And we don't know anyone in the other Clans who can either. And since we don't know what the books are about, none of us feels comfortable handing the translation off to an outsider."

"Okay, then what about an online translation—"

Bear gasped before Ski could even finish his suggestion. Ski's brothers only used modern technology when necessary. But they were like medieval monks when it came to books.

Books were to be treasured. Loved. Adored. Like a good woman. And no matter what happened in this technologically advanced society they lived in, that belief would never change.

"All right. Understood. But what about the Crows? That Clan has Russian speakers."

"We checked . . . just her."

"Just her? You mean Jacinda Berisha?" Bear nodded. "So? From what we saw last night, she understands Russian *and* English. Which sounds perfect. Why would we not use her?"

"Because she's insane and no one wants her around the books. What if she flips out and rips them all apart? Can you live with that?"

"You'd be amazed what I can live with."

"That only saddens me. These are books we're talking about, Ski. *Books.*"

Ski took a moment. Just breathed in. Breathed out. He would not allow himself to get . . . terse. His brothers didn't like it when he became terse.

"May I suggest," he finally said, "that we offer the opportunity, and I'll keep a close watch on her. I'm sure it'll just be for a week. Two at the most." Bear frowned at the suggestion. "Just to get an idea of what we're dealing with and whether it would be safe to go to an outside vendor. She'll look at titles and things. One of us will always be by her side," he added.

"If you're sure . . ."

"I'm sure. It'll be fine."

Ski waited until Bear walked out, closing the door behind him, before he fell back on the bed. Salka placed her tiny paw against Ski's head and snuggled her nose against his jaw. They'd both just started to doze off again when Bear knocked on the door—it was more of a banging, actually—and asked through the door, "You're not falling asleep, are you?"

Salka scrambled up and darted out the window Ski left open for her so she could come and go as she liked. The tree outside his window made it easier for her. Then, about a minute later, he heard Bear howl in pain. "Get off me, Salka! Off! Off!"

Ski grinned. He loved that intolerant cat.

Jace woke up with very little memory of what had happened the night before and feeling *great!*

Which meant only one thing . . . she'd "flipped the switch" again.

That's what Erin had always called it. "Jace flippin' the switch."

Oh well. It wasn't her fault. The Russian had brought it on himself.

Jace touched her face. She still had a welt on her forehead and her nose was unbelievably sore, but it was all healing well and by tomorrow at this time, she'd be right as rain.

Stretching and yawning, Jace began to smile when a big furry head brushed up against her leg. She looked down at the puppy she was supposed to be fostering but that everyone in the house knew was now *her* puppy. Lev. Short for Lev Niko-layevich Tolstoy, one of her favorite authors. She'd had him only a few weeks, but already he'd grown. Substantially.

No one seemed to mind Lev. He was still a baby. But she saw

Chloe, the leader of the Los Angeles Crows, watching him. She hadn't been happy when Kera brought in her one-hundred-pound pit bull, Brodie Hawaii, and something told Jace that she wouldn't like a full-grown Lev much more. At least not in the main Bird House. "Our insurance doesn't cover vicious breeds, ya know," she'd remind them. But Lev was not vicious. As Jace liked to say, "He's a lover, not a fighter." And he was. Nothing he liked better than lying in bed with Jace and letting her scratch his ever-growing barrel chest.

Big, lazy, and not the brightest, he just wanted to be happy. Jace adored him like the moon.

After spending about fifteen minutes playing with Lev on the bed, Jace grabbed clean clothes and walked to her bedroom door. She eased it open and looked down the hallway to make sure no one was around.

Together, they snuck down to the closest bathroom. It wasn't that Jace didn't want to see any of her sister-Crows, she just didn't want to *talk* to any of them.

Jace was not a naturally chatty girl. She liked silence. She liked to hear the birds tweeting and the wind blowing and pretty much anything but the drone of human voices.

Not that she didn't love people. Jace was a people lover. She just didn't feel the need to actually be *around* people.

She took a quick shower, brushed her teeth, and dealt with her curls. A small chore in and of itself. Then she brushed Lev's teeth. He pulled his lips over his gums so that she could easily get to them.

She loved her dog.

After his teeth, she gave his coat a good brushing, picked up all the hairs that fell on the floor, put her clothes on, and to-gether, the pair snuck back down the hallway. They were al-most at the stairs when she heard several of her fellow sister-Crows coming toward her.

Jace dove into a nearby closet, Lev right behind her. She thought the voices had passed and was about to crack the door when it was snatched open from the other side.

"Oh. Hi, Jace," one of her sisters greeted before grabbing a few boxes of tissues beside a crouching Jace. "See ya," she said and closed the door.

Jace let out a relieved breath and waited a few minutes longer until she was sure the coast was clear.

She eased the door open and darted into the hall, down the stairs, started to go for the kitchen, heard voices coming from the other side and spun around, accidentally ran into the wall, cursed in Albanian like her grandmother used to do, and limped in the other direction, rushing into the game room and out the glass doors that led into the yard. She closed the door and limped around the corner, freezing in her tracks when she came face-to-face with Kera, Erin, and their Raven buddies, Vig, Stieg, and Siggy sitting at a glass table, enjoying breakfast.

Erin grinned. "Trying to make a break for it?"

"No."

"Liar."

Although Erin seemed the most antisocial of the group, she wasn't. She loved being around people . . . just so she could fuck with them. It brought her joy the way silence and a good book filled with others' misery brought joy to Jace.

"Eat something," Ludvig Rundstrom said, pulling out a seat. She knew it was meant as a kind invitation, but Vig had a way of making everything sound more like an angry order. Poor guy was so painfully shy, he barely looked Jace in the eyes. He'd sort of come out of his shell, though, now that he was spending time around Kera.

After years in the Marine Corps, Kera could get along with pretty much anyone. She knew how to talk to people. Knew how to interpret body language. Knew when people were comfortable and when they needed a hasty exit. Jace wondered to herself whether Kera would one day lead the Crows after Chloe retired or, you know, died in battle. The decision was always Skuld's choice, who among her brethren ran her Crows. Just because Tessa was second in command did not mean she would one day be their leader. It always came down to what was happening at the moment.

Hell, a few weeks ago, an ancient goddess was nearly un-leashed into the world, and if that had happened . . . they would have needed a battle chief, not a politician, which Tessa sort of was. But they'd thankfully stopped that from happening and then they'd gone back to their lives.

Except for one thing. Poor Betty Lieberman. An older Crow, she'd been badly hurt going headfirst out the window of her office in Culver City. At first, when officials assumed it was a suicide attempt, she'd been taken to a an emergency mental facility, but when she didn't wake from her coma, the Crows had arranged to have her come back to the Bird House, where they could take care of her.

It was strange, because not a lot of Crows fell into long-term comas. Usually, they either died from trauma so bad they couldn't recover, or they were up and around by day three or four. But it had been three weeks and Betty was still uncon-scious.

The good news, though, was that there was definitely brain activity. The bad news, there was no ETA as to when she would snap out of it. And they always needed Betty. Not sim-ply because she was a powerful seer for the Crows who could divine things that others couldn't, warning them of danger when necessary. But, more importantly for many of Jace's sister-Crows, she was also one of the biggest entertainment agents in all of Hollywood.

Without Betty, they all felt a little blind these days. They needed her back or someone who could take her place, but that would be up to Skuld, and she hadn't said anything to Chloe one way or another.

Before sitting down, Jace looked around for Lev. He was fine, though. Currently circling a big landlocked group of birds in the middle of the back lawn. Crows—the birds, not the women—loved hanging around the Bird House. Although they were usually in the trees, not in a large flock on the lawn. It was weird, but not weird enough to cause her to go over there and investigate.

As Jace took a seat and reached for the fresh croissants in the basket in the middle of the table, she called out to Lev, "Don't mess with those birds, Lev. They'll kick your ass."

But Lev wasn't looking for a fight. Instead he barked, jumped back, lost his footing, fell over, flipped onto his feet, and started again.

"So we're invited, right?" Siggy asked Kera.

"Of cour—"

"No," Erin quickly cut in. "You're not invited. This is a Crow-only party to celebrate the arrival of our newest sister, Kera. What we don't need are some Ravens there to ruin it."

"Vig gets to come," Siggy complained.

"He's fucking Kera. So we're *allowing* him to come."

"Since it's my party," Kera asked, "shouldn't I have a say in who gets to come?"

"It's a party in your honor. No one said it's *your* party."

Kera looked at Jace, and she gave a little head shake to let her friend know that, "Nope. That made no sense at all."

Kera opened her mouth to argue the point with Erin, but the redhead cut her off with, "Just leave the planning to me. That's what I do."

"Do you want to borrow my clipboard?"

"So I can beat you to death with it?"

"You shouldn't fear the clipboard," Kera solemnly intoned. "For the clipboard knows all. For the clipboard shall rule all, reigning supreme among—"

"Shut *up*."

Jace was so proud of how far Kera had come in her new life. At first, Jace had been really concerned. The former Marine was used to things being done in a certain way, and it seemed like Kera would never fit in with the others. The Crows were not known for good organizational skills or following anyone's regulations but their own.

Plus, Kera seemed really uncomfortable with the idea of killing what she liked to call "random people on the street." It had to be explained to her, more than once, that if the Crows came calling at your house looking for blood, it was because you'd done something shitty enough to earn their attention.

But with time and the help of Vig, Kera had found her way. True, she still questioned whether certain people had to die, but Jace didn't have a problem with that. The Crows needed a good moral center. It kept them from ending up on the wrong side of the other gods.

And, in the end, Kera's sound logic had kept the Crows from getting into a war with Thor's Giant Killers and had prevented Gullveig from entering this world.

One of the Vanir, Gullveig was only mentioned once in the stanzas of *The Poetic Edda*. She came to meet with the Aesir— Odin and his brethren—and by the time she was done, they'd tried three different times to burn and stab her in the heart with spears. So not only did the other gods hate her, but she'd been impossible to kill.

Using their combined powers, the gods had tossed Gullveig's battered essence into another realm, but she'd never stopped trying to find her way back. And considering it was said she was "ever the delight of an evil woman," it was probably a very good thing she never made it through.

"Are you sure we should have a party with Betty upstairs?" Kera asked. "You know . . . in a coma."

"If it were anyone else *but* Betty, I'd say no." Erin shrugged. "Maybe a good party will wake her up."

"I heard her wimpy assistant has taken over since Betty's been gone. She's been firing people left and right. Kicking out clients. Stealing big clients from other agents. It's been a blood-bath."

Erin gazed at Siggy. "How do you know that?"

"I read *Variety*. And people talk to me. I'm very charismatic."

Erin began to argue that point, but Jace shoved a muffin in her mouth before she could say the words. The redhead had a lethal tongue. As vicious as the powerful flames Skuld had given her as an extra gift. Jace had seen her decimate people without raising a finger. Or a talon.

Siggy was just too easy a target.

Using a napkin, Erin coughed and spit out the muffin she didn't want, but she wasn't angry at Jace. Instead she laughed and asked, "I didn't even say anything yet!"

The sliding glass door behind Jace opened and a shadow fell over her. She'd just bitten down on a piece of bacon, but the way the Ravens tensed, eyes glaring, bodies ready to fight, as they stared at something behind her, she nearly spit it out. The Ravens could be moody, just like the god they represented on earth, Odin. But this change was so fast, she immediately turned to see what was behind her.

Danski Eriksen stood there in all his chiseled perfection. He wasn't nearly as big as the Ravens sitting with her. He was leaner. But every muscle on him was cut. Light brown hair hung in his bright green eyes but the back was a little shorter, more . . . clean cut. The Protectors weren't as uptight as the Silent, a Clan that managed to look down on pretty much the entire human race while still talking about protecting it. But the Protectors didn't talk about protecting the human race— they just did. Every day, in big and small ways.

With his head tipped down to look at her, Ski was forced to push the wire-rimmed glasses he wore back just as he smiled a bit.

"Hello, Jacinda," he greeted. "I was told I'd find you back here."

Another Protector, Gundo—she didn't know him by any other name—stepped out on the back patio, but Jace had little interest in this one. He was cute but Danski Eriksen was *really* cute.

Like, keep-a-girl-up-at-night cute.

"So, what?" Stieg abruptly demanded of Erin. "You're just letting Protectors in without question now? Is that what you're doing?"

Erin started laughing. Hard. So hard, she laughed for a good long while before she gasped out, "I love how you think you have any say here! Like you're important!" She slapped her hand against the table several times, still laughing. "That's the best!"

Eriksen watched the pair, head tilted to the side a bit before he blinked behind his glasses and finally said to Jace. "I'd like to offer you a job."

He couldn't have shocked Jace more if he'd said, "*I'd like to set you on fire for a ritual sacrifice.*"

But before Jace could reply, Siggy piped in with, "Don't take it, Jace. It's a trap. They're trying to trap you. Admit it, you're trying to trap her."

Eriksen stared at Siggy and asked, "How?"

"I don't know. You just . . . are. Admit it."

Gundo began to say something but Eriksen raised his hand to cut him off. "No, no. Let's follow the logic."

"What logic?"

Eriksen leaned down a bit so he could look Siggy in the eye. "Let's try and work this out, shall we? How could the two of us asking Ms. Berisha about a job in front of all of you be a trap? If she went missing, wouldn't you automatically *know* it was us?"

Siggy pointed a finger at both men. "It doesn't mean you wouldn't at least *try*."

Kera and Erin winced at that, both knowing the big guy was just really attempting to use what he considered a form of logic. And Jace simply appreciated he was so protective of her. It was sweet.

Gundo gazed at Siggy for a moment before noting, "It must annoy you. That tiny little brain of yours pinging around in that big, bulbous head. Like a Ping-Pong ball inside a bowling ball bag."

Siggy tried to flip the table over so he could go after the Protectors as dramatically as possible, but Vig and Stieg shoved him back down. They simply were not going to let that happen . . . not when they weren't done eating.

"Sit," Vig ordered.

"Yeah, but—"

"*Sit.*"

Siggy dropped back into the seat and Eriksen refocused on Jace. "It's for some translation work. Russian to English." He gave her that gorgeous smile. "Would you like the job?"

Jace deliberately made eye contact with Eriksen. Always important when dealing with job offers or interviews of any kind. Then she replied, "No."

Ski didn't know what kind of response he'd expected from the quiet but powerfully beautiful Jacinda Berisha, but "no" was not on the list. Had that idiot Raven worried her with all his talk of "traps"? It was true. Protectors were the onetime enemies of all Crows and Ravens, but that had been a very long time ago. Several centuries, in fact.

Then again, Crows and Ravens were known for never forgetting an enemy.

"Uh . . . we're not asking for you to do this for free," he stated, deciding to assume she was haggling for more money, like any self-respecting Crow would do. "We'll pay you well."

She nodded, smiling, and replied, "No."

"You'll be safe," Gundo promised, also assuming that idiot had ruined everything. "There's a very good treaty between our Clans since the eighteen hundreds."

"Oh, I'm not worried about that. I know I would be safe with all of you."

"Okay then. Great. So you'll think about it?"

"No." She stood, her head reaching Ski's cheek. She was all curves and simmering heat, and he'd really been hoping she'd take the job so he would have the opportunity to get to know her a little better. To find out if there was more behind that shy smile and those big blue eyes.

"I really wish you'd reconsider," he tried again. "You're kind of our only hope among the local Clans."

"Oh. I didn't realize that, but . . . no."

She eased past him as that idiot Siggy Kaspersen laughed.

Ski locked on Kaspersen, but Gundo was the one who rammed his foot into the man's chair, sending both flipping across the lawn.

The Ravens were up, including Ludvig Rundstöm, one of the most feared Vikings among all the Clans. He came from a long line of killers, his bloodline reaching back as far as Ski's, their ancient kin fighting through the ages.

But before anyone could do any more, Kera slammed her hands against the table. "*That is enough!*" she bellowed.

"Oh, come on," Amsel pushed. "Let 'em fight."

"Shut up. And no one's fighting."

"This has nothing to do with the Crows," Stieg Engstrom explained, his eyes still on Ski. "This is Raven business."

"But you're on Crow land."

"Nice!" Amsel patted Kera's arm. "Look at you getting the hang of all this political bullshit."

Kera's face lit up. "Not bad, right? I just thought of that!"

"Stay out of this, Kera," Engstrom warned.

In reply, Kera called out, "Brodie."

And from that pile of black crows in the middle of the back lawn—which Ski had thought was very odd, but had chosen to ignore—something rose, the crows still holding on. It took a moment for Ski to realize that in the midst of all those birds had been a dog. A big pit bull. It shook itself, the crows squawking in protest as they flew off. Then it yawned, and began walking over to the small group.

Stieg Engstrom looked over at Kera. "Am I supposed to be scared of your dog?" he asked.

Kera replied by raising her eyebrows, and when Engstrom looked back, the dog was suddenly right in front of him . . . eye to eye.

Shocked, Ski gawked at the dog. It had wings. Crow wings. How was that even possible? And now that unholy thing hovered in front of Engstrom, cold dog eyes locked on him, front paws pressed against his chest.

"Okay, but I don't—"

The dog growled, leaning in close to Engstrom.

"I get it, I'm just saying—"

The dog leaned in even closer, teeth bared this time, low growl still rolling along.

Engstrom gave up. "Fine!"

Hearing the answer it apparently wanted—which alone was disturbing Ski on all sorts of levels—the dog lowered itself to the ground, its wings disappearing beneath its thin fur. Head high, tail up, it turned around, and took off after the puppy that Ski just realized Jace had gone to play with. The three of them ran around the yard, Jace laughing, the two dogs barking, until they disappeared around a corner.

"Well, after that," Gundo finally said, turning on his heel, "I won't be sleeping tonight."

CHAPTER THREE

Jace had just opened her book—*Germinal* by Émile Zola. A wonderfully depressing tome about a mining town. When Jace wanted to relax, she looked for books that would make most people suicidal. But for Jace . . . The darker, the better. But before she could get past the first paragraph, Erin's head suddenly appeared in the nearby opening. Erin had always been one of the few Crows who could find Jace no matter where she might have hidden herself.

Like under the house.

"Hey."

Jace bit back her desire to tell her very dear friend to "go the fuck away" and instead said, "Hey."

"Rachel's looking for you."

Jace frowned. Rachel was looking for her? Rachel? A former bodybuilder and now a Crow clearly hoping to be Clan leader one day, Rachel usually left Jace alone. She thought of her as "trouble. Because she can't control that fucking rage of hers."

Which was kind of funny coming from her, since in her bodybuilder days, Rachel took copious amounts of steroids until she became a rage-a-holic, which eventually led to the death that landed her here. She was great in combat, but in day-to-day situations, Jace would rather work with Satan himself than deal with Rachel.

Unlike Chloe, Rachel simply didn't know how to adjust to different personalities and temperaments. She thought all the Crows should act the same way . . . like her.

"Why?"

"I guess she heard about last night. It seems she's concerned."

Jace rolled her eyes and begged, "Kill me now."

"She's gonna track you down. So, you wanna come with me?"

"Where are you going?"

"Food shopping. For Kera's party."

Jace rolled her eyes again, now annoyed for a different reason. "Seriously?"

"Come on, it's great! She's such a sucker. I could fuck with her all day."

And clearly that was Erin's plan. To fuck with poor Kera all day long. Because the caterer had been called, arrangements made, invitations sent out. The party was going to be exceptional, but Erin was ready to convince the poor newbie of all sorts of ridiculous shit. For no other reason than she could. Because that's what Erin did. She fucked with people. Happily.

All day long.

"Besides, if you come, she'll believe it."

"I'm not lying for you."

"You don't have to. Just don't talk, which you barely do anyway."

"Is she over there?" Rachel demanded a few feet away.

Erin stood and Jace heard her say, "No. She's not here."

"You're such a bad liar, Amsel."

Actually, Erin was a great liar, but she'd been among the Crows long enough for all of them to know when she was lying.

Rachel's very large head appeared. "You're under the house?" she demanded, because Rachel demanded everything. "Why are you under the house? Maybe you need therapy."

"She doesn't need therapy." Erin pushed Rachel over a few centimeters—about all she could manage with a woman that large and unwilling to move—and stuck her hand out for Jace to grab. "She's fine."

"You're not helping by coddling her."

Jace grabbed Erin's hand and let the smaller woman yank her

out from under the house. Lev, who'd been resting against her leg, trotted out after her, briefly stopping to bark at Rachel. The little guy already knew who bugged Jace the most and acted accordingly.

Rachel glared down at the puppy. "Are you actually keeping this thing?"

Jace tossed her book aside and quickly scooped Lev into her arms. She wasn't giving up her dog. She didn't care what anyone said. Lev would stay.

Jace quickly took off after Erin, but Rachel decided to follow them.

"You have to get control of this rage, Berisha." Rachel was a big fan of using everyone's last name. As if they were in the military. Even Kera, who had been in the military, didn't do that here. Of course, her brain hadn't been addled by past steroid use. "You can't just go around blowing up our assignments because someone pisses you off."

They were near one of the outside patios, where a group of unemployed actor-Crows were sitting around, chatting about Hollywood jobs they *hoped* to get.

Erin, still walking, grabbed Lev from Jace's arms and tossed him to the first Crow she saw.

"Hey!"

"He'll be fine."

And he was. Jace's sister-Crow caught the puppy and grinned, holding him close. "I'll walk him with Brodie later today," the Crow promised as Erin grabbed Jace's arm and hauled her inside.

But Rachel was still on their heels. And still talking.

"You can't ignore this, Berisha. It's become a problem."

Jace wasn't about to argue with the woman. Arguing with Rachel took a special kind of patience that Jace didn't have. A special kind of patience she didn't *want* to have.

They cut through the house and were near the front door.

Rachel was reaching out to put her hand on Jace's shoulder when a fist punched it out of the way and Kera stepped between them.

"Leave her alone."

"Maybe you should stay out of this, Watson."

"Maybe you should make me."

Jace didn't want a fight to happen between Kera and Rachel. They'd already had their problems, and the bottom line was, they simply didn't get along.

Not every Crow got along with other Crows. Like the birds themselves, there was always in-fighting. It was in their nature to be kind of dicky. But in-fighting among their own didn't mean they didn't have each other's backs when it came to outsiders. Crows who had been known to hate each other personally, would often risk their lives for their enemy sister.

"Loyalty unto death to our sister-Crows," was one of their oldest mottos. But when there was no outside battle to distract them, trouble could easily explode inside the Bird House.

Jace didn't want that.

Ever since they'd first met, Kera had been very protective of Jace. Jace had no idea why, but it didn't offend her the way Rachel's concern did.

Or maybe it was just Rachel herself who offended her. The woman could be truly offensive without much effort on her part.

"Kera," Jace attempted to soothe, "it's okay."

"No. It's not okay," Erin said. "Get her, Kera!"

Instead of following Erin's ridiculous order, both Kera and Rachel glared at the petite redhead.

"What is wrong with you?" Rachel asked.

"Actually . . . nothing. I'm amazing. And beautiful. And charming. And *sassy*."

Jace snorted out a laugh. This was why she'd put up with Erin all this time. Her insanity had a way of diffusing bigger problems. True, she could be annoying, but she had a way of making it all work out in the end.

"Now, come on, Kera. Let's get you some Cheez Whiz and crackers for your party!"

Flabbergasted, Kera faced Erin. "Cheez Whiz? Seriously? I got a better send-off from the Marines."

"What did they do?" Jace asked.

"Nothing. They did absolutely nothing because they figured I'd be back. Surprisingly, the whole stabbed-to-death-then-taken-by-a-goddess thing didn't really occur to my COs."

Erin put her hands on her hips, shook her head. "How can you be against Cheez Whiz? As an *American*?"

"God, I hate you," Kera complained before yanking the front door open and walking out.

Laughing, Erin followed and Jace realized they'd left her alone with Rachel.

When the bigger woman opened her mouth to speak, Jace skittered out the door, slamming it behind her.

"This isn't over, Berisha!" Rachel yelled after her.

"What is that woman's problem?" Kera asked Jace as they walked toward the big circular driveway.

"She just worries about me."

"She obsesses about you," Erin corrected. "For a while there, she was obsessed with Kera. But then Kera became a soulless killing machine after her time in Asgard—"

"Gee, thanks."

"—so now she's back on poor Jace. Like a tiny, weak mouse who can't get away from the big, former steroid-using house cat."

Jace stopped. "I am *not* a mouse."

"Rat?"

Kera shook her head. "You know, Erin, it amazes me that no one has killed you a second time."

"I know, right? And the best part? They can't kill me the same way!"

"I have no idea what that means."

"What killed me the first time was being shot in the head. Someone shoots me in the head again . . ." She shrugged. "Nothing except a headache and annoyance. And if someone tries to stab you in the chest again, chances are the knife will break?"

"That's just weird. Why do you tell me weird things?"

"It's weird, but also exceptionally cool. Skuld doesn't want you dying the same way twice. Think about it . . . that would be embarrassing if you died the same way you died the first time. Or if I got shot in the head again. Or if Jace died . . . the way she was originally killed. Whatever way that was."

All the Crows knew it had been Jace's ex who'd killed her the first time but no one asked for details. Maybe they just didn't want to know.

"You can't tell me that's not a great thing." Erin stopped walking and gestured to the car she'd chosen to go shopping in.

Kera gazed at it. "A Chevrolet Impala convertible?" she asked.

"Very good eye."

"Does it bounce up and down, too?"

"Racist."

"Can we be a little less LA about this? And take a nice, *sensible* car to the store?"

Erin parked the Hummer in the grocery store parking lot, making sure to take up two spots before jumping down from the driver's seat. When she came around the front, Kera was already standing there, glaring.

"*This* is a nice, sensible car?"

"In Los Angeles . . . yes."

Jace walked by the pair, eyes practically rolling out of her head.

Erin knew the quiet woman would rather be back under the Bird House, reading her book and rubbing her puppy's belly, but that was not to be. Anytime she went full-rage during a battle, there was some kind of blowback for several days following the episode. Not from Chloe. She appreciated having a berserker on her team. But from a few of the others. Although Erin didn't know why. The ones who had a problem with it, like Rachel, weren't even part of their strike team.

Rachel had her own damn team to manage, so why did she insist on fucking with theirs? Was her life really that boring?

Grabbing two carts, the three women worked their way

through the store, Erin making sure to buy the most cliché, cheapest, ridiculous crap she could find for Kera's "party."

None of it did she plan to use. And, in the end, she'd probably give it all to some homeless shelter. But seeing the look of disappointment and insult on Kera's face kind of made Erin's day.

Okay. So maybe her life was that boring, too. Because there was nothing she loved better than messing with the former Marine. She was just so serious about damn near everything, fucking with her was all sorts of entertaining for Erin.

Grabbing several bags of the most generic, plain, cheap tortilla chips she could find, Erin dropped them into her filled cart and announced, "Okay. That's it."

"Gee," Kera said flatly. "Really?"

"I think we have more than enough. I mean . . ." Erin blew out a breath like she was thinking really hard. "I know our strike team is coming. And a few of the other Crows said they'd *try* to make it. I think you invited Vig, and of course he'll be there because he kind of has to . . . so, yeah. I think we have enough."

Kera looked at Jace. "Seriously?" she demanded. So insulted, that one.

Jace stared at Kera for a few seconds before shrugging her shoulders and pushing the cart toward the checkout stands.

See? That's why Erin didn't have a problem with Jace's silence. Who needed someone chatty when silence often worked so well in Erin's favor?

Erin paid for the food and they made it to right outside the store before Kera stopped Erin. "Maybe we should cancel this thing. It sounds like no one's coming. It's gonna be lame."

"Oh stop! It'll be fine. Right, Jace?"

Jace gazed at both women, eyes darting back and forth before she gave a forced, closemouthed smile and pushed her cart toward the Hummer.

"You can't force me to go through with this. You can't!"

"You owe it to your sister-Crows," Erin told her.

"You mean the ones who aren't coming?"

"They'll try!"

Kera's eyes narrowed and Erin was sure the woman would finally spot what bullshit this all was, but then her head turned and her expression went suddenly blank.

"Hey," she said, tapping Erin's arm. "Who's Jace talking to over there?"

Erin looked toward the Hummer. Jace stood by the passenger door. She no longer had the cart, and it looked as if she'd put the purchases in the back.

There were four of them. Three women and a man. The females stood around her while the male spoke.

"I don't know who they are. Don't recognize them."

"Does she have friends outside the Crows?"

"Not if she can help it. Maybe they're trying to sell her something."

"Oh, or get her to sign some petition or something." Kera's face scrunched up. "Let's rescue her." Like any proper Marine, Kera hated the ones she called "crunchy-granola hippie types." And anyone trying to get her to sign some petition fell into that category. And the gods forbid the poor petitioner was anti-government. More than once Erin had been forced to drag Kera away after a ten-minute-long yelling match. Especially once she heard the sirens and knew the cops were coming.

But before either of them could get over there to rescue poor Jace, their quiet friend did something extraordinary to the people speaking to her . . .

She backhanded one across the face. Punched another in the throat. Kicked the one standing behind her in the leg, breaking the woman's femur. And the male she grabbed hold of by the back of his head and began slamming into the door of the Hummer while screaming.

"*Oh shit!*" both Erin and Kera yelped before they took off running.

She hadn't seen them since before she'd been killed. But she'd seen others. They'd hissed at her when she'd walked into the courtroom to get the permanent protection order. They'd hissed and called her a sinner before the judge had them thrown out.

But none of them had ever bothered her after that. She didn't even think they knew where she lived.

She thought, after openly working with federal prosecutors, she'd be dead to them.

But here some of them were. They'd surrounded her, not allowing her to get into the Hummer. Immediately, he started speaking for all.

Telling her they understood why she'd done what she'd done. How it wasn't her fault. How they'd forgiven her for her sins. They'd forgiven her for her betrayal.

Then, he had told her that she was still one of them.

And that's when Jace got angry.

She didn't want to be one of them. It hadn't been her choice. It had been forced upon her. Just like this conversation. Leaving her no way out.

Only this time, she took a way out.

By beating the holy shit out of them.

He was bleeding and crying by the time Erin and Kera reached her. Kera, the strongest of them, tried to drag Jace away. But she wasn't done.

She tossed Kera off, startling them both. But then she reached down and grabbed him by the head again, pulling him to his feet.

She remembered him. His name was Bobby and he was still loyal. He always would be.

They all would be.

But not Jace. Not anymore.

"If you come around me again," she whispered against his ear. "If you call me. Drive by my house. Send fucking smoke signals. I will kill you. I will cut your throat. I will bathe in your blood, and I will watch you die. *Do you understand me?*" she finished on a growl-scream, her teeth clenched tight.

Now both Kera and Erin had hold of Jace and they dragged her away.

Erin released her long enough to unlock the Hummer and get the door open before she and Kera shoved her inside. Kera pushed or dragged the others away from the vehicle. Then she leaned in and demanded of Erin, "Give me cash."

Erin, who was now in the driver's seat, tossed her wallet to Kera.

Kera walked over to some poor kid who'd been recording the whole thing on his phone. She took the phone from him and crushed it in her hand. Then she took a wad of cash out of Erin's wallet and chucked it at him.

She returned to the Hummer, jumping in beside Jace and slamming the door. "Go!"

Erin gunned it out of the parking lot and out onto PCH, heading back toward the Bird House.

After a few minutes, Kera suddenly gripped Jace's chin and turned the berserker's face toward her.

"Oh shit," Kera muttered.

"What?" Erin demanded. "What's wrong?"

"She's not raging."

"What?" Erin stopped at a red light and turned in her seat to look at Jace. She gawked at her for several seconds before asking, "You're not in a rage?"

"No." At least, not in the rage they were talking about. A berserker rage that involved complete loss of control.

If she had been in a rage, all four of those people would be dead now. Not just wounded. Not just sobbing. But dead.

Erin glanced at Kera before turning back around and moving forward with the rest of the traffic.

"Just so we're clear," Erin told them, "I'm pretty sure this is one of the seven signs of the Apocalypse."

Wide-eyed, Kera looked at Jace, but Jace gave a quick shake of her head. So she wouldn't worry.

And Jace was almost positive she wasn't lying . . .

CHAPTER FOUR

It took less time than Jace would have liked for what had happened at the grocery store to spread through the Bird House like a virus.

And nearly everybody asked her about it.

They wanted to know why she'd beaten the crap out of four people for no obvious reason. Not that any of them had a problem with that. And Jace had a feeling if she'd said, "I didn't like the shoes they were wearing," more than one sister-Crow would nod her head sagely and reply, "Totally get that. You should have seen what Dora wore the other day. She's lucky I didn't beat *her* to death."

Even worse, the story had transformed from Jace kicking some ass to killing four strangers. But Kera and Erin were quick to tell everyone that was *not* what had happened.

Soon the news spread to the Ravens and then the other Clans, so that by the time Jace showed up for her time to sit with the comatose Betty, the Holde's Maid who was helping with her care—at least the mystical aspect of it—immediately asked as Jace walked into the room, "Hey. Heard you killed like thirty people because someone got your taco order wrong. Is that true?"

Jace gawked at her. "*No.*"

The Maid looked so disappointed, her lip stuck out in a pout as she packed away the candles and potions that the Maids used daily on poor Betty in an attempt to bring her back. So far nothing had been working.

She walked past Jace, briefly stopping to tell her, "You don't have to use that tone. *I* didn't get your taco order wrong."

Jace closed her eyes and fought her desire to scream, "*It wasn't about tacos!*" She was not going to open that can of worms and reveal her old life, though.

Once the door closed and she knew the Maid was gone, Jace dropped into the big, comfy chair beside Betty's bed.

She wished Betty would snap out of it. Whatever "it" was. She wished the older Crow was here. More than once, Jace had gone to Betty for her counsel. As a Seer, Betty didn't need Jace to say anything to her. All she had to do was hold Jace's hands and she could "see" everything. Understand everything.

And, like any good Hollywood agent, she knew how to keep her mouth shut. She never talked to anyone about what she'd seen from others. What she'd learned. It was just between the Seer and the Seen.

Jace could really use that right now.

After a moment, Jace pushed herself out of the chair and leaned over Betty, gazing down into her face.

Then she yelled, "Betty! *Betty, can you hear me?*" When that got no response, she snapped her fingers three times in the woman's face.

Nope. Nothing.

With a sad sigh, Jace dropped back into the chair and opened the book she was going to read to her friend: *You'll Never Eat Lunch in This Town Again.*

She had a feeling that Betty would like the behind-the-scenes drama of Hollywood even if it was a little out-of-date. Last week she'd read her, *The Kid Stays in the Picture: A Notorious Life: Robert Evans.* Even though the book didn't bring Betty out of her coma, she did seem more relaxed.

A few of Betty's past assistants had tried to get books on their old boss published, but Betty had crushed those brief dreams like she was holding Thor's hammer. Eventually, no one bothered to try. Not where Betty was concerned.

Of course, Jace didn't really know that Betty. The Hollywood Betty. Scary Agent Betty.

She only knew her as Betty, the Crow, the Seer, the chocolate-chip cookie thief after an ugly episode involving a Holde's Maids bake sale during one of the Clan tournaments. Jace didn't know the terrifying, ruthless, cruel Betty Lieberman, Hollywood agent.

And to be honest, she didn't want to know that person. Just like Jace didn't want to know the sociopath that Annalisa once was before she died and Skuld gave her a conscience. Or the mean rich girl Alessandra once was, who tormented everyone around her out of boredom. They were different now, and that was all that mattered. At least to Jace.

Jace began to read where she'd left off the day before and was so fascinated by the machinations of terrible people that it took a little while before she realized that it wasn't one of the local crows pecking at Betty's window but someone throwing pebbles at it.

Marking her spot, she placed it on the side table and walked over to the window. Pushing it open, Jace rested her hands against the sill and leaned out, staring down at the yard.

"Hi."

Startled by the voice coming at her from the tree in front of her, Jace jerked up to see Danski Eriksen perched on a branch. He watched her with those big pretty eyes behind designer glasses that managed to make him look geeky and sexy all at the same time. Plus, she kind of expected him to hoot at her from there. What with the Protectors' owl wings, powerful legs, powerful hands, and ability to turn their heads almost completely around.

"What are you doing?" she whispered.

"I need your help."

"I don't want a job," she insisted, becoming exasperated. "Stop bothering me."

"It's not about the job. Well . . . it is. But not about you wanting the job."

"What?"

He reached into the back pocket of his jeans and handed her a legal-sized sheet of lined yellow paper with a list of names.

"What is this?" she asked.

"Names of potential Russian translators that my brothers came up with. Thought maybe you could steer me in the right direction."

"What makes you think I would know?" she asked, a little more testily than she'd meant to. "I don't even leave the house if I can help it."

"Which is probably good since I heard you just killed a busload of nuns earlier today." She didn't say anything, but her expression must have been clear because he laughed and said, "You should see your face right now. Good thing I can fly."

She glanced down at the list. "Look. I don't really want to get involve—"

"Please," he said. "They're driving me nuts. Really, Bear is driving me nuts, but then they all sort of join in and it becomes a chorus of seriously obsessive compulsive guys bothering me, which is something you should understand . . . right . . . nun killer?"

"I didn't—"

"I know," he said, still laughing. "I *know*." He gestured to the list. "Just take a look. Please?"

As soon as she looked down at the list, she held her hand out and snapped her fingers. Without thinking, Ski gave her a pen and she began scratching names off.

"No on this one, this one, and this one. They're all gangsters. You'll end up killing them after they try to blackmail you. Or steal something you value." She stopped, read a few more, began scratching their names off. "They have an American sensibility about Russia. And they don't know enough about the early dialects to help you with some of those books, I'm guessing." She cringed. "Definitely not this one. He did the worst translation of *War and Peace* that I've ever read. And these three will not keep their mouths shut about what they discover. And this one is a high-level sorcerer. He'll steal important information from the books and possibly start a world war or something."

She handed the sheet back to him. "There you go."

She'd scratched out every name.

Every. Name.

"Uh . . . that was very helpful. Thank you."

"You're welcome."

"But perhaps you can—"

She closed the window on him before he could ask if she knew anyone who could help him *and* whom she would approve of, and then shut the shades.

Unreasonably annoyed—women were usually a lot more helpful than this with him—Ski sat there a few moments, thinking on what he should do, when a Raven noisily landed on the branch behind him, his weight making the poor wood creak, and snarled, "What the fuck are you—"

Turning just at the waist, Ski grabbed the Raven by his head and rammed it into the tree trunk several times before tossing him out.

With a sigh, he looked down at the decimated list. "Back to the drawing board," he muttered before jumping out of the tree, landing by the Raven, who was trying to pick himself up.

Erin Amsel sat at one of the outside tables, a big umbrella blocking the sun. She sat with a few other Crows who didn't seem too interested in him or the Raven groaning on the ground.

He nodded and Erin gestured to a pitcher. "Iced tea?"

"No. But thank you."

"Sure."

Carefully folding up the list and putting it back in his pocket, Ski returned to his car.

"He likes her," Alessandra noted about the Protector after he'd left. The Protectors had great hearing, and it was wise for her to wait.

"Probably," Erin replied, flipping the page on her tattoo magazine.

"Should we help them out?"

"Nope."

"Yeah. You're probably right after she killed all those people."

Erin looked up at her sister-Crow. "She didn't kill anybody."

"You don't have to protect her. It's not like we'll think less of her."

"Shut up," Erin snapped, tired of explaining what had gone down earlier in the day.

"Are you going to help me?" Stieg Engstrom barked. His words muffled because his face was still buried in the dirt.

Erin looked over at the Raven, stared a few seconds before replying, "No."

CHAPTER FIVE

After taking Lev and Brodie for another walk—good thing both dogs loved to walk because they got a lot of it with the other Crows taking their turn—and spending some time hiding behind the couch in the living room so she could get some more reading in, Jace decided it was time to find something to eat. She tended to forget when she was reading. But her stomach growled, giving her no other option.

She did briefly stop to think about *why* a stomach growled. What was actually happening inside a person when their stomach growled? She decided to look that up later and began her sneaky way toward the kitchen. But just as she reached the swinging door, Rachel grabbed her arm. "There you are."

"What?" Jace asked, immediately beginning to panic. "What's happening?"

"Chloe's looking for you."

"Yeah, well . . . uh . . . I—"

"I don't want to hear it." Still gripping Jace's arm, Rachel dragged Jace—literally—down the hall to Chloe's private office.

"Found her," she announced, yanking Jace into the room.

Chloe looked up from her laptop. "You dragged her here?"

"What was I supposed to do?"

"Not that."

"She wasn't coming on her own. I could see it in her eyes."

Chloe took a moment to rub her brow with both hands.

"What?" Rachel snapped. "Now what did I do?"

"Forget it." Chloe had little patience for those who would not hear. Instead, she gestured to the two chairs in front of her desk. "Sit, Jace."

Jace tried to pull her arm away but Rachel wouldn't let go. There was a brief tug-of-war, but when Jace finally got loose, she began slapping at Rachel, who slapped her back. That went on for a bit until Chloe cleared her throat.

She'd trained them to know that a throat-clear from Chloe was as good as a nuclear weapon from an anti-American country.

Both women, still glaring at each other, sat down in the chairs across from Chloe, and their leader smiled at Jace.

"How are you feeling?"

"Okay."

"I heard you killed a bunch of people today."

Fed up, Jace immediately started yelling, "*I did not*—"

Chloe held her hand up, a big smile on her face. "Stop. I know exactly what happened. Kera came in here to tell me you didn't kill anyone because she was so outraged that the rumor had spread and there was a lot of desk pounding and words like 'morally' and 'outrageous' and 'God,' and 'America' was in there somewhere at some point. To be honest, I stopped listening because I didn't care. I just . . . I just didn't. And you know how she is. She can just . . . go. With no brakes on that car that is her mouth."

Chloe let out a breath. She did that a lot now that Kera was part of the Crows. "But after last night and today . . . I have to say we're getting a little worried about you."

"You don't need to—"

Chloe held up her hand again. "Let me finish. Now, some of the Crows think, and I do have to agree with them, that you just don't get out enough."

"Chloe—"

"Look, I get it. You're a shy little flower in a wilderness of squawking Crows. That can't be easy for you."

"But—"

"But if you get out more, I'm sure you'll learn to tolerate people better."

"You don't under—"

"So Rachel had a good idea."

Jace reared back. "Rachel?"

"Yes," Rachel snapped. "I had a good idea. I get good ideas."

"Really?" Jace couldn't help but ask. "Steroid use is a good idea? That heart attack at thirty-three, a good idea?"

"*Before,*" Chloe bellowed, "*this gets out of hand!*" She blew out a breath, lowered her voice. "Why don't you just hear the idea first?"

"Okay."

"How about you get a job?"

Jace began to blink. "A . . . a job?"

"Uh-huh. Nothing big. Something part-time. But it gets you out. Gets you around people. Doesn't that sound nice?"

"No. No, that doesn't sound nice at all."

"You don't wanna work?" Rachel asked. "You're lazy? You want everything handed to you?"

Jace's hands curled into fists and Chloe quickly jumped in.

"What I'm sure Rachel means—and maybe she should shut up now—is that a little contact with the outside world would be very good for you. Staying here, cooped up all day, reading those extremely depressing books, can't be healthy. But a little fresh air, a little time out meeting new people . . . this could really help."

That's when Jace realized they still didn't get it. None of them got it except maybe Erin and Kera. After all this time her fellow Crows didn't understand.

"In fact," Chloe went on, completely oblivious to the panic Jace was now feeling, "I've already talked to the other Crows who have offices. And they are more than happy to give you a job. Receptionist. Or secretary. Office management. There's a lot of different options for you. You just have to pick one."

And now Jace knew Chloe had made up her mind. No

amount of rationalization was going to save Jace. Nothing she said or did now would change Chloe's mind. Over the years, she'd seen others go up against the Great Wall of Chloe Wong and no one had ever breached those walls. Because she, again, had her mind made up.

Which meant . . . Jace needed another option.

When Chloe opened her mouth to start speaking again—offering her more office jobs that required talking to people most likely—Jace raised one finger. "Can you give me a couple of minutes? I'll be right back."

Chloe shrugged. "Sure."

Jace stood, walked out the door, carefully closing it behind her, moved down the hall, grabbing the backpack she always left by the front door, opened the door, walked outside, closed the door, then took off running.

Chloe watched Jace run past her office window.

"Is she running away?" Rachel asked, already on her feet.

"No, no. Sit."

"But—"

"Sit."

Rachel dropped into the seat. "You sure she's coming back?"

"She said she'd be right back." Chloe shrugged. "I've never known Jace to lie to me. Besides," she added, unable to stop the smile, "I kinda want to see what the fuck she's up to."

Ski pulled open the front door to the Protectors' Pacific Palisades' home and blinked in surprise at the panting, sweaty Jacinda Berisha standing there.

"Hi, again."

"Hell . . . hell . . . o." She took in deep breaths.

"Are you all right?"

She held up her hands for a moment, then placed them on her knees and bent over at the waist. Ski patiently waited until she could speak again.

"Uh . . ." she finally got out, "is that . . . is that job still open?"

"Sure, but—"

"Great . . . I'll . . . geez . . ." She took more breaths in. "I'll take it."

"Are you sure? You seemed pretty adamant that you didn't—"

"*I'm taking it.*"

"Okay." Now Ski held his hands up, but for a different reason. "Actually, that would be great."

"Okay, good." She finally stood straight, but her hand rested against her side like she had a stitch in it. "So if any of the Crows call asking . . . I've taken the job. I'm working with you. Understand?"

"Sure, but . . . why would they ask?"

"Just . . . just promise me you'll tell them that if they call or ask."

"Of course."

"Great."

She turned to go.

"Don't you want to know how much we're paying?" he asked casually, fascinated. "Where you'll be working? How long? What you'll be doing? Any of these questions interest you?"

She shook her head. "No. See you tomorrow. I'll start to-morrow."

"Okay. Great."

Then she took off running again.

"What was that about?" Gundo asked from behind him.

"We got her. Jace. She said she'd do the translations for us. She'll be starting tomorrow."

"Oh. Okay. What changed her mind?"

"No idea."

"Where did she go?" he asked, looking out the door.

Ski pointed. "She took off running that way."

"Running?"

"I could be wrong . . . but I think she's running back to Malibu."

Gundo blinked. "The Bird House is like twenty miles from here."

"Yeah."

They stared at each other a second before shrugging and going back into the house.

Jace was running down the sidewalk when she heard a car horn. At first, she refused to look, in no mood to field lecherous attacks from idiot men, but the horn didn't stop. So she put on her best glare and looked over, nasty words in Albanian on her lips. But it was Danski Eriksen.

"I can drive you," he said through the open passenger window.

With a stitch in her side and sweat pouring down her face, Jace decided that might be a good idea.

Flying she might be good at and could do for hours, but running . . . clearly not her strong suit.

She walked to the corner, and the car stopped in front of her. She got in and closed the door.

The car was nice. Really nice. A top-of-the-line Mercedes. Like her father, Jace had a weakness for cars. She didn't drive much, though. In fact, she'd only gotten her license two years back when she'd become a Crow. And she'd never driven her sister-Crows anywhere. Ever.

Eriksen pulled back into traffic. When they stopped at a light, he brought up the Bird House address on his GPS and let it do the rest of the work.

They drove in silence for a good twenty minutes until Eriksen asked, "So, what made you change your mind? About working for us?"

"Does it matter?"

"It might. You're a Crow. For all I know the whole lot of you could be up to something."

"We're not."

"Well that's good."

Jace continued to stare out the window, believing the conversation was over.

It wasn't.

"So what made you change your mind?"

"Timing."

"Ah. I see. Timing is always very important."

"Uh-huh."

"Will your sisters have a problem with you working with us?"

"I don't know."

"Are you worried?"

"No." But she was worried this conversation would never end. Why wouldn't it end? Was he going to insist on talking to her while she was working, too? She doubted that. They needed the translations done, so she doubted Eriksen or any of the Protectors would waste precious time by insisting on painful chitchat.

Jace knew that almost all of her sister-Crows would take this time to get to know someone as handsome as Danski Eriksen. Except that Jace didn't really have anything to say. Nothing of importance anyway.

And she'd promised herself two years ago, when she'd landed in her Second Life, that she would never force herself to indulge in "small talk" ever, ever, *ever* again.

Even for someone as adorable as Danski Eriksen . . . who was *still* talking.

Studying everything around her outside of the car, Jace made her move.

Ski heard the passenger door close, and he looked to see the seat beside him empty.

"Did she combat-roll into the street?" he asked absolutely no one.

Hitting the brakes, Ski stopped his car and jumped out, gazing over his roof while ignoring the honking horns and cursing coming from the drivers around him.

Mouth open, he watched Jacinda Berisha run across the Pacific Coast Highway—managing somehow not to get mowed down by anyone—and run up John Tyler Drive.

"Thank you!" she yelled out as she kept running. Running like the devil himself was behind her.

"Move your car, asshole!"

Annoyed, Ski snapped his head around. The female driver squeaked in shock, and Ski realized he was not keeping control of himself. It was never good to show the Unknowing—as they were called by the Clans—what his kind truly was. They simply couldn't handle it.

Ski got back into his car and drove until he could make a legal U-turn.

She is really shy, he thought to himself. Because that had to be the answer, right?

He couldn't be *that* repulsive, could he? Could anyone?

"See," Chloe pointed out to Rachel. "There she is."

Hours after having left, Jace ran into Chloe's office, dropping to her knees right inside the door and panting hard.

Patiently, they waited for Jace to get her breath back.

When she did, she practically screamed out, "I have a job!"

"What job?" Rachel demanded in that tone that pretty much ensured she'd never be the leader of the LA Crow Clan. She was just too bossy. They'd all rise up and kill her one day.

"With the . . . the . . . the . . . Protectors. Translating text. From . . . Russian to . . . something."

"Most likely English," Chloe filled in for her.

"Probably."

"That's great," Chloe said.

"It is?"

She glared at Rachel. "Of course it is. It's a job that's out of this house. All good."

"I start . . . tomorrow."

"Excellent."

"Wait." Rachel shook her head. "The Protectors? Isn't their house in Pacific Palisades?" Eyes wide, she demanded, "Oh my God, did you run all the way there and back?"

Jace, now curled into a ball on the floor, shook her head. "Danski Eriksen drove me part of the way back, but . . . but . . . he kept *talking* to me."

"About what?"

"Just chitchat!"

Rachel leaned down a bit and asked the struggling-to-breathe girl, "Would it have killed you to make small talk with someone? *Anyone?*"

"*Yes!*" Jace screamed, startling them both. "*It would have!*"

CHAPTER SIX

Jace passed Lev's care off to one of her sister-Crows, knowing she'd take care of her baby.

Yes, she was now at the point where she considered Lev her "baby." She'd never thought she'd be one of those dog owners, but here she was.

She smiled a little, thinking how annoyed her grandmother would be. Nëna considered animals either food or protection. There was no in between for her.

"Don't get so attached to that goat, little *inat*," she'd say. "He's probably tomorrow's dinner."

Her grandmother never said those sorts of things to be cruel. In her mind, she was just toughening up Jacinda to the harsh world around them.

"You are too sweet, little *inat*," she liked to say, using the Albanian word for "ire." "You can't be so sweet. Boys will only use you to make their lives easier. And I never want that for you."

Jace stopped walking. She couldn't keep thinking about her grandmother. It only hurt her heart. The memory of Nëna's face when she'd tried to see Jace but they'd stopped her. She hadn't seen her grandmother since. Jace had been too ashamed to let her grandmother know how weak she'd been for staying so long.

And, of course, for choosing. Jace had made a choice and for that Nëna would *not* forgive.

After giving herself a moment, Jace started off again. She

made it downstairs and was about to head toward the hallway when a hand clamped down on her arm and another around her mouth. Then she was yanked back until she was under the stairs.

A few seconds later, she saw Rachel and a couple of Crows from Rachel's strike team appear in the hall. The three women stood there, looking around.

Looking for Jace.

Jace rolled her eyes. Rachel was trying to push herself into this, too. Trying to "help" Jace out.

Jace couldn't express, in words or actions, how much she did *not* want any help from Rachel. Not when it came to her life in general. During a fight? Sure. Help away. But any other time, Rachel just irritated the fuck out of Jace. She wouldn't say she hated her or anything. Jace didn't hate anyone.

But the more annoying a person became—and Rachel was really annoying—the less time Jace wanted to spend around that person.

After looking around, Rachel gestured to her team. "I doubt she left yet. I want to talk to her before she goes. Find her."

The three women split up, heading in different directions to track down Jace.

Once they were gone, the hands on her loosened and Jace turned to see that it was Erin and Kera who had rescued her.

Loyal sister-Crows to the end. Protecting her from annoying *yentas*. One of the few Yiddish words her grandmother used extensively when talking about women who annoyed her, but whom she didn't actively hate.

Without saying anything, the three of them made a run for it. But as they went around one corner, they quickly realized that Rachel had gotten her entire strike team involved in tracking Jace down. Probably so she could give Jace one of her irritating "pep talks."

They froze, the back of their sister-Crow to them, and waited a few seconds before darting down another hallway, into the dayroom, out of the dayroom, and into the next hallway over.

They all slid to a stop when they realized that Rachel was there. She was just turning toward them when all three dove into the nearest closet.

Clinging to each other like terrified orphans, they watched Rachel stomp by through the crack in the open door. When she disappeared, they let out a breath and Kera began to ease out the door just as Annalisa was walking by. She frowned at the sight of them huddled in the closet, but before she could say a word, Kera mouthed, *Rachel*, and pointed.

Annalisa smirked. She wasn't a big Rachel fan, either. She suddenly pushed Kera back into the closet and stood in front of the door.

Rachel reappeared, stopping in front of Annalisa and looking her over. "What are you doing?" she finally asked.

"Just thinking about my day. What are you doing?"

"Trying to find Jace. Have you seen her?"

"Trying to find her? Why? Is it because she's Albanian?"

"I'm trying to . . . wait . . . what?"

"You hate her because she's Albanian?"

"I don't hate—"

"Is it just Albanians you hate, or is it all East Europeans?"

"What are you talking about?"

"Wow. I had no idea you were like this."

Another sister-Crow showed up. "Like what?"

"Rachel hates Eastern Europeans."

"I do not!"

"So you hate *all* Europeans? Is that what you're saying?"

"No!"

"My God, Rachel." The other sister-Crow shook her head, disgust on her face as she walked off. "I'm really disappointed in you."

"Wait . . ." Rachel glared down at Annalisa. "Jesus Christ."

"So you hate the Christian God, too?"

"Oh my God! Shut up!"

Rachel stormed off, calling after the sister-Crow who'd been so disgusted with her, and Annalisa opened the closet door. "Anglo guilt . . . it's so my favorite thing."

★ ★ ★

Ski opened the front door and again found Jace Berisha standing there. This time, however, she wasn't panting like she'd run a desert marathon.

She also wasn't alone.

With a sigh, she said, "I couldn't shake them."

"We helped you escape," Annalisa Dinapoli stated as she pushed her way past Jace and stepped into the hallway. "The least you can be is grateful."

"We just wanted to make sure everything was on the up-and-up," Kera said, giving a small smile before adding, "Nothing personal. We would do this with any of the Clans."

"No problem." Ski pulled the door all the way open. "Please, come in. Have a look around."

"That isn't necessary," Jace said, still standing outside the doorway.

"Will it make your friends feel better and go away?"

"Probably."

"Then they can look around." He winked and gestured her inside with a head nod.

"Beautiful place," Kera said.

"Eh," Erin muttered.

"Thank you, *Kera*."

He heard Erin chuckle.

"How are you enjoying your Second Life?" he asked.

"I like it," Kera said with real eagerness, eyes bright.

"And has your dog had wings for long?"

"Since I have." She shrugged. "Brodie enjoys it."

"She wasn't with you when you were dealing with the Russians."

"She makes Chloe nervous. So we only bring her in when things get really bad."

"Because she's a dog with wings?"

"No. Because she's a breed that the insurance company won't cover."

"Do all the Protectors live here?" Erin asked.

"No. Just me and sometimes Ormi."

"Why you?"

"Because I'm the Keeper of the Word."

Ski stopped when he heard Jace suddenly choke and begin coughing. He went to her side, lightly placing his hand on her back.

"Are you okay?"

"Fine." She waved him off and stepped away from his hand. "I'm fine."

He didn't believe her, but he wasn't going to argue with her.

"So where are the books?" she asked, probably assuming that the quickest way to get rid of the Crows was to involve dusty old books written in Russian. He doubted she was wrong.

"The library. It's right down this hall . . ."

Ski stopped and let out a breath, eyes briefly closing. He should have seen this coming. But he'd been so distracted, he'd forgotten to deal with this very situation.

And now . . . he was stuck.

It looked like every local Protector from Southern California was filling up that big, beautiful hallway with the marble floor and walls, where their god Tyr's rune—the Tiwaz, which resembled an arrow pointing at the sky—was subtly designed into everything.

With arms crossed over chests, they stood and stared down the small group of Crows.

Eriksen glanced at Jace. Poor guy looked mortified as he asked the Protector everyone called Bear, "What are you doing?"

"Making sure our books are safe."

"That's my job."

"It's not that we don't trust you . . . we just don't trust you."

"What?"

He pointed. "You allowed *her* in here."

They all turned to Erin, who looked over her shoulder before turning back around, pointed at her chest, and asked, "Me? What did I do?"

"You spit flame."

"I don't spit anything." She held up her hands and grinned. "I use my hands," she growled, wiggling her fingers.

"Yeah," Bear said, "she's not allowed around the books."

"You seem very protective of the books, Marbjörn Ingolfsson," Annalisa noted. "Have you always been this way? Since childhood, I mean. Did your mother like books?"

"Don't answer her!" another Protector ordered. "At least six of my patients are in prison because of her."

Annalisa smirked. "They were hardly innocent. And it's not my fault you were snowed by your sociopathic patients." She gestured to the Protector. "My friends, this is my fellow forensic psychologist—"

"I don't care," Erin whined.

Annalisa shrugged at her colleague. "She doesn't care. About you. Or your sagging, sad career."

The man's eyes narrowed. "You are such an evil witch."

"Awww. Thank you. It's so sweet you noticed. I do still try to be that girl I once was. Tormenting the innocent. Destroying the will of the good." She sighed. "I miss those days."

"You are *freaking* me out," Bear finally stated.

Deciding she was done with this conversation and realizing that everyone was focused on "Fire Hands" Erin and former-sociopath Annalisa, Jace pressed her back against the wall and carefully slid past the Protectors until she reached the library.

As she stepped inside, her mouth dropped open. This wasn't some rich person's McMansion library. This was a *real* library. There were at least three floors, shelves filled with books lining each wall and then stacks across the floor, as well. Near the entrance were wood tables and chairs for people to do research. Several were filled with studious young Protectors. Teen boys who were taken from their families by the time they were eight or so and trained in the art of war and reason in a special boarding school hidden somewhere in the Midwest—but fully accredited so the teens could move on to prestigious high schools and then Ivy League universities.

Tyr was the god of war, battles, and justice. Unlike the other gods, Tyr never lied and was all about self-sacrifice, integrity, and honor. When a Protector made an oath of any kind, a man could know without a doubt that the oath would never be broken. However, if the one who made an oath with a Protector broke his side, his suffering would be legendary. The Protectors, with all their mighty integrity, could be the cruelest bastards in the known universe when crossed. So no one went into a deal with the Protectors lightly.

Which was why Jace, much as she didn't want to be here today, would go through with her commitment.

Of course, now that she was actually *in* the Protectors' library, she was shockingly happy she'd made the agreement with Danski Eriksen.

Her hands clasped together, Jace picked the first bookshelf she came to and began studying each title as she walked down the length of it.

"I see you made a break for it," a voice teased.

Jace glanced up. Gundo towered over her, smiling.

"Would you like me to show you around?"

No. She really didn't want him to. But, instead, Jace said, "No."

Wait . . . that wasn't what she'd meant to say. Although it's what she did mean.

Gundo smirked. "Would you like me to introduce you around?"

"God, no."

"I see. Is it me?" he asked.

"No."

"Is it because Crows and Protectors were once sworn enemies?"

"No."

"Is it because you're truly *not* a people person and you'd rather walk through fire than have polite conversation?"

Instead of answering, Jace just stared at him.

Gundo nodded. "Understood. If you need anything, let me know."

And, much to her relief, he walked away, smiling, which she appreciated.

"Sorry about that," Eriksen said as he reached her. "They really don't want Amsel in here."

"They're holding me hostage!" Erin yelled from the doorway.

"No, we're not," a Protector helping to block her replied. "You can leave at any time. In fact, we'd prefer if you left *now.*"

That's when Erin warned, "The more you tell me to go, the longer I'll stay."

Ski led Jace to the large wood table where they'd placed their newest acquisitions.

"Here we go," he said, watching her drop a very large backpack onto one of the chairs.

"The ones on the table are from the first box," he explained. "There are six more boxes right here." He pointed at the wood boxes beside the table. "Those are the older books. Bear wouldn't let us touch those, though, without the proper—"

Before he could finish, she pulled out a big box of disposable latex gloves.

Teasing, he asked, "Shouldn't those be white cotton?"

"No." She gawked at him. "White cotton is the worst thing you can use on old books. They can still transfer oils and debris from your hands to the paper, which would eventually destroy it over time." She shook her head. "What kind of librarian are you?"

"I'm just the Keeper of the Word. I basically have to make sure no one sets the place on fire. It's a job that was given to me. A sacrifice even Tyr himself might make."

"Books are never a sacrifice."

"I see I chose well. You should do okay here."

"You don't like books?" she asked.

"Of course I like books. But I'm equally happy reading on my phone as I am reading a print book."

The entire room gasped and they both looked around at the younger Protectors gaping at Ski.

He sighed. "And on that note . . ."

"So, what do you need from me? Exactly."

"First, we need titles, authors, date of publication. Once we get that sorted, then we can decide what, if anything, needs to be translated and what can be filed away for later. For instance, we don't need you to translate the Russian version of Stephen King's *Christine*."

"Why not?" she asked flatly. "It's a good book."

"If you say so. But since we can get it here in the language it was originally written in, not sure why we would pay you to do it."

"That's a valid point."

"Thank you."

They both grinned at each other and, for the first time, Ski felt they were connecting.

"And what if there's nothing here?" she asked. "Nothing of use?"

He pointed to the bookshelves. "Then we'll code them and shelve them as we do all books that come our way. Does that work for you?"

"Sure."

"Do you want to discuss payment?"

She kneeled on one of the chairs, her gaze locking on the books before her. "Not particularly."

"You just want me to leave you alone?"

"Yes, please."

Understanding her more and more, he turned to leave but asked, "And your friends?"

Without taking her eyes off the books, Jace reached into her backpack and pulled out a pencil. A pencil she threw across the room the same way he'd seen her throw the long blade of the Crows during battle. It hit Amsel in the head, stopping her from tormenting Bear by doing "jazz hands" with fire, flicking the flames between her fingers.

"You can go away now," Jace muttered at her friends with a toss of her hand.

Annalisa stopped in the middle of torturing the defense lawyers and social workers of the Protectors by arguing for something regarding the death penalty—Ski couldn't shake the feeling that she actually didn't care one way or the other about any of that, but was just enjoying the way some of his brothers were getting red and frustrated at their discussion—and walked away.

Erin started to leave but stopped and jerked her hands toward the library. No flame appeared but poor Bear threw his big body right in front of the doorway, ready to go to Valhalla in the attempt to protect the books.

The redhead gave what Ski could only call an evil, throaty cackle and turned to go. But Kera walked around Bear and asked, "Are you sure, Jace?" She glanced at Ski. "We did hold this one hostage once."

"I wasn't really a hostage," Ski reminded her. "I was just insurance. So no hard feelings."

There was that forced smile from Kera. It came out anytime she didn't understand Viking life. He wondered if Ludvig Rundstöm saw that expression a lot, since word among the Clans was that the pair had become quite close.

A remarkable thing considering how smart and caring Kera Watson seemed to be and how Rundstöm appeared to be the polar opposite.

"Jace?" Kera pushed when the other woman didn't respond.

Frowning, Jace looked up. "What?" Her frown deepened at the sight of her sister-Crow. "Why are you still here?"

"Okay, then," Kera said. "I'll take that to mean you're fine. Call me when you're ready to come home."

With that, the Crows were gone, leaving devastation and horror in their wake . . . something they were known for, so it wasn't exactly surprising to Ski, but his brothers turned to him, all of them glaring.

"Don't look at me," Ski told them. "It was Bear who insisted we needed a translator for these books."

"I didn't know she'd bring her insane friends!" Bear feebly

argued, because *of course* Jace had brought her insane friends. Crows never went into another Clan's territory without at least one of their own.

Although less for protection than as a witness.

Ski glanced down at Jace to see if she was offended. She wasn't because she wasn't listening.

He'd lost her to the books.

CHAPTER SEVEN

Jace didn't know how long she was sitting in the same spot, but every time she bothered to glance up from her work, something had been added to the table. First it was a high-priced laptop, already set up with a spreadsheet so she could begin inputting information about the books. Then, a little later, a small printer that could print out about a hundred pages at a time, plus a few reams of plain white paper. Another time she found a Russian-English dictionary, in case—she assumed—she needed help with a word here or there. Then there was that bronze statue of an owl.

It was the owl she couldn't stop staring at. What did it mean? Owl statues were often used to scare off crows from someone's house or a building. Especially if a large number of crows were leaving a healthy load of shit everywhere. But what exactly were the Protectors trying to tell *her* with this? Were they threatening her? Trying to scare her away? Playing a joke? Or just . . . putting an owl statue down?

It was hard to tell from the statue itself. Those cold, bronze owl eyes were not friendly.

"You have to eat."

Jace finally turned away from the owl to find Eriksen standing over her. "I'm not hungry."

"You have to be hungry. You haven't eaten since you arrived. You haven't had any water. I don't think you've even urinated."

"Probably because I haven't had any water."

"I tried to get you some earlier. But my brothers *physically*"—and he sounded so annoyed—"dragged me back to the kitchen."

"I understand that. Until we know how important the books are, we shouldn't have food and water around them. It could damage the—"

"I don't care. I just need you to eat."

"But I'm not hungry."

He crouched down, staring at her through those glasses. "I don't care that you're not hungry. What I'm *not* going to do is have the Crows think I'm starving you. Because they don't complain quietly or calmly."

"It's not even lunchtime."

"It's three in the afternoon."

Jace turned and looked out the big windows. The sun had moved, suggesting a later hour. "Oh."

"Yeah. Exactly. So . . . please?"

Jace looked down at the books. She wasn't nearly as far along as she'd like to be. She'd only just started on the first box of books after finishing the ones on the table and she—

"They're not going anywhere," Eriksen practically snarled, cutting into her thoughts. "So get your cute butt up and let's get you something to eat."

Jace blinked. "Cute?"

"Very." He smiled. "Didn't you know?"

"Don't really look. But . . . thanks."

"Welcome."

Jace grabbed the desk and lifted herself off the chair since she was still resting on her knees. Once she had her feet on the ground, though, her legs sort of gave out from under her and she was suddenly sitting on her ass.

"By Tyr's missing hand!" Eriksen snapped, sounding angry. "Is this literally the first time you've gotten up since you arrived this morning?"

"Well . . ."

He crouched beside her, putting his arms around her waist. "I see I'll need to keep an eye on you to prevent you from losing your legs from blood loss."

"Don't be so dramatic."

He lifted her into his arms and stood. "You can't walk. I think I'm allowed to be dramatic. Isn't it bad enough I have to take care of these guys? Now I've got to take care of you, too."

"I can take care of myself."

"Clearly not."

He walked out of the library, with Jace still in his arms. As they moved, she gazed up into his face until she finally asked something that had been bothering her since she'd arrived here, "Why do you and most Protectors wear glasses? And I'm pretty sure some are wearing contacts. Why didn't Tyr give you all better eyesight?"

"He gave us excellent eyesight. And if we were just running around, hunting our enemies, none of us would need glasses. But the glasses help us adapt so that those around us don't notice the . . ."

"Freakiness of your owl eyes?"

"They're not freaky. They're unique."

"You can also turn your heads three hundred sixty degrees."

"No, we *can't,*" he quickly corrected her. But then, a few seconds later, he added, "It's more like two hundred seventy degrees."

"A difference of ninety. Uh-huh."

"Tyr likes owls. They're very thoughtful predators. So he gave us many of their wonderful attributes to enhance our fighting skills."

"How come you don't have talons, like we do?"

"We have talon-like skills when we fight, but Tyr thought his warriors having actual talons would not be very masculine. He's still a Viking, you know?"

"Uh-huh."

They walked into the kitchen, where several Protectors were already sitting at the table. None of them were talking. They were all either writing or reading, each of them seemingly deep in thought.

Eriksen walked up to one of his brothers and kicked the chair. Then he grunted at him.

"What?" the brother asked.

"Move."

Growling, the Protector picked up a large load of books and papers and moved down the large wooden table to another free spot. Then Eriksen placed her in the vacated chair, her feet against the seat, her knees raised.

"What do you want to eat?" he asked. But when Jace just stared up at him, he shook his head. "Forget it. I'll give you something to eat, and you'll eat it."

He walked away and Jace rested her chin on her raised knees. That's when she realized the other Protectors were staring at her. And they kept staring until she finally demanded, "What?"

"So, what have you discovered?" Bear asked. Or demanded, depending on your perspective.

"About society?" Jace replied.

And Ski, who'd been buried arms-deep in their big refrigerator, had to look up from what he was doing to see if she was seriously asking that question.

She was! She was gazing at Bear with that kind of blank expression, waiting for his answer.

Poor Bear, he didn't know what to do with that.

"No. About the books."

"You'll have to be more specific. That is too vague a question."

Bear looked at Ski, but all he could do was shrug and point out, "That was a very *broad* question."

Bear tried again. "Are the books helpful? Are they a waste of your time? Are they informative?"

"So far they've been all three. Kind of like life," she added, glancing up at the ceiling. That's when she grinned. "A skylight. How beautiful. No wonder you guys eat in here."

As one, Ski's brothers looked up. He was sure that none of them had ever noticed the skylight before. Even Ormi never noticed. Ski had it put in during a holiday weekend. The few brothers who'd come in and out, for whatever reason at that time, walked by the construction guys like they weren't even there.

"That is nice," one of the brothers noted. "Has it always been there?"

Shaking his head, Ski pulled the fixings for a sandwich out of the refrigerator and placed them on the kitchen island. He then pulled out several bottles of cold water. He opened one and walked over to the table, holding it in front of Jace's face. Her gaze slowly moved down from the skylight to the bottle. After a moment, she smiled, and admitted, "Thank you, I am a bit thirsty."

Of course she was. She hadn't had anything to eat or drink in hours.

He knew that he'd have to keep an eye on her while she was doing this job. She was like his brothers, easily consumed by things that interested her and hiding from things that didn't.

At least four of his brothers had lost their homes and/or cars over the last few years because they'd forgotten to take care of important personal business like mortgages and loan payments. They didn't like dealing with money, so they didn't bother and then they'd watch, stunned, as their car was towed away from the front of the house or they'd return to their home or condo to find the locks had been changed and a sheriff's deputy waiting to serve them with papers.

It became so bad that Ski finally hired a financial manager. He didn't trust anyone from the other Clans to deal with the rather large sums of cash that many of the Protectors had access to, but he didn't want someone who could expose them to the world. So he'd settled on a shifter. A man and wife team who, when not managing the Protectors' money, could shift into leopards and lounge in trees. Something they often did in the backyard of their Beverly Hills mansion.

The shifters—a rather bland moniker for those who could shift into another species with a thought the way the Protectors could fly—didn't actually like the Nordic Clans. In fact, from what Ski could tell, they sort of loathed them, especially the

Crows. But they did like Clan money. And with both groups needing secrecy to function, they put aside their differences and found ways to work together to each other's benefit.

Jace tipped up the bottle and took a drink. Then she took a longer drink. By the time Ski went back to the counter, grabbed another bottle, and brought it to her, she'd finished the first one and was eagerly reaching for the second.

"You need to remember to take breaks," he told her. "If you die at the desk, your friends will make our lives hell."

"She can't drink around the books," Bear reminded him. "Or eat. What if she dumps water on them? Or gets food crumbs in the pages?"

"The world will end?"

"That's not funny."

Ski chuckled. He thought it was kind of funny.

He went back to the island and began to put together a nice large sandwich for their guest. While he did, Gundo asked Jace, "Are you Russian?"

"No. I'm Albanian on my father's side."

"So why do you know Russian?"

"I was forced to learn multiple languages in order to find evidence of the end times in the writings of other cultures."

Ski debated putting mayo on the sandwich. Something told him she wouldn't be a mayo fan. He could ask, but he'd rather figure it out on his own. Maybe a vinaigrette for the top of the sandwich would work well with the turkey and kale.

"The Crows made you learn languages to do that?"

"I didn't think the Crows cared about any of that," Bear muttered.

"Not my sisters," Jace replied. "The cult I was forced into when I was a child made me learn. As the wife of the Great Prophet it was considered one of my duties. As was smiling . . . and talking . . . and being loyal."

Holding the top of the seeded wheat bun over the sandwich, Ski looked up in shock, his gaze meeting Gundo's. They stared at each other until Bear asked, "You were in a cult?"

"Since I was ten."

"What cult?" Gundo asked.

"The Patient Dove Congregation out of the Valley."

Ski dropped the bun top onto the sandwich before leaning in and asking, "The group the Feds referred to as 'Another Waco about to happen'? *That* cult?"

She nodded, the second water bottle still gripped in her hand.

Borgsten pointed a finger at Jace and said, "You're the wife that leader guy tried to kill. He buried you in the backyard."

"He buried my *corpse* in the backyard. The ATF caught him while he was tossing dirt on me. Skuld brought me back . . . and I woke up cranky."

Ski's brothers stared at her for a long time until Bear asked, "Do you know Aramaic?"

"Yes. Plus, Greek, Latin, Hebrew, Arabic, several of the romance languages. Ancient Egyptian. Some African languages like Setswana and Hausa, but I read those better than I speak them. Most of the Slavic languages, reading and speaking. And since I've been with the Crows, the fundamentals of the Scandinavian languages, which wasn't too hard because I already knew German; and I've been taught to curse in Japanese, Korean, Hindi, and since Kera arrived, Tagalog. At some point I hope to get to Cantonese and Mandarin. I asked Chloe about it, but she's, like, third-generation Chinese American and she just stared blankly at me. And that's when I realized I'd be better off taking a class at UCLA . . . preferably without her."

"Those people you attacked the other day . . ." Gundo said, staring at her. "The ones everyone are talking about, they were from that cult, weren't they?"

"Yes. They were."

"Because why else would you beat them up?"

"Everyone else thinks I killed them."

Gundo snorted. "No. You suddenly snap and start killing random people, the Crows will put you down themselves." When Jace stared at him, a little confused, he added, "The

Crows don't talk about it, but they don't tolerate that level of crazy. So when the rumor spread through the Clans that you wiped out an entire old folks' home—"

"Oh, come on!"

"—we all took it with a grain of salt."

Bear suddenly pointed what seemed to be a damning finger at Jace and said with grave concern, "We might have some extra work for you translating things when you're done with the Russian books."

Jace jerked slightly, as if she'd been expecting him to say something else. Then she nodded and replied, "Okay."

Bear nodded. "You're not as worthless as I thought you'd be, Crow."

Ski placed the food in front of Jace. "Bear meant that as a compliment."

Appearing mildly confused, she replied, "Yes. I know." She paused, then added, "What else would it be?"

"Jacinda?"

"I'm not hungry," she told the persistent Protector. Earlier the man had actually come to her and asked if she'd "used the bathroom in the last three hours."

What kind of question was that? And why was he so concerned?

Of course, with him staring down at her with those big green eyes, she'd finally gotten up to use the toilet, only to discover she really did have to urinate. Then she'd heard not-as-funny-as-he-thinks-he-is Gundo remark, "We may have to get that one a diaper to prevent accidents."

Har-har-har.

But, Jace was forced to admit, she did like working around the Protectors. Unlike her sister-Crows whom she loved so dearly, the Protectors were wonderfully, unabashedly, almost obsessively *quiet*.

Not one of them was an actor or a musician or a model or a superstar with an entourage. They were all lawyers, social workers, judges, police detectives. They took the ideal of justice very seriously and tried, in their own Viking way, to give back to the community.

She admired that even while knowing she could never do it herself. Their jobs required too much time talking to people. Listening to them. *Dealing* with them. Since she was a child, there was nothing Jace hated more.

Much to her grandmother's great annoyance, Jace would often disappear with a pile of books and a candy bar, forcing the entire family to come looking for her. She was often found up in trees, under the house, in the backseat of someone's car, or in the attic of a family member. Any place she could find peace and solitude was where one could find Jacinda Berisha.

But that idyllic life had ended when her mother had come for her. When she'd taken her to the cult, where peace and solitude were not allowed. Alone time meant introspective thoughts that, even at a young age, Jace knew would lead to life outside the cult. Something the Great Prophet of the time would never allow. So, for sixteen years, Jace never had any time to herself except when she was studying or searching out proof to back up the current Great Prophet's claims about the end of the world.

Then she'd become a Crow and all that had changed. True, in the beginning, the Crows tried to make her feel welcome. Tried to get her to join in. But, eventually, they realized that she didn't want any of that. She mostly wanted to be left alone, and when she didn't, she'd let them know. Much to her surprise at the time, the Crows were fine with that.

Until Rachel, for some unknown reason, had decided to make Jace her personal pet project.

Maybe she was hoping to show Skuld that she would be a good leader, but from what Jace had seen of other Crow leaders she'd met, including Chloe, they didn't have to show anything. They just were and Skuld knew it.

The problem with Rachel, though, was that she was painfully hardheaded. Explaining to her that none of this would help her or Jace was just a waste of breath. She believed exactly what she wanted to believe until proven wrong. And it was

hard to *prove* that being left alone was in a person's best interest. It was human nature to assume that everyone wanted to be
part of a pack. That everyone wanted tons of friends, popular-
ity, and things to do on a Saturday night.

In Rachel's mind, Jace was just a tragically shy girl who
would get her rage under control once she went barhopping a
few times with "her girls."

Jace realized the Protector hadn't walked away and she glared
up at him. "I said I wasn't hungry."

"I'm not offering you food," he replied. Although he didn't
sound angry, more amused.

"Then what do you want?"

"For you to leave."

"Huh? Why?" She rushed to explain what she'd been doing
all day, pointing at the computer they'd given her. "I already
have the first two boxes of books listed with title, author, and
basic theme. I haven't gotten to the other boxes, but I will soon
and—"

"Jace, I'm not firing you."

"You're not?"

"No. I'm telling you to get out because we don't allow non-
Protectors in the library when we're not here."

"Where are you going?"

"On a job."

"In the daytime?" she asked, shocked. Did Tyr protect his
warriors in the day? Why didn't Skuld do that for her Crows?

But instead of answering her, the Protector grabbed the back
of her seat and turned the entire thing around so that she was
facing the big, floor-to-ceiling, UV-protected windows. It was
dark outside.

"Oh."

"Yeah." He turned the chair back, the scraping noise of the
non-wheeled legs making her wince, and stepped beside her.
"We've got work to do. We are nocturnal, after all."

Eriksen was wearing the typical Protector fighting outfit. A
white, sleeveless hoodie T-shirt, revealing his god's rune branded
onto his left upper bicep; blue jeans; thick work boots. Like

the Ravens, he carried no weapons. Unlike the Ravens, the Protectors didn't turn everything around them into weapons. Their hands and feet did enough damage on their own.

"And, unfortunately," he went on, "I can't have you stay while I'm not here since you're my responsibility."

"I am?"

"If you suddenly snap and destroy all the books, that'll be on me."

"Most say if I suddenly snap and kill everyone in the room."

"We care more about the books."

So did Jace.

"Okay. So you want me back tomorrow?"

"I'm sorry, did you think you were done? Because the guys already have a list going."

"A list? For what?"

"The jobs they want you on after this. Nedolf is a public defender and he has several clients for whom English is a second language, and for some reason he doesn't trust the current translator he's working with. Sevald has been working with several Eastern European countries on some political issues, but his Polish and Ukrainian are sketchy at best, and he's afraid he's pissing people off."

"He probably is."

"Yeah. Then there's Fredgeir—"

"Who wants a better name than Fredgeir?"

"No. He needs you to—"

"Forget it. Forget it." She waved her hands to stop him. "Forget I asked."

"You don't want to be involved?"

"I didn't say that. I just mean . . . I can only deal with one stress at a time and I'm pretty into these books right now. They're my whole focus at the moment."

"Good. Because that's exactly what I want and the reason I started the list. I love my brothers, but one must get control of them from the very beginning or risk panic and whining. I hate the whining."

He smiled and Jace thought about looking at something else

in the room. He was just so . . . handsome. But then she couldn't think of a reason to look away. Her divorce had been final for ages, her lawyer getting it through the system as fast as humanly possible along with a permanent protection order against her ex.

But as Jace gazed into this particular handsome face, she began to worry. So she asked, "You don't pity me, do you?"

The smile faded. "Why would you ask me that?"

She scrunched up her nose a bit. "The cult thing."

"Oh." He thought a moment and she appreciated he didn't reply with an immediate—and most likely bullshit—"No, no. Of course not. No!"

After several seconds, he replied, "I was surprised you told us about it. Because it's clearly something you don't discuss. Otherwise, it would have been fodder for the other Clans long before now." He thought a little more. "But . . . I am glad that you trusted us enough to tell us about it. Still . . . in answer to your question, no. I don't pity you. But I must admit, my heart did break a little for the girl you once were. And that your freedom was taken from you without your consent."

Jace was shocked at such a thoughtful and caring answer. Not only did she appreciate it, but she adored the way he didn't just react. Crows and Ravens were all about just reacting.

"Thank you," she said. "I appreciate that."

"Of course. But if those people bother you again, let us know. We have connections with the police, politicians, everyone. You don't have to fight them alone."

Jace had to smile. "I'm a Crow. I never fight alone."

"True. But you don't have to physically fight them either. So if you'd rather take a more rational approach . . . the Protectors are here for you. *I'm* here for you."

Jace got the feeling he was trying to tell her something beyond what his words were saying, but before she could reason it out, a banging at the windows startled them both and they looked to see Stieg Engstrom standing on the other side of the glass, glaring.

"Do I need to kill him?" Eriksen asked.

"No, no." She quickly shoved her few things into her back-pack. "I'm sure he's here for me."

"He couldn't come to the front door like a normal person?"

"Stieg? No. He rarely does what normal people do."

Jace slung the backpack over her shoulder and motioned to Stieg. "Front door!" she yelled at him. "Go to the front door!"

"Are you sure you'll be all right with him?" Eriksen asked after Stieg slowly moved away, his glare locked on the Protector.

"I'll be fine with him, though I doubt you would. He's not a Protector fan."

"You two together?"

"We'll be together in the car."

Eriksen frowned in confusion, then said, "No. Are you two together? Like dating. Or something."

Jace laughed. "There's no one in the world who would let that happen."

Ski opened the door and allowed Jace to walk out. As he did so, he made sure to keep his gaze fastened on the Raven glaring at him.

Actually, they glared at each other.

There was simply no love lost between Ravens and Protectors. They tolerated each other the way cats and dogs tolerated each other, which was to say not at all unless they were in a situation that required it.

"Why are you here?" Jace asked the big, slow-witted Raven.

"Kera asked me to pick you up." Still the Raven stared at Ski. "I can't believe they let you come here and stay here . . . alone. With *them*."

"Are you just going to keep staring at him?" she asked Engstrom.

"Maybe."

"It's weird."

He finally looked down at her. "Whose side are you on?"

"My own?"

"Typical."

"Can we just go?" she asked, walking toward the car. "And I'm driving myself here tomorrow."

"Do you even have a license?" Engstrom asked, *still* staring at Ski.

"Ski, you ready?" Gundo asked from behind him.

So, Ski turned just his head around so that he could look at his friend. He heard the Raven growl.

"Fuck! I hate when you bastards do that."

Ski swung his head back. "Then fucking leave, Raven."

"With pleasure," he shot back, arms thrown wide in obvious challenge as he walked backward toward the car.

Jace tossed her backpack into the car, then returned to grab the Raven by the back of his neck.

"Ow!"

"In the car! Jeez!"

She pushed the Raven toward the vehicle and waved at Ski and Gundo. "See you tomorrow."

They waved back and watched her get in the car and drive off with the Raven, the pair bickering the entire way.

"They dating?" Gundo asked.

"She says no."

"Good. Because you like her."

Ski nodded "I do." He faced his friend. "I don't think she gets that, though."

"Oh no. She doesn't get it at all."

"Why do you always have to be a dick to them?" Jace asked Stieg. "Can't you be nice? For once?"

"No."

She let out a sigh and stared out the window.

"And I don't know why you're being so bitchy to me. It's not like he was any friendlier."

"That's not the point. You're on their territory and you bang on the window like a mental patient!"

"I did that to protect you."

"Protect me from what?"

"He was giving you 'the look.'"

"The look? What look?"

"The I-want-you-to-be-my-concubine look. Like he would have been more than happy to toss your chunky ass over his shoulder and carry you off to his pompous, book-lined Viking boat."

"My ass is not chunky."

"Well, it ain't small."

Jace pressed her fists against her forehead. "Explain to me again why we're friends?"

Stieg shrugged. "You're one of the few people I get along with."

"And that doesn't tell you something?"

Chapter Eight

After leaving Stieg in the car, Jace walked into the Bird House.

As soon as she entered, Rachel was there, her mouth open to speak. And, to be honest, Jace didn't want to hear it, which was why she said, "Shut up." Shocking Rachel into immediate—if temporary—silence.

She'd had such a good day, she didn't want to hear anything from anyone.

Jace paused and let out a whistle. A whistle her team used in order to track each other down during battle. She received a whistle back and tracked her team into one of the small living rooms. Except for Tessa, they all sat on the couch watching TV or working on their electronic gadgets.

Kera turned around and smiled. "How did it go?"

Jace stopped. Blinked. "What happened to your face?" she asked, horrified. The entire right side of Kera's face was swollen and black and blue. Jace immediately looked at Erin. "What did you do?"

"It wasn't me! Why do you guys always assume it's me?"

When that got nothing but snorts and giggles, Erin looked back at the television.

"She's right," Kera said. "It wasn't her. It was a one-hundred-pound Rottweiler momma who wasn't a fan of me trying to rescue her babies. The puppies aren't here," Kera quickly added when Jace squealed and clapped her hands together.

"Why not?"

Everyone on the couch looked at Jace and she realized she might have sounded a wee bit . . . terse.

But come on! You couldn't talk about puppies and not have them here for her to play with!

"Right now I'm working with another rescue group in town until I get mine going. So the puppies and their momma are being cared for by them. I'm paying for food, boarding, and veterinarian costs."

By now Lev had heard Jace's voice and run into the room. On his hind legs, he pawed at her denim-covered calf with his claws until Jace reached down and picked him up. "Well, you need to get on that, Kera."

"To help the American vets who'd risked their lives for our freedom and now need a little extra help at home . . . or so you can have easy access to puppies?"

"Why can't it be both?"

Maeve, sitting on the couch, bundled up in a blanket, held out a thermometer. "I'm sick."

Erin sighed. Loudly. "You are not sick."

"I am. It's either the flu . . . or I'm dying."

"Dying?" Erin demanded. "Really?"

"My lymph nodes are swollen," she argued, pressing the tips of her fingers against her throat. "My nose is running. I'm sneezing. My sinuses are killing me—"

"Did you take your allergy meds?" Jace asked, pressing her nose against Lev's. That was when he started licking her face and nibbling on her chin.

"Allergy meds?"

"The last time you had those symptoms, turned out it was your allergies. As opposed to some virulent form of bird flu."

"Oh." Maeve lowered the thermometer, thought a moment. "I did forget to take my allergy pill this morning."

Erin rolled her eyes; shook her head. "Oy."

"Hey, check it out." Alessandra grabbed the remote and turned up the sound. "Isn't that Betty's old assistant?"

It was. The leggy blonde looked amazing as she smiled on *Entertainment Tonight*, talking about "covering for poor Betty Lieberman while she recovers from her recent accident."

"That's a lot of fuckin' gold jewelry," Erin noted. "What is she? A rapper? She looks like she's joining Public Enemy."

With a snort, Kera asked, "Is that the most recent rap group you've heard about?"

Erin laughed. "Nah. Just one of my mom's favorites."

Tessa walked into the room, stopping beside Jace to pet Lev's head. "Okay, ladies. We have a job tonight. Let's gear up."

"What?" Erin asked. "Again? We just had a job last night."

"The other Strike Teams are out. So we're up."

"Is it a full moon or something?" Maeve asked, between dramatic coughs . . . which everyone ignored.

"Surprisingly no." Tessa waited a moment before snapping, "Bitches, get up!"

Groaning and complaining, Jace's sister-Crows got to their feet and headed up the stairs.

Tessa turned to Jace. "Did you tell Rachel to shut up?"

"Yes. But in my defense, she was going to ruin my day by talking to me. I wasn't going to let that happen."

Tessa gave a small shrug. "That was probably a good plan."

Ski perched on the roof of the bar outside Bakersfield. He'd come with Bear's team again.

They all perched and waited. Of course, what they were waiting for, he didn't know. He just knew what he had to protect.

"Uh-oh," Borgsten groaned.

Ski briefly closed his eyes, the sound of motorcycles roaring through the parking lot of the bar irritating him more than he could say.

"By Tyr's right hand," Gundo complained, "why them?"

"Because we're having a bad night."

The engines of the bikes were shut off, hammers were unslung and rested on big shoulders. The Protectors watched Thor's human Clan, the Giant Killers, lumber their way toward the front doors of the bar. And Ski knew that as soon as that Clan stepped inside, the screaming would start.

When Ski had been a little boy, he'd never thought there could be anyone dumber than Ravens. He'd quickly learned he was wrong. There was dumber.

Thankfully, though, Frieda was with this group. She was the leader of the Los Angeles Giant Killers. She wasn't actually smart, per se. But she wasn't painfully dumb, either. That helped.

Ski raised his hand and signaled his team to move. They had to do this quickly and quietly, which wouldn't be easy. Not with Thor's Clan.

Suddenly Ski found himself wishing he was dealing with the Ravens instead. Something he rarely ever thought.

Ski launched himself off the roof and landed hard in front of Frieda.

She immediately stopped, her hand tightening on the handle of her weapon. Her team stood behind her, ready to start swinging those ridiculous hammers at any moment.

Like Thor himself, there was nothing subtle about those stupid hammers.

"Danski Eriksen." Frieda pursed her lips as she looked Ski over. "What are you doing here?"

"We can't let you do this, Frieda."

She gave a harsh laugh. "Oh? Ya can't? And why's that?"

"This place is under our protection."

"A bar? You losers are protecting a bar? I'm shocked."

"The owner is a favored priestess to Tyr. Now, if she has something that belongs to Thor, I'll personally retrieve it for you. But you're not about to go in there and start killing everybody."

"We're not?"

"And who's gonna stop us?" one of the older Killers asked. A Killer who'd been slammed around so many times in fights with the Crows and Ravens that Ski was pretty sure the man had permanent brain damage. Like a professional football player who'd been hit one too many times on the field. "You . . . Urkel?"

Frieda lifted the hammer off her shoulder, slapping the head into the palm of her hand. Ski cringed. That had to hurt.

"Bring it," Frieda urged. "We're more than ready."

"I don't want to fight you, Frieda."

"Why? Because you're a pussy?"

"I don't like that," Haldor announced. One of the Protectors who wasn't just quiet—the man could literally go for months without saying a word.

Frieda gawked at him. "You don't like that? So?"

"I have a daughter and I'm trying to teach her self-respect in a very male-centric world. And suggesting someone's weak by calling them female genitalia bothers me. Viscerally."

"What-erly?" one Killer asked another.

"As a woman," Haldor went on, "you really should be more conscious of—"

"Shut. Up!" Frieda roared. "Now, are we going to do this or not? Come on, Protector!" she challenged. "Let's fight!"

Except Ski didn't really want to fight . . .

Pastor Bruce Maynard sat back in his chair and watched his wife take a stack of bills off the table where all the money they'd made for the night had been counted out.

She held it under her chin, grinned. "How do I look?"

"Rich."

She laughed and kissed his forehead. "I'll go home. Get the party started."

"I won't be long."

She walked to the exit, stopped, and reminded him, "No hookers tonight."

"I said I wouldn't."

She rolled her eyes, chuckled, and walked out.

Bruce stood and took a moment to walk around his tent. He was going to be here for another few days. Selling the Word of God. Providing some healing. And earning some money. It was what he was good at. The best long con he'd ever come up with. He even had TV interest. And that was where the real money was at. If he could get the masses pumped up and his wife could do her amazing song and dance, they'd have that private jet in no time.

He heard something on the wood stage behind him.

She crouched there, watching him. She was pretty. A hot little redhead dressed all in black. She couldn't have been at the sermon, though. He'd have noticed her. Would have had one of his security guards bring her to his trailer. So, who she was?

And where did she come from?

"Hello?"

She stood, arms crossed over her chest, but said nothing.

He walked toward her but heard something behind him again. Turned. This one was Latina. Very pretty. Long blond hair, big brown eyes. Also dressed in black, but she wore a long skirt slit high up on both sides. She smiled at him. He smiled back.

A throat cleared. He faced the redhead again. She was no longer alone on that stage. There were two more women. One black. One white with long, curly brown hair. Both attractive enough.

"Can I help you, ladies?" he asked. Hoping they were here for more than just help.

It was the Latina behind him who spoke.

"We listened to your sermon." She laid her hand on his shoulder, slowly walked around him until they were face-to-face. "It was . . . interesting. Your message." She dragged one of her manicured nails, painted a deep red, down his chest. "About God . . . and His apparent need for money."

Who were they? Some uptight broads complaining about the money taken from their grandparents? How boring.

"Our Lord and Savior—"

"No," she cut in. "You can't mention His name. It upsets us so. It's sacred. Like the people who worship Him. They're sacred."

"Perhaps you should talk to my—"

"We're here to talk to *you*." She smiled, her hand moving steadily lower. "And you're going to listen."

She grabbed his balls and twisted, nearly had him on his

knees. But she quickly backed off the pressure, even though she didn't release her hold.

"You keep selling those lies, taking these poor people's money, and we're going to come back here, and we're going to rip your soul from your body."

"Are you insane?" he asked.

Wings extended from her back. Big, black wings.

They all had wings.

At first, Bruce thought it was a trick. They were in Barstow. That was only, like, a two-hour drive away from Los Angeles. Movie territory. It could be some movie mogul's parents he'd gotten money from. And they'd set up this whole thing.

But then the redhead flew across the room to reach him. She *flew*. Landing in front of him.

"Do you understand what she's saying to you?" the redhead demanded. "Do you understand what we can do to you? We're giving you a chance here. One chance." She leaned in and whispered, "You heard what we did to Sodom and Gomorrah, right? That was a whole city."

"I—"

She lifted her hand, flames danced through the fingers, and Bruce tried to lean away but another one of them, wings extended, stood behind him, pressing him forward.

"So," the Latina said, "you'll give back the money. You'll preach the *real* Word. You won't try to steal any more money from these people. You'll get right with our Father or we'll come back here and we'll decimate *everything* you could possibly love. Do you understand?"

"I understand! I understand!"

She pushed him away. "Do not fuck up again, Bruce."

"I won't! I swear! I won't!"

Her wings went up, then down, and she flew out the hole at the top of the tent.

The redhead leaned in and removed the weird bracelet from his wrist that his wife had purchased for him from some high-end jeweler she really loved, who also cleaned their money for them sometimes.

"And I'll be taking this," she said as she tucked it into the back of her black jeans.

"Why?"

She leaned down until their faces were nearly touching, her hand raised, a ball of flame in the palm. "What did you say?"

"Nothing! I swear!"

"That's what I thought." Then she was gone. They were all gone. And all he could do was cry and tell God he was so sorry.

Big Bavarian pretzels were the bar's well-known specialty. And as the priestess handed them out to each Protector, along with mugs of cold beer, they ate and stared at the spot where the Killers were no longer standing.

"That was a little less satisfying then I thought it would be," Gundo mused.

"Were you in the mood for a fight tonight?" Borgsten asked.

"Not really. Still . . . opening doorways, shoving them through. Not exactly Viking-like."

"If we were going to be Viking-like, we would have killed all the Giant Killers and fucked their corpses." When Borgsten's brothers stared at him, he added, "At least that's what my bloodline was known for. Thankfully, we've since moved away from that."

"Thankfully," they all said in unison.

"You do know, Alessandra, that you held his balls for a really long time?" Erin asked.

"I know, dude, but they were *huge*. And his dick was like an elephant's."

Kera cringed. "Surprisingly, that does not sound as hot as you'd think it would."

"It explains why he's so confident."

They perched in the trees overlooking the revival tent and watched the pastor run out. He was crying and tripping over his own feet. And there was now a yellow stain on the front of his white pants.

They'd only come for the bracelet. He hadn't used it. Didn't even know what it was. Erin could have stolen it and that would have been that.

But after a little research and watching a few minutes of his online videos, Kera wanted to send a message. Her very religious mother used to fall victim to assholes like him all the time. If she could stop even one of them, she'd feel like she'd accomplished something with her life.

You know . . . besides helping to save the world from Ragnarok and all.

"So, what do you guys think?" Erin asked. "Think he'll really change?"

Annalisa shrugged. "I don't know. It's nearly impossible to change a sociopath. And you kinda have to be one to steal from the poor by using their religion against them. Even I was never that shitty. And I was really shitty. But I will say, I do enjoy pretending that we're angels."

"I heard the Pope hates when we do that," Alessandra said.

"He hates everything we do."

"No." Erin shook her head. "Not everything."

"Wait," Kera cut in, beginning to panic. "How does the Pope know about us? How are we involved with the Pope at all? Why does he hate us?"

Erin chuckled. "I do love ex-Catholic panic."

"I don't know which is worse," Jace suddenly said, her voice soft as she watched Pastor Bruce's car speed away. "The ones who don't believe what they're saying and steal from you . . . or the ones who do believe and still steal from you."

"Wow," Annalisa said, "that's some deep shit."

"Anyone else hungry?" Erin asked. "I am so in the mood for waffles."

"We passed a twenty-four IHOP off the freeway."

They all nodded and the others unleashed their wings and took off. But Jace was still sitting there.

Kera carefully moved across the tree limb to perch beside her. She still wasn't as confident as the others that the trees could hold her weight, but she was getting more comfortable with the intricacies of her new life. Jace kept telling her it would take time, "but it'll be part of your every day before you know it."

"Jace? Are you okay?"

"Yeah," Jace replied a little too fast. "I was just thinking."

"About lying pastors?"

She smiled. "You could say that."

"I've met a few myself. My mother used to send them money all the time. Drove my dad crazy. Especially when they came over to the house and he'd find them in his living room, drinking his coffee and stealing his money. He said they were like cult leaders."

"No," she said with a shake of her head. "They're not like cult leaders. Not at all."

And with that cryptic bit of information, Jace unfurled her wings and was gone.

CHAPTER NINE

Ski woke up extremely early when Salka pawed the back of his head. That meant someone was in the house. Usually it was the cleaning people, but this wasn't their day.

So Ski got up, Salka draped around his neck since she was in no mood to move. He walked downstairs and found a few of his brothers just coming through the front door, grunting a greeting at him before heading to the kitchen to get their first cups of coffee.

But Salka wouldn't wake him up because of his brothers. She knew them almost as well as she knew Ski.

Yet Salka also wasn't panicking. She wasn't alerting Ski to any major danger, just letting him know a non-Protector was in the house.

Over time, the cat Ski had found sick and nearly hairless in the rosebushes out back had turned into the true protector of this sacred place. Even Tyr liked her. Then again, he liked any animal that didn't try to remove the only hand he had left.

Ski stopped, tilting his head. He heard a page turn. Smiling, he headed to the library. He found Jace sitting at the table, her feet up on the chair, a book resting on her knees. Eyes wide, mouth slightly open, she was deeply involved in whatever she read.

It was definitely one of the books they'd retrieved the other night but it didn't look important. Or interesting. The binding was rather old, but not ancient. He wondered what she'd found in there that had her so transfixed.

But before he could ask, Ski heard a bark.

While still reading, Jace reached one hand back and patted the top of the beige carrier resting behind her. "It's okay, baby. Go back to sleep."

"What is *that* doing here?" Ski demanded, pointing at the carrier set up near the table.

Still reading, she replied, "No one could take him this morning. So I brought him with me. Kera will pick him up later."

"He can't be in here."

"He's fine."

"There are no dogs allowed in our library."

"Is that because Lev is a canine and Tyr lost his hand to the wolf Fenrir? Is this some kind of canine bigotry?"

"More like canine disgust—and what are you reading?"

"Victorian porn in Russian."

Ski wasn't sure he'd heard her right. "Pardon?"

"Victorian porn. I'm guessing they dressed it up in this boring cover so that Lenin and his uptight cronies wouldn't know it was filled with imperialist dogma in the guise of wild-wielding sex."

She finally lowered her book and looked up at Ski. Jace frowned and stared a little bit before noting, "You have a cat on your head."

"Yes."

"You can have a cat, but I can't have my dog?"

"She lives here. And cats aren't nearly as filthy as dogs."

"Do you mean morally or because dogs like to roll around in their own feces?"

"Both. And Bear is going to lose his OCD-riddled mind when he finds out you brought your dog to his precious library."

"He's in a carrier. And he's a *baby*. I can't leave a baby alone."

"Dogs of a young age are not babies. They're puppies. Puppies that don't wear diapers."

"He has a diaper on."

Ski folded his arms over his chest. "You put a diaper on your dog? And you don't see anything wrong with that? Psychologically, I mean."

"I put it on him so there wouldn't be any leakage."

"That's disgusting."

"He'll be fine," she insisted, going back to her book.

"Have you finished logging in all the other stuff in those boxes?"

"Not . . . no."

"Then could you put your porn reading off to a later date?"

"It's just so fascinating."

"I'm sure it is, but I'm almost positive we won't need you to translate that for us. Nor will we *pay you* to translate that for us."

"Fine," she sighed out, placing the book off to the side.

Ski asked, "Did you have breakfast?"

"I don't eat breakfast."

"I'll make you something to eat."

"I don't want anything to eat."

"You'll eat."

"What are you? My grandmother?"

"Obviously someone has to watch out for you," he said, heading toward the kitchen. "Starving yourself over porn."

"I was not!"

Jace heard Eriksen call out that breakfast was ready, but she chose to ignore him and kept working.

She was reaching for one of the books she'd piled on the table when she felt her entire chair being lifted off the floor.

"Hey!"

"I called," Eriksen replied. "You ignored."

With amazing ease, he carried her and the heavy wooden chair through the halls of the house until he reached the kitchen. The table was already filled with Protectors but they didn't even look up from their books, papers, laptops, or phones to watch as Eriksen set her down.

He placed a plate piled with sausage, bacon, eggs, and toast in front of her. Next to that, he placed another plate filled with a stack of pancakes.

"Isn't that . . . a lot?" she asked.

"For who?"

Deciding she didn't want a debate, Jace just shook her head and looked back at the plate. Pulling her legs up so that the heels of her feet rested on the seat, she reached over and took a slice of bacon.

She was quietly munching on it and staring out the window when she sensed someone standing very close to her. Too close. She turned her head, bacon hanging from her mouth, to see one of the Protectors eyeing her hair.

"Can I help you, Haldor?"

"Your hair . . ."

"Yes?"

"It's like my daughter's."

"Oh. Okay."

He leaned in closer. "Can I braid it?"

"Why?"

"Yeah," one of the other Protectors asked, looking away from his paperwork. "Why?"

"She wants me to take her to a Viking fair. It's like a renaissance faire, and she wants to go in costume and she wants her hair braided. Except I don't know how to braid hair. So I bought a book." He held the book up. "And thought maybe I could practice a bit before I tried it on her."

Jace remembered that Haldor's wife had died a few years ago, leaving just him and his little girl. He'd raised her himself with the help of babysitters and nannies, of course, but from what she'd heard, he'd taken it fully upon himself to give his daughter as normal a life as possible.

As normal as possible when one's father had wings and one's Valkyrie mother had died during a battle with demons.

"Sure," Jace said with a shrug.

"Thank you. That's great." He handed the book to Jace. "Which do you like?"

She looked over the styles, which were probably very popular in 1596, and randomly picked one. It didn't look too complicated and she guessed it wouldn't take too long.

"This one."

Haldor nodded. "Nice choice." He looked over the page,

closed his eyes a moment, then put the book on the table. Closed. That's when she knew he had an eidetic memory. Something Jace had always wished she had. Then again, if she could remember everything perfectly, it would be no fun rereading her favorite books like *Crime and Punishment* or *War and Peace*.

While Haldor used his extremely large hands to carefully separate her hair into sections before beginning the braiding, Jace nibbled on dry toast and stared out the window or up through the skylight.

Jace was having a nice day.

Bear walked into the Protectors' house and immediately went to the library to see how far along the Crow had gotten with the books. He stopped at the entrance and stared at the empty desk. Where was she? And where was the chair?

Several teen Protectors walked past him and into the library to work. The teen Protectors were only sent to this location for their final battle training. Usually transferring to the local private high school in their junior year. Younger boys went to what was called a "private boys' school" but was really a training ground for future Protectors. There they were taught general education and simple battle techniques, how to fly, and how to read and translate runes as well as use them for power and magic. You know . . . the basics.

Deciding to see if he could find the Crow—she was probably in the kitchen—he turned to go but stopped when he heard a sound.

What was that? What kind of noise was that?

He heard it again. A "yip."

Head turning and tilting to the side, he heard panting and whining coming from a carrier of some kind by the desk.

Bear went to it and lifted it from the ground until he was eye to eye with whatever was inside.

It yipped again and Bear's eyes narrowed, and a little growl eased out of his throat.

★   ★   ★

Ski had never seen one woman take so long to eat three pieces of toast. But all she did was nibble. Slowly. Sometimes she'd stop to take a drink of water. Or nibble on a bit of bacon. But mostly she just nibbled on that toast while Haldor worked on her hair with his big, somewhat clumsy hands.

Then it got weirder.

Suddenly Jace was surrounded by several Protectors who'd decided to help their brother out. They didn't touch her hair, but they pointed out what Haldor should do to get the style right.

And Ski just watched. Fascinated by the whole thing. Haldor's need to do something for his beautiful daughter; his brothers' need to help a fellow Protector with something they knew absolutely nothing about; plus, Jace's amazing amount of patience.

The whole time she didn't complain. She didn't look uncomfortable. Nor did she engage in the conversation going on around her.

She just nibbled and stared.

That's when he finally understood.

Jace Berisha wasn't painfully shy due to the tragic past that had led to her eventual death and rebirth as a Crow.

She was an antisocial introvert who didn't hate people . . . just small talk.

No wonder she'd bolted from his car like he'd come at her with a knife. He was trying to have polite conversation with her and she'd rather do anything *but* that.

Realizing he'd figured out the puzzle that was Jace made Ski feel like he'd accomplished something amazing. He just didn't know why.

One of the teen Protectors walked into the kitchen, paused briefly to stare at what his older brothers were doing, then shook his head and came over to Ski.

"Uh . . . Mr. Eriksen?"

"You really don't have to call me that, Karl."

"At this time in my existence, I'm more comfortable with calling you mister."

Not willing to argue that point, Ski said, "Okay."

"Uh . . . anyway . . . that . . . uh . . . animal. In the case. In the library."

"Yes?"

"Yeah. Mr. Ingolfsson took it. Outside. While muttering. Personally, I've always found his muttering . . . unsettling."

Ski straightened just as Jace spun around in her chair and the Protectors stopped fussing with her hair. They all stared at each other a long moment before they bolted out of the kitchen and back to the library. One of the sliding doors was open and they all slammed into it together, getting jammed there except Jace, who crouched and dived out before she could get caught.

"One at a time, gentlemen!" Ski ordered before pulling himself out of the pack and taking off after Jace.

He easily caught up to her, and as they rounded a large hedge, they found Bear holding the puppy around the middle with the animal facing away from him. He held him high in the air with both hands and Ski thought for one tragic, horrible second that his brother was going to throw the thing down to the ground in a rage.

He didn't.

Instead, he loudly commanded the puppy to, "Urinate! Urinate, puppy!"

Jace looked at Ski, but he could only throw up his hands. He had no idea what the hell was going on.

Taking a breath, Jace slowly walked over to Bear and stood beside him.

"What are you doing?" she asked softly. Gently. So as not to startle.

"Allowing this animal to urinate. Here. In nature."

"Uh-huh. He might be more comfortable doing that if you put him down on the ground."

Bear glanced at Jace. "Are you sure? He might run away."

"He might . . . but chances are you'll catch him. He still trips over his own feet. He's only about two and a half months old."

"Oh. I see."

Bear placed the puppy on the ground. Then he ordered, loudly, "*Urinate!*"

"Uh . . ." Jace put her hand on his forearm. "You don't need to . . . order him to urinate. He'll do it. If he needs to. The . . . loudness of your voice might scare him."

"Oh. I see."

He faced Jace. "The cat defecates in a box."

"Yes. I've never had a cat, but I do know that."

"Dogs don't, though. And he's young. So you shouldn't leave him alone. He was whining. He sounded sad."

"He was probably lonely. Wondering where I was."

"You shouldn't leave him alone. Not in a new place."

The smile broke across her face like a bright sun. "You're absolutely right, Bear. I shouldn't have left him alone."

He suddenly looked her over. "I like your hair."

"Thank you. Haldor did it."

Bear nodded. "For the Viking festival." He turned to Haldor, who had come up behind them. "I think this will work."

"I think so, too."

"He's done," Jace said.

Bear reached down and picked the puppy up. He gazed at him with that expressionless face before noting, "I like him. He doesn't try to rip my face off."

When Bear looked at Ski, Ski rolled his eyes and reminded him, "Then you shouldn't wake Salka up. You know she's not a morning cat."

Kera stopped in front of the Protectors' house and turned off the engine.

"Your dog's breath stinks," Erin complained.

Both Kera and Brodie gawked at her, mouths open.

"Rude," Kera told her and Brodie barked in agreement. "And we didn't need you to come. We're just here to get Lev. Don't you have a job tattooing people?"

"Not until I'm done with your party."

"The party that's going to suck?"

"That's the one!" Erin cheered before stepping out of the car.

"Why do I bother?" Kera sighed, but that's when Brodie rubbed her big pit bull head against Kera's jaw and neck.

Smiling, Kera kissed the top of her snout. "I love you, too, baby."

Kera rolled the windows down all the way. "I'll be right back."

When Kera stepped out of the car, Erin shook her head. "Leaving your poor dog in a hot car? She could *die*."

"I can't bring her inside."

"You'd let your dog *die* before you'd upset the Protectors?"

"Don't the Crows have enough enemies?"

"Don't you love your dog? Your poor, giant-headed dog?"

Not liking that description of her head, Brodie leaned out and snapped at Erin.

"I meant it in the nicest way possible!"

Kera walked around the car and stuck her head in the back window. Brodie licked her nose.

"Do you want to come in, Brodie? Or are you okay here?"

Brodie leaned back, sitting regally with her snout up.

Kera walked past Erin. "See?"

"You do know that Skuld did more to that dog than just give it wings and that psycho metal muzzle, right?"

"Brodie is not an 'it.' Brodie is a 'she.' And I don't care what Skuld did. Brodie's here with me now and she's one of us. Besides . . . why don't you just admit you like her?"

"Because I don't. I'm more a cat person."

"Liar. Cats hate you. They actively attack you."

Kera reached the front door, Erin right behind her.

"I know. I can't even say it's because I'm a Crow. When I was eight, my aunt's old cat almost tore my lip off. I don't know why, though," she added, smiling. "I am *such* a lovely person."

"You know, you're actually not."

Erin laughed and Kera raised her fist to knock on the door. That was when she realized the front door was open.

Grabbing Kera's arm and pulling it away from the door, Erin pushed the door all the way open.

"Why are we doing this?"

"Because we're nosy."

"What is this 'we' shit, white girl?"

Erin chuckled and walked into the house. Together they made their way down the big halls toward the library.

To Kera's surprise, no Protectors came out to greet them. Or, more accurately, stop them. From what she'd heard, the quickest way to get a Protector to rip your head off—literally—was to "invade" one of their precious libraries without permission. And that was the word they used. "Invade."

But she and Erin walked on, seeing no one . . . until they reached the library. That was where they froze. Right outside the large double doors that stood wide open.

They froze and gawked. Looked at each other. Then gawked some more.

Because Kera really didn't know what was going on.

Wasn't life weird enough these days? Why did it keep getting weirder?

One big Protector was braiding Jace's hair. Intricate, pretty braids that looked straight out of some historical TV show where people get beheaded or poisoned and a king rules with an iron fist while his queen plots.

Standing around him were three more Protectors, giving him tips and pointing to a couple of books they held.

But that wasn't the weirdest part.

Another Protector, the one Kera knew they called Bear, had Jace's puppy around the waist, holding the dog up over his head and turning in a circle. As if he was showing Lev something. "This is not a room to poop in, puppy," he announced . . . to the dog.

The *dog*.

"You shall not poop in this room. Nor shall you chew on anything. Or urinate. *You shall not urinate in this room!*"

He brought the puppy down and turned him around so he

and Bear were eye to eye. "Do you understand me?" he asked . . . the dog.

The *dog.*

Still not the weirdest part.

Another Protector, wearing latex gloves, carefully pulled old-looking books out of a big wood box and placed them on the table. When one of his brothers tried to touch a book, he slapped hands or punched stomachs and told them, "Until the Crow says you can touch, you don't touch."

"I just want to look."

"No."

"But—"

"*I will kill you!*" the Protector bellowed.

Still not the weirdest.

The weirdest part? That was Jace.

Because Jace wasn't trying to find a table to crawl under or a car trunk to hide in. She wasn't actively trying to avoid all the weirdness.

And yet, Kera had seen Jace practically run from a room screaming when the Crows began to argue about some reality show they'd all been watching.

She wasn't doing that now. Instead, while some strange dude with absolutely gigantic hands braided her hair, she was playing . . . Scrabble.

She was also winning, the Protector she'd just beaten throwing his hands up in the air while several of his brothers politely applauded and laughed.

Bear put the puppy on the floor. "Now that you know the rules, I expect you to abide by them. Understand?"

The puppy barked and Bear seemed to take that as an acknowledgment and agreement to his terms. Did the man not realize Lev was just a dog and was probably barking because . . . well . . . because he was a dog?

"Good. Now go forth and try not to annoy."

At that point, Kera looked at Erin and she shrugged her shoulders in reply.

They turned to leave and found Danski Eriksen standing behind them. Not only had he not made a sound as he'd moved up behind them—creepy enough, thanks—but he also had a large white cat on his head.

A cat.

On his *head*.

He smiled at them—at least that wasn't creepy—and said softly, "Lev will be fine."

That was good enough for Kera. She nodded and walked around him, glancing back to see Erin move out of range of that cat's paw as it slashed at her, claws extended as much as possible.

Snarling, Erin turned toward the cat but before she could do or say anything, Kera grabbed her elbow and yanked her away and back down the hall.

When they reached the car, they both got in. Brodie was still in the backseat, her gaze bouncing back and forth between them.

After a moment of silence, Kera asked Erin, "Starbucks?"

She nodded. "Starbucks."

And they headed out for a coffee and a few hours of analyzing what the holy fuck they'd just seen.

Yardley King, movie star, paparazzi favorite since her accidental sex tape, and Los Angeles Crow, sat in her trailer and waited until she heard the knock.

"Come in."

Her agent's assistant opened the door and leaned in, smiling.

Yardley had to fight her desire to narrow her eyes in a show of obvious distrust, but she wanted to be better than that. It wasn't as if Brianna had done anything wrong. Not really.

She'd done what anyone in Hollywood would have done after their boss had apparently thrown herself out her office window. She'd taken over.

And yet . . . Brianna's boss wasn't just anybody. She was Betty Lieberman. An elder Crow. A mighty seer. And a kick-ass agent.

Betty had taken Yardley under her wing as soon as Yardley

had woken up in the Bird House. Betty had not only handled Yardley's battle training, she'd managed her career. Taking her from a former teen star who, at that time, couldn't get a job to save her life to a fifteen-million-per-film movie star in little more than three years with a whole redemption story attached.

She'd shown Yardley the ropes among the Hollywood vipers and the local Vikings. She'd taught her how to read a room at a media event and how to rip off a face with her talons while leaving her victim still breathing.

Betty had been like a mother to her. Actually, she'd been better than Yardley's own mother, who'd been the one to pin Yardley down on her bed and shove a copious amount of drugs down her throat until she'd overdosed. But that was a long story she really didn't want to get into.

Instead, she just wanted Betty back, but Yardley was contractually trapped here while one of her closest friends was in some kind of a weird coma.

And Yardley didn't believe for a second that Betty had tried to kill herself. Because that woman wouldn't give anyone in the industry the satisfaction. Not Betty.

So then, what did happen? Yardley didn't know.

All she knew was that she was on this location shoot with this idiot director. An emotional mess of a man who had convinced the world he was an *auteur*.

Betty had warned her. Not by using her seer powers, either. Instead, she'd just said, "You really want to do this movie, sweetie . . . ? Because he's an idiot."

Dammit, Betty had been right! As always, Yardley should have listened.

"How ya doin', hon?" Brianna asked, stepping into the trailer and closing the door behind her.

Yardley didn't like how familiar and comfortable Brianna had become lately, either. She didn't need the woman kissing her ass, necessarily. But Yardley would definitely prefer that Brianna not act like they'd been best friends since the beginning of time.

"The man's a mess," Yardley immediately stated. "I mean . . . he's a mess, Brianna."

"Yeah . . . I was just talking to the producer and all the double-talking . . . definitely an issue there." She took a few steps closer and Yardley couldn't help but notice the copious amount of jewelry on the woman. She was sure that Brianna had given herself a much bigger salary than Betty had approved, but wow . . . that was a lot of gold. And diamonds. So many diamonds. "Is he really in a tent somewhere . . . crying?"

"Yes. He cries every day. Over nothing. The slightest hiccup and the man bursts into tears. This entire movie is a fucking disaster."

"I heard the studio is going to bring another director in. They just have to work out a deal to get rid of this one."

"I don't want to work with another director on this thing. I just want out."

"But hon—"

"*Get me out of this.*"

"Well . . . you did sign a contract."

Yardley stared at Brianna. The way Betty had taught her.

"Don't speak, sweetie," Betty had always counseled. "Just stare . . . and wait. You have to be willing to wait. It freaks people out every time."

So Yardley waited and, after several long minutes, Brianna finally threw up her hands and said, "Okay. I'll see what I can do. Why don't you just go back to the hotel?"

"Fine."

"I'll call you later."

Brianna left and Yardley's security team—several of her fellow Crows who were paid well to protect the one movie star who probably didn't need it—came in to help Yardley pack up. As far as she was concerned, she was out of here. If the media wanted to turn her into a diva over it . . . so what?

Thankfully, her sister-Crows knew how to get Yardley to lighten up. After only a few minutes, they had her laughing and talking about past boyfriends until sometime later, they heard a horrible scream.

Always Crows, they ran out of the trailer without thought to their own safety. Much of the film crew was running past her.

Running away. Some people were screaming. Others crying. One big guy, some union driver, stopped, leaned over, and threw up.

Shocked, Yardley and the others pushed forward until the producer crashed into her, trying to push Yardley back.

"No, babe. You can't see this."

Babe? Did he just call her babe?

"What? What are you talking about?"

"Just go back to your trailer. I'll be in—"

Yardley pushed the producer off her as one of her sisters walked out of the director's tent and motioned to her. She quickly walked in, ignoring the producer's demands for her to stop.

As soon as she stepped inside, though, she did pause.

Yeah. She paused.

Gazing down at the man she now felt a little bad for, Yardley asked her fellow Crows, "Where's his skin?"

Jace relaxed back against her chair and pressed the tips of her fingers against her closed eyelids, taking a moment to rub them. They were dry and she wished she'd remembered to bring some eyedrops just to lubricate them.

"Tired?"

Pulling her hand away, she looked up at Ormi Bentsen, leader of the Southern California Protectors.

"Just my eyes. I'll be fine."

"It's late, Jacinda. You should go home."

"But I just found this book on runes and—"

"It'll be here tomorrow."

Jace took a moment to study Ormi. His wings were out. She looked over her shoulder at the floor-to-ceiling windows and realized it was dark.

"Gosh, I'm sorry."

"Never apologize to *me* about working too hard. I love hard workers."

"It's just been pretty fascinating. I mean, some of these books are completely useless to you guys. But others, I think, will be quite an addition to your collections."

"That's what I needed to know. Now . . . I'm assuming you'll be staying with us through the full translation process."

"Uh . . ." Jace rubbed her nose. "I think I was just supposed to translate titles and authors and get the general gist of each book. Although I've been told there's some kind of list for other translation services."

"Those will wait until you're done with this."

"Are you sure?"

"Of course I'm sure. You fit in perfectly here."

Jace had never heard that before. "I do?"

"You're quiet. You do your work. But when you do have something to say, it's concise, useful, and doesn't bore anyone with unnecessary, vapid content. For a Protector that's pretty much the 'whole package,' as they say."

"I really like coming here," she admitted. "But some of this translation may take time. Some of it is in seriously ancient Russian. Plus, there's some Mongolian in there and some of the books are just written in runes. Which . . . for me . . . would actually be an amazing challenge. But I don't want to waste your time. I'm sure a Holde's Maid could translate the runes much quicker than I can—"

"Perhaps," Ormi cut in. "But they will annoy me."

Jace frowned. "Isn't your wife a Holde's Maid?"

"And she annoys me. Love her to death," he quickly added, "but to work with her? Rather get my toes eaten off by rats. *That's* how annoying she is. Demanding. Demeaning. Rude. Pushy. It's true, I find her very attractive and our sexual life is quite fulfilling—"

"Oh."

"—but when it comes to my work here and my brother Protectors . . . I must think of their welfare. And mine. My wife has no patience with them."

"What makes you think I have patience?"

"You beat Kilmar at Scrabble, but not once did you try to remove the eyes from his head. My wife can't say that."

"I don't know why he got so bitchy, though. He said Latin words were included."

"He didn't know anyone knew Latin as well as him."

"Well, he was wrong."

Ormi laughed and gently closed the cover on the laptop they'd loaned her. "Go home, Crow. We'll see you tomorrow."

Jace stood, taking a moment to stretch her muscles.

"Are you leaving?"

Jace smiled as Bear walked toward her, Lev asleep in his arms.

"Thank you so much," she said with real sincerity.

Bear grunted and handed Lev over.

"I don't know what happened to Kera. She said she'd be here to pick him up."

"She was," Eriksen said, walking into the library with a set of keys in his hand. "Her and Erin Amsel."

"Really? Why didn't anyone say anything?"

"Bear had Lev handled. Didn't you, Bear?"

Another grunt.

Bear started to walk away, but stopped and leaned in to Jace. His face looked really angry, but she didn't shrink from it. She had a feeling that would just . . . hurt his feelings.

Which was kind of a strange reaction to a man who seemed moments from threatening her life.

"Tomorrow," he practically snarled. "You can bring him back. He was very good. He only pooped and peed outside."

"Uh . . . okay."

"He poops a lot, you know," he added.

"Did you feed him a lot?"

"He appeared hungry to me."

"He's a dog. Dogs will always appear hungry, even if they've just had an entire slab of cow. That's just their way. They don't have an 'off' button when it comes to eating. So it's up to us to monitor what they eat and adjust accordingly."

Bear straightened up, gazed down at Jace before replying, "Excellent point. Tonight I'll read books on dogs. By tomorrow . . . I'll know more."

"I don't have to bring—"

"You can bring him. Good night."

"'Night, Bear."

The large man lumbered out and Ormi grinned at her. "See? My wife would have hexed him by now and all his skin would have fallen off long before that conversation ended." He patted Jace's shoulder. "You're perfect."

Ormi walked away without another word, and she turned to Eriksen. He shrugged at her. "Told you. This job is for you."

"He wants me to do all the translations. Is that because of you?"

"I didn't say a word. But the list on the refrigerator is filling up. You are going to be booked for quite a while. Besides, even if I had said something, Ormi still does what Ormi wants to do. So you must have impressed him. All on your own." He held up the keys. "Lift?"

"Oh, I can fly—"

"With the dog? He'll be shitting in panic all the way home."

Dammit, the man was right. But another long, painful, chitchat-filled drive back to the Bird House? Oy.

Jace forced a smile. "Okay."

Eriksen stared at her a moment before laughing and walking off. She had no idea what that meant, but she girded her loins for the nightmare to come.

Ski pulled up to the front of the Bird House and shut off the engine, the doors automatically unlocking.

"See ya tomorrow."

Jace glanced at him. "Are you mad at me?"

"No. Not at all."

"Did I do something wrong? With the work, I mean."

"Are you kidding? You even got Ormi's seal of approval. His own *wife* can't get that. Why?"

"Well . . . you didn't say anything."

"Did you want me to say anything?" When she struggled to answer, he said, "Let me put it this way. Did you want me to talk to you about general, nonsensical things? Or keep quiet until I have something interesting to enthrall you with?"

"You make me sound horrible."

"No, no. That's not what I meant. You just don't like bull-shit. But as second in command of the Protectors, I spend a lot of time bullshitting. I work with the other Clans. Occasionally I have to work with the gods because Tyr really has no patience for them anymore. And I *am* good at bullshitting. But I only do it when I need to. I am more than happy to sit and be quiet until I have something of actual interest to say. And I just assumed that's what you'd prefer."

She smiled in relief. "Actually, I would."

"Then there you go. So, see you tomorrow?"

Her grin widened. "Yes!"

"Great."

Ski watched her grab hold of her backpack after situating her dog in her other arm. She hadn't even realized she'd left the dog's carrier back at the house.

Ski reached across to open the door for her.

"Thank you."

"Welcome. Hey," he said before she could get out. "Would you like to go out some time? You know . . . like, on a date?"

Still smiling, she shook her head. "No."

Ski blinked, then asked. "So you don't like me."

"No, I like you."

"Okay. You don't find me attractive."

"No, you're really attractive," she said with a laugh.

"But you won't go out with me?"

"No." She was still smiling.

"Could you tell me why?"

"No."

"O-okay. Well . . . see you tomorrow."

"Okay! See you tomorrow!" She got out of the car, using her cute ass to close the door. Then she ran up the stairs and disappeared into the Bird House.

Confused, he went to start the car, which was when he realized someone was standing beside it.

He looked up and saw Vig Rundstöm glowering down at him.

★   ★   ★

Jace walked into the Bird House. She was still smiling as she closed the door.

"Hey, *chica*," Kera said, coming around the corner. "You look happy."

"I just got asked out on a date."

Kera in her cut-off shorts and United States Marines T-shirt, plus bare feet—the woman was not big on shoes—clapped her hands together. "Eriksen, right?"

"Yeah."

Appearing more excited than Jace, she asked, "So you guys are going out?"

Still smiling, Jace shook her head. "No."

The grin on Kera's face, however, faded away. "No?"

"No."

"So you don't like him?"

"No, no. I like him. I think he's really hot."

"But you're not going to go out with him."

"No."

"You gonna tell me why?"

Jace started toward her room. "No." She waved at her friend. "See ya!"

They stayed like that for several long minutes. Ski staring at the Raven and the Raven staring back.

They all called Vig Rundstöm the Pit Bull. Not normally to his face, but they weren't above doing that. Unlike the other Ravens who just seemed stupid, Rundstöm seemed . . . off. The fact that Kera Watson, a former Marine and even-tempered female who was sorely needed by the constantly emotional Crows, had taken up with him had become a source of discussion. Two people couldn't be further apart in personality.

But Kera was new to the Crows and perhaps she had no real understanding of the man she was lying down with most nights.

Vig Rundstöm, of the Rundstöm bloodline, known for their berserker-like tendencies in battle since the early days of the gods.

Which was why Ski seriously thought he'd be forced to kill

the man right there, in the Crows' driveway, until Kera Watson walked out of the house and yelled, "Ludvig Rundstöm! Stop that right now!"

"He started it," Rundstöm argued, forcing Ski to cringe at what the Ravens called "logic."

"You mean he started it by breathing?" the pretty Crow asked.

The disturbingly big Raven shrugged enormous shoulders and replied simply, "Yes."

Shaking his head, Ski started the car, and pulled out of the driveway.

Maybe it was best that Jace had turned him down. She was close friends with Kera Watson, which might mean eventual double dates—and Ski didn't think he could spend time outside of Clan work with that idiot.

Chapter Ten

Again Jace was already in the Protector library by the time Ski woke up. Although he did get a later start than usual.

He was exhausted. As soon as he'd returned after dropping Jace off, he'd been pulled into another job with two teams.

It could be his imagination, but it seemed as if they were working more than usual. And the previous night had been messy, the group walking in on a sex rite that included an orgy and several human sacrifices.

It had been kind of horrifying. Not the sex part. Ski wasn't against sex magic in general. But including death in rites that usually celebrated life and pleasure was . . . strange. Something not normally done. And these weren't Satanists, who could be all kinds of trouble. These were pagans. Of different faiths.

Honestly, Ski didn't know what to make of it all. He just knew that shutting the whole thing down before too many lives were taken had involved a lot more work than he'd expected.

But seeing Jace hunched over the table, pencil in hand, deep in translation work did nothing but cheer up his morning.

He felt that pang of regret again. Not quite sure why she wouldn't go out with him. But he was part of the honorable Protectors. Unlike the Giant Slayers or Ravens, he wasn't about to start pestering her until she finally gave in just to get him to stop. That was not his idea of the start of a healthy relationship.

Kilmar sat at the table also. He seemed to be doing the logging work that Jace had originally been hired for.

That didn't bother Ski. He could tell she'd been dying to dive in to some of the books she'd had her hands on.

He did have one problem, though . . .

"You're writing it out longhand?"

Slowly, sheepishly, Jace raised her gaze to his. "Well—"

"No. We have technology. You will use it."

"But—"

"No," Ski said again, determined on this point. "Kilmar, please get our guest another laptop."

The younger Protector frowned. "But wouldn't longhand look nicer?"

"Kilmar," Ski pushed, tempted to slap his brother.

Kilmar shrugged at Jace. "Sorry."

"Where's that dog?"

"That dog," she shot back, "is at the Bird House playing with Brodie."

"Bear will be disappointed."

"Is there a problem with my dog?"

"Not at all—until he chews up the first book. Then expect all Helheim to break loose."

Sighing, she leaned back in her chair.

"So Kilmar knows Russian?" he asked, motioning to the book Ski's brother had been logging in.

"No. Those books are all written in Latin. Strange, since they were published in the forties." She waved her random thought away. "We all know that Kilmar has a *basic* understanding of Latin."

Ski smirked. "That was mean."

"Just a little." She crinkled her nose, letting him know she was just teasing. Not surprising, since Ski was pretty sure she'd never let Kilmar near her if she didn't like him. "You look a little tired today," she noted.

"I am. Busy night. Ever heard of sex rites that involved human sacrifices?"

"Satanists?"

"No."

She frowned. "That's unusual."

"That's what I thought."

"We had a job last night, too. We've had a lot of those lately. Each Strike Team usually only goes out once, maybe twice a month at the most. But lately, each team has been going out every week. *That's* strange."

"We've been busier than usual, too. I'll mention it to Ormi."

Kilmar returned with one of their most expensive laptops, still in the box and untouched. Ski smirked, realizing how much his brothers liked the Crow; they didn't usually give out their best equipment to just anyone.

"Do you know how to type?" Ski asked, watching as Jace opened the box and pulled everything out.

"Yes."

"Are you going to eat?"

"I'm not really—"

"I'll make you something."

"Why do you ask when you don't even lis—"

"I'll make you something hearty."

"Jace? *Jace.*"

Jace looked up and saw that her Strike Team stood around her, dressed for battle.

She leaned back in her chair and cracked her knuckles. "What are you guys doing here?"

"We have a job."

"Oh. Uh . . . yeah . . ." She went back to her work. "Just come get me when we have to go."

"We have to go now."

Surprised, she looked at her team leader. "In the day?"

Tessa stepped back, gesturing to the ceiling-to-floor windows the way Ski and Ormi had recently done. It was becoming a definite pattern. "It's nighttime, sweetie."

"Oh. Uh . . . okay."

Nodding, Jace pushed her chair back and realized that she might have been sitting too long in one position because she couldn't move her neck.

Leigh immediately saw Jace's problem and gently placed her

hands against the tight muscles. "Relax and breathe," she told Jace.

Leigh's First Life had been as a massage therapist. A good one, too. She immediately tweaked the tenseness out of Jace's muscles with just the tips of her fingers.

As Jace felt the pain drift away, she saw Erin reaching toward the table. "Don't touch the books!" she snapped.

Leigh's hands stopped moving and everyone froze.

Jace sighed. "I'm not raging. I just don't want anyone to touch anything."

"Oh," they all said together, going back to what they were doing, except for Erin, who'd been the one about to touch the books.

"I have everything where I need it," Jace went on. "And some of these books are ancient. They need to be handled carefully. Not by someone who uses their hands to force ink into the flesh of another."

Erin's brows peaked. "You have one of my tattoos."

"So I know what I'm talking about."

Tessa looked around the now-empty room. "Were the Protectors nice to you?"

"They're great to me."

"Because they leave you alone?"

"Pretty much."

"And you like that," Annalisa noted.

"It was heaven."

"Why didn't you just tell us?" she asked.

"Tell you what?"

"That you're an introvert. It would have made life easier for those of us—"

"She means Rachel," Erin muttered.

"—who thought you were just shy."

"I don't know. It seemed rude to just come out with, 'I'm not a people person. Get the hell away from me.' I'm pretty sure the only one who wouldn't have been insulted by that was Erin."

Erin nodded. "She's right. I'm the only one who wouldn't have been insulted by that."

Once she felt she could move her neck without screaming, Jace stood, taking the clothes handed to her by Kera.

She quickly changed from her blue jeans, black T-shirt, and running shoes into the Crow combat outfit. Black jeans, steel-toed black work boots, black bra, and black racing-back tank top that allowed her to easily unleash her wings.

Once dressed, she carefully folded the clothing she'd just removed and looked at her team. That's when she realized they were staring at her. Almost gawking.

"What?" she asked.

"Wow," Alessandra announced. "You are *really* not shy."

Erin handed Jace her two blades and she placed her foot on the seat of her chair so that she could strap the weapons to her leg.

Jace tugged her jeans down to cover the leather holster and dropped her leg back to the floor. She then unleashed her wings, shaking them out and loosening up her shoulders so that flying would be easier.

"I can't believe the Protectors left you alone in their precious library."

"They had a job tonight. And I'm not really alone."

Jace motioned to the top of one of the book stacks. Ski's cat, Salka, sat there, licking her paw and keeping a close eye on her.

"She's been watching me since Eriksen left. I get the feeling if I tried to do anything to destroy even one of these books, she'd rip my throat out."

Erin nodded. "That's a good cat."

The team headed toward the exit.

"What's the job tonight?" Jace asked, hoping she wouldn't be out too late. Having several gods-related assignments in one week was unusual and exhausting. Plus her mind was already thinking of the books she'd left behind. She couldn't wait to get back to it all in the morning.

"This should be an easy job," Tessa told her. "In and out."

★ ★ ★

In the fetal position, Jace hit the window and went through it, glass exploding around her and falling to the ground thirty stories below.

She spun out into the air, floating for a few seconds before gravity stepped in and her body dropped.

She loosened her shoulders and unleashed her wings, catching the air and immediately heading back up. She tilted forward and dived through the now-open window and into the midst of the battle.

Jace rammed her body into the man who'd thrown her, wrapping her arms and legs around him and dropping them both to the floor.

He threw her off again and Jace flipped across the carpeted floor. Once she stopped, she rolled over onto her stomach, then up on all fours, and charged again.

"Fuck!" the man screamed out, quickly crab-walking back, away from her. "Get this bitch away from me!"

Jace landed on him again, placing her hands against his shoulders and shoving him to the ground. She pinned him there by his throat and grabbed hold of her fighting blade with her free hand.

"Wait—"

She cut off his words by ramming her blade into the side of his neck, severing the artery. She yanked the weapon out, then slammed it in again. Just to be sure.

That's when another set of hands grabbed Jace by the hair and yanked her up and off, tossing her away.

"You bitch!" someone screamed. "You killed him! You killed him!"

Jace was just getting to her feet when she was kicked and sent flying into a ceiling-to-floor glass mirror.

The glass shattered and she went down with all the pieces crashing around her. She closed her eyes and tried to cover her face to protect it, but she could still feel her body being cut.

"Jace!" she heard Kera call out. But Kera was in her own fight. They all were.

★ ★ ★

Ski gazed up at the ceiling. "How did they get all those bodies pinned up there?"

"No idea," Gundo replied. "But it is one of the more interesting sacrifices I've seen in a while."

"Now we know why Ormi sent you out with us." Borgsten walked around the ten-thousand-dollar-a-night bungalow, looking for more clues. "Is it just me, or does this seem like too nice a place for a sacrifice?"

Borgsten was right. Most sacrifices they'd come upon over the years were either done out in nature or in the cheapest hotel or motels that could be found. Because no one asked questions in those places. Not when there were drug dealers and gunrunners in the other rooms.

But a five-star hotel-and-bungalow complex in Palm Springs?

"We need to find out who rented this room."

"And why they needed so many offerings."

"How many do you count?" Ski asked. There were whole bodies pinned to the ceiling with thick metal spikes, but there were also some body parts scattered across the floor.

Gundo sighed. "I don't know. Ten. Twelve."

"Thirteen?"

"Maybe."

"Thirteen is usually the anti-Christians," Bear reminded them. He never wanted to call them Satanists, but Ski had no idea why. Maybe he thought the term was too limiting.

"Should we call the Pope?" Gundo asked and they all turned to face him. That's when he laughed and added, "Just kidding."

Borgsten shook his head. "You know the Protectors haven't dealt with a Pope since the Crusades."

"That was an ugly time."

"It wasn't our fault!" Bear argued. Like he always did. "Things just got a little out of hand."

"Do we have to go over this again?" Ski asked. "Really? It was nearly a thousand years ago. I can't believe we're still talking about this." Everyone fell silent but then Ski just had to add,

"And it was *totally* our fault. The Inquisition was not our fault. But the Crusades . . . all of them . . . *absolutely* our fault."

"But—"

"Let's just leave it at that."

They went back to searching for evidence when Gundo suddenly gasped, "Holy shit!"

"What?"

"You need to see this."

Ski walked into the sunken living room. There was a gorgeous fire pit right in the middle surrounded by big, comfortable couches and a fur rug. As he stepped around the couches, he saw all the jewelry. Had to be millions of dollars' worth.

"Is that stuff . . . is it real?" he asked. He knew watches, but he'd never been big on sparkly jewelry and he'd never dated women who were into much of that, either.

Gundo crouched beside the mound and picked one piece up. He held it up to the light, head tilting, eyes adjusting.

"I don't have a loupe but . . . I think so."

"So they offered up humans . . . and gold and diamonds?"

Bear now stood beside him, arms crossed over his massive chest. "Are the Crows *really sure* they got rid of Gullveig?"

Ski scratched his head. "Ormi's going to have to go back to Chloe. Because I'm not doing it."

"That won't go well," Gundo guessed. And he was most likely right. Chloe did not like to be questioned by the other Clans. About anything.

Still staring down, Gundo gave a small grunt.

"What?" Ski asked.

He reached down and picked something up from under the jewels. "Is this . . . is this straw?"

"Why would there be straw on the floor of a ten-thousand-dollar-a-night bungalow?"

"I think we need to let Ormi know what's going on," Borgsten said from the doorway.

Ski nodded. "Yeah. I want to get back and—"

He turned, head tilting until he'd almost turned it upside

down. But it was that sound. What was that sound? And where was it coming—

She appeared from smoke, ramming her hand into Bear's chest, sending the big man flying across the room and into Borgsten; the pair disappearing from view.

She turned toward Ski, but he heard something behind him and spun around. His hand shot out and he grabbed the neck of another female. With just a twist of his fingers, he had her screeching and bent awkwardly at the waist.

It was the *Mardröm*—the Mara for short—female demons who made their victims physically experience the nightmares they gave them. They were powerful and ancient and Ski had never seen one before, but he'd heard that the Crows and Ravens had fought them when they'd gone to stop Gullveig's reincarnation on this plane. The two Clans believed they'd destroyed them all.

Apparently they'd been wrong.

How these idiot dude-bros, as Erin called them, could get their hands on a powerful Rhine gold necklace forged by the gods, Jace didn't know. Even more fascinating was their decision to cut the necklace into pieces and sew it right into their bodies. That move gave them enhanced strength and fighting ability.

Human bodies weren't really made for that sort of power, though, and at some point, they'd probably burn themselves out. Until then, however, they could still do a lot of damage so the Crows couldn't risk them getting out of here like this.

"You killed him!" she heard again before being lifted and thrown to the other side of the room.

Jace hit a door and went through it. She flew right over a bed and into the far wall.

Her attacker followed. It seemed that bit of gold sewn into his chest gave him a steroid-like anger.

He again grabbed her by the hair and dragged her to her feet. While he held her hair with one hand, he slapped her with the other. The whole time chanting, with each hit, "You killed him! You killed him! You killed him!"

As he reached his hand back to slap her for the fourth time, Jace remembered she still had her blade tight in her fist. She brought it up, ramming it into his groin and ripping up.

She tore a line right up his gut until she reached his chest bone. She tilted the blade and dug it in deeper, tearing into the man's heart. She moved the blade around, then yanked it out.

He released her then, stumbling back, his hands over his bleeding stomach and groin.

"I killed him," Jace said, her breath harsh. "And now you."

She plunged her weapon into his eye. Then the other eye. He moved his hands to his head, screaming as he stumbled away from her.

Jace shoved him to the ground and tore open his T-shirt. She saw the scar left after he'd put the gold inside his body. She used her talon to rip that flesh open and plucked the item from his chest.

As soon as she did, he stopped screaming, he stopped fighting, and his body seemed to deflate into the floor.

Now holding one piece from the necklace, Jace closed her fingers over it and began to chant an ancient incantation she'd read in an old Nordic grimoire.

She chanted, eyes closed. She chanted and ignored the new screams she now heard. The shocked gasps of her sisters. She chanted and waited until the one gold piece in her hand was joined by all the others.

Panting, she opened her eyes. The necklace was covered in blood and flesh, but it was whole again.

Slowly she walked back into the living room. The other dude-bros were on the ground, the parts of their bodies where they'd sewn in the gold now torn open.

Tessa took the necklace from Jace. Smiled. "Nice work, sweetie. See how well you do when you don't flip out all the time?"

"Couldn't you have just left it at 'nice work'?"

"Coulda . . . didn't."

Kera approached, her face cringing.

"What?" Jace asked. "Why do you have that look?"

"We need to get you home. And . . . sewn up."

Jace blinked. "Wait . . . what?"

Another Mara landed on Ski's back, her legs around his waist, her hands digging into his hair.

Then the two females sort of . . . waited. Like they expected him to do something specific.

That's when he twisted his fingers more and snapped the one Mara's neck. It didn't kill her, but it seemed to hurt like a bitch. Her screech rang out, but stopped when Ski kept twisting and pulling until he'd yanked the witch's head off, black blood flying.

The female still on his back screeched and dug her claws into Ski's face. The tips extending into his flesh.

He roared in pain and caught the Mara's hands, yanking them away and flipping her off his back. He slammed her into the ground, lifted her, and slammed her. Lifted. Slammed. Lifted. Slammed. Until she was nothing but broken pieces.

That's when the hissing sound intensified and smoke began to fill the large room.

"Out," he ordered his brothers. "Out. Now."

He backed away, toward the exit, as the Mara appeared. From smoke to something almost human. Except for those rows of tiny black fangs, meant to tear and rend their victims. Some of the Mara crawled on all fours across the ceiling, while others eased along the walls. One led them. Naked, covered in blood, she moved across the room toward Ski.

"So beautiful," she hissed at him. "And what is your name, pretty Viking? What can I call you when I come to you at night? When I take you inside me? When I make you mine?"

Ski gave a small smile. "You? You can call me the Viking who took your heart."

With that, Ski rammed his right hand—the hand his god, Tyr, had sacrificed in the mouth of Fenrir the Wolf—into her chest. Ripping past bone and flesh until he could grip her heart.

Holding it, he continued on until he'd torn out to the other side.

Shocked and gasping, she gawked down at the part of his arm she could still see and then, slowly looked up at him.

Her heart still beat in his hand, so Ski silently squeezed until it turned to pulp in his grip and oozed down to his wrist.

The lead Mara gasped one final time and dropped, hanging from his forearm.

He pushed her off and looked at the others. Taking a step back so that he was on the other side of the doorway, Ski unfurled his wings, spreading them wide.

"*Protector!*" one cried in a panic.

The Mara began to back up, some beginning to turn to smoke, others rushing toward the walls they'd already come through.

"In the name of the mighty Tyr," Ski intoned, his blood-and-heart-covered right hand now drawing his god's rune in the air, "I bring you justice . . . and I bring you *death*."

The walls turned black and the lights overhead turned red. Everything shook and the walls crumbled in, trapping the Mara underneath the rubble. Until there was nothing but darkness and their far-off screeching.

Ski let out a breath and faced his brethren. Each closed his eyes, nodded his head, silently praising their god and giving Ski their blessing for his actions.

He walked out of the crumbling bungalow and once outside, spread his wings again and took to the skies, his brothers behind him.

CHAPTER ELEVEN

Jace was dressed and ready to head to work, practically skipping down the stairs. She stopped, though, when she heard the doorbell. No one else was around, so she went to answer it herself.

"Oh my God!" she gasped before thinking. "Your face!"

"*My* face?" Eriksen asked from the other side of the doorway. "What happened to *your* face?"

Jace immediately touched her cheeks, her fingers gliding along the stitches Tessa had put in the night before. She'd completely forgotten about them.

"Oh. That."

"Yeah. That."

"I was thrown into a mirror. And out a window." She thought a moment. "I think that's it."

"Oh well, that's good."

She frowned. "The sarcasm is unnecessary."

"Is it?"

Ormi, who stood beside Eriksen, leaned in and said, "Jacinda, dear. Would you mind taking us to Chloe? We need to see her."

"Oh sure." She turned and headed off to Chloe's private office.

"Aren't you going to ask us why we're here to see Chloe?" Eriksen asked.

"No."

"Why not?"

"You might tell me."

She heard Ormi laugh and Eriksen grunt.

They reached Chloe's door and Jace raised her hand to knock. But she instantly froze when she heard Chloe screaming from the other side, "*I know you're fucking that Valkyrie whore from Vegas!*"

"So?" a male voice shot back. "I know you're fucking that plastic surgeon from Beverly Hills! *Is he why your tits are suddenly bigger?*"

Something crashed against the wall, and Jace spun around to face the two Protectors. "Why don't we go see Tessa? She loves helping! She was a nurse!"

Without waiting for either to reply, she pushed past them and walked back through the house; the screaming still coming from Chloe's office thankfully fading away as they moved.

She cut through the living room, where the Crows who worked from home or were waiting for acting jobs to come in looked up from painting their nails or watching TV, silently observing Jace and the Protectors walk by.

She opened the sliding glass door and led them out to the back patio, where Tessa was having breakfast with the rest of Jace's Strike team except Kera. Based on Kera's absence and the extensive paperwork covering the large, round table, that meant they were in the midst of finalizing the plans for her welcome party.

Poor Kera was still convinced by evil Erin that her party would consist of six people and processed cheese.

"Tessa, the Protectors are here to see Chloe."

"Oh, just take them back—"

"But Chloe just found out that Josef is dating a Valkyrie who is also a stripper and he just accused her of getting her tits done, soooooo . . . yeah."

Tessa dropped her head into her hands. "Seriously?"

"Things are being thrown."

Without lifting her head, Tessa pointed at Annalisa. "Go deal with it."

"Why me?"

"You deal with hardened criminals every day as a psychiatrist. I'm assuming you can handle two people who can't move on from their shitty marriage."

"Of course I can handle it," she said, getting to her feet. "I just don't want to."

"Well, you might as well sit." Tessa gestured to Annalisa's empty chair, then the breakfast foods. "Melon ball?"

Ormi blinked. "Uh . . ."

Jace heard a whistle and looked over her shoulder.

"Couple of guys here to see you," her sister-Crow said.

Jace frowned. "To see *me*? Are you sure?"

"They asked for you. One's a Claw. The other's some black guy." The other Crows stared at her until she threw up her hands. "What? He is."

"I'll deal with it." Jace gave a small wave to Eriksen before walking back into the house.

As she followed her sister-Crow, Lev ran up to her, and Jace stopped long enough to pick him up and snuggle him close, laughing when he chewed on her nose.

She was led into the study by the front door, but Jace stopped as soon as she walked inside.

Her feet felt like lead once she stood in that room and, she had to admit at least to herself, all she wanted to do was turn and run. Especially when she saw the expression on the face of the man she knew so well. A combination of apology and regret.

Norris Bystrom was a lifelong member of the Claws of Ran. He and his brethren still ruling the seas, dragging boats and the contents down to the bottom of the ocean just as the Nordic goddess Ran and her nine daughters once did to the Vikings when the mood struck them.

This Claw was also the ATF agent who'd been the first to see Jace at her absolutely most terrifying two years ago, when her Second Life had just begun.

Now he and the federal prosecutor who'd handled the case stood in the Bird House study, waiting to speak to her.

The prosecutor had always been so kind to her, too, and he

wore the same expression as Bystrom. Apology and regret. She hated that expression. Hated it more than most things.

Both men tried to smile.

"Hi, Jacinda," the federal prosecutor said. His name was Dave Jennings. He was tall. Handsome. Of black and Mexican descent. And was steadily working his way up in the prosecutors' office. She had no doubt that he would be attorney general one day.

But not today.

"Hello."

"How have you been doing?"

"Fine."

Lev whimpered and snuggled close to her neck.

"He's kind of big to hold, isn't he?" Jennings asked, trying desperately to lighten the mood.

"He's not even three months."

"Seriously?" Jennings's eyes briefly widened. "He's going to be huge."

"Jace—" Bystrom began.

"Let me handle this." Jennings gestured to the couch. "Why don't we sit down?"

"That's okay."

"No. Really. I think you should sit and—"

"He's out," she said for them, when she saw they were doing that thing that men do when they hated telling a woman something. They'd sit her down, hope to keep her calm. Offer to get one of her friends. Or some tea. Anything to avoid the torrent of tears they were expecting.

Although maybe *dreading* was a better word than *expecting*. They were *dreading* those tears. And this conversation.

"Jacinda—"

"It's all right," she said, deciding to let them off the hook. Because they didn't understand. They never did. No matter how many times she told them, explained to them, they kept treating her like a traumatized wife rather than a woman who'd seen everything. Understood everything because she had no choice.

Her husband had never bothered to hide anything from her. He'd considered her property, and why would you hide anything from property? She didn't hide popping her zits from Lev.

"I told you this would happen," she reminded them. "I told you that you'd never keep him in."

"We haven't given up," Jennings quickly insisted.

"The cops caught him *burying* me, and you still couldn't keep him in. So maybe you should give up."

"We still have the weapons charges."

"Weapons charges, but the judge let him out? Yeah . . . okay."

"We have very high hopes—"

"You shouldn't. You should never have high hopes. The others, my husband's . . . parishoners, will protect him with their last breath. All of them will. You'll never get them to turn. Ever."

"You could testify."

"I'm his ex-wife."

"You can't testify about what he told you as his wife, but you can testify about what you've actually seen. No one can stop you from doing that."

She wished she could say she was frightened by Jennings's words. She wasn't. Instead, she was irritated. She'd spent so much time explaining to him how this would work. This wasn't just some hick cult with no pull. True, it would have been if her ex-husband had started it himself. He didn't. His father did. A man who turned a long con into an actual religion. And to protect himself he'd made sure his group had contacts, connections, and anything else that got him control.

She'd tried again and again to explain that to Jennings, but he was one of those guys who believed justice ruled all. He really thought that someone as dangerous as her ex would get thrown into prison and stay there because that's how it was *supposed* to work.

The man understood so little about this that he thought Jace was afraid of testifying against her ex. She wasn't. She was afraid of what she'd do once she was in front of that court. In front of *him.* She could easily see herself climbing over the witness box and wrapping her hands around the bastard's throat in the midst of her testimony. Choking the life from him right there. In front of the world.

So . . . no. Testifying against him would not work to her benefit.

She felt her rage welling and she worked hard to calm it down. To get it under control. She had to. Jennings was an outsider. Not one of the Clans, unlike the Claw who'd hauled her away from her ex after Skuld had brought her back. Bystrom had immediately known that she was a newly spawned Crow because he was descended from the Vikings who used to fight them. He was one of the Claws of Ran, West Coast. A human clan that was still female led, and still didn't much like the Crows, often sending seagulls to attack the avian Clan when they were forced to travel over the Pacific. But Norris had always made an exception for Jace after realizing it had been her husband who'd killed and buried her in the backyard of the compound.

Norris suddenly glared at Jennings. "I thought we weren't going to discuss testifying until later."

"It seemed as good time as any," the prosecutor said, glaring right back. He was the prosecutor, after all. Norris was just some ATF agent who didn't understand these things. At least that's how she was guessing Jennings saw this situation. But *he* didn't understand. He would never understand.

"Well, that was a dumb thing to do." And then, Bystrom looked behind Jace and she knew, without looking, that her sisters now stood behind her. They stood outside the glass doors. They sat on the chairs. They crouched on the staircase banisters.

Like a scene from Hitchcock's *The Birds,* they had appeared in order to protect one of their own. And they'd done it without Jace saying a word because they just knew. They knew something was really wrong.

Bystrom's body tensed, recognizing how dangerous this all was.

But Jennings merely saw a bunch of nosy women who apparently lived in an expensive rehab center, which meant they were rich. He might have even recognized a few faces from TV or movies. He didn't understand the fear that was welling up in his gut. Instead he would ignore that fear. Tamp it down. Pretend there was nothing to be frightened of.

Oh, how wrong he was.

Not wanting the situation to get out of hand—and it was about to—Jace said, "I need to think on this." She turned toward the glass doors, but Jennings caught her arm. Not harshly. She knew harsh; this wasn't close.

But Bystrom took in a sharp breath and she could feel the eyes of every Crow locking on where Jennings's hand touched her elbow.

"Please, Jace, you have nothing to be afraid of. We'll get you protection. We'll take you someplace where you'll be safe. And when the trial is over, we'll put you in witness protection. He'll never find you."

Jace patted his hand, forced a smile like she used to when she stood beside her husband and greeted newcomers too foolish to realize what they'd just given away. Their freedom.

Jennings was such a sweet man, and he believed every word he was telling her. That he would manage to protect her. Protect her from a past she understood all too well.

"Let me think on it," she insisted before pulling away.

One of her sister-Crows opened the door from the outside and she walked through and away.

Norris watched the Crows closely. This was why he'd wanted to take Jacinda out of here to have this discussion. But no. Jennings didn't want to "take her out of where she's comfortable. She's already been through so much."

Which was very true. The woman had been through hell. But if she were like most people, she'd still be dead. The reason she wasn't dead was because of who she was deep down inside. Because of her power. True power. Not that typical human shit, but the kind of power that frightened the hardest of true men. Of Vikings.

And with reason.

She hadn't even said a word and the Crows had sensed her need. Her growing rage.

Gods, how could Jennings not see it? The man always wore a small gold cross around his neck. Did his Christian belief system really make him that blind?

The Crows continued to watch them as Jennings hemmed and hawed about whether they should keep trying to talk to Jace now or wait. But it wasn't long before Chloe Wong walked into the room.

She smiled sweetly at both men, but Norris wasn't fooled. Not by her.

"Gentlemen. It's good to see you again," she greeted. "What brings you here to Giant Steps?" She dipped her head a bit, dark brown eyes locking on Norris. "Little drinking problem?" she asked.

Norris started to reply to that bitchy remark—everyone knew he didn't have a drinking problem because he could out-drink everyone at the yearly Tournaments—but Jennings placed his hand on Norris's shoulder.

"We came here to talk to Miss Berisha."

"About that horrible ex-husband of hers?"

Jennings glanced down before admitting, "He's getting out. The charges have been dismissed."

Chloe looked at Norris. "I thought you and several other ATF agents caught the man in the act of burying her."

"We did but—"

"Those charges," Jennings interrupted, "were dismissed due to problems in my office. I take full responsibility."

"Problems?"

"Information that was not properly passed along to the defense."

"So her ex has contacts in your office who are helping him."

"I doubt that."

"I don't." She put her hands together. "So what's the next move?"

"We move ahead on the weapons charges."

"But he's already out."

"We'll get him back in."

"Uh-huh. And other than to inform Jace about this, why else are you here?"

"Well, that's between me and Miss Berisha."

Chloe turned her gaze to Norris, and he knew he couldn't ignore her question the way Jennings could.

"They want her to testify in court against him," Norris explained. "About what she saw. About the organization."

"I see. Skylar?" Chloe called out.

Norris knew Skylar. Still had scars from that time she'd slammed her talons into his back during an ugly Clan fight, nearly destroying his kidney in the process.

Jennings knew her, too. Had his ass handed to him in court on more than one occasion by that woman.

"Gentlemen," Chloe said, placing her hand on Skylar's shoulder. "From now on you'll be dealing with Skylar Nosek on any issues regarding Jacinda."

"That is unnecessary—"

"Is it?" Chloe asked, held tilting to the side, her face mockingly scrunched up with bullshit concern. "You let this motherfucker loose and then you come here and have the nerve to ask that poor girl to face him in court. You must be kidding."

"We'll put her in protective custody right now."

"You will leave this house. Right now. And if you want to discuss anything with Jace, you can talk to Skylar first. Right, Skylar?"

Skylar's response was to smile. Her bright white teeth flashed.

"Okay," Norris said, grabbing Jennings's arm, "time to go."

"We're not done here."

"We are so done here."

He pulled the protesting man toward the hallway, the Crows silently parting. As the last of them split into two groups to allow them to pass, Norris was brought up short by Danski Eriksen, second in command of the Southern California Protectors and his Clan leader, Ormi Bentsen.

But it was Eriksen who was staring Norris down, and Norris was wondering why the uptight Protectors, with their books and glasses and ideals about justice, were in the Bird House. He knew when he got out of here he would need to give his own Clan leader a heads-up. Rada wouldn't be happy. She never liked when the other Clans got along.

Finally, Eriksen growled at Norris, "You failed her."

Not willing to listen to shit from an uptight Tyr lover, he shot back, "Fuck you."

Eriksen had Norris by the neck, powerful fingers digging into thick flesh. Norris knew what the Protector could do with that move. He'd seen the man tear heads off of beings with far thicker necks than his.

Norris released Jennings and grabbed Eriksen around the waist, ready to break the man in half.

"Gentlemen!" Chloe barked.

Without looking away from each other, they knew they were surrounded by Crows.

If they had this fight here, they'd have to kill Jennings and get rid of his body. Something the Crows would not like happening on their territory.

But it was Ormi Bentsen who pulled them apart.

"Not the way to handle this," the older man chastised his second in command.

Still unable to let it go, though, Eriksen said in Norwegian, "Nice fuckup, asshole."

"Suck my big Claw cock, book reader," Norris shot back in Swedish.

"Isn't that the same insult your mother uses?"

Norris almost had his hands on Eriksen again when Bentsen grabbed him by the throat. The strength of his tensed fingers told Norris it would take nothing for this man to crack his neck like so much kindling.

Bentsen nodded toward the completely confused Jennings. "Just go."

Letting out a breath, trying to get his anger under control, Norris yanked away from Bentsen and grabbed Jennings by the arm. He pulled him out of the house and to their government-provided car.

"What the fuck was that about?" the prosecutor demanded.

Norris looked at him, shrugged, and replied, "Nothing . . . why?"

Jace made it as far as the garages where they kept the Bird House cars. From high-end to used-simply-to-abuse, they had every kind of auto and motorcycle currently available. Vehicles that could be driven at any time by any Crow. It was one of Jace's favorite places. She liked to find a quiet spot to settle down and read. But she hadn't been out here since she'd started to work for the Protectors.

She stood beside a bright blue Bentley. A special order that Chloe must have gotten. She had a thing for Bentleys.

"You have to come with me."

Jace faced Eriksen, her mouth open, aghast.

"Come on," he pushed.

"Seriously?" she asked. "You really think I need *your* protection?"

He frowned. "What are you talking about?"

"You, big, strong Viking, are here to protect me from my ex-husband, right? Because I can't do it on my own, right? I can't protect myself. That's what you're saying, isn't it?"

"No, actually. I was sent to get you out of here before—"

"Jacinda, we need to—"

Without thinking, Jace spun toward the familiar voice entering the conversation and punched with her left fist. Hitting Rachel right in the throat . . . and possibly breaking something important.

The bigger woman stumbled back, swayed, then fell over, landing hard on her side. Jace covered her mouth in horror.

"Oh shit!" She looked at Eriksen. "I panicked," she admitted. "I heard her voice and I panicked!"

He grabbed her arm and dragged her toward the front of the house.

"We have to help her!"

"No. Tessa and the others have to help her. What I have to do is get you as far away from that very angry female as quickly as humanly possible because she looks like she's about to kick your ass."

Running behind Eriksen, Jace looked over her shoulder and saw that Rachel was trying to get to her feet, teeth gritted together, eyes raging . . . even though Jace was pretty sure the woman couldn't swallow.

She might have crushed Rachel's windpipe. An action that would kill a typical human in several short minutes. But a Crow? She could last awhile like that. And keep fighting to boot.

By the time they reached the car, Ormi already had the motor running and Eriksen shoved her into the backseat and closed the door. A few seconds later, he opened the door again and Lev tried to jump in, but he didn't quite make it. He dangled there a moment, front paws tearing across the nice leather interior, little legs trying to push himself the rest of the way.

Hand under his ass, Eriksen shoved him in and jumped into the front seat. He slammed his door closed and barked, "Drive."

Jace held Lev in her lap and turned so she could look out the back window. Rachel was trying to run after the car, but now Erin, Kera, and Alessandra were holding her back as the rest of the Crows streamed out of the house and joined in.

"It was an accident!" Jace argued with absolutely no one.

"Was it?" Eriksen asked, sounding less than convinced.

"Of course it was!"

"Did you think it was your ex-husband?" he asked.

Jace flinched. "No."

"Did you think it was one of the cult members?"

Now she let out a sigh. "No."

"Then it really wasn't an accident, was it? You knew it was her!"

"You don't understand. She's very irritating!"

He looked at her. "Why? Because she won't stop talking to you?"

Jace scrunched up her nose before admitting, "Maybe."

Rolling his eyes, Eriksen turned back around and kept shaking his head.

Ormi looked at her in the rearview. "I have to say, Jacinda, I really enjoy having you around. It's all so exciting when the Crows have come to town, as my grandfather used to say."

Slowly, Eriksen turned his head to look at his leader and snapped, "Shut up."

CHAPTER TWELVE

Jace wasn't thinking when she placed Lev on the ground as soon as she entered the Protectors' house. She just put him down and immediately headed to the library.

"Why is this puppy roaming the halls?" she heard Bear growl just a few seconds later.

She hadn't even sat down at the table yet.

Bear walked into the room, the puppy tucked under his arm. "I thought we discussed the rules regarding this . . ." He stopped and stared down at her.

"What's wrong?" he suddenly asked her.

"Nothing."

"You're a bad liar."

"Actually I'm not. I'm a very good liar. I just don't use the skill often."

"You're unhappy. Why are you unhappy?"

Finally dropping into the chair, Jace sighed and said, "It's a long story—"

"Her ex-husband is out of prison," Gundo explained as he walked in. "He was just released."

"Or it's a short story," she amended. "Depending on your perspective."

"Why is he out?" Bear demanded.

"The federal prosecutor screwed up," Gundo explained. "At least his office did."

Actually, the only thing Jennings had done wrong was not

take Jace's warnings seriously. But no one understood her ex-husband as well as she did.

Eriksen suddenly reappeared with a mug of tea. "Here," he ordered, pushing the tea toward her. "Drink this."

"I don't want tea."

"Drink it anyway."

"Give me that," Bear snarled, covering the steaming top of the mug with his hand and pulling it away from Eriksen while at the same time dropping poor Lev. "What do you think you're doing?"

She caught Lev before he could hit the ground and pulled him into her lap.

"I'm giving her tea."

"Here? What if she gets that female thing where her hands shake from fear or whatever, and she gets the tea all over the goddamn books?"

"She just caught that dog in midair," Gundo helpfully pointed out.

"She could snap at any time," Bear insisted before leaning down and informing her, "But you're safe here. You don't have anything to be afraid of."

"I'm not afraid."

"Really?" he asked, big head tilted to the side.

"He's already killed me once, Bear. And, unlike most people, when I die again, I know where I'm going." She glanced at Eriksen. "Kera's already been there and she said she had a blast."

"Kera Watson's been to Valhalla?"

"Yeah. She went with Vig and his sister." She briefly studied the three Protectors. "Not sure you three will have as good a time, though. Didn't hear anything about libraries in Valhalla."

Bear appeared crestfallen. "That's depressing."

"Can we worry about our deaths later?" Eriksen snapped.

"I've got an idea," Gundo cut in. "Have the Ravens kill your ex-husband."

"Pardon?"

"It makes complete sense. That way you and society won't have to worry about him at all."

"Well, if you're so worried, why don't you kill him?"

"Because I'm a Protector," Gundo patiently explained. "I'll protect you because that's what we do. But outright murder? That's a mindless enterprise that seems much more . . . Ravenesque."

"You just think the Ravens are stupid."

"They *are* stupid," Eriksen muttered.

"My hand's burning," Bear suddenly announced.

Eriksen gritted his teeth. "Because it's over the hot tea."

"A sacrifice I'm willing to make to protect our sacred books."

"*Then don't complain!*"

Jace kissed Lev's now-sleeping head. "Why are you yelling?"

"Because I'm upset! Why aren't you upset?"

"I am upset. But you are looking for hysterical. I don't do hysterical."

"Unless it's Rachel?"

"That was an accident."

"Uh-huh."

Bear took an abrupt step backward. "Come on," he ordered.

"Where?" Gundo asked.

"Just come on." He walked out, probably to put the tea Jace had never wanted into the sink and put some ointment on what she would bet was now a bad burn on the palm of his hand.

With a shrug, they all followed Bear into the hallway. He pointed toward the front door while he went to the kitchen.

When he met them outside a few minutes later, he had his poor hand bandaged. Eriksen snorted and she slapped his arm. "Be nice."

"But—"

"Nice."

"Come on," Bear said again, motioning to a large red SUV parked down the curved driveway a bit. Probably the only thing the big Viking could fit in.

As they walked toward it, a motorcycle raced into the driveway. It was one of those speed bikes rather than a Harley, Jace's preferred mode of motorcycle transportation. Not that she'd ever been on either, but she just thought Harleys looked so cool.

The bike pulled up to the corner and stopped; there were two people on it. The motor shut off, the one in the front pulled off her helmet, short red hair dropping in front of big green eyes. And Kera was riding behind Erin. She jumped off the bike as soon as it was still, stumbling backward while pulling off her helmet at the same time. Gundo moved forward, barely catching her before she hit the ground. But she didn't seem to notice since she was too busy chucking her helmet at Erin's head.

Thankfully, the laughing redhead ducked in time.

"What?" Erin asked.

"Crazy bitch! You could have gotten both of us killed!"

"You wanted to get here quickly."

"Fuck you!" Kera pushed away from Gundo. She was so angry. It was all over her face. But anyone with sense knew not to go riding on a motorcycle with Erin Amsel. She took crazy chances and, more importantly, she was self-taught and didn't actually have a motorcycle license.

Not that Jace was going to say so at this moment. That would be a very poor decision on her part.

Bear pointed at the two women. "Do you like them?" he asked.

Not sure why he was asking, Jace replied, "Yes."

"Okay." Then he picked Kera up with one arm and Erin with the other. Holding them the same way he'd held Lev.

"Hey!" both sister-Crows barked, pounding on Bear's arms and shoulders, trying to get him to let them go, but he ignored them. Reaching the SUV, he patiently waited until Gundo opened the back door for him. Bear then pushed the two women inside before gesturing to Jace. "Come on."

She glanced at Eriksen, but all he could do was shrug. "Might as well," he added when Jace hesitated.

Snuggling Lev closer, she got into the back of the SUV, where Kera and Erin were now arguing with each other.

Eriksen sat in the front passenger seat and Gundo got into the second row. Once the doors were closed and Bear was behind the wheel, they set off.

But where they were going . . . ?

CHAPTER THIRTEEN

Ski stood at the hiking trail by a large set of boulders and gazed down into an open valley.

"This is nice, Bear."

"Yeah."

Erin stood beside him, but she shook her head and said, "This place looks familiar. And I'm not a hiker." She looked at Bear. "Where are we?"

"Old Santa Susana Stage Road." When no one reacted, he added, "This used to be called Spahn Ranch."

Ski still didn't know what that meant but after a few seconds, Erin stumbled back, her mouth open in shock.

"Spahn Ranch? *The* Spahn Ranch?"

"Yeah."

"What's Spahn Ranch?" Kera asked.

Erin put her hands to her forehead and began massaging what Ski was guessing might be a headache. "That's where the Manson family lived."

Ski and Gundo turned to their brother. "Bear!"

"What?"

"Why would you bring us here?" Ski growled, beyond angry.

"Because she needed a safe place to talk."

"So you take us to the hangout of a murderous cult? That really seemed like a good idea to you?"

"I knew she'd like it."

"Why would she like this?" Kera asked. "She's trying to get *away* from cults. Not relive someone else's nightmare."

"I knew her dark soul would connect with this place."

"Hey!" Ski barked.

"I didn't say evil. I said dark. There's a difference." He gestured to Jace. She had her back to them, her hand resting against one of the boulders. "Ask her."

Ski walked over to Jace, placed his hand on her shoulder. "Are you okay?"

Jace looked at him. There was absolute peace on her face, her smile wide. "Yes."

"You . . . fascinate me," he told her, not knowing what else to say.

"Yeah." She gazed over the open valley. "I know."

"You don't have to say anything, honey," Jace heard Kera say. "We're just here for you."

Frowning, Jace asked, "Don't have to say anything about what?"

An awkward silence followed while everyone stared at her.

Finally, not surprisingly, it was Erin who said, "About the whole . . . life-in-a-cult thing. Chloe gave us all a short rundown, which is why Rachel came looking for you."

"Oh. That." Jace shrugged. "I can talk about the cult thing. I don't care. Don't want to talk about waking up in a grave, though," she added. "That I will not discuss."

"If you can talk about being in that cult," Erin asked, "why haven't you before?"

"No one asked."

"Everyone asks a Crow about her death," Kera pointed out.

"Actually, almost everyone *volunteers*, but I didn't want to talk about my death unless I was asked. Besides, I figured Chloe would have told all of you by now"

"No," Erin replied. "All Chloe told us was that your husband had killed you and at that point, what was there left to ask? I mean, sadly, that's how a lot of our ladies end up as Crows."

"That's upsetting," Bear admitted.

"Isn't it? But Chloe never mentioned a cult or anything else until today. We all just knew that Skylar helped you get a permanent protection order against your ex and that you'd tried to kill him, which made sense to all of us."

"Skylar knows everything. She worked with me from the beginning. Used her connections to get me a divorce lawyer, while she got me the permanent protection order."

"And now she'll be handling whatever's going on with that federal prosecutor."

"Yes. But don't blame Jennings. He didn't know what he was dealing with."

"So are you going to tell us?" Bear asked.

"Tell you what?"

"About the cult."

"Bear!" Eriksen barked.

"What?" Bear demanded. "She said she could talk about it."

Jace patted Bear's arm and gestured to one of the big boulders. He grabbed her around the waist and gently placed her on top of it.

"Thank you."

"Sure."

"So," Jace began, "when I was six years old, my father died and my mother disappeared. Everyone said it was the grief. She couldn't handle it. My father's mother raised me. She was Albanian by birth on her father's side, but her mother was Romanian and that's kind of how she lived. Anyway, when I was ten my mother suddenly returned. My grandmother wouldn't let me see her, but she showed up one night and asked me to walk with her. I did. That's when she and her new friends took me. It turned out her new friends were loyal cult members of the Patient Dove Congregation. An end-of-the-world cult that was convinced their leader was an immortal prophet sent by God to protect them during the Rapture. He wasn't. Martin Braddock was a con man from Fontana who knew how to play people like puppets. He got a lot of money from the first members he had, and he used that money to gain power with those who had any kind of control in government or finance. He wasn't above blackmail. In fact, he really liked it."

Jace smiled a little when Lev nuzzled her neck before going

back to sleep. "Anyway, Braddock became very, very rich in very short order and enjoyed having his own puppets to order around all day. Then the immortal prophet found out he was not so immortal. He got cancer and passed everything on to his only child, Davis Henry Braddock. The problem was that Davis believed his father was a great prophet and that with his death the power had passed on to him. He truly believes the Rapture's coming any second. He truly believes he can even help it along. He truly believes he's a great prophet. He truly believes he will sit at the right hand of God."

"What does he truly believe about you?" Eriksen asked.

"That I'm truly his property. That I belong at *his* right hand, monitoring the women and leading the children. That is my role." She glanced off. "I was promised to him when I was ten."

Kera let out a breath, but Jace quickly held her hand up. "Don't panic. We didn't get married or have sex until I was sixteen. When I was eighteen, I also became the Finder of the Word." She scratched Lev's neck and smirked at Eriksen. "Now you know why I choked when I heard your title. Anyway, it was my job to track down any information about the End of Days. I used that as an excuse to learn multiple languages, so that I could decipher ancient texts. I always had an easy way with languages and already knew Albanian, German, Romanian, French, and Spanish. While he thought I was researching information that would help him end the world as we know it so he could start his own reign—and no, I'm not joking—I was actually reading anything I could get my hands on: *Pride and Prejudice* in Russian, *To Kill a Mockingbird* in Greek, and *The Narcissist Next Door* in Polish. But things got really bad between us when I read *Raven: The Untold Story of the Reverend Jim Jones and His People's Temple* in Italian. That's when I knew exactly what I was dealing with and how bad this was going to get. I guess he could read the concern on my face. At that point, he made it his business to subjugate me even more. He never hit me. Not before that last day. Just words." She sighed, closed her eyes. Such words.

"And I took it," she admitted regretfully. "Like I always took it. Until one day . . ." She shrugged. "I snapped. Started yelling at him. Told him I hated him. Wished he was dead. Said I'd call the cops about all the guns. But it was when I told him he was nothing special, that he *wasn't* God's prophet . . . he threw me to the ground, started beating me, then he put his hands around my throat and the next thing I knew . . . I was talking to Skuld. When she sent me back . . ."

No. She couldn't talk about that. The dirt falling on her. The feeling of being suffocated a second time. She couldn't go through that again.

"I tried to kill him then," Jace went on. "Would have, too, if Norris Bystrom hadn't been one of the ATF agents there. They'd come to search the compound because they'd finally gotten a witness to talk about the guns and Jennings had gotten a warrant based on that." She shook her head. "I would have killed all of them that day. My husband. The agents. The rage had me. All I wanted was his blood covering me. To know I'd finished him. But Bystrom stopped me in time, which is good. Braddock should properly pay for his crimes like everybody else."

"He'll come for you," Kera said, her voice low.

"Of course he will. I'm his property. He wants his property back. Like a bratty child who won't give up his tricycle to his little brother even though he's moved on to his big bike."

"So we track him down and we kill him," Erin announced, but Jace shook her head.

"No. We're not doing that."

"Why not? I mean . . ." She glanced around at the others. "Isn't that what we do?"

"He's not an assignment from Skuld. He's stolen nothing mystical, nor involved himself with our gods in anyway. He's not our problem."

"If he's your problem, he's *our* problem."

"So then you'd be doing this for me?"

"Of course."

"Then stay away from him."

"Jace—"

"No. I'm serious. I love you guys more than I can possibly say. And knowing that you will always have my back means the world to me. But I'm not going to kill him, and you guys aren't going to kill him, either."

"Why not?" Erin asked.

"Because we're not murderers. He is, but we're not."

Bear pointed at Erin. "She kinda is."

Erin slowly faced the big Viking. "Thank you," she said with great sarcasm.

A sarcasm that was completely lost on Bear.

He shrugged. "You're welcome."

It took Tessa longer than she thought it would to repair Rachel's crushed windpipe.

She wouldn't say that Jace had been *trying* to kill her sister-Crow, but if she was asked under oath, Tessa didn't think she could deny it, either.

Jace had hit the woman with some force. But the beauty of being a Crow was that you were no longer the normal frail human you once were. True, they could all die again, but it took a lot more effort to kill them the second time.

Rachel, whom Tessa had to knock out in order to get her to stop trying to follow poor Jace so she could—most likely—beat her up, was still out cold in the Healing Room. So Tessa tracked down Chloe in her office. Their leader sat at her desk, feet up on the mahogany wood, her gaze focused out the big bay window.

"Find out everything about Jace's ex," Chloe ordered.

"She doesn't want us involved."

Chloe looked at her. She was still pissed about whatever argument she'd had with Josef. According to Annalisa, he'd stormed out before the thing with the federal prosecutor went down, so Tessa had had no time to help them work out anything. Not that she ever could. Tessa was sure Chloe and Josef enjoyed arguing too damn much.

"Okay, okay," Tessa said quickly. She didn't want to argue with her leader at this moment. "Ormi and Ski Eriksen stopped by."

"Yeah, why the hell were they here anyway?"

"You're not going to like it."

"At this moment, I don't like anything."

"Well, don't get pissed, okay? But . . . they walked in on a massive sacrifice site last night. They found gold, jewels, and the Mara. So . . . Ormi is wondering if we—"

"Really stopped Gullveig."

"Right."

Tessa expected Chloe to explode. She was already in a bad mood over her ex, then the shit with Jace, and now another Clan was questioning what she'd said and had believed.

Yet Chloe didn't explode. Instead, Chloe replied, "I got a call."

"From?"

"Yardley."

"Everything okay?" Yardley had been on a location shoot for a few weeks now, but she never called Chloe about anything unless there was a problem. Otherwise, she went directly to her own team leader.

"No. But her call makes sense now."

"Do we need to move on something?"

"Not yet. We keep this between us."

"Okay."

Chloe dropped her legs to the floor and turned her chair. She motioned to Tessa with a jerk of her chin. "Close the door."

Ski settled down on the boulder beside Jace. She'd had her eyes closed, silently meditating for the last fifteen minutes.

"How can you find peace here?" he asked.

"Because I see beyond the evil of one man to the land beneath. This is beautiful country."

She finally opened her eyes, looked around, and asked, "Where'd everybody go?"

"It suddenly occurred to them that we're on a hiking trail with no water, food, or supplies. They went back to the SUV to pick up a few things. Bear took Lev because he seems to really like that dog. But they shouldn't be too long. The Isa"—

the Viking goddess Skadi's human Clan—"runs this place now that it's been folded into the park and I can promise they know exactly where we are at this very moment."

"Okay."

"You seem very . . . calm. Considering."

"I knew that it was coming. And now that it's here . . . it's here. You know?"

"No. I really don't know what that means."

"I don't have to worry anymore because it's happened. He's out. I always knew he would be, but now it's a done deal. I can stop worrying, because he's out."

"And when he comes?"

"I'll deal with it."

"You know, you may be able to keep the Crows from getting involved in this. But the Ravens like you. And Rundström is the wild dog they have on a really cheap leash. Preventing him from going after your ex will be next to impossible."

"Yeah, but they're a little scared of me. No one likes when I get rage-y."

"I don't mind it."

"Seriously?"

"Well . . . if I wasn't one of the mighty Protectors, then I would mind; of course, because you'd beat me into the ground. But Tyr blessed me with awesome strength."

"Do you see Tyr a lot?"

"Yeah. He comes to the library all the time. He likes to chat. So . . . be forewarned while you're working with us. I know how you hate chitchat."

"I don't *hate* it."

"You just hate it with me."

"No. I'm just not good at it. It's awkward and uncomfortable. And when I was in the Congregation, I had to pretend-chat all the time."

"Why?"

"It was my role as his wife." She frowned at Ski, her face earnest. "I never believed, you know. Not for one second."

"I know."

"How do you know?"

"Because it sounds like you took every opportunity to expand your mind even though you were trapped in a pretty horrible situation. If you believed, even for a moment, you wouldn't have bothered."

"I was lucky. I had my grandmother. That woman taught me two very important things before I was taken. How to make learning new languages easy . . . and how to trust goddamn nobody."

"Well, what you need to remember is that you're not alone in this. You've got the Crows."

"True."

"The idiots."

"Why do you hate the Ravens so much?"

"They're stupid. Purposely stupid. I have no time for that. Or patience."

"They're really not that stupid." She cringed. "I mean, they're *not* stupid."

"You probably had it right the first time. And, to continue our conversation, you now have the Protectors."

She smirked. "Really?"

"You got the Ormi seal of approval. Let me rephrase that. You're a *Crow* and got the Ormi seal of approval. That just doesn't happen. Plus, Bear—of all people—is out making sure your puppy has water. And I haven't seen that man show interest in anything that wasn't between two covers in . . . forever."

"He is myopic."

"Very. But it works for us. And then there's me."

"The big man who's going to rush in to protect me?"

"No. I'll respect your boundaries. As boring as that may be."

"Because you're a progressive male?" she asked, laughing.

"No. Because you're a Crow and if I get in your way, you'll just tear my face off with your talons. One of the first things my dad taught me . . . 'never get between a Crow and her prey.' According to him, you guys hate that."

"We do hate that." She turned on the boulder, sitting Indian-style so that she could face him. "You do understand why, though? Why I won't go after him?"

"I understand. You're not the girl that you were. To kill him would give him the ultimate power, because it would mean he still mattered to you."

"That's it exactly."

"But *you* need to understand, he'll never stop. Men like him never do."

"I know what my ex-husband can do. I know what he's willing to do. I also know that if he does come for me, I'll be ready. But I'm not going to him. I also won't have my sisters hunt him down like an animal."

"Even though they're really good at that?"

"Yes."

Ski turned to her, sitting the same way she was. "Can I ask you a question?"

"Sure."

"Did you turn down going on a date with me because of your ex-husband?"

"No."

But she kind of snapped that at him and said it really fast. So Ski kept staring at her until her mouth twisted a little in frustration and she finally admitted, "Maybe."

"I thought you were beyond him now," he teased.

"I am. I just . . . I've never been on a date before. He's the only man I've ever been with." She let out a breath. "What if you go out with me and realize I'm . . . a mess?"

"You're a Crow. Of *course* you're a mess."

And he was glad when she laughed.

"But," he quickly added, "I'm a Protector. They took me from my family when I was six. I knew how to kill a grown man by the time I was twelve. I'd actually done it before I was eighteen. You're Clan, Jace. You're gonna be a mess. All I'm saying is, why don't we be a mess together? One date. That's it. We give it a try."

She cringed. "Except I hate the idea of dating."

"The *idea* of dating?"

"Yeah."

"Is this the chitchat thing again?"

"Yeah."

"You have to talk to someone sometime."

She cocked her head to the side. "Do I?"

Now they both laughed.

"Okay, okay," she said. "How about . . . you come to the party this weekend? At the Bird House."

"The one Kera was complaining about all the way here?"

"Yeah."

He forced a smile. "Because it sounds like such fun."

"No, no. It'll be fun. She just *thinks* no one will be there."

"Why would she think that?"

"Because Erin's a dick."

"Oh. Yeah." He nodded. "She is."

"So you'll come. We'll hang out. See if that works."

"All right. I'll give it a try."

"And bring Bear."

"Why would you say that?"

"Because I know you'll bring Gundo. And you'll bring Borgsten. But you won't bring Bear. Even though you should."

"But he'll cramp my style," Ski joked.

"What style?"

"All right, then . . ."

Chapter Fourteen

Jace was up and dressed when her cell phone rang. She never used her cell phone, rarely gave her number out, and most of her sisters who would call her for some reason were hanging around the house today. So she stared at it for a really long time before she answered. But by the time she picked up, the call rolled over to voice mail. She had dropped it back on the dresser, when the phone rang again. This time she picked it up more quickly but didn't say anything.

After several seconds, "Jace?"

"Yeah?"

"It's Ski."

"Who?"

She heard what sounded like a deep sigh. "Eriksen."

"Oh. Yeah. Hi."

"You call me Eriksen in your head, don't you?"

"Maybe."

"Anyway, I wanted to point out to you that you don't have to come in on Saturdays or Sundays. Those are your days off until the job is done."

"Okay."

"And today is Saturday."

"Oh." She looked around. "Oh! Right. It is." She rolled her eyes at his laugh. "It's not that funny."

"It kind of is."

"It's Saturday."

"Yes."

"You're coming tonight, right?"

"Definitely."

"And Bear?"

He sighed again. "Are you sure?"

"I'm sure. He needs to be more social. It'll be good for him."

"I can't believe you, of all people, is saying that."

"I'm saying that about Bear, who probably wants to be around people, but he doesn't know how. I'm not talking about me."

"All right. We'll all be there."

"Great. And thanks for letting me know—"

"What day it is?"

"Again. Not that funny."

Jace disconnected the call and dropped her backpack at the end of her bed. She motioned to Lev. "Come on, you. Break time."

He leapt off the bed, crash-landed rather badly, shook it off, and ran . . . into the door.

Jace walked to the door and pulled it open for him. He took off and she followed, mumbling a greeting to her sister-Crows as she passed.

She entered the kitchen, where most of her Strike Team was sitting at the table, strategizing that evening's party. But still no Kera, which meant she still didn't know.

"How are you getting her out so that we can set up?" Tessa asked Erin.

"I've got it covered. We'll be out of here in another fifteen. Twenty at the most."

"Good."

Jace pulled open the sliding glass doors and let Lev run outside to relieve himself. She then poured herself a cup of coffee and took a long moment to sip it and stare out the window, smiling as she saw Lev play with the crows lurking in the yard.

"Oh," she said to Erin, before she forgot, "I invited the Protectors."

"To what?"

She faced her team. "To the party."

"Why?"

She wasn't about to tell them she'd invited them so that she and Erik . . . uh . . . Ski, yeah, Ski. So that she and *Ski* could find out if they should start dating. She loved her fellow Crows, but some reactions she wasn't ready to deal with. "Just a nice gesture," she lied. "Get the guys out."

Erin frowned. "Do they know how to relax? Or are they going to try to organize us into proper rows or something?"

Not in the mood to even attempt to respond to that, she said, "Just let whoever is managing the front door know. Please."

"Okay."

Jace spied chocolate glazed doughnuts on the table and was reaching for one when Brodie ran into the room, quickly followed by Kera.

Papers were quickly hidden, laptops quickly closed, phones and tablets quickly flipped over. Jace couldn't remember her sisters ever moving so fast when food, liquor, or battle wasn't involved.

Swinging a broom, Kera dived under the table after Brodie.

"What's happening?" Tessa asked, leaning down so she could see what Kera was doing.

"Vermin!" Kera snarled. "We have vermin! I will not tolerate vermin in this house!"

Maeve ran out of the room. Without a word. Alessandra lifted her feet off the floor and made a disgusted squealing sound . . . that didn't really stop. Leigh grabbed one of the knives from the table. Tessa and Erin leaned down further to see. Annalisa watched it all and noted each person's reaction because nothing she loved more than monitoring varied human emotions to outside stimuli.

"What vermin?" Tessa asked. "Rats?"

Alessandra, always kind of a princess, squealed louder.

Something shot out from under the table and Kera and Brodie went after it. The thing went out the open sliding doors and its stalkers didn't stop.

"Oh," Erin said, waving her hand. "It's just a squirrel."

There was a minute of silence as everyone started to go back to what they were doing . . . then there was that moment. That moment when everyone looked up, mouths open, gawking at each other. The panic beginning to spread. Even Maeve walked back into the room. They stared more. Then everyone dropped everything and ran toward the sliding glass door. But they all tried to go through at the same time. The others got trapped but Jace dropped and wiggled through their legs.

"Kera! No!" Tessa screamed just as Brodie caught hold of the squirrel, shook it, flipped it in the air, caught it, shook it some more.

The rest of the girls made it past the door, but they could do no more than stand beside Jace, staring in horror.

"*Kera!*" Tessa screamed.

"*What?*"

"Get Brodie to drop that squirrel!"

Kera lowered the broom. "Oh my God. It's got plague or something, right?"

"It's . . . it's not just a squirrel."

"What?"

Brodie was now running around the yard, her prize in her mouth. And she was still shaking it.

"What do you mean, it's not just a squirrel? What is it then?"

Tessa pointed at Brodie and the squirrel. "That's Ratatosk!"

"It's what?"

"Ratatosk! Messenger of the gods!"

Kera froze, eyes wide.

Hearing growling, she slowly turned. Brodie was right in front of her now . . . Ratatosk still in her jaws.

Kera lifted her hands, Broom still held, kept her voice firm but controlled. "Brodie. Drop it."

Brodie took a step back.

"Brodie . . . *Drop. It.*"

Head down, ass in the air. Play bow.

Fuck.

"Brodie Hawaii, you drop that thing right now! Now!"

At the yell, Brodie took off running—and they all took off after her.

★ ★ ★

Vig stood at the kitchen table with Stieg and Siggy and ate the plate of chocolate glazed doughnuts while they watched Kera and her friends chase after Brodie.

"What's going on?" Stieg asked before shoving another doughnut in his mouth.

"No idea."

"What's Brodie got in her mouth?" Siggy asked.

"Looks like a rat."

Rolf, who'd just walked in, shook his head. "That, my friends, is not a rat. That's Ratatosk."

Vig briefly closed his eyes. "Uh-oh."

Siggy shook his head. "This will not end well."

"Calm down." Stieg picked up what was left of the chocolate glazed doughnuts, but Vig quickly yanked the plate from him.

"Not the chocolate, idiot." He replaced that with the plate of jelly doughnuts. "This."

Stieg walked to the open sliding doors and yelled out, "Brodie! Doughnuts!"

The dog stopped and spun, facing Stieg. She practically spit Ratatosk out of her mouth, then charged poor Stieg.

Jace cringed when Brodie hit Stieg right in the chest with her full weight, knocking the big Viking to the ground.

Annalisa winced and muttered, "Damn."

Tessa ran over to the Raven. "Stieg? Stieg, can you hear me?"

Jace went to Ratatosk. His home was the World Tree—*Yggdrasil*—and not only did he transport messages between the gods and the underworld, but he was also a major, grade-A shit starter.

Literally, that was his job. To start shit and keep the rage going. At one time, that was his *only* job. Then the human Clans came along and Odin gave him something new to do—get messages to each Clan leader as needed.

Of course, Ratatosk didn't make things easy. He didn't necessarily deal with each Clan leader. Especially if that particular Clan leader had pissed him off once. And sometimes, he'd only speak to a Clan's seer. Or sometimes he'd make a leader guess the message by doing pantomime.

In other words, Ratatosk was just a dick. As many squirrels were.

With the LA Crows, Ratatosk currently only dealt with Betty. But, of course, she was still in a deep coma. A coma no one really knew when she'd be coming out of.

Jace crouched beside him, but she couldn't get past the fact that he really was a squirrel. Just a normal little squirrel. That was immortal and talked to gods.

"Is it dead?"

Trying to see if he was breathing, Jace leaned in closer . . . and that's when Ratatosk reared up, planted his claws on Jace's face, and crawled up until he sat on her head.

Jace fell back, screaming.

Annalisa caught her hands before she could slap the fucking thing off her head and Jace heard barking, Lev trying to protect her with his little body and paws.

"Get it off me! Get it off me!" Jace screeched, panicking.

"I think he's supposed to be there," Annalisa said, using her best, "*I have a psychotic here!*" voice.

"*Fuck you!*"

Chloe walked out of the house and yelled, "*What is going on?*"

"*Get it off me!*"

Chloe came over, smiled.

She smiled!

"Ratatosk. Hi! Do you mind not fucking with my girls, sweetie?"

The vermin sitting on the top of Jace's head chittered. He was laughing at her! Bastard!

Jace sat up, Annalisa still holding her hands.

Lev jumped in Jace's lap, paws on her shoulder, as he barked incessantly at Ratatosk.

"Awww. He's being protective."

"Because there's a rat on my head," Jace snarled.

"He's not a rat. He's a squirrel," Chloe patiently explained.

Gawking, Jace warned, "I'm about to get *really angry.*"

"Okay. Okay." Chloe quickly reached down, holding her hand out toward the rodent sitting on Jace's head. "Come on. You've upset her enough."

The little bastard scrambled onto Chloe's arm and up to her shoulder.

Now Lev was standing in front of Jace, barking wildly at Ratatosk, who chittered back.

"Feel better now?" Chloe asked Jace.

"I feel like turning in a circle and screaming, 'I'm unclean! I'm unclean!'"

Annalisa pulled Jace to her feet. "That, out of context, can have many meanings."

Jace bent over at the waist and brushed her hair with her hands. "Did he shit on me? I feel like he shit on me!"

"He didn't shit on you. Your hair's fine."

Jace straightened up, glaring at the mocking rat. "It better be." She reached down and swooped a still-barking Lev into her arms, holding him close.

The fact that he felt so protective of her made her love the dog even more. Something she didn't think possible.

Chloe looked at the vermin on her shoulder. "Betty can't talk to you right now. So you'll have to talk to me. And I don't play charades."

Jace's lip curled in disgust as the immortal animal placed its tiny claws against the side of Chloe's forehead.

Kera walked over, her hand holding Brodie's collar. White powder and raspberry jelly covered the pit bull's entire snout.

Standing together, the friends watched their leader close her eyes and nod her head several times.

"Okay," Chloe finally said, nodding. "Thank you."

Ratatosk jumped off her shoulder and took off running. Kera yanked Brodie back as the dog's prey drive pushed her to go after him.

"You don't want my dog here," Kera pointed out to their leader, "but you'll allow that *rat* in the house?"

"He's not a rat. He's a pain in the ass, but he's not a rat. And that animal," she reminded Kera, glaring at Brodie, "isn't covered by our insurance."

In reply, Brodie barked at Chloe and she winced. "What is on that dog's face?"

"Jelly doughnut residue. And perhaps a little of Stieg's blood."

Chloe sighed and turned away when a sister-Crow called for her from the house.

"What is it?" Chloe yelled back. Because gods forbid she should go inside and find out herself.

"Phone!"

With a nod, Chloe walked off, pushing past the Ravens, including poor Stieg, who now held a bag of frozen peas against the back of his head.

"Dog," he said, pointing with his free hand at Brodie.

"You had a plate of jelly doughnuts," Chloe told him as she passed. "What did you expect?"

Vig crouched in front of Brodie with a towel and wiped off the dog's snout. When he was done, Brodie put her paws on his shoulder and licked his face. She'd grown to love Kera's Viking, which was good. Kera and Brodie were a locked deal. One would go nowhere without the other.

Well, in big picture, existential terms, of course they wouldn't go anywhere without each other. But when it came to walks and car rides with other Crows, Brodie was always up for that and often deserted Kera for a few hours away from the house. Kera still wasn't used to it, but she was complaining less.

She still called the dog a "whore," though.

Once Brodie finished licking Vig's face, he stood and grabbed Kera around the waist and pulled her in.

Laughing, Kera tried to push him away. "You're covered in dog! Do you know what she was just licking ten minutes ago? And it wasn't a jelly doughnut!"

Behind Kera, Vig, and the other Ravens, Jace could see Erin. The redhead motioned to Jace with a jerk of her head and, placing Lev on the ground, she followed Erin as she stepped farther into the yard and away from the house.

"I'm about to get Kera out of here so the rest of the girls can set the place up for tonight."

"Okay."

"You should come with me."

They stopped as they neared the end of the house. "I thought you needed me to help out here, too."

"I did. But Rachel's looking for you."

"Oh fuck! Come on!"

"Don't sweat it. She just thinks she's being helpful. Come with me—we'll take the dogs to get groomed or whatever. Maybe get some lunch, and be out for a few hours. Tessa will talk to Chloe about getting Rachel to back off. By tonight she'll be so over it all."

"Yeah. Okay."

Erin started to walk off, but then she stopped and suddenly grabbed Jace by the shoulders, pushing her away.

"Go!" she whispered.

Knowing that Rachel was heading her way, Jace quickly walked to the end of the house. She'd cut around and meet Kera and Erin out front. But she heard Lev's bark and knew that she had to grab him since part of Erin's plan required getting poor Kera out of the house with a lie about dog grooming.

Jace stopped and faced Lev, but her dog was looking past her, barking. And the crows in the trees were angrily squawking. Then a hand fell on her shoulder.

Without thought, she spun around and punched.

She thought she was hitting Rachel. Again.

It wasn't Rachel.

Davis Henry Braddock barely had time to catch his head preacher as the man fell back, his hands around his throat. He was trying to breathe.

Davis looked down and realized that his parishoner's Adam's apple had been shoved back into his neck several inches.

By the woman who was Davis's wife.

Shocked blue eyes peered at him. He'd been planning to have John just grab Jacinda so they could get her out of this place and back where she belonged. By his side. The wife of the Great Prophet. But her reaction had been swift and decidedly brutal.

She took a step toward him, but someone called out her name. A few seconds later, two other women came around some large hedges. One was a short redhead. The other was a giant. An oversized female with muscles on top of muscles.

For a moment, he thought his wife was going to call for help. She didn't. Instead, she slapped her hand around Davis's mouth and yanked him off to the side of the house.

The other women quickly followed, dragging his still struggling-to-breathe second in command behind them.

"What's going on?" the redhead asked.

His wife slammed Davis against the house and held him there with one hand. "This is him."

"Oh fuck," the mammoth muttered.

"I can't believe you came here," his wife said. "I can't . . ."

She stopped speaking, head dropping, body beginning to shake.

The two women seemed terrified.

He thought they feared him. Why wouldn't they? He was God's chosen son.

Then his wife lifted her head and eyes red as blood bored into him. Muscles pulsated under vibrating skin. And her once-pretty face, now covered in fading scars, contorted into a mask of pure evil.

She wrapped her hands around his throat, words coming out of her mouth he didn't understand.

Her hands tightened and he gripped her wrists, trying to pull her off. But her strength . . .

She leaned in close, her harsh breath pelting him as she continued to viciously whisper to him in some devil's tongue.

The redhead suddenly appeared, her hands raised like she was dealing with a wild animal. Afraid to spook it into a horrifying mauling.

"Listen to me, sweetie. I need you to listen. You do anything to him that gets everyone's attention and Kera will know. She'll know and the party will be over. Because you know her concern will be to protect you. That's all she'll care about. So I need you to let him go. I need you to walk away. Can you hear me, Jace? Walk away."

His wife's body shook more. Hands gripped his throat even tighter. She closed her eyes, lowered her head. He realized that her feet were on either side of his hips. She was off the ground using just her hold on his neck, her feet pressed against the house.

When his wife lifted her head and opened her eyes, they were blue again. Her face no longer contorted into something . . . unholy.

But she was struggling to maintain control. Her body still tense and her hands still around his throat. Her feet still against the wall.

She jerked forward, and he instinctively slammed back, his head colliding with the wall behind him.

"Come here again . . . bother me again . . . and there will be nothing to protect you *from me.*"

Her voice ended on a growl and the red began to come back to her eyes. Again she lowered her head. Again she fought it. Finally, she released him, jumping down. She was still panting and she started to speak in that devil's tongue again to the redhead.

"English, sweetie. I know a little Yiddish and that's about it. So you need to hit me with English."

His wife swallowed, slowed her breathing. "Get him and his friend out of here, Rachel. Don't let Kera or the others see. Can you do that for me?"

The mammoth nodded. "I got him. You go."

Taking slow, deep breaths, she patted the big woman on the

shoulders and walked off. Someone called for her inside the house and she picked up her step. The redhead went right behind her.

Then the mammoth yanked Davis by the hair until he was in front of her and twisted his arm around until she held it against his back. The pain cut through him, and he gritted his teeth.

She whistled and another oversized female ran toward them.

"What the hell?"

"I'll explain later. Get the other one."

The new female grabbed John and lifted him with her bare hands.

These women . . . they were too strong. It was unnatural. They were unnatural.

And they'd infected his wife with their unholiness.

They forced him around to the front of the house, but yanked him back when his wife, the redhead, some black girl, and some Asian female came out the front door and headed to an SUV.

"Where are we going?" the redhead asked, her arm around his wife.

"I'll tell you when we get there."

"Do we really have to go?"

"No," the Asian female replied. "But I want you to go. Because they like Jace. So she'll soothe. They hate you. So you'll irritate."

"Why am I going?" the black girl asked.

"Just get in the fucking car. You ask too many damn questions."

The women holding him waited until the SUV drove off. Then they quickly pushed him to the van he had waiting to carry him and his wife out of here.

His people opened the side door and the woman holding him threw him at Ezekiel. That wasn't the name he'd been given at birth, but the name Davis had blessed him with.

They crashed into the van and the other woman handed John in. He was no longer moving. Not even struggling.

"You better get him to the hospital," the mammoth said. "And don't come back here. We'll kill you all if you come back here."

Then she used those frighteningly large arms, and slammed the door closed in his face.

As they pulled away from the house, he stared out the small back windows of the van. They'd tossed him away. Like trash.

Those . . . females had treated him like some common person. Like they were better than he. Like they were stronger and more important than he was.

"He's not breathing, Brother Davis."

Davis looked over at Ezekiel. For a moment, he didn't recognize him. He didn't recognize anything or anyone except his outraged hatred.

This was his wife's fault. She'd caused this by being weak and letting that evil into their lives.

She'd have to be cleansed.

But for now . . .

"Get me a knife and a straw."

"A tracheotomy? Here? Now?"

"We can't go to the hospital," he said calmly, barely thinking about John. "Get me what I need. We'll do what we can."

First John. Then he'd figure out how to bring his wife to heel and back to his side where she belonged.

For eternity . . .

CHAPTER FIFTEEN

Jace stared up at the gothic-style building in the middle of downtown Los Angeles.

"Why are we here?" Kera asked, sounding panicked.

"Because they asked me to come."

"Nuns?" Kera turned away from the St. Mary Magdalene Convent of All Saints and faced their leader. "Nuns asked for you to come here? Nuns?"

"Why do you keep saying that over and over with that tone? Yes. *Nuns* asked me to come here."

"Why?"

Chloe patted Kera's face. "So much for the new girl to learn."

"Why are you still calling me that?"

"Until tonight, until the rites, you'll be the new girl."

Kera glanced at Erin. "What rites?"

"You haven't told her yet?" Chloe asked.

"I thought it was just a party."

"Well . . ." Chloe shrugged. "There will be punch. And some beer. You like beer, right? And Cheez Whiz!"

"Again with the Cheez Whiz?"

Laughing, because she enjoyed emotionally torturing others as much as she enjoyed the royalty checks from her historical fiction books, Chloe headed toward the convent.

Kera pointed a finger at Erin and snarled out between clenched teeth, "There better not be fuckin' Cheez Whiz at my party. Understand me?"

"All right. But you don't know what you're missing out on."

"I was in the military. I know *exactly* what I'm missing out on."

She stomped after Chloe, and Erin began to follow, but Jace caught her arm.

"You stopped me," Jace said, her mind still scrambled from all that had happened in the last hour.

"I did."

Focusing on the ground, Jace said, "Thank you."

Gentle fingers gripped Jace's chin and lifted her head until she was forced to look Erin in the eyes.

"You didn't do anything wrong, Jace. Not a damn thing."

"I knew he'd come. I knew it. And I was going to be very calm and rational. I wasn't going to let him get to me." Jace could feel tears beginning to well. She fought her desire to cry. This wasn't the time.

"But now I've shown him weakness. I've shown him a way back in. Even if it is just to irritate the living fuck out of me until I snap."

"Narcissists do like any attention. Even bad attention."

"I've just handed him power."

"Let me kill him for you, Jace. He'll just disappear and you'll never have to worry about him again. It's not like I have any moral center to stop me."

"Don't even try that bullshit with me," Jace snapped, yanking her face away, residual anger still moving through her veins. "You have a very high moral center no matter what lies you tell everybody else. But don't fucking lie to me!"

"Okay, okay!" Erin laughed, hands up to placate. "I'm a very moral person. Except when I'm fucking with Kera."

Jace let out a breath. She refused to let her anger gain control. Even though it was always waiting. Waiting to snap. "Besides . . ."

"Besides what?"

"I don't think it's a task for us."

"What does that mean?"

"When I touched him, I . . ."

"You . . . what?"

"I don't know. Just leave him alone. Promise me."

"Jace—"

"*Promise me*," she spit out between clenched teeth.

"*Fine.* No need to get homicidal."

"Are you ladies coming?" Chloe loudly asked from the steps of the convent. "Or do you bitches need a special invitation?"

Erin smirked. "I love how Chloe yells curses from the convent steps every time she comes here."

Jace shook her head. "It's just so embarrassing."

Alessandra didn't have a lot of time to get the party set up. Everything would be out back and, when Erin returned, she would be the one to get Kera downstairs for the "rituals" before the former Marine could see anything.

A lot of work just to fuck with the new girl, but even Alessandra had to admit . . . she was having a blast!

Snatching the front door open, she glared at the caterer standing there. "You're late," she accused.

"Do you want the food or not, freak?"

This was the problem with working with these people. Shifters, they called themselves. They could literally change from human to some predatory animal with no more than a thought.

But they weren't the freaks, according to them. Instead, they were genetic gifts from God.

The *Crows*, however, were freaks because they weren't born with wings, talons, and enhanced skills, but they had to die and be brought back that way. That slight change in the "natural order of things," as they called it, seemed to offend their shifter sensibilities.

Interesting, since the woman standing in front of Alessandra was six-nine with brown and gold hair and could change her entire body into a grizzly bear. She also smelled of honey. Like she'd bathed in it or used it as a perfume.

Yet Alessandra and her girls were the freaks.

"Get in, set up . . . be *nice*."

The She-bear stepped into her, over her, glowering down into Alessandra's face. "Or what?"

"Or I destroy your goddamn business in this town. And trust me, sweetie, I'm the one who can do it." Alessandra moved back so the bear and her team could come in. "Now get your big, fat ass out there, and get to work."

Growling just like the bear she was, the caterer lumbered into the house, her team of fellow shifters behind her. Varying, Alessandra assumed, in species and breed based on the body size and hair colors streaming through the Crows' doorway. Some had to be about seven feet tall. Others didn't even reach Alessandra's shoulder.

"And don't even think about spitting in our food!" Alessandra remembered to yell after them.

Alessandra snapped her fingers at two of her sister-Crows and pointed at the caterer, silently signaling them to follow Her Lady Bitchiness and her Bitchy Animal Menagerie.

Before Alessandra could close the doors, the chairs and tents arrived. A company also owned and staffed by shifters. Then security. Men and women so large, she would have guessed they were all Vikings except they ranged in race . . . and apparently species.

The shifter-owned companies were overpriced, the management and staff rude, with a tendency to snarl and/or bark. But there was just nothing better than being able to unleash one's wings during a great party, while still having someone else serve you. It was the only reason the Crows and Ravens hired shifters. Because the Clans didn't tell anyone about the shifters' ability to chase their own tails and the shifters didn't tell anyone that the Crows and Ravens had a molting season.

It was an agreement that worked as long as some hyena didn't hit on some tipsy Valkyrie who responded by cutting his throat and laughing. That was usually when trouble really began.

But that was why Alessandra had also hired a shifter-owned security company. Just to prevent that sort of thing. So she had high hopes all would go well this evening.

The DJ and her staff made it in, and Alessandra ticked them off the list on her tablet.

Seeing that the entire staff was now here, she began to close the door for the last time. But a hand slapped against it and pushed.

Startled, she stepped back, then grinned. "Yardley! You made it, girl!"

"Yeah." She tossed her luggage in. Most stars had their security team or assistants handle their luggage. But Yardley's entire team was made up of Crows . . . and they knew the woman could handle her own goddamn luggage. "The shoot is currently on . . . hiatus."

"What? Why?" Alessandra owned a Spanish-language TV network, so she loved hearing industry gossip. And rumors about the director Yardley had been working with were swirling everywhere. She was dying to hear the scoop.

"Well," Yardley began, "they found the director without his skin. So that sorta halted production for a while."

Alessandra gasped. "*What?*"

"Yeah. Guess I'll have to go to his funeral tomorrow. And he turned out to be such an asshole. But I'll need to at least make an appearance."

"Wait. Hold on. His *skin* was missing? What the fuck happened?"

"Not really sure. But there's every chance . . . Brianna ripped it off him."

Alessandra's arms dropped to her sides and she gazed at her sister-Crow in shock.

Not surprisingly, before either woman could say another word, a number of Crows were suddenly surrounding them, having overheard and being naturally downright nosy.

Leigh held up one finger. "I'm sorry . . . what?"

"Brianna?" Alessandra asked. "Betty's Brianna?"

Yardley scrunched up her nose in a way that had made her "one of the sexiest ten women alive" according to some men's magazine a year ago. "Yeahhhhhh."

Maeve grabbed Yardley's hand and dragged her toward the living room. "Come with me. I must hear *everything.*"

And considering Maeve didn't like touching anyone because of the whole "germ transference thing," as she called it . . . this was huge.

So while the shifters got the party set up outside, the Crows got the dirt.

They were sitting in the waiting room outside the Mother Superior's office. The Mother Superior was out of town, but her second in command, the one who'd called the Crows, was in attendance. And she, like the Mother Superior, was not to be ignored.

Because in the Crows' world, there were nuns . . . and there were nuns.

And then there were the Sisters of St. Mary Magdalene Convent of All Saints aka the Chosen Warriors of God.

Since the dawning of Christianity, the Sisters had been working in the background to protect the world from itself and to prevent the End of Days. In a lot of ways, their goals were no different from that of the Crows, but the two groups had a bloody history. One filled with violent sneak attacks, assassination attempts, revenge killings, and a particularly ugly event that brought on the Salem witch trials. But when that led to a bad time for boths sides, a treaty was born that still held to this day.

A treaty that was, at best, shaky.

Jace reached for a magazine on the coffee table in the middle of the room, and noticed that Kera had a nervous tic. She was using the ball of her foot to bounce her leg the way one might nervously tap one's fingers against a desk.

At first, Jace didn't mind. But five minutes in and she was getting annoyed.

Jace was about to gently lay her hand on Kera's leg—she probably didn't even know she was doing it—but Erin barked, "The leg, dude! What is wrong with you?" before Jace had the chance.

Of course, Kera was immediately defensive, which was why Jace had planned to try something different.

Sitting across the room, Chloe read the latest *Vanity Fair* with a nearly naked Yardley on the cover while Jace did her best to separate Erin and Kera as they slapped and punched at each other *over* Jace, who sat between them.

"Are you going to help me?" Jace asked their leader.

"Help you with what, babe?" She didn't even look up from her magazine, but she did say, "I can't believe nuns have a subscription to *Vanity Fair*. Like, shouldn't they be reading something called *Nun News*? Or *Daily Nun*?"

Fed up, Jace forced her two friends apart, screeching, "Stop it! Stop it now!" as four men entered the waiting room and sat in the chairs across from them.

Big and buff, they flipped through magazines or talked on their cell phones while Jace's sister-Crows settled back into their chairs and muttered curses at each other.

Jace didn't think much about these men because she already knew them. But when one winked and smiled at Kera, making her friend smile back, Jace knew she had to step in.

Jace had no worries that Kera would even *think* about cheating on her boyfriend. Kera loved Vig with all her heart. And most women enjoyed a little light flirting. Not catcalls, but light flirting. But these were not men to flirt with.

"Stop it," Jace said, keeping her voice low.

"Stop what? I barely touched Erin."

"Not that. Stop flirting with him."

"I'm not. He's flirting with me. I'm just appreciating it."

"Every girl likes to know she's still got it going on," Erin noted, her mini-fight with Kera already forgotten. The girl was not big on holding grudges once the initial heat wore off.

"You don't want to flirt with those men," Jace informed her friends.

"Why not?"

"Because they're the Four Horsemen."

Kera blinked. "The Four Horsemen of what?"

Jace and Erin gazed at her for a moment before Jace said, "The *Apocalypse.*"

Kera snorted and gave a little laugh. "Now *you're* fucking with me, Jace? Did Erin tell you to do this? Like when she told me I'd have to sleep with all the Valkyries so Odin would allow me to shack up with one of his Ravens."

"Erin!"

"I didn't say she had to," Erin corrected. "I said I'm sure Odin would appreciate it."

"You're an asshole," Kera barked.

"You act like you're telling me something I don't already know," Erin shot back.

"Both of you stop before I get terse," Jace warned, and the women immediately settled back in their chairs.

But Erin Amsel was a born shit starter. It was like she couldn't help herself.

Still, Jace initially had no idea what Erin was doing when she grabbed Jace's hand and gently placed it against Kera's forearm.

She said something in Old Norse, and when Kera looked across the room toward the Horsemen, her entire body jerked out of the chair, her back slamming against the wall, her arms up to protect herself.

"*Jesus fucking Christ!*" she bellowed. "*Where's his face!*"

Erin, laughing, leaned forward and gave the man a little wave. "So you must be Pestilence. Nice to meet you."

Jace used her thumb and forefinger to briefly rub her eyes. "Is there something psychologically wrong with you?" she asked her friend.

Erin stared at her. "Yes."

The Mother Superior's office door opened and one of her assistants stepped out. "Ladies," she said, her hand gesturing.

Kera was still in the corner of the room, her eyes closed tight, her body turned away. Jace was reaching for her, but Chloe got there first. She yanked Kera over and shoved her through the door. "Get over yourself. Trust me when I say, they won't be the worst things you'll see in this life."

"How did you do that?" Jace asked Erin.

"It's something Betty taught me. Want me to show you?" Erin grabbed Jace's arm, but Jace slapped her hand off and pushed her. Erin pushed her back.

"Would you two bitches get in here?" Chloe yelled. "Now!"

"Awww, come on, Chloe," one of the Horsemen lightly complained. "I was enjoying that."

"Let me guess who you are—" Erin began, but Jace grabbed her by the back of the neck and pushed her into the office.

Jace forced a smile. "Gentlemen," she said to the Horsemen before quickly walking into the Mother Superior's office and closing the door.

Sister Theresa Marie Rutkowski, the Mother Superior's second in command, sat at the large wood desk, dark eyes calmly gazing at them.

Smiling, Sister Theresa asked, "And how are you ladies doing today?"

Chloe put on her best fake smile and replied, "Wonderful, Sister, and you?"

That was when Jace knew this might not go too well . . .

Ski was sitting in the backyard, his feet up on another chair, while he read a book about the Jonestown cult from the perspective of a survivor.

He wanted to know more about the life Jace had lived. So many questions he wanted to ask, but after what she'd been through, he wasn't going to do that. If she wanted to tell him, he'd be there to listen. But he wouldn't push her for details she was not ready to give.

So, instead, he'd found about twenty books on different cults in the twentieth and twenty-first centuries and had read nineteen of them in the last two hours. He'd found them interesting, but Jace was so different from the survivors he'd read about. He'd believed her when she'd told him she'd never bought into the cult's belief system. She wasn't in denial. She really hadn't been part of that life—at least not emotionally—

otherwise her Second Life would have been much harder. Yet she'd happily joined the Crows, never looking back except when she had to.

That even as a ten-year-old she'd avoided being brainwashed said so much about her. Manipulating the situation so that she could expand her mind with languages and books . . . simply amazing.

"Hey," Gundo said, dropping into a chair at the patio table, a Diet Coke in his hand. The man was drinking from a curly straw.

A grown man.

"Did you know her grandmother isn't dead?"

"Whose grandmother?"

"Jacinda's."

Ski shook his head. "What are you talking about?"

"She constantly speaks of her grandmother. The one who raised her before her mother took her. The way she spoke of her, though, made me think she had passed. She hasn't. She's still quite alive. And with an extensive criminal record."

Now Ski laughed. "What?"

"I know. Shocking! I mean Jace is so . . . non-criminal. Even though she's a Crow. But her grandmother and other members of her father's side of the family cannot say the same. Several have actually done hard time."

"It sounds like her grandmother was the only one who—"

"—kept her from being psychologically trapped in that life." Gundo nodded. "Exactly. I'm just wondering why she hasn't contacted her since she became a Crow."

"Some of the Crows never lose contact with their families. Some never want to see them again. It's a personal choice."

"But the ones who don't want anything to do with their families are usually the ones who were killed by their families. That's clearly not the case here, and the way Jacinda speaks of her—"

"You've already called her grandmother, haven't you?"

Gundo gave a small shrug. "I left a message."

"By Tyr's missing hand, Gundo!"

"I know, I know. I didn't think I'd find a number. But I did. And I kind of ran with it."

Ski closed his book, ready to give his "*You can't just do things you want to because you think it's the right thing to do*" speech, when something hit the metal patio table, startling both men.

It was Ratatosk. He'd landed on his back, little arms and legs spread out wide from his small body, panting heavily. He looked like he'd been through hell.

Gundo leaned in to take a closer look. "He's bleeding. And I see teeth marks."

Ski sighed and asked in Icelandic, "Who did you piss off now, little rat?"

Having dealt with Ratatosk personally since the day Ormi had drop-kicked the little bastard across the library floor, Ski was sure he'd pissed someone off. It was Ratatosk's way. Running between the eagle at the top of *Yggdrasil* and Nidhogg— the dragon who would one day bring about Ragnarok—at the bottom, for no other reason than to carry bitchy words back and forth between the two was a job created for an asshole. But no matter what Ratatosk might say, he enjoyed his role among the gods and the Vikings.

Ratatosk placed the back of one claw against his forehead and moaned. Dramatically.

Ski rolled his eyes and Gundo dropped back into his chair, already ignoring the long-tailed rodent.

"Do you have something to tell me or not?" Ski pushed.

"*He's here to tell you about an All-Clan meeting on Monday.*"

Ski stood, looking around for the voice that boomed at him from all sides, and desperately covering his ears. His poor neighbors for about ten miles would think they'd just experienced a small earthquake.

"Could you not do that?" Ski asked.

"*Sorry!*" Tyr, the god of war, battle, and justice, cleared his throat since his voice was still booming and said in a more human tone, "Sorry. I forget."

Tyr stood by the glass doors leading to the patio. He didn't actually look the way one would expect a god to look. Not in that black Led Zeppelin T-shirt that had probably been purchased at an early seventies concert—the Nordic gods did love Zeppelin so—and thick black work boots that appeared just as old as the T-shirt. His brown and gray hair reached to his waist in a long, loose braid. A thick dark beard hit just above the collar of his T-shirt and covered the lower half of his face, several braids woven in. His arms were covered in tattooed runes except for his right forearm, which had the face of an angry wolf branded onto it. Where his right hand should have been was a metal glove covered in powerful runes and created by ancient dwarves. It allowed Tyr to use it as if his hand was still there.

A string of tattooed runes also circled his very thick neck, and a brutal scar went from under his chin, across his mouth, abruptly ending in the middle of his cheek.

It made Tyr appear terrifying, but he was one of the most cheerful and pleasant gods Ski had known. He only became angry when he felt a true injustice had been done.

And no one wanted to deal with an angry Tyr.

"An All-Clan meeting? Why?"

"I think you already know why."

Ski sat back down, shrugged. "Gullveig."

"Gullveig. The Crows and Ravens didn't stop her. Although they made quite the effort. So I don't hold it against them."

"I don't see the other gods being quite so forgiving. At least not of the Crows."

"We remember Gullveig. She's a deceitful female. That she fooled the Crows, the most distrusting of the Clans, was no easy task. Sadly," he said on a sigh, "it's not really *us* the Crows need to worry about."

CHAPTER SIXTEEN

"So let us discuss the big, huge, ridiculously bad mistake you ladies have made."

Jace winced, watching Chloe's jaw tense. That was never a good sign.

"You're blaming this on us?" Chloe growled.

"Who else should we blame it on? You had a chance to stop her and you didn't."

"We thought we had."

"Well, you were painfully wrong. Sacrifices are up—"

"There are always sacrifices."

"Natural disasters have grown substantially since the day you thought you'd stopped her. Earthquakes in Iowa. That pesky little flood in the Gobi Desert. And the five hundred miles of rain forest that turned into ice. You don't think that's because of her?"

"Perhaps. Or maybe that Fallen bastard you people can't seem to keep control of has gotten out of hand again. Or maybe he's bred another Antichrist. Or maybe these are just signs."

"The sacrifices aren't signs. They're offerings and you know it. And the longer she's here, the more her power grows."

"*I know!*" Chloe bellowed, her patience snapping. "Oh, I know," she said, calmer. "And we'll deal with it."

"Then fucking *deal* with it, pagan. Because once we step in—"

"Don't threaten us, Christian. As we both know, the Clans don't take kindly to it. Let us not forget what was started in 1618."

"And I'd hate for there to be another episode like the Salem witch trials. Remind me again, Crow, how many of you were left by the time it was all done?"

Chloe stood, her chair thrown back, her hands landing hard against the table. And Sister Theresa Marie was there to meet her, their noses and fingers nearly touching as they leaned in close to each other, eyes locked in a centuries-old battle begun long before either woman's great-great-grandparents had even been born.

Jace took in the rest of the room. She saw hands move toward hidden weapons. Bodies tense. Gazes dart.

This was seconds from getting out of hand, so she readied herself to step in, hoping to prevent that from happening.

But then Kera was there, slapping her own hands on the desk, leaning in, and screaming, "*Am I really the only one completely freaked out by the Four Horsemen sitting around a waiting room?*"

"New girl?" Sister Theresa Marie asked Chloe, neither angry gaze wavering from the other.

"New girl."

"You know I'm right here!"

Theresa Marie laughed. "Your ex-Catholics are the *best,* pagan."

"Best. Worst. Whatever."

"Gullveig returning to this world is a bad thing," Tyr told Ski and Gundo. "A bad thing for everyone." Tyr's shoulders hunched, his two hands—the metal and flesh—twisting together. "I'm not saying what the family did to her was right. It wasn't. But there's something about that female. Wherever she goes, she brings despair. As she walked around Valhalla that day, in and out of all the rooms, coveting all the gold . . . every time she smiled, my bones literally filled with dread.

"If she can, she will unbalance this world just to get even with us." He sat back in the chair, the poor metal squealing in protest. "She needs to be stopped. Now."

"Excuse my directness," Gundo said. "But I'm not sure why

none of you are doing this. She's a god, all of you are gods . . . you can all do god things together."

"She's not in Asgard. She's here. And here is protected by you. All of you. Because Gullveig will bring Ragnarok if she can. I believe that's her goal."

"We'll do whatever we have to," Ski told his god.

"Good. But this also means that you, Ski, will have to work with the other Clans."

"Of course."

"You have more skill with that than Ormi, and he'll be prepping with the other Clan leaders for battle."

"I understand. Anything you need."

"Of course this also means you'll need to work with the Ravens."

"Why do you hate me?"

Gundo laughed and Tyr shook his head. "Still with this?" the god asked.

"There's just so much stupid."

"You manage with the Giant Killers well enough. And they're stupid."

"The Killers are what the Killers are."

"Right. Stupid."

"But the Ravens don't have to be stupid. They *choose* to be. Am I the only one here who really finds that offensive?"

Tyr and Gundo shared a look before both shook their heads and replied, "No."

"Maybe we could all calm down," Jace suggested.

Erin pulled Kera over to a corner, attempting to keep her from spinning out.

Sister Theresa Marie slowly turned her head to look at Jace. Her eyes deadly cold underneath that prim habit, a smattering of brown and gray bangs peeking out.

Finally, the nun said, "You are such a lovely young lady, Jacinda Berisha. I truly don't understand what you're doing with these evil, godless bitches."

Skin met skin as Chloe's hand cracked across Theresa Marie's face.

The nun stood there for a moment, eyes focused on a spot behind Jace's head, a small trickle of blood forming in the corner of her mouth until it slowly rolled down her chin.

When she finally turned her head back toward Chloe, it was so Theresa Marie could crack her neck.

Jace stepped closer to the desk. "Perhaps I was not clear on the meaning of the word 'calm'?"

"I expect you to do the right thing, Danski Eriksen," Tyr told him.

"Even if it's incredibly painful?" And Ski knew he was whining. Most of the Nordic gods didn't stand for whining, but Tyr was extremely patient.

Plus, Ski was sure that Tyr knew he was kind of kidding. Kind of.

"Yes. Even if it's painful. Do you think it's easy dealing with Odin? Or, by all that is in my name," he said on a sigh, "Thor?" He shook his head. "Thor. It is so tragic when your hammer is smarter than you are."

Gundo quickly covered his mouth and looked off, working hard to keep his laugh in. Ski just used what he called his "blank expression." It was a true skill he'd honed over the years working with the other Clans.

"But," Tyr said, his voice filled with conviction, "we must overlook the weakness of those beneath us and fight to keep the world right. Understand?"

"Is this where we chant your name?" Ski asked.

"Are we Ravens now?" Tyr demanded. "If you're performing some kind of magical rite or sacrifice, feel free to chant away. Otherwise . . . don't. You know too much noise annoys me unless I'm in battle or celebrating a victory."

"We'll deal with this, Tyr," Ski promised. "We'll start at the All-Clan meeting Ratatosk is going to tell me about."

The god finally looked down at the immortal squirrel. "What's he doing?"

Ratatosk was still lying flat on the table, eyes closed—groaning dramatically.

"We've been ignoring him. He hates that."

Tyr rolled his eyes and asked the squirrel, "Why are you still here, little rodent? I'm sure you have messages to get to the other Clans and I can fill my loyal sons in on the pertinent information."

Ratatosk chittered and Tyr's usually placid expression filled with rage, his fist slamming down on the metal table, crumpling it.

The squirrel scrambled off before he was trapped among the twisted wreckage.

Tyr shot to his feet. "*Odin said that?*" he roared. "*Then let that one-eyed bastard say it to my face!*"

Ski held up his hand, halting his god. "Source, Tyr," he reminded him quietly; yelling was never effective when dealing with any god of any pantheon. "Note the source of this information."

Tyr let out a breath, nodded. "Of course, dearest Ski, you are right as always." He flicked his middle finger and Ratatosk flew. "Away with you, vile rodent. Tell your lies to someone else!"

Ratatosk hit a bush and disappeared.

"I don't think anyone has ever accused Ratatosk of being a liar," Gundo remarked for some unfathomable reason.

"Shut *up*," Ski warned his friend.

Thankfully, Tyr seemed oblivious as he sat back down, the metal chair squealing again at all that weight forced into it.

"You are always very reasonable, Danski Eriksen. Just like your ancestor Bárðr 'The Friendly' Eriksen. He may have pulled that twelfth-century monastery down stone by stone to get to the gold within and taken all the young monks as slaves, but he was very reasonable when he slaughtered the other Christians."

"Thank you, Tyr."

"Of course." He gestured to the remnants of the table. "And I will pay to replace this."

"No need."

"I insist. How much?"

"Twenty thousand."

"Dollars? *Are you mad, boy?*"

Ski winced at his god's bellow. "It was handcrafted by an Icelandic designer."

"I don't care if Brokkr himself made it," Tyr snarled, talking about the dwarf who helped his dwarven kin create Thor's hammer, Freyr's ship, and Odin's spear. "Who spends that kind of coin?"

As kind and good-natured as Tyr definitely was—especially as gods go—he was definitely tight with a buck.

"Why can't you be more thrifty, like your Boston brothers?"

"They're not thrifty," Ski corrected. "They're poor."

"Of course they're poor," Gundo interjected. "They're all college professors . . . in the *arts*."

Tyr shook his mighty head and muttered the phrase he always did when discussing finances with Ski or Ormi, "You LA people."

Chloe's body collided with the office door, taking it down, and rolled back out into the waiting room.

Pestilence laughed. War cheered. Death looked annoyed. And Famine appeared mildly concerned.

Adjusting her short habit, Sister Theresa walked out after Chloe.

And before Jace could stop her, Erin followed, wrapping her arm around the nun's throat and pulling her back.

If that had been it, both Jace and Kera would have stepped in to stop Erin. But two other sisters and two laywomen with tattoos and old scars jumped in. Jace still wanted to stop any of this from getting worse, but one of the laywomen pressed a switchblade against Kera's neck.

That's when Jace no longer cared if Erin burned the whole convent down and the Crows laughed in the ashes.

"Let Kera go or I will tear your heart out through your pussy!" Jace growled.

"Okay," Erin said, immediately releasing Sister Theresa and

putting her hands up. "I don't know what Jace just said, because she didn't say it in English."

"It was Slovakian," War interjected, "and it was *rude*."

"But when she starts speaking in different languages," Erin went on, "everyone needs to calm the fuck down."

"She's right," Death said, grabbing a copy of *House & Garden* magazine from one of the end tables. "She's about to put me to work, so maybe you babes should think about taking it down a notch. Because I'm not in the mood today to start grabbing souls that aren't already on my list. Me and my brothers are going surfing tonight," he added, as if that would mean anything to any of them.

Sister Theresa smoothed down the front of her plain white, button-down shirt and simple greenish-blue calf-length skirt. An ensemble that hid a woman who'd been a Chosen Warrior of God since she was fourteen. She'd been fighting demons, the warriors of other pantheons, and every form of pure evil known—and unknown—to man for decades.

And these ladies were even more secretive about their activities than the Crows. Only a select few of the Vatican priests even knew these warriors existed. The rest thought they were just nuns—there to serve God and them. According to the Mother Superior, that was for "men's own good. You know they can't handle too much. It's best for everyone they lead their lives in ignorance."

The switchblade was moved away from Kera's throat and Jace's rage disappeared.

She didn't realize until that moment how protective she was of her new friend. She really liked Kera. Not just as a sister-Crow, not just as a team member. But as an actual girlfriend. Something Jace had never had before. Of course, maybe she should have realized all that when she didn't mind Kera coming by her room just to chat. It didn't annoy Jace like when the others tried to do the same thing. Then again, Kera's chit-chat was *never* small talk either. The woman did love to discuss big issues of the day.

Erin helped Chloe back to her feet.

"You're psychotic," Chloe accused Sister Theresa.

"And you're an idiot. Do you really think I have the Four Horsemen sitting in our waiting room for shits and giggles? I can actually *see* what they look like, you know?"

"Hey," Famine complained, "I thought you liked us."

When Sister Theresa and Chloe just stared at him, Famine shrunk back in his chair, pouting. "Forget it."

"You know how this works, pagan," Sister Theresa practically snarled at Chloe. "If even just one of our end of days is set off, it leads to all the others. From Ragnarok to us to the Hindus, to the Muslims, to the Greeks, to the Romans, and on and on and on until it's all gone. Is that what you want?"

"Of course not."

"Then fix it, Crow! Gullveig is your problem, not ours!"

Chloe made a move as if she was about to go after Theresa again, but Erin yanked their leader back by her shoulder, if for no other reason than because Chloe should really stop making moves on Sister Theresa. Sadly, this was not the first time the nun had thrown the Crow leader through a door. These Christian warriors were well trained and insanely powerful. Some took the vows to be nuns. Some didn't. But they all fought the same fight for the future of the human race in the name of their higher power.

And the Crows wouldn't have been any kinder if the roles were reversed. Nothing pissed off the Clan leaders more than when the Christians couldn't keep their demons or archangels in check.

Chloe took a deep breath, trying to rein in her temper. "We have an All-Clan meeting on Monday. We'll discuss this further then. Happy?"

"Ecstatic. Bitch."

Chloe went for her again, but Erin caught her around the waist and dragged her to the front door and out into the hallway, leaving Jace and Kera alone with warrior nuns, warrior laywomen, and the Four Horsemen.

Kera began, "Uh—"

Jace slapped her hand over her friend's mouth and led her to the door.

"We'll handle it," Jace promised, pushing Kera out into the hallway. She nodded, first at the Horsemen. "Gentlemen." Then at the sisters and laywomen. "Sisters. Ladies."

With nothing else to say, Jace closed the door and let out a relieved breath.

"Those women are *nuns*? Are we sure?" Kera asked.

"Some of them are. Some are laywomen who were orphaned street kids the nuns take in and train to be the Chosen Warriors of God. If they have the calling for that role."

"Those nuns seem stronger than I remember from when I was a kid."

"Really?" Jace asked. "I haven't met a nun yet who hasn't had strength. She'd have to, don't you think? Just to take her vows. To commit to this life. I mean . . . could you?"

They stared at each other a moment, then moved off down the hall without bothering to reply.

As they walked, they passed three tall, exquisite men.

Jace greeted them by name as she always had since the day her grandmother had introduced her to them. They'd been having tea in her grandmother's kitchen "Michael. Raphael. Khamael."

"Hey, Jace."

"Hey, sweetie."

"Jacie-girl! How you doin'?"

Kera stopped and focused on the three men walking into the office they'd just left.

"Jace, was that . . . are those . . ."

"Do you really want to know, Kera? Do you really think you can handle knowing exactly who those men are?"

Kera shook her head. "No. I really don't think I can."

Jace put her arm around Kera's shoulders and led her to the front door of the convent. "Come on. Let's get you some ice cream."

"I thought we were going to get the dogs groomed."

But that would mean going back to the house to get the dogs . . . where they were still setting up for Kera's party.

"That can wait," Jace said casually. "Especially when you look like you need the ice cream more than Brodie needs a bath."

"Ice cream. Liquor. Whichever."

"So what do you think, brother?" Gundo asked after Tyr had given them details of the All-Clan meeting before wandering off.

"That we should allow for traffic when we decide what time to leave for the Crows' party tonight."

Gundo shook his head. "Not that, you eager idiot."

Ski grinned. He was a bit eager. He couldn't wait to see Jace. He was a bit sorry he'd told her it was Saturday. It would have been nice to have her hanging out in their library again.

"I'm talking about Gullveig."

"Oh," Ski replied. "Well . . . if Tyr says she's here, she's here. The Crows failed to stop her. It's not good, but it happens."

"Still, Chloe won't like being questioned about this."

"No. But I wouldn't worry too much. Compared to leaders of some of the other Clans, Chloe Wong is calm and rational."

"You didn't even try to help!" Chloe accused Kera from the front seat of the SUV that Erin was driving back to Malibu.

"They were *nuns!*" Kera yelled. "I was raised Catholic!"

Chloe turned in her seat so she could look at Kera behind her. "That was your First Life! In this life, they're your enemy!"

"They didn't do anything wrong! You started it!"

Chloe gasped. "I did not!"

"Suggesting Thor swung the hammer that drove the nails into the cross was a *great* way to calm down the situation."

"I was joking!"

"*Not funny!*"

"It was kinda funny," Erin muttered.

"Shut up!" Kera snapped.

Jace's phone vibrated in her back pocket and she quickly checked it, assuming it was about the party.

See you tonight.

It took Jace a moment to realize the text was from Ski. For two panicked seconds, she thought it might be from Haddock, and she hated him more for once again tainting her Second Life.

She quickly shook the anger off, though. She wasn't going to let him do this to her. Not again.

She replied:

Yes. See you tonight.

She almost put her phone away, but it vibrated again.

And don't forget . . . it's Saturday.

Rolling her eyes and smiling at the same time, she texted back two words.

Shut up.

Again focusing on the argument happening right next to her, she heard Kera bark, "You really are a piece of work, you know that?"

Chloe unbuckled her seat belt so she could fully turn around in her seat, rising up on her knees, and pointing a finger at Kera. "Look, I don't care what religion you came from, little girl. Now you're one of us! And that means when a nun throws a right cross, you *back me the fuck up!*"

"It was a left jab, and *you deserved it!*"

"Your nose is broken, by the way," Erin pointed out to Chloe.

Growling, Chloe grabbed her nose between both hands and jerked one way, then the other until she'd sort of forced the pieces back into place.

"And let me explain something to you," Kera went on, ignoring the cracking sound that went along with Chloe fixing her nose. "When I was growing up with my crazy mother, it was the nuns who helped me. It was Sister Mary Angelic who noticed the occasional bruises. It was Mother Mary Francis who told my mother if she did it again, the wrath of God would fall upon her, because the only thing my mother feared was the wrath of God since she never took the social worker assigned to our case ever a little bit seriously. And it was Sister Mary Typewriter who suggested I join the military after high school graduation to get away from my mother rather than getting pregnant by my boyfriend at the time."

Erin glanced back. "Sister Mary Typewriter?"

"She was the senior class typewriting teacher, and that's what we all called her. I don't remember her real name."

"Look—" Chloe began, but Kera cut her off.

"So if you think I'm just going to start attacking nuns on your say-so when you *started it,* our Second Life together is going to be *very* strained."

Chloe reached for Kera, and Jace quickly leaned in between them, just as the SUV suddenly stopped and Chloe flew back, her body landing in the foot well, the back of her head slamming into the glove box.

Erin glanced over. "Sorry, Clo."

"Bitch."

"I had to stop. There's a car."

No, there wasn't.

Jace leaned forward and patted the leather seat. "Sit, Chloe. And put on your seat belt."

"But—"

"It's unsafe! Seat belt!"

Growling, their leader did as Jace ordered.

"Don't worry, Chloe," Erin said as she started up the SUV again. "I'll always have your back with the nuns."

Kera slapped her hands against her thighs. "Because they clearly hated you, Amsel!"

Erin's laugh was happy and boisterous. "They do! Even before I became a Crow. In high school. Junior high. Kindergarten. They hated me! I still don't know why."

"Why were you going to Catholic schools?" Chloe asked. "I thought your mom raised you Jewish."

"She did. But she had a way of pissing off our rabbis. So we always ended up with the nuns and priests since my dad was Catholic."

"In other words," Kera remarked, "your ability to piss people off is in the blood."

Erin nodded, grinning. "It really is."

Jace sighed. "Am I the only one who's concerned that we seem to have failed to stop Gullveig from entering this world and that she's probably here to start Ragnarok?"

"Of course you're not the only one concerned," Chloe said, finally sounding a little more reasonable. "We're just in denial about it, but we'll deal with it."

"But don't you worry, Kera," Erin added, giving her a thumbs-up. "This will not ruin your party tonight!"

Slowly, Kera's gaze moved over to Jace. *Help me,* she mouthed.

But there was no help for poor Kera. She'd have to suffer through the upcoming indignation just like the rest of them had done . . .

CHAPTER SEVENTEEN

There was chanting.

So. Much. Chanting.

Plus, there were a few chickens in cages, and a goat.

Dear God, where had Erin found the goat?

Jace glanced over at poor Kera. She was still on her knees in front of the big Fates statue. It had been made in the twenties when the first Crows had moved into this territory.

The bronze statue had been quite a source of pride, as well as the location of the occasional sacrifice back in the day. But the Crows, like many Californians, became less comfortable with using animals for anything other than pets. In fact, these days there was an entire Strike Team out of Portland that was openly vegan.

Right now, however, the statue was being used for no other purpose than to torture poor Kera.

That would be her name for a while now. Poor Kera. Because Erin was really making the kid's life a living hell.

Especially when the chanting—something Erin had taped days ago using the Crows' *worst* singers, and then made into a continuous loop so that it played over and over again, ad nauseum—was completely nonsensical! And had been going on for an hour!

Thankfully, one of the sister-Crows peeked around the pillars and motioned to Alessandra, letting her know everything was set and the party was in full swing.

Letting out a relieved sigh—because to be honest, Poor Kera

wasn't the only one suffering through this—Alessandra motioned to Erin, letting her know it was time to wrap this shit up.

Some were hungry, most needed a drink, and all were more than ready to party with the others.

Erin nodded and reached down, pulling Kera to her feet. Very necessary, since she'd been on her knees so damn long, she probably couldn't stand on her own.

"Come, sister. We're at the final step."

"Thank God," Kera complained. She hadn't hidden her annoyance at this for one second. Everything seemed to be pissing her off. She sighed constantly. Rolled her eyes. And there was definitely some growling. It was clear she just wanted this to be over with.

Of course, so did the rest of them.

Dressed in white robes that Erin had borrowed from the set of a sword and sorcery TV show that one of the sister-Crows worked on as a costume designer, they walked up the long flight of back stairs that led them into a room where Erin had fixed up a table filled with the boring, cheap food she'd insisted on buying, including some cans of Bud Light beer, more cans of Cheez Wiz than seemed necessary, and a sheet cake from the local grocery store with "Welcome Insert Name Here" written on it in pink frosting.

Disgusted, Kera faced Erin. "Are you kidding?"

"Wait, wait! Don't get too excited."

"Excited?"

"One more step before we can begin the festivities."

"Kill me now."

"Again? You were already killed once."

"Can we just finish this, please? So I can watch some TV or set myself on fire."

"But this will be fun!"

"What is it?"

"We strip and dance naked in the moonlight. Covered in goat's blood, of course."

"Don't touch that goat, and there is no moon tonight."

"Pretend there is."

Kera sighed and shook her head. "I'm done," she said, pulling the robe over her head and tossing it at Erin. She wore shorts and a black tank top under the robe, even though Erin had told her she had to be naked. "I am *so* done."

"But—"

"No. I'm not dancing naked. There will be no blood. I'm not kneeling anymore. I'm not singing any more goddamn Zeppelin songs. I'm not getting hit any more with sticks."

"That was Odin's staff."

"Shut up!"

Erin grabbed Kera's arm. "Calm down."

"Let go of me."

"Would you stop?"

"*Let* go of me."

"Let's just go outside and—"

"You want to go outside?" Kera asked, finally snapping. She turned and grabbed hold of Erin by the throat. "Be my guest, sister-Crow!"

Using Erin like a shotput, Kera threw the smaller woman at the back door, the force taking the whole thing down.

Kera cracked her knuckles and followed. She reached down and again grabbed Erin by the throat, lifting her up until Erin's feet didn't even touch the ground. Jace raced outside and grabbed her friends, desperately trying to separate them.

"Kera, let her go!"

"Just let me snap her neck, Jace. Or choke the life out of her. *Just let me choke the life out of her!*"

Realizing Kera was too angry to see anything but the one irritant in front of her—namely Erin—Jace grabbed Kera by the hair and snatched her back and around until she was forced to drop Erin.

"Ow, Jace! Get off me!"

Jace swung Kera around again, forcing her not to look, but to *see.*

Three hundred Crows from around the States, Europe, and Africa gazed at the "new girl."

Kera froze, mouth open.

Chloe—who'd told Kera she wasn't coming to the ritual "out of principle, nun-lover"—stood in front of the crowd of women who were all dressed in black, their wings out and proud.

Chloe grinned at Kera, her arms crossed over her chest. "Ni-iiiiice," she purred, staring at Erin.

Gasping and coughing, Erin got to her feet. "Welcome to the Crows," she finally wheezed out.

"I don't . . . what . . . I can't . . . what's happening?"

"This is your party," Jace explained. "Your *real* party."

"Surprise!" Yardley called out, but when Kera's dark eyes locked on her, she stepped back into the crowd of wings and designer black clothes, attempting to hide.

Kera rounded on Erin. "This whole thing was a prank?"

Erin's chuckle was shockingly oblivious. Even for her. "Pretty good, right?" she asked, her grin revealing how proud of herself she was. "Like I'd ever give you a shitty party."

"Why would you . . . what purpose . . . why can't you . . ."

Erin shrugged. "Is it my fault you're so fucking gullible?"

Kera's head dipped down—Alessandra called it "Kera's angry bull look"—and Jace tried to grab her, but Kera caught hold of Erin first, lifting the redhead off her feet, unleashed her wings, and took off, flying higher and higher until they could barely see either of them.

Jace went to follow, but Annalisa put her arm around her shoulders and held her in place.

"Let Kera handle this."

"But—"

"No. It's something she needs to do."

"I don't know why you're getting so mad!" Erin argued from far up in the night sky. "I was just kidding! Don't you know how to take a joke?"

"This has been a long time coming," Annalisa added.

"You're being unreasonable! I don't know why you're acting like—hey! Hey, hey! Wait! Shitttttttttttt!"

They heard a splash that suggested Erin had gone headfirst into their Olympic-size pool, meaning Kera had used her new gods-given strength to throw Erin down rather than merely dropping her and letting her wings save her.

A few seconds later, Kera landed, brushing off her hands. "Now . . . where were we?"

"See?" Annalisa said to Jace. "They just needed to work their shit out."

Chloe motioned to Rachel.

"Music!" Rachel called out and the DJ rolled some tech because Erin had found out that was Kera's favorite dance music.

"Feel better?" Jace asked Kera.

Her smile was small, but there. "A little."

"Well, then." Jace hugged her. "Welcome to the family, Kera."

Ski stood beside his brothers in front of the Bird House, their heads tilting so far over they were nearly upside down as they gazed up at the seven-foot man staring down at a clipboard.

"Your names aga—" His eyes widened at the sight of the Protectors. "What's going on with your necks? What are they doing with their necks?" he suddenly called out.

One of the Crows quickly stepped up, smiling at Ski. "Don't worry. That's normal for them."

"Freaks," the man muttered, again looking at his clipboard.

"Alessandra said to be nice to our guests. So be nice." The Crow gestured to Ski and his brothers. "Untwist your necks, guys. You're freaking the freaks out."

"I'm not a freak. I'm a grizzly."

The Crow giggled. "I like how you say that as if it's supposed to be normal or something." She gestured at the door. "Why don't you guys go in? The party's already at full swing."

But before Ski and his brothers could step inside, the Ravens appeared beside them.

In fact, it seemed as if *all* the Ravens were there.

"Name?" the large man asked.

"Ludvig Rundstöm."

The grizzly gestured with a jerk of his head. "Go."

Rundstöm stepped between the grizzly and the Crows and

went inside. The rest of the Ravens attempted to follow but the man threw up his big hand. "Name?"

"Stieg Engstrom."

The grizzly quickly flipped through the many pages of names, then said, "Nope."

"What do you mean 'nope'?"

"I don't know how much clearer 'nope' can be."

"What about Rolf Landvik?"

"Nope."

"Wait," Siggy Kaspersen cut in. "Are you saying the rest of us Ravens weren't invited to the party?"

Ski watched Gundo physically recoil from that sentence structure.

The grizzly shrugged. "If you're not on the list . . ."

"Vig was invited," the Crow pointed out. "Not you."

"But we're his brothers."

"Oh, I'm sorry," the Crow replied, expression earnest. "But tragically we don't care." She pointed at Ski. "You and the Protectors can go in, though."

"But," Ski said, "I was so enjoying . . ." He turned to stare at Engstrom and finished, "the *burn.*"

Engstrom was reaching for Ski when the grizzly stuck his big arm between them. "No fighting, freaks." He motioned to the other security members. "We're not afraid to maul. And we already have permission if things get out of hand."

"I'm sorry," Bear said, staring at the bigger man before him. "I'm confused by you people."

Ski and Gundo winced in each other's direction because the man they were talking to was African American.

The shifter's eyes narrowed. "You people?"

"Yes," Bear went on, oblivious. "Are you genetically a bear? Or just mystically?"

"What?"

"I was wondering that, too," Haldor pushed. "Is your DNA strain different from other humans? I mean, we're enhanced mystically, but genetically we're no different from anyone else. But I've heard that you people test differently."

Borgsten, who dabbled in science on the side, leaned in. "You do? In what way?"

"I heard they can't involve themselves in anything that might lead to blood testing of any kind, like the Olympics, or professional sports."

"That must be disappointing for you," Gundo noted. "Since you could win all the Olympics all the time. Are you angry about that? Do you have a form of grizzly rage? They are a very aggressive animal. Are you aggressive like that?"

Haldor nodded and asked, "And are your children born furry?"

Kera received really warm hugs from Crows out of the Philippines, and promises in Tagalog to get together for dinner soon.

The Philippine sister-Crows walked away and Kera realized she didn't remember their names. She didn't remember anyone's name. There were so many people here! Crow reps from all over the world. All here to see her.

And to drink.

Kera knew these ladies were also here to drink. Heavily.

Someone tapped her shoulder, and Kera took a breath, ready to meet someone else whose name she'd never remember. But to her relief, standing behind her was Vig.

She threw her arms around his shoulders, hugging him tight. "I'm so glad you're here!"

"You knew I wouldn't miss it." He kissed her, his hands tight on her waist. "How has it been going?" he asked when he finally pulled back.

"I dropped Erin in the pool."

"Well . . . that doesn't really surprise me."

"Did you know about this? About the party fake-out?"

"Yeah."

"And you didn't tell me?"

"You didn't ask."

Kera stepped back. "I have to ask you if someone's faking me out?"

"Only if it's another Crow. I'm not getting between you and

the Crows. That way only leads to death. Or, at the very least, harsh, *harsh* criticism."

With a sigh, Kera turned in time to see her dog bopping through the dancing crowd. Wings out, Lev on her back. Everyone greeted Brodie. It was like they all knew her. Even people she'd absolutely *never* seen before.

"I think everyone likes my dog better than me."

Vig put his arms around Kera from behind, his chin resting on the top of her head. "Yeah, they do."

Erin came up to them. She'd changed into dry clothes— black denim shorts, black racer-back tee, and black flip-flops— and her wet hair was in two short ponytails. She had a Long Island iced tea in one hand and a mini-pizza in the other. Smiling, she moved to the music.

"So?" Erin asked. "What do you think of your party?"

Kera tried to make another grab for her, but Vig wouldn't release her.

"If you're hoping that she's even thinking about what happened an hour ago," he whispered against Kera's ear, "you'll be very disappointed."

"I dropped her into the pool from, like, three hundred feet in the air."

"She just doesn't care."

Kera wasn't sure she believed him until she watched Erin for a good minute.

The redhead raised her glass in the air, greeting the Japanese Crows walking by. Then she snapped her fingers at one of the waiters and took several of the hors d'oeuvres from the silver platter since the mini-pizza was long gone.

"This is Kobe beef," Erin explained before shoving one in her mouth. "Yummy!"

"Oh my God," Kera whispered to Vig. "She really doesn't."

"Erin never holds grudges. Not the way you and I hold grudges, I mean."

"I threw her through a door."

"Doesn't matter."

The Los Angeles Valkyries walked into the backyard. They

didn't wear much. Mostly bikinis or very tiny shorts and T-shirts. But it was all silver. And headbands with wings. The leader threw her arms in the air and screeched out, "*Valkyries in the house, bitches!*"

"You invited the Valkyries?" Kera asked Erin.

"No, but they come anyway."

"I thought we had security."

"My sister's a Valkyrie," Vig reminded them.

"We do have security," Erin went on, ignoring Vig. "But our security is made up of shifters, which means that like all wild animals, they are slaves to their basest instincts." She gestured to the now-dancing Valkyries. "So, yeah, who's going to stop the whores from coming into the party?"

"Again," Vig said, "my sister."

Kera glanced around. "Where's the guys?" she asked Vig and when he stared at her, "Your Raven brothers?"

"Outside."

"Yeah." Erin held up her empty glass, gesturing at one of the waitresses for more alcohol. "They have been denied access."

"Why? I like the guys."

"Yeahhhh, but this really irritates them, which amuses me, sooooooo, yeahhhhhh—"

Kera shook her head. "What is wrong with you?"

Annalisa suddenly appeared beside them, as if she'd been waiting for just such an opening. "You know, many have asked me that about Erin. And you'd think she must have some kind of personality disorder. But surprisingly . . . she doesn't. Erin is just kind of a dick."

Erin gratefully took the fresh Long Island iced tea and, grinning, nodded her head in agreement.

Jace perched in the trees overlooking the party. Birds surrounded her on all sides, the crows and ravens keeping her company as she watched her sisters dance, laugh, and have a good time.

She wished she could say she was unhappy being up here.

She wished she could regret not feeling comfortable enough to be part of the action.

But that would be a lie.

Jace was so very comfortable right now, being a part of and *apart from* everything. She used to dream about living this way in those days when she was the Great Prophet's wife. Those days when she had to be right by her husband's side, smiling, shaking hands, holding conversations with idiots not smart enough to realize they were being used and manipulated. Being part of everything. Fully involved.

Gods, how she always hated it so.

But when Jace had become a Crow, during her own welcome party she'd gone to the trees and the Crows hadn't said a word. They'd noticed. They'd cared. But when they realized Jace was more comfortable observing rather than participating, they'd backed off and left her to her own devices. Then such a show they'd given her, filled with fights and laughter and rude pranks directed at each other and the visiting Clans. They'd made sure that Jace had something fun to watch.

Her party had been amazing.

Kera's was turning out to be even better.

The birds surrounding Jace suddenly took flight in a large panic of wings. When they settled back down, they were all on Jace's left, staring.

Jace looked to her right to see what had her friends so concerned.

Ski and the Protectors were now perched beside her. Some had plates of food. Others had drinks. After a few minutes, they politely switched with each other. They were sharing.

It was so civilized. Not what she was used to at all. A fight over bread sticks broke out among the Ravens once at an Olive Garden. That's what Jace was used to.

Ski smiled at her. Gods in the heavens, he was just so damn handsome.

"Sorry I'm late," he said. "The guys were harassing the shifters."

"We weren't harassing," Gundo argued. "We were just asking questions."

"But they certainly are sensitive for wild beasts," Haldor said between bites of Kobe beef and chicken wings.

Jace winced. "You didn't call them that to their faces, did you?"

"No. Of course not."

"Of course not," Ski repeated. "They just called them wild animals and freaks."

"In our defense, Jacinda," Haldor added, "they did call us freaks first."

Jace didn't bother to argue and instead pointed out, "You guys don't have to sit up here with me, you know. You're more than welcome down there with everyone else."

The Protectors suddenly looked uncomfortable.

"Well," Haldor finally said, "the crowd is so large—"

"—and the music is so loud—" another Protector chimed in.

"—and there is so much pushing and shoving—"

"That's called dancing," Ski muttered.

"—and whoever invited the Giant Killers should have told the men that deodorant is not optional but a mandatory accoutrement—"

"—which is to say—"

"—we'll be much happier up here—"

"—than we would be down there—"

"—if it's all right with you, Jacinda," Haldor finished for them all.

"It's absolutely fine with me," Jace replied, understanding the language of introverts better than any other language she knew. "Whatever you guys want to do. That's what Crow parties are all about. Within reason, of course. No random murder. Chloe hates that. And no grabbing entire trays of food and going somewhere to sit down and feed . . . everyone else hates that."

"Wait." Bear's eyes grew bright. "Does that mean we can—"

"*No*," Ski stated firmly. "You can't harass the shifters."

"Questions are *not* harassment."

"That grizzly was moments from tearing your head off. I promised Ormi no one would die tonight."

"Actually," Jace said, "I chatted with one of the bartenders before I came up here—"

"You chatted?" Ski asked.

"About global warming."

"Of course."

"—and she's a neuroscience major studying for her master's. She was exceptionally friendly for a shifter, and I'm sure she'd be more than happy to answer your questions as long as you refrain from calling them freaks or wild beasts. Want me to ask?"

"No," Ski said.

"Yes, please!" the others replied.

Ski waited until Jace flew off before glaring at his brothers. "Really?" he asked.

"We're curious," Borgsten replied for them all.

"Curiosity killed the owl."

"No. It killed the cat. The owls flew away."

Jace returned. "Whenever you want, stop by the bar. Her name is Wendy. She's actually an African wild dog . . . and yet," she went on, obviously fascinated, her wings keeping her aloft in front of them, "*not* black. Korean American, fifth generation. But she apparently comes from a very long line of African wild dogs." Her grin was wide. "Fascinating, right?"

"Fascinating!" his brothers parroted back to her, their grins equally wide.

They weren't mocking. They really found that information fascinating.

Jace perched on a branch next to Ski, and he looked over at Borgsten.

Ski raised his brows and tipped his head. Borgsten frowned. Shrugged. Oblivious as always.

Ski mouthed, *Go away.*

"Oh! Yeah." Borgsten pointed to more trees across the yard. "Gentlemen, we're going there for a better view."

Bear looked at the distant trees, then back at Borgsten. "A better view of what?"

"A better view of everything."

"But I'm comfortable."

Borgsten pointed. "Move."

With an annoyed grunt, Bear flew off and the others followed. Borgsten stopped long enough to wink and blatantly nod at Ski.

Idiot.

"They are so cute," Jace said, laughing.

At least she was laughing.

"I think you mean oblivious."

"Why oblivious? Because they won't allow themselves to be forced into society's norms of good behavior?"

"No. Because they can't tell when one of their brethren wants to spend time alone with a beautiful woman."

"Who?"

Ski closed his eyes, shook his head. "Gods, no wonder you get along with them. You're oblivious, too."

Oh. He meant her.

He meant her!

"Uh . . ." Jace didn't know what to say.

"Are you blushing?"

"No. Shut up. No. Asshole."

Ski laughed. "I didn't mean to embarrass you."

"I know. I'm just not used to compliments."

"Because no one gives them or because you're too busy ignoring everything and everyone around you?"

"Uhhhh . . ."

"Yeah, that's what I thought."

Rolf waited until Josef handed the keys to his Bugatti to the valet before he approached.

"They won't let us in," Rolf told him.

"What?"

"They won't let us in. They let Vig in, but we're 'not on the list.' And the grizzly at the front door is being kind of a dick about it, and Stieg and Siggy are about two seconds from starting a *National Geographic* documentary–style fight on the African plains."

"All these years and you still haven't figured out how to get into a Crow party?"

"Not since you divorced their leader, no."

"I didn't divorce her. She divorced me."

"Do we really have to have this discussion again?"

"I say we fly in there," Siggy volunteered.

"And get pecked to death by those crows? I mean the birds, not the women."

"The raven birds will back us up."

Rolf studied his brother. "You're really relying on actual birds to protect us from other actual birds?"

"Everyone calm down," Josef said. "I've got this covered."

"You gonna divorce Chloe again?" Stieg asked.

Their leader's eyes narrowed. "You are *such* an asshole." Josef motioned to a small truck that had followed him in.

Three men came out, pulling something from the back of the truck's cab.

Josef walked to the front door with the Ravens behind him.

The grizzly didn't even look up. He just sniffed the air— which was weird—and said, "Again . . . you're not on the list, fellas."

"Can you grab one of the ladies of the house, please?" Josef asked. When the grizzly finally looked at him, he added, "Before you start getting lippy, we can drag you up and drop you from five hundred feet in the air before your friends can even flash a fang. So just get whoever is running this shit show. Thanks."

A minute went by, then two before Alessandra arrived at the front door. Rolf quietly let out a breath he'd been holding. He'd been worried it would be Annalisa. Of all the Crows, he found the former sociopath the most disturbing to deal with. It seemed she could just look at a person, instantly figure out what their insecurities were, and design a way to fuck with them in a matter of seconds.

And honestly, Josef was just too easy to torture.

"Gentlemen," she purred, looking hotter than ever. "Can I help you?"

"We're here for the party," Josef replied.

"I know you are, but Chloe hates you. She hates you a lot. And with good reason. Valkyrie stripper, Josef? Really?"

"I can't believe you're judging another woman."

"I might believe your lame attempt at feminism if I didn't know the only reason she's a Valkyrie is because of Odin and his love of big-tittied strippers."

"Odin knows what he likes."

"Maybe he should leave the Valkyrie decisions up to Freyja."

"Those are god decisions I don't involve myself in. I suggest you do the same. But for now—"

"Yeah, sorry, but—"

"I brought a gift."

"Come on, Josef. Do you really think you can *buy* your way into a Crow party?" She chuckled and turned to go back into the house.

"Even if I brought *Barrique de Ponciano Porfidio?*"

Rolf had no idea what Josef was offering or why the man was suddenly speaking Spanish, but Alessandra froze in midstep and several Crows appeared in the doorway.

Slowly, Alessandra faced Josef. "Are you lying?"

"No. I have one hundred bottles just for you lovely ladies."

"Are they counterfeit?"

"Got them from a Norwegian Raven brother who was in Japan recently."

"The Japanese *are* the biggest buyers," Leigh Matsushita said to her sister-Crows, voice low.

"Show us one," Alessandra prompted.

Josef, always one who enjoyed being the center of attention—just like their god, Odin himself—silently gestured to one of the three men behind him.

The man came forward, holding one of the handcrafted bottles in his hands.

"Alessandra."

The beautiful Crow leaned in and studied the bottle. Rolf had seen her do the same thing with diamonds. The woman knew expensive.

"It's the real deal," Alessandra said. "One of the best tequilas to come out of Mexico. At least two grand a bottle, and our dear Josef there says they have one hundred bottles for us."

Leigh pushed past Alessandra and opened her arms wide. "My Raven brothers! Welcome!"

"I have absolutely nothing to say to you."

Ski nodded at that out-of-nowhere statement from Jace. "Wow. Okay."

"I wish I did. I wish I could have sparkling, fascinating conversation with you. But I'm sitting here, looking at you . . . and there's nothin'."

"Okay. I get that. You're not a big conversationalist."

"I'm really not."

"But you wish you were."

"Not really. I mean . . . I wish I had something interesting to say to you. You know, so I could entice you into my sexual web."

"I'm a guy. A Viking guy. Enticing me into your sexual web is pretty much you breathing. So no worries there."

"Good to know."

"But, to be honest," he admitted, "I was hoping for more than just—"

"A one-night stand?"

"Yeah. But if that's not what you want . . ."

"I'm really not a one-night stand kind of girl. When I think about it, it just makes my skin crawl rather than get me all worked up. So . . . yeah. That's not the issue."

"But talking to me is?"

"I don't mind talking to you," she matter-of-factly replied. "I just have nothing to say."

"Well . . . what have you been thinking about? While you're sitting here next to me."

"Ivan the Terrible," she instantly replied.

"Uhhh . . . okay. I make you think of Ivan the Terrible?"

"No, not at all."

"I guess that's something."

"It's just . . . I saw a documentary on him last night. It was really fascinating. Did you know that he dragged out a man he'd been having tortured in freezing cold water just so he could boil him alive later?"

"What did he say to piss Ivan off?"

"How did you know he pissed Ivan off?"

"Why else would Ivan bother doing all that? Do you know how much effort it takes to get a big pot, fill it with water, get a fire going, then bring it to the point of boiling? Then you have to get the guy *in* the boiling water. Or keep him in the water while it gets to the boiling point. So the tortured guy must have said or done something to piss off Ivan. What was it?"

"He told him hell was coming for him."

"That'll do it. Especially because Ivan the Terrible was very religious and believed, like most monarchs of that time, that he was chosen by the Christian God Himself, so to imply that he had fallen from the grace of his God . . . Plus, Ivan did have what I'm sure many psychologists of this time would call paranoid personality disorder."

Eyes wide and bright, she leaned forward, placing her hand against his forearm. "I thought the same thing last night!"

"Have you studied personality disorders?" Ski asked her. "I'm sure that every monarch, dictator, and terrorist leader has suffered from one if not several."

"I've been realizing that. The more history I read, the more nothing seems to change."

Ski smirked at her. "Want to figure out the personality disorders of the Tudors?"

"No." A beautiful grin spread across her face. "The Borgias! Oooh! And the Medicis."

Laughing, Ski nodded. "You're on!"

★ ★ ★

"Did you even notice we were stuck outside?"

Vig looked up from his plate of fried chicken and replied to his Raven brothers with sincere honesty, "No."

Rolf laughed, but Stieg and Siggy were just pissed.

Still, as they sat down at the table with him, they already had at least two plates of food each, piled high. And microbrew beer from Germany and Norway. With all that food, they weren't about to get into it with Vig about deserting them.

"Where's Kera?" Rolf asked.

"Dancing with the Crows."

As one, they all turned to look out over the nearby dance floor. Kera was with Erin, dancing and laughing, their past issues forgotten. Vig was so happy for her. She'd found her place. She'd found where she belonged. It wasn't easy for some of the Crows, coming into this world. A new world the rest of the Clans were mostly born into. New Crows had so much to learn, so much to get used to, but they also had each other.

The Crows weren't an easy group to get along with, but once you found your place, you found your home—in this life and the next.

Jace walked by with a Protector. The one Stieg always called Pointdexter. They were in a deep, animated conversation . . . about serial killers.

"Don't you think Ted Bundy was overrated?"

"No way," Jace said, talking more than Vig could ever remember. "Between his body count, his high IQ, and the fact that people around him were completely unaware of his sociopathic tendencies because he was so good at faking everyone out . . . he's definitely not overrated. But then you have your Henry Lee Lucas types . . ."

The Ravens turned back toward the table—and found their food gone.

They looked around, Vig wondering if the staff hired for this event had whisked their plates away for some reason. But he didn't see anything.

After they stared at each other for a few seconds, they shrugged and stood to get more food.

Sitting in the trees above the party, the Protector brothers enjoyed the food they'd stolen.

"Isn't it almost *too* easy?" Haldor asked Gundo and Borgsten around a large rib eye.

"No!"

"I have to disagree," Bear said. "You need a real challenge."

"Which is?"

"Steal liquor . . . from the Killers."

When Gundo and Borgsten smiled, Haldor quickly reminded them, "We promised Ski there'd be no fights."

"There can only be a fight if they catch us."

Kera danced with Vig's Valkyrie sister, Katja, because Erin had suddenly walked off the dance floor.

Erin wasn't pissed, but something else had her attention. It took Kera a while to figure out that was just Erin. She didn't say "good night" or "good-bye" or "I'll call you later" like most people. She just . . . walked away. It was one of the few times when she wasn't purposely rude or instigating a fight. She just figured the conversation was done so . . .

"Are you having a good time?" Katja asked Kera over the pulsing music.

"Yes! This is great!"

Erin returned, two cold beers in her hand and a Diet Coke. She handed the beer from Sweden to Katja; and the one from Boston to Kera. The Coke was for her.

"So, you still pissed at me?" Erin asked Kera.

"I should be, but—"

"My charm has won you over?"

"You have no charm. I'm surprised you hadn't been killed sooner than you were."

"Well—"

"I'm surprised your parents didn't suffocate you in your crib.

That schoolchildren didn't stone you. That the United States government didn't send you to a war-torn country . . . by accident. That you weren't tossed into a zoo's lion display during a school trip. That you weren't—"

"Okay!" Erin barked, while Katja bent over at the waist from laughing so hard. "I get your point."

"I wouldn't say that I've dealt with worse than you during my time in the Marines. But I have dealt with the equivalent. And I figure if I could put up with guys as annoying as you, I can give the same opportunity to a fellow female. But I only do that out of my innate feminism and because Jace will yell at me if I don't."

"Thank you," Erin replied dryly. "I appreciate your goodwill."

"As you should."

"Oh, by Odin," Katja choked out between laughs. "You two are *priceless* together. You should take your show on the road."

"Shut up," Kera and Erin snapped.

It was one thing for them to mock each other, but to get it from a Valkyrie? Uh . . . no.

Chloe was choosing between the Mexican food table, the tapas table, and the fried food table—she eventually decided to hit all three—when she realized that she was surrounded by fellow Crows.

The leaders of the Alabama Crows, the Maine/Canadian Border Crows, the Tri-State Crows, the Florida Crows, and all four of the Texas Crows—representing Houston, Dallas, Austin, and San Antonio—gazed silently at her.

Without their saying a word, Chloe knew what they wanted to discuss.

"Yes," she told them, "I know my ex-husband's here. Whatever."

"We don't give a shit about your ex-husband, darlin'," Serena of the Alabama Crows replied. "Lord knows, I have four of my own, and they just ain't that interesting."

"You got in a fistfight with a nun?" Neecy of the Tri-State Crows asked. "I mean . . . really? A nun?"

"Oh, like you've never been in a fight with a nun."

"Of course I have. They're a bunch of ball-crushing, soul-destroying, demon-stomping bitches who I happen to adore."

"Only because the New York ones are nice to you."

"I survived a Catholic orphanage. That gives me automatic acceptance points with the nuns."

"Look"—Serena pushed her hair behind her ears—"we've all had our run-ins with the Chosen Warriors of God. I still have the scars from where one of them tried to destroy my spleen. But none of us purposely fucks with 'em. It's not like the old boys' network from the Vatican. These ladies can actually do some damage."

"I didn't seek them out. They came to me."

Sadie, of Maine, held up her hand. "Instead of going around and around about this . . . why don't you just tell us what's going on? I sense it will be easier that way."

"Okay," Kera said, sounding exasperated. "Then who is Fenrir again?"

"He's the giant wolf that bit off Tyr's hand when Tyr bound him," Erin patiently explained. "Because it's foretold that he will one day begin Ragnarok."

"Tyr?"

"No. Fenrir."

"And why don't they just kill him? I don't understand!"

"Because you're using logic. How many times do I have to tell you that logic and gods are not a mix that will ever happen? *Ever.*"

Erin watched Kera grapple with the backstories of all the Nordic gods and giants. She was clearly struggling . . . which Erin had to admit she was thoroughly enjoying.

Erin motioned to one of the waitresses for more drinks. Not so much for her as for Kera. Her years in the Marines had taught Kera well how to hold her drink, but not exactly when to stop. Erin, however, had hit her two-drink limit a while ago.

"Hey!" a Giant Killer suddenly yelled in the middle of the party. "*Who the fuck is stealing our liquor?*"

Kera gazed at the screaming Killer for a long while before she asked Erin, "How many monster children did Loki have?"

"Loki has lots of children, but the ones you have to worry about are the three children he had with the giantess Angrboða. Fenrir the wolf. Jörmungandr the serpent. And Hel. All *delightful* beings," she joked.

"*Where's our liquor?*"

Kera pointed at the still-screaming Killer. "Should we be worried—"

"Nope."

"Okay, then."

A waitress placed a beer and a diet Coke in front of Kera and Erin.

Stieg Engstrom suddenly appeared beside them, his eyes across the dance floor. "What's that?" he asked.

"What's what?"

He crouched beside Erin and Kera, and pointed. "That."

They looked where he was pointing, and Kera replied, "That's what we in the *normal* universe—"

"The Nordic gods *are* the normal universe," Erin reminded her.

"—call a hookup."

"And you're okay with this?"

Erin glanced at Stieg. "You act like they're fucking on the table."

"A Protector with Jace? It's not right."

"Do you have a thing for her?" Kera asked.

"She's like a sister."

"A sister you want to fuck? Like a stepsister?"

Stieg gazed at Erin. "What is wrong with you?"

"It's a valid question."

"It's a sick question. I'm just protective of her. She's weak and . . . docile."

Erin and Kera again looked over at Jace. She sat at one of the tables—shocking, really, because Jace usually stuck to the trees when there was a party—with Ski Eriksen. They were both laughing and talking.

Jace Berisha was talking. Willingly!

Only a Raven could have a problem with that.

"I think they're a cute couple," Kera argued. "And he's so sweet to her. How could you have a problem with this?"

"Ignore him, Kera. Engstrom's just pissed because the Protectors call the Ravens stupid. Like Thor stupid."

Stieg leaned in to Erin because he was probably going to yell at her, but a Giant Killer stood in front of the table and screamed, "*Did you steal our liquor?*"

Erin shrugged. "No."

With a grunt, the Killer walked to the next table and yelled, "*Did you steal our liquor?*"

"We are *not* Thor stupid," Stieg insisted, the three of them watching the Killer walking to all the tables and yelling the same sentence. "We'll never be *that* stupid!"

"Sweetie," Kera reminded him, "that's not saying as much as you think it is."

Jace had no idea how they'd ended up at this table near the dance floor. She usually stayed in the trees but Ski had said he was thirsty, she'd decided to come with him to get a soda, and they'd never quite made it back to the trees. Instead, they sat at a table and continued their conversation.

Their lovely conversation. About the Second Punic War.

True. She couldn't think of many people who would find the war between Rome and Carthage as interesting as Jace always had, but she adored Roman history.

Was glad she'd never lived it, but still loved reading about it and, now that she was free of her First Life, watching movies about it. Couldn't get enough.

The movies, filled with battles and good-looking British guys with tight abs, always caught the interest of her fellow sister-Crows and the viewing room filled up quickly, everyone passing around popcorn and candy, cheering during the battles or pointing out battle-technique flaws. It was one of the few things Jace enjoyed doing with other people. But trying to talk to any of the Crows but Chloe about the real history behind those movies and . . . forget it. Her sisters' eyes would glaze over or they'd start making "I'm bored" noises. So Jace didn't bother.

She wouldn't have bothered discussing any of it with Ski, either, except that he was well versed on most military history, from the earliest wars in Mesopotamia to the recent battles throughout the world.

Shockingly, he knew way more than she did. He could rattle off statistics—the death toll, the number of legions involved, how many cities and small towns were decimated, even how many slaves were sold for some of the Roman wars and battles, because the Romans kept such meticulous records of everything—while thoroughly understanding the politics that drove the world at that time.

He was magnificent. Smart *and* good-looking.

God, was she drooling? She felt like she was just staring at him and drooling.

She was pathetic, wasn't she?

It wasn't like she had much experience with men. Dealing with her ex-husband and his sycophants just didn't count as real experience. And hanging out with the Ravens recently because of Kera didn't count much, either. They all treated her like a little sister with a hair-trigger temper. And because they had no interest in her sexually, she could talk to them without worry. She wasn't trying to entice them, just preventing Erin from insulting them or Annalisa from messing with their heads.

Yet listening to Ski Eriksen . . .

Listening. Shit. She wasn't listening. She was just staring at his face and he was asking her something.

"Sorry?" she tried not to wince.

"I asked if I was boring you. Guess I am."

"No," she said too quickly. "No, it's just . . ."

"It's just . . . what?"

"I just really don't know what I'm doing."

"What you're doing? What do you think you're supposed to be doing?"

"I don't know. That's the problem. I don't know what I'm supposed to be doing. I just enjoy sitting here, listening to you go on and on about death tolls and the number of horses and elephants in Hannibal's cavalry. I could listen to you go on for days about that, but that's not exactly a dialogue that helps a relationship grow."

"No. It just makes me your college professor."

Jace shrugged. "I wouldn't know. Never went to college."

"You should. The Crows will pay for it. Although you should understand, you already know way more than any of your professors will know. That might irritate some of them and bore you."

"Doesn't matter."

"Trust me, it does when you're sitting there listening to them completely screw up the Viking portion of their Norwegian history class. It's almost physically painful."

"No, I mean, it doesn't matter—at least not yet—because I don't have a high school diploma."

Ski frowned. "You don't?"

"I was"—she raised her hands and made air quotes with her fingers—"'homeschooled.' Because *those* people were only going to teach me evil and lies."

"I don't understand. Then how did you learn so many languages?"

"Well, once you get the basics of Latin, which my father started teaching me before he died, the Romance languages become almost frighteningly easy. Plus, my grandmother taught me Romanian, which has a lot of French and Italian and Spanish at its heart. She and my uncles also taught me Albanian, which is an Indo-European language. And then the cult insisted I learn Hebrew, ancient Persian, ancient Sumerian, Coptic—which is ancient Egyptian—Arabic, and Aramaic."

"And, um . . . the Russian?"

"My grandmother started me on Russian, and by learning

Russian, you can learn Polish, Czeck, etcetera, much easier, and I enjoyed Russian so much, it was really easy to teach myself what my grandmother never had time to do."

He gazed at her for a moment before admitting, "I know Old Norse."

"Yes, you do. And you should be proud of that. It's hard."

"You already know it, don't you?"

Jace shrugged and admitted, "Sorta."

"Yeah." Ski sat back in his chair. "We need to get you your GED, so we can get you in and out of college as quickly as possible."

"Why?"

"So you can earn your master's and PhD in languages."

"Why?"

"Because talent like yours can't go unnoticed. And, to be quite honest, if it hadn't been for Bear being quite the annoying pain in my ass, it would have."

"So I know different languages? So what? What's the big deal?"

Ski leaned over and spoke to the Giant Killer sitting at the next table. He spoke in Norwegian. After glaring at him, the Killer snapped back, "English, dude. This is *America*. Duh."

Now Ski stared at her. "That's why. *Duh*."

Jace shook her head. "What do you mean, the Protectors have been stealing the Killers' liquor?" she asked in a whisper, having easily understood what Ski had said to the Killer.

Ski laughed. "They've been doing it all night."

"Don't pick on the Killers," she laughingly chastised. "They serve their purpose."

Resting his arms on the table, Ski leaned in and asked, "Which is?"

Jace thought long and hard on her answer . . . because she really didn't have one. But, at the last second, she came up with, "We'll understand their purpose," she said, raising her index finger for emphasis, "when Ragnarok comes."

"Very nice save."

"I thought so!"

★ ★ ★

She found the Great Prophet sitting in the backyard, gazing up at the sky. When she looked, all she saw was stars and clouds, but she knew the Great Prophet saw so much more. He always had. Even as a child, he'd been . . . a presence. A presence in this world that they were all undeserving of.

These people who tried to entrap him, tried to jail him in the hopes of containing his truths . . . they would suffer greatly when the world ended. All of them would.

But especially that girl.

She'd been given the greatest gift of all. The gift of being his wife. The *wife* of the Great Prophet and she'd turned away from it. Like a fool. A lost, heartless fool.

In the end, that girl had deserved nothing she'd been given, and her suffering for letting it go would be great. In this world *and* the next.

Sitting beside him, she patiently waited for him to speak.

He'd requested her and she'd come. Without thought, without question. As it should be.

He didn't speak for ten minutes, but when he finally turned to her, she felt awed by his presence. By the mere fact that he was looking at *her*.

"She needs to come back," he said. "We need to save her. She'll talk to you."

She swallowed and asked, "And if she won't come?"

"Make her."

With a nod, she left him. She'd put a small team together that would help. But he was right, of course.

Jacinda would talk to her. She was, after all, Jacinda's mother . . .

Chapter Eighteen

Kera suddenly sat down beside Jace. Directly on her chair, pushing her over until they were both barely on it.

"Hi, Kera."

"Hi, Jace." She smiled.

And then she kept smiling.

"Enjoying your party, sweetie?" Jace asked.

"I am. I am *so* enjoying my party."

"Kera . . . are you a little drunk?"

"No. I'm a-lotta drunk. But it's that bitch's fault," she said, pointing . . . around. Since Erin was off somewhere. "She just keeps giving me drinks."

"You don't have to take them."

"But they're just so tasty." Then she began quietly chanting. "Tasty, tasty, tasty, tasty."

Jace thought Kera was going to keep going, but she suddenly pointed at Ski. "You, with the penis."

Ski's eyes widened behind his adorably dorky glasses, his lips pressed together to stop the laughter.

"You treat this girl like she's a goddess. Understand me?" Tears suddenly formed in Kera's eyes. "Do you know why?" she asked, choking a bit. "Because she's the only one who hasn't abused my clipboards."

Ski scratched his head and quickly looked off. All the other Clans had heard about the recent Clipboard Incident. There'd been a bonfire. And dancing. And a "We Are the Champions" sing-along.

It had not been pretty.

But the Crows saw Kera's clipboards as an attempt at controlling them, and it was the one thing the ladies would not stand for from anyone but their goddess and their leader. Kera, as the "new girl," did nothing but bring out the panic.

Yet Kera was a true Crow—she'd not soon forgive or forget what had happened that night.

Sadly, that was confirmed when Kera suddenly pointed around the party and yelled, "*Unlike these treacherous bitches here!*"

As was the Crow way, Kera's drunken outburst was greeted with joyful cheers. Because they were Crows and all of Jace's sisters were ridiculous.

"You see?" Kera asked Ski. "They're *all* bitches. But not my Jace." She put her arm around Jace's shoulders and hugged her. "Never my Jace. So if you hurt her . . . I will have Erin burn that pretty face of yours *right off!*"

"Okay," Jace said, pushing Kera's arm off—it was now squeezing her so hard, it was starting to really hurt . . . and possibly break something—"perhaps we should get you to bed."

"Why?" Kera looked around. "The night's young!"

Ski could tell that Jace was embarrassed about her friend, but he didn't know why. These were the descendants of Vikings. Drinking and then embarrassing themselves at parties was what they did.

Even the Protectors, after a few drinks, had finally come down from the trees and were standing around, watching everyone else on the dance floor.

But was Ski embarrassed by them? No. And Jace shouldn't be, either. The best thing about drunk friends? They were pretty honest. Sometimes that meant very hurtful things were said, but in Kera's case it just showed how much she cared about Jace. She didn't seem to have enough nice things to say about her.

"Sorry, Jace," a low voice rumbled and Ski looked up to see Vig Rundström. "She got away from me."

"It's okay," Jace said with a little laugh.

"Isn't he amazing?" Kera asked them. "I love him."

One side of Rundstöm's face lifted. One might call it a smile. Maybe. Or a small stroke.

"Look what he gave me!" Kera held her arm out, nearly punching Jace in the process. A slim silver chain bracelet dangled from her wrist. "Isn't it pretty? Look." When Jace and Ski both smiled and nodded, the woman's eyes narrowed. "I said *look*."

Now afraid not to, both Jace and Ski leaned in.

"It's a boat."

"It's a *snekkja*," Rundstöm grumbled. "A long boat."

Ski grasped the charm between two fingers and removed his glasses so he could take a closer look. So much detail in such a small item. He could make out the sails, the round shields, the oars, even the small heads of the men. It amazed Ski to think that a butcher like Vig Rundstöm could craft such beautiful work.

"You did this yourself, Raven?"

"Yes."

"I didn't know you had the skill. Not with those hands."

A deep snarl rumbled up from the dark face hidden behind black hair and a big beard.

The Rundstöm bloodline had not changed since the 600s. Vig Rundstöm was so very Viking. More than most. He was just missing the round shield and fur cloak to complete the picture. There was absolutely nothing modern about the man, so it didn't surprise Ski that he'd chosen a warrior Crow to be his mate. It just surprised him that Kera, a very evolved female, would tolerate the Neanderthal.

But, as Ski's grandfather always said, "To each their own."

"You made that *Mjölnir* necklace, too?" Ski asked, now examining the representation of Thor's hammer around Kera's neck, and an obvious slap at the Giant Killers who had giant hammers—not their god's rune like the rest of them—branded on their bodies. Seeing that necklace around the throat of a Crow must greatly annoy them.

The Raven grunted in response.

"Nice work."

Another grunt, but this time Kera patted her Viking's chest. "Be nice. He looks rich."

Ski grinned. "I am."

Jace coughed, but quickly dropped her head.

"See?" Kera said. "He's rich. Be nice, he'll buy your stuff. Right? You'll buy his stuff?"

"Well—"

"I said," she growled, voice low, "you'll buy his stuff . . . right?"

Ski didn't dare look at Jace. "Right."

"Good." Kera stood, stumbled, although she wasn't actually moving, straightened. "Maybe some coffee?"

Rundstöm grunted, nodded, wrapped his arm around her waist, and carried her off.

Ski shook his head. "By Tyr's justice, he's *such* a Viking."

"So . . . that's where we're at," Chloe finished to her fellow Crow leaders.

They were silent until Neecy asked, "Still didn't really explain why you swung at a nun."

"Because she was irritating me," Chloe snapped back. "Isn't that good enough?"

"No."

"But you're sure," Serena asked, "that this Brianna girl *is* Gullveig?"

"What else could she be?" another Crow leader asked.

"An LA agent?" When all Chloe got were blank stares, "You people have no idea what it's like in Hollywood. Betty was nicer to that minotaur she took on once than she was to that studio head she thought was trying to screw over her client back in the nineties. When she was done with him, the guy ended up joining a kibbutz in Israel. He's not even Jewish."

Serena leaned forward. "Well, darlin', you better confirm she's the one and Gullveig isn't roaming around inside some dog somewhere."

"And you need to find out before that All-Clan meeting,"

Neecy added. "The Silent are looking for any excuse to push the Crows out of the Nine. Don't give 'em a chance."

Chloe thought a moment. "The director—"

"The one who lost his skin?"

Chloe nodded at Neecy's question. "His funeral's tomorrow." She glanced at her watch. "Make that today. Yardley has to go, and I'm sure Brianna will be there."

"Why?"

"The director won an Academy Award for some artsy film he did. A lot of names will be there to make an appearance, get their picture taken, schmooze."

"At a funeral?" Serena's lip curled in disgust. "Well, isn't this a godless little state."

"It used to be just Southern California, but since the tech boom, Northern California's been catching up." Chloe blew out a breath. "Okay. We'll send Yardley to the funeral with her team. And I'll send a team to Brianna's office and her home. See if we can find anything else. Although I don't know what we should be looking for." She shrugged. "An altar of skin?"

"I saw one of those once," Serena admitted. "It was nasty. And surprisingly stinky."

"Look for something," Neecy pushed. "You can't go into that All-Clan meeting with no information. The Silent will crucify you."

Serena looked out the window as a group of women and one man walked by, her eyes narrowing. "What is your ex-husband doin' here with all them Valkyries?"

"Trying to goad me into a fight, but I promised Erin that if there was any fighting at this party, it wouldn't be because of me."

"Especially after you punched that nun," Neecy muttered.

"You really need to let that go."

Serena stood. "With you havin' so much on your mind, why don't *we* entertain your ex-husband?"

Chloe smirked. "Ladies—"

"Oh, come on! It'll be fun. You focus on your little Gullveig problem—"

"I'm not sure a god forcing her way into this world is a *little* problem."

"Shut up, Neecy. And we'll keep your ex out of the way."

Chloe stared at Serena. "And how are you going to do that?"

"Don't you even worry. Trust us to handle it."

"See, that's where we have a problem." Chloe laughed. "I don't trust any of you bitches."

"You want something to drink?" Ski asked.

"That would be great."

"What would you like?"

Jace panicked. She'd never done the drinking thing, so she really didn't know what to order. So she blurted out one of the drinks she'd heard ordered throughout the night by her sister-Crows. "Dirty martini!"

Ski gazed at her with those sometimes-unblinking eyes.

She tried again. "Uh . . . Kamikaze?"

His head tipped to the side.

"Southern Comfort on the rocks?"

Still staring.

"Singapore Sling!"

"What's in a Singapore Sling, Jace?"

She rubbed her chin. "Liquor?"

"Jace, what do you really want?"

"Sprite."

"Why didn't you just say that?"

"Well, everybody else is drinking."

"Yes. Everyone else is drinking." He looked over the dance floor. It was not pretty.

Wings were out. Dance moves were attempted . . . and failed. Some, like Kera, were just standing there, holding a beer and moving their heads, sometimes jerking their hips, eyes closed. Kera wasn't actually moving to the music playing, but to something she was hearing in her head.

Then there were Alessandra and several Valkyries, with their arms in the air, writhing.

So much writhing.

Then there were the Ravens. Eesh.

Big men shouldn't really try to dance. Unless they were Siggy.

Siggy could move his ass with the best of them, even keeping up with the Tri-State Crows, who were known for their skills on the dance floor.

"That's what drinking gets you, Jace. As you know," Ski went on, a little smug, "the Protectors don't get that kind of sloppy drunk."

Jace didn't respond. She just pointed. Gundo had his head buried in some Giant Killer's voluptuous boobs and Borgsten was resting against Gundo's back while they all slow-danced to a fast song. The others were in a line, arms around each other's shoulders, singing along to a song that had no words. In Norwegian.

Ski cringed. "Well . . . that's disappointing. I'll get your Sprite."

"A freezing cold bottle please."

Ski walked off and Erin quickly replaced him. "What are you doing?" the redhead demanded.

"You think I should have gone with the Singapore Sling?"

"Not the drink, dweeb. You've got flippin' Ski Eriksen making moves on you and what are you doing? Talking?"

"He's not making moves."

"What are you standing against?"

She glanced back. "A wall."

"Right. A wall. And do you know why a guy like Ski Eriksen maneuvers a hotsie-totsie like you against a wall? So he can make out with you. But you keep fuckin' talking. Usually we can't get you to say a word, but now you won't shut up."

"We've been having a great conversation."

"Yeah. About *Stalin*."

"You know I find dictators fascinating. Caligula. Hitler. The Dalai Lama."

"The Dalai Lama?"

"Don't trust those warm, caring eyes. They hide a dark soul."

"Okay, I see you need my help, Jace."

"I really don't."

"But that's what friends are for."

"Most friends would just leave me alone."

"Not *good* friends."

Ski returned with her Sprite and a Norwegian beer for himself. He handed the unopened bottle to Jace.

Grinning, he said, "Bear is chatting up that shifter bartender. I think she likes him. Why, I don't know, but whatever."

"Don't be mean. Bear is very likable."

"Is he?"

Erin put the tips of her fingers to her temple. "Even *Bear* is getting some?"

"He's just talking to her," Jace corrected.

Ski shrugged. "Which for Bear is him getting some."

"See?" Erin asked Jace. "You need me."

"I really don't."

"What are you guys talking about?"

"Erin's trying to get me some."

"Oh. Thanks, Erin."

"Don't thank her. She'll just continue the bad behavior. Like Lev licking his butt. You have to tell her, 'No. Bad.' And shake your finger at her until she learns not to keep up the bad behavior."

Ski laughed, but Erin just rolled her eyes.

"I need to get you guys out of here," Erin said.

"Or you could let us handle this on our own."

"But you've already done so poorly."

Jace raised her fist, but Ski quickly grabbed it and pulled her next to him.

"We could just leave," he said, giving Jace a little wink.

"And have everybody talking about it?" Erin leaned in and whispered, "You know how these bitches are."

"Insane like you?" Jace asked.

"I bet I can distract everybody."

"Oh, please don't distract everybody," Jace sighed.

Erin watched a Giant Killer stumble by, her eyes locked on him in a way that Jace had only seen in nature films about predators and prey.

"Hey, Geirr Eklund," Erin called out. "You do know the Ravens have been stealing your liquor all night, right?"

No, they hadn't, but Erin never let a little thing like honesty get between her and a goal.

Eklund stopped and tried really hard to focus on Erin's face. "What?"

"You heard me!" She dramatically pointed at a still-pretty-sober Stieg. "It was him. Get him! *Get the thief!*"

Poor Stieg only had a moment to look shocked before Eklund dove at him, the two big men hitting the ground hard. From there, it took seconds for other Ravens and Killers to jump in. The Valkyries cheered them on and the Crows kept dancing.

"What is your problem with Stieg?" Jace demanded, but when Erin turned to reply, a Killer came at them. He was seriously drunk and Jace wasn't sure he was even aware of what he was doing. Pushing Erin out of the way, he lunged awkwardly at Jace.

She had her fists up, ready to back him off, when Ski reached out and caught the bigger man with one hand. Fingers tight around the Killer's neck, Ski twisted and had him down on his knees.

The Killer reached up and caught Ski's arm, but as soon as he took hold, Ski shoved him to the ground, then jammed his foot against his back, pinning him in place.

It amazed her that Ski, who was probably a good fifty to seventy pounds less than the Viking under his foot, managed to keep the Killer down on the ground, but she'd heard that it was a gift all the Protectors had, no matter their size. From what she'd read, that was how owls caught and held their prey.

Which to Jace meant Protectors had incredibly strong

legs . . . and the thighs that went with them. Like professional soccer players.

She watched Ski as he calmly gazed at the man he had pinned to the ground. No matter how much the Killer struggled, he couldn't get away. What Jace enjoyed, though, was Ski's calmness. To others it might come off as coldness. Detachment.

It wasn't. Nor was he pissed or out of control with Viking rage. Nor was he joining in for the hell of it.

In the middle of a pit fight, Danski Eriksen was the epitome of sound, clear reason.

And, just as she was having that thought, he looked up with those large green eyes . . . and smiled. At her.

Jace's breath left her lungs, her knees felt a little weak, and her hands shook.

She was either having an aneurism or she was incredibly turned on.

Since she'd never experienced either—but had read about both—she wasn't really sure.

Ski began to panic. He didn't understand the expression on Jace's face.

He'd forgotten his father's wise words, "*Never get between a Crow and her prey*," which was exactly what he'd done by stopping the Killer from stupidly going after Jace. Of course, he hadn't actually been protecting Jace from the attack as much as he'd been protecting her from decimating the Killer and then waking up tomorrow to a lot of guilt over it.

He simply didn't want to spend several hours nursing Jace through one of her rage-induced crying jags, so he'd reacted rather than thought the move through.

She was probably pissed now and their great date would end anyway.

Determined to at least get another date out of this, Ski opened his mouth to apologize but Jace's hand suddenly slipped into his.

Startled, he stared at her smaller hand wrapped around his

big one. When he finally brought his gaze up to hers, she smiled and asked, "Um . . . wanna see my—"

They both quickly leaned back as a bottle of very good Swedish beer flew past them and crashed into the wall behind their heads.

"—room?" Jace finished after brushing glass and a little beer off her shoulder.

Did he want to see her room? No. Did he want to dive headfirst into her bed?

By Tyr, *yes*.

"Uh-huh," he managed, desire goddamn choking him.

He swung his leg, sending the man under his foot flying— and slamming into Stieg Engstrom, who'd just barely managed to pull himself out of that pile-on.

Sadly, Ski didn't feel the tiniest bit sad for him. Even when the Raven got thrown back into the fight he'd been trying to get away from.

Erin had done what she'd promised. The distraction was perfect. Everyone was so focused on the fight, drinking, fighting and drinking, or the fresh mac and cheese that just came out of the kitchen from the caterer, that no one noticed when he and Jace slipped out of the party and up the three flights of stairs to Jace's room.

Jace pushed the door open and led Ski inside. He had his arms around her waist and Jace pushed against the wall before he could even think about anything. Because he couldn't think about anything but her.

Jace didn't seem to mind, though. Her hands dug into his hair.

Ski pulled her in closer, flush against him, and lowered his mouth to hers. She already had her chin lifted, her lips parted. She wanted him to kiss her, and he didn't want to overwhelm her.

She wasn't like her sister-Crows, who'd mostly had normal First Lives. Jace had only been with one man before Ski, and that man had been a colossal asshole.

So Ski was worried.

At least he was until he kissed her. Until his mouth touched hers and he felt her entire body sort of unwind even as her fingers tightened around the strands of his hair.

She was still a little nervous, though. He could feel it as he took her mouth. But once his tongue slid across hers, the nervousness seemed to vanish and she became bolder, pressing her body against his as she raised herself up on her toes.

Ski slid his hands down and gripped her ass, pulling her hips in tight to his groin, loving the breath that caught in her throat.

He was so hard now, he could barely think. Could barely breathe. Could barely—

Growling, they pulled back a bit and gazed at each other, both wondering if they'd heard what they thought they'd just heard . . .

The knock on the door came again.

"If that's Rachel," Jace whispered, "I will kill her."

"I'll help you bury the body."

"Jace? It's Kera. Open the door."

Neither moved, really hoping sweet but drunk Kera would go the fuck away.

"Open the door or I'll have Vig take it down."

Jace's jaw tightened. "Kera, *you* could take it down."

"Oh my God." Kera drunkenly giggled. "I totally could. I'm so fucking strong now."

Jace closed her eyes, released a breath. "It's open."

The door opened a bit and Kera leaned in. Yeah. She was definitely drunk.

"Hi, Ski."

"Kera."

"Yeah. I just wanted to give you this, sweetie." Kera reached in with one arm and placed something in Jace's outstretched hand.

"I'm gonna go throw up now," she shared. "And Vig's gonna hold my hair."

The door closed and Jace adjusted her hand so that she could release the very long strip of condoms that Kera had handed to her.

Wide blue eyes gazed first at the *extremely* long strip of condoms, then at Ski.

"This . . ." She cleared her throat, tried again. "This seems like a lot."

"Actually, for a Viking . . . it's just kind of a good start."

"Oh." She glanced off, gnawed at her upper lip for a bit, then looked back at him with a shrug. "Yeah. Okay."

CHAPTER NINETEEN

Ski glanced at the bed. "Do you want to lie down?"

He was being really sweet right now, trying not to spook her.

Jace appreciated that. She really did.

But sweet wasn't what she needed. Her entire sex life with her ex had been pretty much perfunctory. She was his wife, after all, and not nearly as interesting to fuck as the wives and girlfriends of the men who worshiped him and followed his orders. Those were the ones who got the freaky, fun sex.

Jace, of course, had always been okay with that. The less she had to do for that man, the better.

But she was now with someone she *wanted* to be with. Someone she actually desired and who desired her right back. Who didn't consider her property.

She was with Danski Eriksen, who had killer abs under that white, sleeveless hoodie and big white wings. Not only that, but when she said things like, "The Rubicon I will not cross," he actually knew what she meant! He knew things! Handsome, smart, and *not* an egomaniac.

What did that all mean to Jace?

That she wanted freaky.

"I don't want to lie down."

"You don't?"

"No. I want it here. Now. Up against the wall."

"You do?"

"I want Viking sex, Ski. Can you give me Viking sex?"

"If you want Viking sex, I can give you Viking sex. But I want to make sure that's what you want. And if at any time you start feeling remotely uncomf—uh . . . that's my ear you're biting."

"Uh-huh."

"That feels really good."

"Yeah. I read about it in that Russian porn book." She nipped his neck. "I read lots of other stuff, too. Now I want to try them. You know, on you."

"Well," he teased, "when you mention Russian porn . . . how can I say no?"

That made her laugh.

"What?" he asked. "You look surprised."

"Joking. Laughing. During sex. Didn't know that was an option."

Ski pushed his hips forward, pinning her against the wall. "I'm a firm believer that sex should always be about fun. Otherwise, what is the point?"

"Progeny?"

"That's what the condoms are for."

She laughed again. One of the sweetest sounds Ski had ever heard.

He hated to think what Jace had already been through or, as she would probably phrase it, what she'd "put up with." But this wasn't the time for that.

Jace wanted fun. She wanted "Viking sex." And she'd picked Ski to give her that. He had no intention of failing her.

But, first, in order for him to think straight, he needed to give her exactly what she'd asked for first—Viking sex.

Actually, they both needed Viking sex at the moment. The fun, relaxed stuff could come later.

So to speak.

Ski pulled off his glasses and placed them on the top of the tall chest of drawers beside them. Then he reached for her jeans, unzipping them, and Jace quickly followed suit. She unzipped his jeans and the delicious slide of her fingers against his bare ass as she pushed his jeans and underwear down tore up the back of his spine.

He pushed his knee between her legs and pressed her harder against the wall. He wanted to take her right now, but that might be asking too much of her this soon, this fast.

She wanted it, that he wasn't worried about. But he needed her ready.

"Condom," he ordered.

She tore one off the strip and tossed the remainder to the floor before she opened the package. She slid the condom down his cock, and Ski growled in order to pull back on his first response to that wonderful feeling, which was immediately burying himself inside her. Her eyes widened at the noise he made, but she didn't show fear. Not with that grin on her face.

"No," he snarled. "No evil, sexy smiling."

"What if I can't help it?" she taunted.

"Shut up."

Her laugh didn't help, so Ski grabbed both her wrists in one hand and pinned them above her head. Holding Jace there, Ski slipped his free hand between her thighs and stroked his fingers against her pussy.

Gently at first, coaxing a response at this point rather than demanding it. He stroked her mound until the tips of his fingers became slippery, then he slid one finger between her lips, circled around her clit a few times.

Jace went higher up on her toes, her back arching from the wall, her nipples so hard now he could see them through her bra and black tank top.

He also adored how she still had eye contact with him. She wasn't shying away from this or him. She wanted him to know she was as fully invested in this as he was.

She panted and groaned, her tongue sliding across her bottom lip.

Ski slid one finger deep inside her and she whimpered, blue eyes still on him. He slid in a second, moved them in and out, then circled around.

She was so wet now. And hot.

Wet and hot and clinging to his fingers, like she was trying to hold his fingers inside her body. Thinking about that same sensation on his cock nearly had him coming right there.

What was wrong with him? Was he twelve? He needed to get some control here.

But how could he when, still on her toes, Jace began to move against his hand, using her body to control the thrusts?

He added a third finger and her eyes blazed. He almost choked on lust, so Ski pulled his hand away.

Unable to hold himself back any longer, Ski eased his hand around the back of her thigh, tugging her legs as far apart as the jeans around her ankles would allow. He aligned his cock against her pussy and pressed forward.

He pushed the head in and Jace immediately tensed.

Ski leaned in and kissed her, his tongue going past her lips, deep into her mouth.

Jace kissed him back. And the longer they kissed, the wetter she got. He eased his cock inside her body, bit by bit, inch by inch. He didn't know how long it took, but suddenly he was buried deep, his body flush against hers.

Her kisses became urgent, demanding, her hips struggled against him, as did her hands, but she never told him to stop.

So Ski didn't.

He fucked her instead. Viking style.

Jace felt Ski pull back and, for one panicked moment, she feared he was about to stop. But then his hips shot forward and her fear, her moment of panic, turned to an unbelievable amount of joy.

She tried to pull away so she could wrap herself around his body and never let him stop, but he still held her pinned against that wall.

Without a word said between them, Ski took her hard. His fingers tightened on her wrists and thigh; his hot breath mixed with hers.

She couldn't even think straight anymore. She couldn't think past the lust she'd never felt before for anyone.

So this was what it was like. Why her sister-Crows kept going back for more even when the guy was sometimes a douche.
She understood now.

The only thing she wished was different was that they were
both naked. Her nipples were so hard they hurt and all Jace
wanted was to press them against his chest. To let the friction . . . the friction . . .

Jace didn't know what was happening to her body. Everything seemed to be shutting down. It all narrowed to nothing
for a second—then it all exploded out of her. Passion, lust, desire, and screaming.

Jace screamed into Ski's mouth, his body sweating and hot
against hers.

He groaned and shook, his hips moving faster until he
pushed into her once, twice. With the third time, Ski's entire
body lost its strength and he was leaning against her, breathing
hard and losing his grip on her wrists and thigh.

She thought he might hit the floor, but his arms wrapped
around her waist and Ski carried her across the room and over
to the bed.

That's where they landed, still panting and rolling away from
each other. Their jeans around their ankles, sweat pouring off
their foreheads, they both gazed up at the ceiling.

They stayed like that until Jace noted, "Viking sex for the
win."

Chapter Twenty

Jace propped herself up on her elbow. "I'm a little hungry."

"Eat later," Ski told her. "Get breath back now."

"I have my breath back."

"Probably because I did most of the work." He heard something and looked over to see that Jace had thrown her legs up and was trying to wrestle her jeans off without removing her running shoes. "What are you doing?"

"Figured I'd get naked," she replied, her feet over her head. A little more and she would flip over entirely. "It's harder than I thought."

"Maybe if you took your shoes off first . . ."

"At the time that seemed an unreasonable request. Now I'm spotting the error of my ways."

"And yet you still haven't done it."

"Well, now that I've started . . ."

With a growl, unable to watch her do this anymore, Ski rolled to his knees and grabbed hold of her ankles. He held her legs with one arm and then yanked off her shoes before pulling off her jeans.

"Hey! I was making progress."

"I am in no mood for obsessive behavior." He pulled off her tank top and unhooked her bra, tossing both to the floor. "I deal with obsessive behavior all day, every day. I refuse to do it during sex."

"But you handle obsessive behavior so well."

Ski untied his boots, yanked them off, and dropped them to

the floor. His jeans, boxer briefs, and hoodie followed. He then removed the condom he'd forgotten all about and tossed it into the wastebasket by the bed. Naked and comfortable, he relaxed back into Jace's big bed.

"I handle obsessive behavior because that's part of my job," he informed her.

"You're the protector of the Protectors, aren't you?"

"Someone has to look out for them. Otherwise they'd all be broke, homeless, and dangerously unstable. If there's one thing we've learned over the centuries, Vikings need jobs. If they don't have them, they cause all sorts of trouble."

Jace stretched her back vertically across Ski's chest, arms over her head.

"If you're the Protectors' protector, who watches out for you?"

"Ormi."

"And who watches out for Ormi?"

"We all do. And his wife. She's a Holde's Maid. Inka. She's really mean, but she makes us oatmeal cookies, so none of us bothers to complain."

"I'm concerned with your reasoning, but . . . okay."

"They're really good cookies."

Jace rolled over so that she was now on her stomach. With her arms and legs outstretched, she pretended to be flying.

Ski watched her for a bit before he decided to point out, "You do know you can really . . . fly . . . don't you?"

"I know. But this is fun, too."

Without warning, she abruptly rolled off him and leaned over the edge of the bed, giving him a delightful view of her ass. When she again sat up, she had the strip of condoms in her hand. She reached over him to place them by the pillow at the head of the bed, then stretched out again on top of him lengthwise.

"Are you comfortable?" she asked.

"Very."

"Good." She rested her cheek on her crossed arms, and closed her eyes.

Ski watched Jace for several minutes. She appeared wonderfully relaxed.

Her eyes closed, lips parted. All that beautiful curly hair spread across her shoulders and down to just above her waist.

That's when he noticed it. A tattoo from her right shoulder to the middle of her back. It was hard to see through that thick mane of hair, but he saw part of it.

Using the tips of his fingers, he brushed her hair to the side.

The image was a large, black crow, a metal cuff around its ankle and a length of chain that was broken as the bird took flight to freedom.

Jace's tattoo was bold, brilliantly detailed, and strong, saying everything there was to say about her.

"I didn't know you had a tattoo."

"Because it's not for you and the world. It's for me."

Ski smirked. "Not much for sharing, are you?"

"Nope." She opened one eye. "So . . . you get your breath back yet?"

"Get over here and find out."

Instead of moving around so they were face-to-face, she rolled across his chest like a log until her stomach covered his head.

Ski would have laughed but he couldn't breathe, so he slipped his hands under her and lifted Jace up. She squealed and giggled, her legs and arms kicking out.

"Put me down!" she ordered. "Put me down!"

Ski dropped her onto the bed, but before she could scramble away from him, he caught her ankle and dragged her back.

He straddled her legs around his waist and dropped her plump, perfect ass right onto his cock, so that it was caught between them. He hoped the position would keep him from doing something stupid.

Still laughing, Jace put her arms around his shoulders and leaned in, kissing him on the lips.

But as soon as her lips pressed against his, Ski no longer felt like laughing. His hands suddenly dug deep in her hair, turning her head so he could delve deeper into her mouth while he pushed her back against the bed, moving his body over her.

It was like a wildfire, shooting through him. His need to bury himself inside her. Become part of her. Her naked body beneath him feeling smooth and warm, her arms tightening around his neck.

She was kissing him back with the same intensity, her body opening up for him. Welcoming him.

He almost took the invitation. Almost took her right there, but he couldn't do that to her twice in a row. She deserved more. He wanted to give her more.

By Tyr, he wanted to give her everything.

He pulled out of their kiss and Jace almost yanked him back. She'd never had a kiss that managed to take and give all at the same time. Maybe because Ski didn't see her as property. She was a willing partner in what was happening between them and it amazed her, the difference it made.

Her entire body felt alive. She hadn't experienced anything like it since she'd woken up in her grave. But instead of feeling immense rage, she felt nothing at the moment but desire.

Intense, soul-defining desire.

Ski kissed his way to her breasts, stopping to suck one nipple while his fingers squeezed the other.

He switched sides, the wet nipple he left behind becoming even harder in the coolness of her room while at the same time aching for him.

Jace arched into him, opened her legs wider. She wanted Ski inside her again. Taking her with that big Viking dick, forcing her to make sounds she'd never made before.

But he would not be rushed. She lost track of how long he teased and toyed with her breasts. She just knew that she'd started sweating halfway through, and that her hips kept pushing against him, urging him to fuck her.

When he finally moved farther down her body, she began to tremble and locked her eyes on the ceiling. She knew what he was planning to do . . . it would be her first time. For that any-way.

As the Great Prophet's wife, she'd only gotten missionary. Straight, boring, uninspired missionary.

She definitely, at some point, wanted missionary with Ski, but she wanted everything else with him, too. She had the *Kama Sutra* under her bed and she wanted to try every possible position in it.

Jace also had a copy of some Victorian erotica under her bed, and there was this whole thing with a long feather that she'd been dying to try since she'd read the story.

Ski was between her thighs now, his face hovering over her mound. She felt his hot breath against her skin. He pressed her thighs apart, his fingers still gentle on the sensitive flesh.

"Jace."

She continued to stare at the ceiling, almost afraid that if she looked away for a second, it would all end. That she'd lose everything.

That this would turn out to be just an amazing dream. Her Second Life. Her sister-Crows. Ski. Even Lev.

She knew if that happened, she'd never recover from the loss. Not ever.

"Jace . . . look at me."

Swallowing past her fear, Jace looked down at Ski. His smile was warm, but concerned.

"You okay?" he asked.

She nodded.

"Are you sure? We can do something else."

"Oh no. I mean . . ." She forced herself to calm down. "I've never . . . but I really want to. With you. Right now."

Ski's brow creased the slightest bit, and Jace knew exactly what he was thinking as he stared at her. How, in a ten-year-long marriage had two people never gone down on each other?

Well, she wasn't about to explain that at the moment. The last thing she wanted to think about was her ex. She didn't want him tainting this amazing night.

She didn't want Ski thinking about him, either. Not when they were together. Alone and naked. Even Lev was off with Brodie, the big dog taking care of the puppy like she always did when Jace wasn't around. They had this room and this night all to themselves.

That slight crease on Ski's forehead abruptly faded and the smile returned, and then she couldn't see anything but the top of his head.

He began by stroking the length of her pussy with the tip of his tongue. From bottom to top, more times than she could count. Then he'd stop, slide his tongue inside her, and circle it around, before he returned to licking her from bottom to top. He went through the whole process again and again until Jace was once again sweating and whimpering, her hands gripping the sheets as she writhed beneath Ski's mouth, her hips searching out something that Ski wouldn't let her have.

It crossed her mind to beg. She was honestly at that point. Anything to get him to give her what she needed so badly.

She was desperate. Hungry. Needy. And she didn't know how much more she could take.

His tongue stopped stroking past her clit and abruptly centered on it. It rolled around it over and over. When he drew Jace's clit into his mouth and began to suck on it the way he'd sucked on her nipples, the pleasure roared through her.

Everything inside her exploding, her brain short-circuiting.

She didn't realize she was screaming out until she noticed that Ski had reached one hand up and covered her mouth even while he continued to suck on her. With his free hand, he slid two fingers inside her and she came again.

Her hands released the sheets and slapped over Ski's hands to help him silence the scream that came out of her.

The last thing she needed was for her drunk sister-Crows to come storming in here to protect her.

She didn't need protection. She needed Ski.

When he finally stopped, Jace dropped back to the bed, panting and sweating and moaning. But she managed to remember that Ski still needed his payoff.

She reached beside the pillow and grabbed the condoms. She threw them at his face before forcing herself to roll over onto her stomach.

After taking a few more breaths, Jace forced herself up onto all fours.

She looked back at a stunned Ski, her curly hair wet and flat across her face, shoulders, and back. She didn't say a word—and wasn't sure she could even if she'd wanted to—she simply waited.

His cock had been hard since the kiss. Now, as Ski gazed at Jace on all fours, staring at him through that thick mane of sweat-soaked hair, the ends flicking up with each hard pant, he was afraid he'd come right then. Without his cock being touched. Just a random explosion.

He'd never seen anything hotter before in his life. Had never wanted a woman more before in his life, either.

Jacinda Berisha was absolutely everything. Beautiful, sweet, smart, and wanting to be fucked by a Viking.

He couldn't have asked Tyr for more.

Ski quickly tore open the condom package and sheathed his cock. Then he moved forward until he was right behind her. He didn't even have to lift his cock a little bit, it knew exactly where to go and was inside Jace's hot pussy before Ski even realized what he was doing.

It was like the goddamn thing had a mind of its own!

Once he was inside her, he closed his eyes and let his cock just enjoy where it was. It was so happy there.

Jace moved and Ski opened his eyes to see her lean down and lower her head onto her folded arms. As she got into this position, she also managed to push her ass farther onto his cock.

Then she waited for him. Let him do this any way he wanted.

Ski took hold of her hips, moved closer in, then gave himself another moment of just holding still.

But her muscles were still pulsating from her orgasms and he couldn't wait anymore. He tried to be gentle about it, but that wasn't happening, either.

He hammered into her, unable to think of anything but his own pleasure. His own needs.

But that was unacceptable. He wasn't just some . . . Raven. He was Danski Eriksen, a Protector. He had to be better than that.

So he tried to slow down, tried to get control. But when he was able to understand what was going on outside of his cock, he realized that Jace was pushing back against him. She was fucking him back, moaning into the pillow, and he wasn't sure, but he kind of got the feeling she was begging him . . . in Russian.

The only time he'd seen Jace start speaking in another language without meaning to was when she was pissed. When she was about to go into a rage.

She wasn't raging. She was fucking him back. In this with Ski every step of the way.

So he gave up trying to be nice or gentle or in control. He let himself go with the only woman he'd ever trusted enough to do so.

As he fucked her hard, taking her with such force, he watched her wings unfurl from her back, stretching out nearly six feet long.

He would have been impressed with himself . . . if he didn't suddenly realize his own wings were out. In fact, they'd been out since Jace had presented her ass to him.

Shocked—he'd never, in his life, unknowingly unfurled his wings . . . *ever*—Ski realized he was about to come. Like a volcano, he was about to explode.

One hand still on her hip, Ski slid the other around Jace's waist and lowered his hand to her pussy. He clasped her clit between his fingers and twisted and squeezed until Jace buried her face in the pillow and screamed.

That's when Ski let himself come. He came hard and long. It felt like it went on forever, his body jerking with each fresh shot.

When there was nothing left, he finally released Jace. She fell onto the bed and he collapsed beside her.

Panting hard, they both looked at each other, eyes wide in shock, mouths open.

And it was together that each said what the other was thinking . . .

"Holy shit."

CHAPTER TWENTY-ONE

Ski reappeared at the window with two big bowls of that delicious-looking mac and cheese.

Jace opened the window and Ski climbed in, his wings tucking back into his body.

"How bad is it down there?" she asked, taking the bowls from him and placing them on the towel she'd spread out on the floor.

"I think it was starting to break up, but Odin and Thor just arrived. Thor brought beer. Odin brought women."

"Strippers?"

"Probably."

They sat down cross-legged on the floor, the towel between them, and Ski pulled silverware and napkins out of the pockets of his sleeveless hoodie.

"I can't believe he'd bring outsiders to a Clan party."

"Well, by the time he's done with them . . ." Ski looked up and blinked in surprise. It must have been written on her face.

"No, no," he said quickly. "I just mean he'll make them forget. Odin doesn't believe in destroying beautiful women unless they have a spear in their hand and they're trying to kill him first. Plus, I'm happy to say, the mighty Tyr would never let him get away with it."

They ate for several minutes in silence until Jace asked, "Bottled water?"

"I forgot to get some."

"No. I was asking if you wanted any." She turned and

crawled over to the end table built to hide her small fridge. She grabbed two bottles and returned, handing him one.

"You have a fridge in your bedroom?"

"Just a small one. That way I don't have to stop reading when I'm thirsty or need a yogurt."

"So much planning to avoid others."

Jace grinned. "Yeah, I know. Pretty shameless, right?"

"You could be worse."

They fell silent again, enjoying their food. But it wasn't awkward. Jace had the feeling Ski didn't mind quiet times. He didn't need constant noise. Not when he was comfortable and happy.

"Thank you," she said softly when her bowl was empty.

"For what?"

"I don't know." She placed the bowl down. "For being goofy with me. That's not easy for a lot of men. From what I understand and have read, they take their sex very seriously. Which, to me, sounds very stressful. I have enough anxiety issues."

"Jace"—he placed his now-empty bowl on top of hers—"we have wings. I can turn my head nearly two hundred seventy degrees. You have talons. The Crows have a dog that can fly."

"That's Brodie Hawaii."

"Because why would one give a dog a regular name like Spot or Bella?" He lifted his hands, then dropped them as if giving up. "We report to ancient gods who like war so much they are actively trying to avoid Ragnarok while at the same time, *really* looking forward to it because they will most likely go out in a blaze of glory. Downstairs, the All-Father is hanging out with strippers while his brawny son tries to goad the Ravens into a fight they can't win because he thinks his father likes them better. And, to be honest with you . . . Odin *does* like the Ravens better."

"Awww. Thor's not so bad." When Ski's entire face contorted into a mask of confusion and disgust, Jace remained adamant. "He's not. I mean, he's not . . . he could . . . I mean . . . he could use a little . . . it's just . . . he . . ." She shrugged helplessly. "He could be worse."

"I think they once said that about Genghis Khan."

"They did not!"

★ ★ ★

Josef shook his head at the god and placed his opened but untouched beer beside him on the bench. "Thor, we're not fighting you."

"Because you fear me," the giant blond replied, looking really self-satisfied.

"No, because you're a god. It would not be a fair fight for the Ravens."

Thor threw his big arms up and turned toward his human Clan. "The Ravens fear me!"

The Giant Killers raised their fists and cheered. Sadly, however, they didn't see the newest Crow walk up behind them with one of the Killer hammers she'd taken from them when she'd first arrived.

Kera had gone off earlier to be sick. Josef had assumed she'd be gone for the rest of the night. Probably passed out after a good vomiting. But she'd come back, reminding him that she was former military. True warriors did know how to drink.

"Hey!" Kera barked and the Killer Snorri spun around. She hit him with what might have been his own weapon once, sending the much bigger man flying over Thor's head.

Kera lifted the hammer and faced her fellow sister-Crows. She gave a perfectly acceptable battle cry and the Crows cheered until the Killer's leader, Freida, tackled Kera from behind.

The two women hit the ground and the rest of the Crows immediately reacted, diving at the pair, which meant that the Killers dove at the Crows. And Thor wandered off to find more beer. He liked beer.

A typical Clan party, in Josef's estimation.

"A stripper?" a voice asked beside him. "Really?"

"Hey, Serena," Josef greeted the Alabama Crow. "It's always so nice to see someone who can't help but *not* mind her own business."

"Now come on, darlin'. Ain't we friends?"

"No."

She sat down next to him on the bench and pressed her hand against her chest. "Now, that hurts me."

"No, it doesn't." Josef placed his hand on her knee. "You know, Serena, it's okay. You can admit it."

"I can admit what?" she asked, lifting his hand off her leg by grabbing his forefinger.

Josef couldn't help but smirk. "That you're still a little hung up on me."

Serena abruptly dropped his hand. "Hung up on you over what?"

"You know . . . the Trials. The one in Wisconsin."

"Wiscon—good Lord! That was fifteen years ago."

"Yeah, but we had a good time."

"We made out. Once. And to be honest, I was just trying to make my boyfriend jealous. Darlin', you were convenient."

"Okay," Josef said on a sigh. "If you want to play it that way."

"If I . . . have you lost your mind?"

"You were the one who protested our wedding."

"I didn't protest your wedding. I made a toast. And said Chloe could do better."

"*She* could do better?" he scoffed. "Yeah. Right."

"You do understand that Chloe Wong doesn't *need* you, right?"

"She doesn't?"

"No. She doesn't. She successfully leads one of the biggest Crow Clans in the States and has a thriving outside career."

"You mean the little book thing?"

"The little . . ." Serena's hands curled into fists. "She is a best-selling author."

"Yeah. Sure. Best-selling to bored housewives who like a little romance with their historical fiction. It's not like she's writing the Great American Novel or anything."

"Like you'd know good fiction if it kicked you in the balls."

"I read!"

"Not well!"

"Look, I'm just saying . . . if she wants to hook up with some boring surgeon just so she can get her tits done, that's up to her. I mean . . . she's in her forties. I'm sure they've begun to sag."

Serena stretched her arms out, her hands still fists, and Josef thought for sure she was about to hit him, but she slowly shook her head and said, "Thank you."

"For what?"

"That bit of guilt I was having . . . you helped make it go away."

"Hey," he said with real care, "I get it. After all these years you're still hung up on me. And to see me and Chloe together . . . that had to be hard. And now that I've moved on, seeing Chloe pine for me like you do . . . that's got to be hard, too. I totally understand."

"Oh! I'm so glad you do!" She patted his knee. "So glad!"

"But don't worry, sweetie. I know you'll find somebody. One day."

Serena made a weird, whimpering-type noise in the back of her throat before she stood and walked away.

"Poor thing," Josef sighed before picking up his beer and finishing it off, wincing a bit at the bitter taste.

Still seething, Serena stood beside Neecy and watched that idiot finish his beer and signal for another.

"This is taking too long," she finally complained.

"No, it's not."

"You did something wrong."

"I did not." Neecy faced her. "And, my God, what did that asshole say to you?"

"I don't want to talk about it."

"Well, stop snarling at me."

"I just thought a former drug dealer would have a better handle on this."

"Really?" Neecy growled. "You're actually bringing up my First Life?"

"Just pointing out the facts!"

Sadie came up behind them and pointed at Josef. "Check it out."

He was out cold.

Serena grinned and patted Neecy on the shoulder. "Nice job, Dr. Kevorkian."

"Call me that again and I'm gonna snap something off you. Something vital."

"Are you two done?" Sadie asked. "'Cause if you are . . . I'm ready to have some fun."

"Are you guys really sure we should do this?" Neecy asked.

Serena calmly explained to her friend, "If you'd asked me that *before* I talked to him, I might have been swayed by whatever argument your Raven-lovin' ass might have had. But now . . . let's go get him."

"Should we go down and help?" Jace asked.

The last thing Ski wanted to do was go down and break up a ridiculous brawl between the Crows, the Killers, and now the Ravens. He was proud to note that most of his brothers had either left or were watching the brawl from the trees without bothering to involve themselves.

Very proud.

"Do you want to go help?" he grudgingly asked.

"No."

"Then let's assume they'll be fine."

Jace seemed relieved by that response and he began to move away from the window, hoping to lure her back to bed, when he caught sight of something from the corner of his eye. He turned and saw that dog hovering right outside.

Ski didn't know which was more disturbing at the moment. The big pit bull.

The big pit bull with black wings.

Or that the big pitbull with black wings was holding a puppy in its mouth.

Okay. He'd admit it. *All* of it was disturbing.

Grinning, Jace reached out the window and took hold of the puppy. "Thank you, Brodie." Holding the animal close, she asked, "You going back down?"

The dog barked, which meant . . . what? That she'd understood the question? What was happening?

"Remember . . . back up the girls, but no lashing out. Chloe will have a fit."

Another bark and with expert ease, the dog dove back into the fray.

"And that," Ski had to ask, "doesn't weird you out at all?"

"What doesn't?"

"A flying dog? A flying dog that seems to understand what you're saying to her?"

"No. Doesn't bother me at all."

"Okay." In too good a mood to argue about it, Ski went back to the bed and stretched out. Hands behind his head, he closed his eyes and relaxed.

The bed dipped and he grinned . . . until he felt a wet nose sniffing his neck.

"Why is that touching me?"

"That is *my* dog." Jace was stomach-down beside him, and naked, having removed her T-shirt. "We are a pair."

"Which is fine. But it's still just a dog and doesn't need to be here to get an explicit lesson in fucking by watching us."

"*Just* a dog? Do you call that feline *just* a cat?"

"I do, but Salka doesn't. And if you want to keep your eyes in your head, you shouldn't, either."

"You can talk about your cat like it understands what's going on around it—"

"She does!"

"But *Brodie* freaks you out?"

"That dog is not normal."

"Of course she's not normal, but she's cool! She has wings and is great in a fight and she has doggy mom instincts when it comes to Lev. What does that cat do?"

"She watches my back and loves me despite my human weakness."

"Wait a minute." Jace sat up, resting on her knees. "You just think cats are smarter than dogs, don't you?"

"Of *course* cats are smarter than dogs. In what world did you think they weren't?"

Snarling, Jace scooted off the bed. "This discussion is over."

Ski reached out and caught hold of her arm, yanking her back so that she landed on top of him.

Lev barked and snapped, baring his puppy fangs at Ski.

"Well," he said, "that's something."

"What's something?"

"He's protective of you. I like that. He might even be effective one day. You know, when he puts on another hundred pounds or so."

"The vet says he'll probably be about fifty pounds."

"Ech."

"Stop," she ordered, laughing. "He's a medium-sized dog. There's no shame in that."

Ski put his arms around Jace's waist. "Are we going to spend the rest of our time together talking about this relatively useless dog and my amazing cat?"

"The rest of our time together?"

"I meant the rest of our time together tonight."

"Oh."

"Why? You don't want to see me after this?"

"I do. I like you. A lot. And I had a great time tonight. I mean, I'm in it for the long haul if you are." She frowned. "I don't know how to read that smile. Are you mocking?"

"No. I'm just realizing how wrong I was about you in the beginning. You're not shy at all, are you?"

"No. I'm sometimes insecure and that's often misinterpreted as shyness. But if I truly want something, I'm going to go for it. And I want you."

Ski tightened his grip around Jace's waist and rolled until he was on top of her. "Good." He let out a long sigh when he felt Lev clamber to the top of his head and lie down. "We are going to have to do something about this, though."

"Why?"

"I cannot fuck under these conditions, Jacinda. And I find your dismissive laughter offensive!"

CHAPTER TWENTY-TWO

Tessa walked into the Bird House a little after 10 a.m. She hadn't stayed long at the party. She had a husband and kids at home, and getting shitfaced drunk at parties was not something she could do as casually as she once had.

She might have regretted feeling that way, except for the bodies littering the floor of her secondary home.

None of them were dead. Just drunk and hung over.

Putting down her backpack, she began the process of getting non-Crows out of the house. First, she rounded up the well-known ex-drinkers who'd given liquor up for their own personal reasons, and she sent them off to get everyone up the old-fashioned way . . . by kicking and punching them until they got out.

While they took care of that, Tessa placed a call to her favorite cleaning company. They were not shifters like the caterers and security people, but they were used to keeping things quiet. As many assassins in the Southern California area knew, these cleaners could keep quiet, bury bodies, and they did windows, too!

Once she put in the order for an immediate housecleaning—with a warning about vomit and other possible hazardous wastes—she started off down the hall toward Chloe's office.

As Tessa passed the playroom, she found a few other sister-Crows who didn't let drink get to them awake, watching TV, and devouring big bowls of cereal.

Deciding to let them finish their breakfast before she put

them to work, Tessa kept walking, but she froze as soon as she made it past the room.

Not sure she'd seen what she'd *thought* she'd seen, she took several steps back until she could view the TV again.

"Tessa?" one of her sister-Crows asked, her voice trembling, milk dripping from the corners of her mouth.

With a panicked head shake, Tessa ran down the hall and opened Chloe's door. Their leader was already sitting at her desk and working.

"Good," Chloe said. "You're here. I need you involved in this thing today with the funeral and checking out . . ." Chloe leaned back in her chair when she saw Tessa's face. "What's wrong?"

"You . . . you . . ." Shaking her head, Tessa just motioned to Chloe with her hand.

Chloe came out of her chair and quickly followed Tessa back down the hall to the playroom. They stepped inside, and the other Crows stared at Chloe without saying a word.

Chloe looked around the room, but when her gaze caught what was on the TV, she froze, her mouth slowly falling open.

"Oh shit."

Josef hung upside-down from a 405 Freeway overpass, wearing only his boxer briefs and the red paint on his chest that read, "I like strippers!"

Chloe pointed at the TV. "This is just . . . from someone's computer or whatever . . . right?"

"It's on the news. Every local station has it."

"Oh *shit*." Chloe began to panic. "*Oh shit!*"

"Calm down. We can fix this."

"In what way can we fix this?"

"Cops and firemen have arrived," another Crow announced. "Cops look pissed, too."

"Is he dead?" Chloe asked.

"No. He's breathing. But he's out cold."

"Oh my God. *Oh my God!*"

"Yeah," Tessa admitted. "It would be better if he was dead."

"That's not what I meant!"

★ ★ ★

Ski didn't get up when he heard the bedroom door open, whispers, and then squeals that had him wincing as Jace scrambled out of bed, grabbed clothes, and disappeared into the hallway with that dog tucked under her arm.

She closed the door behind her, so Ski went back to sleep.

Sometime later, she'd returned, smelling like several different wonderful things. Mostly flowers and some fruit. He recognized one as a conditioner he'd once used. That's when he knew she'd showered and used all sorts of different products to clean and then moisturize her body and hair.

She kissed him on the lips and whispered, "Gotta work."

"You do know it's Sunday, right?"

"Ha-ha." She kissed him again. "Stay as long as you want. I left a towel and toothbrush for you to use. The boys' bathroom is down the hall to the right."

"The boys' bathroom?"

"The one we have just for guys who stay over because those with penises are kind of gross."

"Thanks."

"You're welcome." She kissed him again, but before he could grab her and pull her back to bed, she was gone.

Yawning and sitting up, Ski realized a shower would be a good idea. He was still sticky from sweat and Jace. A realization that made him smile.

He wrapped the towel she'd left around his waist and walked down the hall to the "boys' bathroom." It was blue and had a urinal. But the shower was roomy and they had a ton of products to use that Tyr would be too cheap to ever consider buying.

After a wonderfully hot shower, Ski dried off, brushed his teeth, combed his hair, and walked out the door. That's where he found Vig Rundstöm.

The big Viking leaned back against the wall, cold, narrow eyes glaring at Ski through all that hair.

All Ski wanted to do was give the man a haircut, for no other reason than to let him see properly.

Knowing it would annoy him, Ski didn't say anything. He just smiled, making sure to show all his teeth.

Those eyes managed to narrow more.

"Here." Rundström held out his hand, big fingers wrapped around what appeared to be clothes.

Ski took them, looked them over. Black sweatpants, black T-shirt.

"Are these for me, Ludvig? How sweet!"

"Kera asked me to loan them to you. For her I make many great sacrifices."

"Well, I appreciate it."

"Shut up."

"Am I the only one who has a problem with what happened?" Kera demanded.

"No," Erin replied, holding an ice pack over the black and swollen eye and cheek left behind by a Killer female who'd knocked her out cold the night before. "But you're the only one who cares enough to whine about it."

They sat at the round glass table out on the back porch, eating breakfast while a work crew took care of scraping their house clean of the previous night's festivities.

"I'm not whining. I'm expressing in clear, concise tones my feelings on this issue."

Erin raised an eyebrow to Jace. "Whining."

Jace hid her smile behind the almond croissant she was eating with two hands. Erin said she looked like a badger eating it.

"Is this something we do?" Kera asked. "Drugging and assaulting men?"

"No one assaulted him."

"What would you call it?"

"Retribution." Erin lowered the ice pack but when Jace cringed behind her croissant, she slapped it back against her face. "And we didn't do it."

"We didn't?"

"No. The Alabama and Tri-State crews did it."

"Which means what? That our hands are clean?"

"That's exactly what it means. Are you expecting a guest, Jace?"

Jace lowered her treat. "Huh?"

Erin motioned behind her with a chin jerk.

Jace looked over her shoulder and smiled. "Hi, Gundo. I think Ski's still upstairs."

"I'm actually here to see you. Do you have a minute?"

"Of course." Jace placed the rest of her croissant on the plate and wiped her hands on her napkin.

"Don't forget," Erin reminded her. "We've gotta be ready to go in about an hour."

"No problem." Jumping out of her chair, Jace went back into the house.

"What's up?"

Gundo smiled and took her hand, leading her toward the front door.

Erin finally lowered the ice pack, quickly realizing what she actually needed was some aspirin to help get rid of her headache. Although it really galled her she'd only had two drinks the whole night and yet she was in the same shape as her sister-Crows who'd passed out from liquor abuse.

"She's happy," she said to Kera. She was hoping to distract her from this ridiculous Josef discussion. Crows fucking with Ravens was as eternal as earthquakes in California.

"She's not happy," Kera replied, pouring herself one of her ridiculous giant mugs of coffee. The woman drank so much coffee. "She's in love."

Erin leaned back. "In love? After one night?"

"She's a one-night kind of gal. You and I may be able to sleep with a guy one night then never see them again and never think about them again. But not our Jace. Trust me, she's in love."

"But what if he's not in love?"

"Well—"

"If he's not in love, too, he may hurt her. We should kill him now. Before he gets the chance."

Kera threw up her hands. *"What is wrong with you?"*

Nothing, actually, but it was just so much damn fun to mess with the woman's head.

"What's going on?" Jace asked Gundo, letting him drag her through the halls.

"I have a surprise for you."

"A surprise? What kind of surprise? It's not weird, is it? I hate weird surprises."

"No, no. Nothing weird. I think you'll like it."

Before reaching the front door, Gundo suddenly swerved into the same room where she'd met with the Claw Bystrom and the federal prosecutor, Jennings.

For one moment, Jace was worried she'd have to talk to Jennings again. Nothing had changed except that Jace was sure if Jennings pushed her to testify, her sister-Crows would kill her ex. Something she didn't care about in a general sense, but she hadn't been lying to Erin.

Her ex needed to stay alive; she simply didn't know why yet.

But as they stepped into the room, Jace immediately recognized the petite woman who stood with her back to her, studying the books that lined the wall.

That white and gray bun messily put together at the back of her neck. The loose, flowing royal blue skirt that reached all the way to the floor and beyond. A skirt that petite body was drowning in. The light, off-white sweater with sleeves that nearly covered her hands and a hem that reached her knees. And those bright, white Keds on unbelievably tiny feet peeking out from under that ridiculous skirt.

After all these years, she still didn't dress for the California weather. Or in the California style. As always, she went out of her way not to fit in. To defiantly remain different even though one could only hear her accent when she was truly angry.

Jace closed her eyes, trying her best to calm her racing heart. To get control of all her jumbled, panicked feelings and—

She heard the sound of that small hand cracking against her face long before she felt the acute pain of it.

Her eyes opened and her grandmother stood before her in all her five-foot glory, blue eyes glaring up at her.

"Two years," Nëna growled at her. "Two years and you don't come to see me?"

Gundo, shocked and now a little panicked by what he'd put into motion, attempted to step in but her grandmother snarled, "*Get out*," and he left. Without question or a word, closing the door behind him. In about five minutes, Gundo would wonder why he'd done that, but he wouldn't have a satisfactory answer.

"Well?" her grandmother pushed. "Why? Do you hate me so much?"

"I don't hate you at all. I failed you and I couldn't face the . . . *stop slapping me!*"

"You're lucky I don't sew your mouth shut for such idiotic words." Arms wrapped around her waist, she began to pace the room. "How could you not come to see me? Instead you send that boy."

"I didn't send him, Nëna, and I never would have come to see you."

"Like a dagger to my heart."

"I'm not trying to hurt you. I'm just telling you the truth."

"You and your truth."

Jace took a breath. "Things have changed, Nëna. Two years ago . . . I'm not . . . I . . ."

She couldn't finish. She couldn't keep going. How could she tell her grandmother about her Second Life? How could she tell her *that* truth?

"You are a foolish, *foolish* girl. Always were."

The door opened again, and Kera and Erin rushed in. Alessandra and Leigh behind them. No one had called to them. They'd just known that something wasn't right. They'd sensed it and they'd come to Jace's aid.

Her grandmother looked at the four women already in the room; more were starting to rouse themselves and follow. Even in their hangover stupor they understood something was wrong in the Bird House.

Kera looked back and forth between Jace and Nëna. "Are you okay, Jace?" she asked.

"I'm fine. Could you guys give us a few minutes?"

Erin shook her head. "No. Why don't you come with us, sweetie? I'm sure Chloe can straighten this all—"

"Quiet," Nëna snapped. "You talk too much, demon child."

Erin opened her mouth to respond but all she could do was gasp. She grasped her throat with both hands, turning to Kera with pure panic in her eyes.

Alessandra spun toward the door. "I'm getting Chloe." But before she could walk back out, the door slammed shut, closing out the Crows who were coming forward and stopping Alessandra from leaving.

"*Nëna*," Jace chastised.

"Did you think I didn't know, stupid girl? That I don't know what happened? I knew when he killed you. I knew when he started to bury you. I knew when that Nordic bitch called for you. And I knew you'd accept her offer before *you* did. Now you owe your life to her. Your soul."

"It was a choice I made. I wouldn't unmake it. Not even for you."

"But you chose," Nëna reminded her. "And I always told you never choose. But you did. Because you're stupid!"

"Could you stop insulting me?"

"I could, but I doubt I will because you are stupid like your father!"

"Jace, what's going on?"

"Kera, this is my grandmother. My father's mother."

"Oh." Confused, Kera shrugged and said, "It's, uh, very nice to meet you, Mrs.—"

"I know what you are."

Leigh stepped forward. "What we are is here for your granddaughter. At Giant Strides, we strive to help those who need it. She's, of course, not an addict, but we are here to help her find a way back from what she went through in that cult. It's one of our hidden specialties."

"Really?" Nëna walked across the room until she stood in front of Leigh. "Hidden specialties?"

"Nëna, don't."

But, as always, Nëna ignored Jace and slapped her hand against Leigh's upper chest. Wings shot out from her back, slamming into Alessandra and sending her flying into the wall behind her.

Alessandra cried out, blood pouring from her nose as she slid to the floor. Leigh panted in shock. She'd been a Crow for many years; her wings didn't accidentally come out.

And they hadn't accidentally come out this time, either. Nëna had *made* them come out.

"Nëna, stop!"

"Do you know why I came today? Of all days?" Nëna asked, facing Jace.

"I—"

"It's not because that man called me. I mean, if you want to play games, *I* can play games."

Jace rubbed her forehead. "I wasn't playing—"

"It's because *she's* coming."

Leigh pulled her wings back in. "Gullveig, you mean."

"No. Actually . . . that's not what I mean."

Vig arrived at the back porch table but no one was there. "Where did everyone go?" he asked.

"Don't know." The Protector held up a pastry. "Danish?"

"Why are you following me?"

"I'm actually not. I'm just hungry and I knew you'd find food. Like an ant sussing out a picnic."

Vig growled a little, entertaining the thought of twisting the Protector's freakish head all the way around several times until he could twist it off his body completely. But Stieg and Siggy were suddenly there, behind him. Word from the Crows was that the Protector had spent the night with the woman they secretly called their "baby sister." Kera had made Vig promise not to beat up Eriksen for defiling Jace, but his brothers hadn't.

So when they attacked, he didn't stop them. But sadly, they were too slow and too loud, the drink and fighting from the previous night still dulling their senses.

Vig blinked and the Protector had the Danish in his mouth—although almost completely eaten—Stieg on his knees, and Siggy facedown on the ground. He held Siggy in place with his foot and used his hand to twist Stieg in such a way that any movement would cause the man intense pain and possibly brain damage from loss of air.

Yardley walked out onto the patio but froze, eyes widening at the sight of the four men.

"No, no, no, no!" She waved her hands. "Don't break each other! I need you guys. Now, what do you think?" she asked, smoothing down the black dress she wore.

"What do we think about what?"

"My dress. It's for the funeral today."

Vig glanced at Eriksen and the Protector replied, "It's . . . it's a little . . . low cut and short."

"It's a Hollywood funeral."

"I don't know what that's supposed to mean. Do you mean it's taking place *in* Hollywood?"

"No, actually it's taking place in West LA. There'll be paparazzi, directors, producers, and probably a couple of actors from those comic book movies. I am *dying* to be a villain in a Stan Lee movie."

"But it's a funeral."

"In this town, a funeral is more a social event than a chance to mourn. So, again, what do you think? Do I look nice?"

Eriksen shrugged. "You look, um . . . very pretty and slightly whorish."

"Perfect. Just what I was going for."

"And why do you need us?" Vig asked.

"Well, I need you guys to go to Brianna's house." She frowned and waved at Eriksen. "Unleash them, Ski. Now."

He did, then grabbed another Danish.

"My team is escorting me to the funeral as my security. Tessa and her team are going to Brianna's office. And I need you guys to go to Brianna's house."

"You have other teams," Vig reminded her.

"Yeah, but we leave in an hour and most of them are still vomiting. Erin said you guys wouldn't mind."

"Erin is volunteering us for shit now?" Stieg demanded. He was moving his head back and forth, desperately trying to work out the pain the Protector's move had probably caused him.

"Can you guys just help me today? Pleeeeeeeease."

"If you promise to never make *that* sound again," the Protector complained. Although Vig had to silently agree.

Yardley clapped her hands together. "Thank you, guys! That means so . . . so . . ." She suddenly looked off. "Something's wrong."

Without another word, she headed into the house and they followed.

The front doorbell rang and Jace asked her grandmother, "Who is that?"

"Why do you ask questions when you already know the answers? You must remember how that irritates me."

Nëna flipped her hand and the study door opened again, and Erin could suddenly speak.

"I do *not* like that, old woman," Erin panted out.

Jace patted her friend's shoulder and pointed her toward Alessandra. Their sister's nose had been broken from Leigh's wing, and blood was flowing down her face and soaking her white T-shirt.

Another Crow stepped into the room. "Someone to see you, Jace."

Jace nodded and waited.

Her grandmother had been right. She'd known who'd be coming through that door, long before she'd even arrived at the house. Jace had known he would send her as soon as she'd had Rachel force him off the property.

But still. At the sight of her mother, it was like Jace's heart had stopped in her chest.

Her mother smiled at her, still doing the Great Prophet's work. "Hello, sweetheart. I've missed you."

It seemed stupid to him. Not getting the Great Prophet's wife back. The Finder of the Word should be back where she belonged. But this part . . . this seemed ridiculous to him.

"Make sure to get the dog," the Prophet had told them before they'd left. "It's a puppy. We can use it to our benefit."

So while the Finder's mother was in there, getting her daughter to understand where she belonged, he was out here . . . tracking down a dog.

In a place this big, there could be a bunch of dogs, but he didn't hear any barking. Or see big piles of dog shit everywhere.

He heard men talking at the back of the house as he eased around the bushes, but then the sounds disappeared inside. So he kept going. The place was pretty quiet except for some cleaning people running around.

But he acted as if he belonged there and they ignored him. They were there to do a job, not keep tabs on pets.

As he cleared around some privacy bushes, he walked into the biggest backyard he'd ever seen. He didn't know lawns like this existed in LA unless they were owned by movie stars. Apparently the rehab business paid really well.

Impressed but still focusing on the task at hand, he moved out into the yard. He didn't have to go far, though. The puppy was right there, gnawing on a chew toy. Cute little thing. And an easy grab.

He walked until he stood in front of the puppy. The dog looked up at him with big brown eyes and immediately, its lips pulled back and the little bastard growled at him.

He reached down and grabbed it, wrapping his hand around its muzzle to keep it quiet.

Still not seeing anything, he turned and started toward the side of the house again. But he'd only gone a few feet before he stopped.

At first, he didn't know why he'd stopped. He just felt that . . . something was wrong.

He looked back into the yard. There was nothing there except several large bags of trash tied up and waiting to be removed. A goat—he didn't want to know *why* there was a goat on their property. And some birds.

A whole flock of black birds sitting on the lawn. A few took to the air and he watched them fly up and over until they landed . . . in front of him.

He knew this would sound crazy, but it was like they were trying to block his way. Three crows? Seriously.

Good Lord, what was wrong with him? He was getting paranoid. It was probably because of that goat. He knew they must be using that goat for something evil.

Yet he trusted the Great Prophet and their mighty Lord would protect him. He had nothing to worry about.

He started walking again, but the crows squawked at him and flapped their wings violently. He stopped again. More crows landed in front of him and he looked over his shoulder once more to eye that pile of birds. That's when he saw the pile begin to rise from the ground. These birds weren't flying but they were all moving up and up until they finally took off, leaving a very large and very angry-looking pit bull.

He stepped back, the goat and birds forgotten; the puppy in his arms whimpering and writhing, trying to get out of his arms.

The pit bull began to walk toward him, then it was trotting, then it was flat-out running.

"Wait . . . oh God! *Oh God!*"

Ski walked into the room to find Erin with her arms around a bleeding Alessandra. An elderly woman stood beside Jace. And a middle-aged woman smiled at them all.

"What's going on?" he asked.

At the sound of his voice, Jace's head snapped around to look at him. Her eyes had turned red, her body was vibrating—from rage.

"Jace, no!"

But she was already moving, flashing across that room until

she had her hand around that middle-aged woman's throat and had pinned her against the wall.

Ski and Vig ran to her, both attempting to pry her off the woman, using all the strength their gods had given them. But it was useless. Jace wouldn't let go.

She was already lost to the rage. Absolutely nothing but blood and death would bring her back. And she was intent on making the woman she had under her hands the sacrifice.

"Jace! Let her go!"

Kera also reached in, trying to separate her friend from this woman who was having the life choked from her while Jace spit at her in what Ski guessed was Russian.

The woman was seconds from dying. She was turning blue.

But then Vig was gone, yanked back by the hair, and the elderly woman stepped in to replace him. She pushed Kera away, as well. Then she slapped her hand flat against Jace's chest and like that . . . the rage was gone.

It didn't leave, it was vanquished. Jace's body stumbled back into Ski's arms.

It was the damndest thing. Not because Jace's rage was gone but because the aftermath—the sobbing or the sleeping—didn't immediately come.

Instead, she just seemed stunned, gazing up at the elderly woman who now had her hand against the other woman's throat.

"I should have killed you when I had the chance, but you were necessary. Now, go," the elderly woman ordered, throwing the other stranger toward the door. The woman rolled across the carpet until she landed on her knees, choking and drooling, her color flooding back. "Get out and do not come for my granddaughter again. Because if she doesn't kill you . . . I will."

Gundo was standing out in the backyard, where most of the remnants of last night's party had been removed except for several large trash bags waiting to be dumped.

A goat ran past him and into the house.

He decided not to think about the goat because he was too busy figuring out why he was standing out here in the first place. He also didn't know why he felt he couldn't go back inside yet. It was the strangest thing.

And crazy! That old woman had no control over him. He was going back inside!

Gundo started toward the house but stopped when he heard rustling in a large bush. He moved closer as that winged dog and his bird friends suddenly began moving off around the side of the house.

As he stepped closer to the bushes, Bear suddenly sat up.

Initially, Gundo thought his friend had simply had too much to drink and had passed out in the bushes. Except, he noted that Bear was naked.

"Where is she?" Bear asked.

"Where's who?"

"The dog?"

Gundo recoiled. "Oh . . . Bear. The pit bull?"

"No! That's disgust—" Bear closed his eyes, took a breath. "The *woman*. The shifter? Who could turn into an African wild dog?"

"Oh. Yes. Well, thank Tyr for that. Because there would be no explaining away—"

"I don't even want to discuss that." He looked around again. "Guess she left me."

"It happens. Especially with shifters. They're a very love-them-and-leave-them form of human being. As most wild animals are. But if we were Ravens or Giant Killers I would just congratulate you on getting laid."

"Why?"

"I don't know, it's just something they do."

Bear nodded and then, abruptly, his head tilted and turned. He was tracking a sound.

Gundo heard it, too.

They gazed at each other for a moment, then followed what they heard around to the side of the house. The crows were in the trees, silently watching as the winged pit bull, her maw wrapped around the thigh of a man, dragged him all over the grass, shaking him.

Most likely attempting to get him to release the puppy he held. Jace's puppy.

Gundo didn't know this man and he wasn't Clan. So who was he? And why was he holding Jace's puppy? She wouldn't like that; he knew that much. She was quite protective of that animal.

Bear started to move but Gundo held him back with his hand on his shoulder.

"Let me. You're naked and might spook him."

Gundo stepped close, and although the pit bull didn't release the man, she did stop shaking him.

"She wants you to release that animal you're holding. Here." He held out his hands. "Give it to me."

Sobbing and blubbering, the man handed the puppy over to Gundo.

"Thank you," he replied before stepping away with the puppy tucked into his arms.

"Wait!" the man begged when the dog began to yank him again. "You said she'd stop."

"No, I didn't. I said she wanted you to release this puppy. You did."

"You have to help me!"

Gundo shook his head. "No. I don't. I can tell just by looking at you that you don't belong here. And to be honest, you're much better off getting your throat ripped out by the dog than being found by one of the ladies. They can be . . . unreasonable when it comes to invaders."

The puppy licked his chin and Gundo smiled. "Come on, little one. Let's get you back to the human who feeds you."

As they walked toward the back of the house, ignoring the screams coming from behind them, Gundo held the puppy close to Bear's face and asked, "Does seeing it make you forlorn for your lost doggy love?"

"I hate you."

★ ★ ★

When the woman didn't leave fast enough, the elderly one snapped her fingers at Leigh and the Crow immediately got the woman up and out into the hallway.

Ski put Jace on her feet. She'd already rebounded from her full-blown rage, something Ski had never seen before from her, and he turned her by the shoulders, leaning down to look her in the eyes. All he saw was the beautiful clear blue he adored. "Are you all right?"

"I'm fine." She pulled away from him, faced the elderly woman. "Don't do that to me again," she ordered.

"Then learn to control yourself. It's been two years."

"Oh! You are—"

And then Jace was yelling at the woman in a language Ski did not understand. Albanian? Romanian? He had no idea. But the elderly woman was yelling back in the same language and he couldn't deal with it. There was just too much going on.

"Everyone, stop it!" he barked.

Both women turned from each other, arms folded over their chests, each tapping one foot.

"By the missing hand of Tyr," he gasped, suddenly understanding, "*this* is your grandmother, Jace?"

The elderly woman turned her head toward Ski. She sized him up with cold blue eyes before she reached out and placed her hand against his chest. He felt a jolt of unadulterated power shoot through him and his wings burst from his back, ramming into an already wounded Alessandra. She screamed and hit the wall, cursing up a blue streak as several Crows went to help her.

"Another Protector," the woman sighed. "Just wonderful." She pulled her hand away and Ski's wings disappeared.

"How did you do that?" he asked.

"She's obviously a witch of some kind," Erin accused.

"Not a witch and watch your tone with me."

"Or what?" Erin pushed, stepping forward, arms thrown wide.

"Are you really about to fight an old woman?" Ski asked, before adding, "No offense."

"I am leaving," the elderly woman replied, not sounding angry or upset so much as just annoyed by it all.

"Good!" Jace snapped back. "Go!"

If the woman heard her granddaughter's tone, she ignored it. "In two weeks," she said, "I'm having a family dinner. You will come, little *inat*. Bring this one." She gestured toward Ski.

"Oh," Ski said, truly pleased. "Thank you." But his smile faded when Jace spun around to glower at him. "What? That was really nice of her to invite me."

"I never said I was going."

"You'll come, little *inat*, or I'll be back," her grandmother warned. "And we wouldn't want that, would we? And where's that other Protector so he can take me back home."

Before Ski could ask for more information, Gundo rushed in holding Jace's puppy. He placed the animal in Jace's arms and then charged after Jace's grandmother, who'd already walked out.

That was around the time he noticed Bear standing there. Naked.

"Where are your clothes?"

"No idea. I think the dog took them."

Kera, who'd been examining Alessandra's poor face, asked over her shoulder, "Brodie took your clothes?"

"No. It was a human dog."

"I don't know what that means."

"Well, get some clothes."

"I thought you could just drive me to my house."

"You do know that you're not getting into my car naked, don't you? You've known me for years. I should not have to explain that to you. That being said, we're not going home. Yardley needs our assistance."

"I do!" she said cheerfully. Way too cheerfully for a woman about to go to a funeral. "We have to leave soon." She looked at her gold diamond watch. "Yeah. Soon. Although I don't think Alessandra should go."

"No," Kera agreed. "She shouldn't. Her nose is pretty bad and I think her cheek is broken."

"I'll take her to the medical room. You guys get ready."

Yardley placed her hands lightly on Alessandra's shoulders, then looked at Ski and Bear, smiled, and said, "Thanks!" before she walked out with her sister-Crow.

Ski had to admit . . . her cheeriness was off-putting.

"I still need clothes," Bear pointed out.

"I don't think even Rachel's clothes will fit you," Erin replied. "At least not the pants. But her stuff might fit you in the shoulders."

Kera pointed at her boyfriend and ordered, "Vig, give him your clothes."

"I already gave the geek my clothes. Let me call some of my brothers to go with us, and the bookworms can go home."

Erin smirked. "Most of your brothers are passed out in our basement by our Fate's statue. And I swear to God, if even one of them pissed on her—"

"No one pissed on her," Vig snapped back, but then he quickly muttered, "And we'll clean it up if we did."

"Clothes, Vig." Kera smiled at the Raven. "Please."

Growling, he walked out of the room.

"I think he wants you to follow," Ski told Bear.

"He does? He didn't say that."

"*Would you come on! Idiot!*"

"Well," Bear sighed, "I hear it now."

He followed, and that was when Ski noticed that Jace was no longer standing there.

Ski looked around the room. "Jace?" He hadn't seen her leave. So where had she gone?

Lips pursed, Kera stalked across the room and using her fist, banged on the top of a large wood cabinet. "*Get out of there right this second!*"

Kera reached down and snatched open the door to the cabinet, and that's exactly where Jace was. Huddled inside with her puppy in her arms. The dog seemed to be handling the forced imprisonment quite well.

Ski crouched down and gazed at Jace. "What are you doing?" he had to ask.

"Just . . . relaxing. With my puppy."

"Jace—"

"*I don't want to talk to anybody!*"

"Most people just walk out of the room. They don't stuff themselves and their dog into a cabinet as if they're attempting to be smuggled out of the country."

He held his hands out. "Give me that animal."

"Can't you call him by his name?"

"Jace."

She handed Lev over and Ski held the dog in one hand and offered his other hand to Jace to help her out of the cabinet.

When she was standing, her fingers nervously brushing her curly hair behind her ears, Jace said, "Soooo . . . that was my grandmother."

"Interesting lady," Erin said softly.

Without even looking at her, Kera reached back and slapped Erin on the shoulder.

"Let's understand," Jace went on, "and I'll only explain this once. My grandmother is not a witch or any variation thereof."

"How is that possible?"

"Witches derive their power through worship, rituals, and sacrifice. My grandmother doesn't. Instead, she's an obtainer of knowledge. And what she obtains, she uses for power and control."

"How?"

"With the power of her mind and sheer will. She worships no one, but knows practically everyone."

Kera took a step back. "Is *that* why those archangels knew you?"

Erin smirked. "Archangels know you?"

"They called her Jacie-girl."

"That's so cute. Can I call you Jacie-girl now, Jace? I have wings."

Jace held up her hand in front of Erin's face to shut her up. "My grandmother is . . . unusual."

"If she has so much power," Erin asked, pushing Jace's hand away, "then why didn't she just come get you from the cult right away?"

"Because my mother said that if anyone tried, the first thing she'd do would be to slit my throat. She'd rather I die in her arms blessed by the Great Prophet than live in evil purgatory with my grandmother."

"Nothing like a battle between a true believer and a true user."

"*Erin.*"

"Don't be mad at her, Kera. She's right. My grandmother is a user. A very brilliant user. And exactly what the gods hate. She can use the power they dole out to others without ever giving them her love or fear. And she only uses her power when it benefits her or the family, never to help others. I love her, but this," she said, gesturing to everyone in the room, "she does not and will not ever understand."

"Why?"

"Because I chose."

"She thinks you chose the cult?" Kera asked, flabbergasted. "You were ten!"

"No. My grandmother doesn't blame me for any of that."

Erin studied the spot where Nëna had been before guessing, "It was because you chose to be a Crow. To be one of us. You chose a god."

Jace shrugged, feeling a little sad. "And for that I'm not sure she can ever forgive me."

CHAPTER TWENTY-THREE

Yardley adjusted her black sunglasses, smoothed down her black dress. The designer silk outfit ended just above the knee, but wasn't so short that anyone would be able to see her blue thong when she stepped out of the limo.

"Ready?" she asked her team.

"You sure about this?" one of her girls asked.

"Don't worry. We've got the easy part. And you guys are all set?" Yardley pointed to her own ear and her team nodded. Each of her sisters had in an earpiece so they could hear what was going on with Chloe and the others. Yardley didn't have one in, though. She was afraid Brianna would see it.

"You hear me, Tessa?" one of the girls asked. "They're ready, Yardley."

"Great." Yardley nodded at her team. "Performance time, ladies." The driver opened the door of her limo and Yardley stepped out. Cameras went off and people filmed her with their cell phones. It was Los Angeles, so there was no sense of proper grieving. Instead, journalists and fans called out her name, acting like this was a movie premiere rather than a man's funeral.

A man who'd lost his skin.

Although that bit of information had been kept out of the news. Most likely by Brianna herself.

Yarldey's team surrounded her and walked with her to the church stairs.

Brianna waited at the top, wearing a sparkling designer gold dress and designer, six-inch gold pumps. Accenting that already bright outfit were diamond earrings, a diamond necklace, and multiple diamond bracelets.

The woman managed to stand out in a crowd of megastars.

That was *not* by accident.

When Yardley reached her, Brianna threw her arms wide, tears pouring down her face.

"Are you okay?" Brianna asked, hugging Yardley tight.

"I'm . . . okay."

Brianna pulled away and Yardley suddenly had the worst feeling. As if dread and foreboding had been wrapped around her entire body.

She didn't know why she felt that way. Brianna hadn't said or done anything to cause it. Her tears seemed real.

"Come," Brianna said, taking her hand, but that's when she noticed Yardley's watch. "A Rolex?" she asked.

"No. A Patek Phillipe. The Ladies Twenty~4."

"How many diamonds?"

"A lot."

"I love it." Brianna lifted her head and purred, "At some point . . . I *must* have it."

Yardley didn't know what that meant. Did Brianna plan to buy her own—a lack of originality that annoyed Yardley in general—or did she mean to take it off of Yardley's dead body?

A situation that would annoy Yardley quite specifically.

Brianna led Yardley into the church, somberly greeting each person by name as they passed.

Brianna moved down the aisle until they reached the front pew.

The family section.

Yardley tried to pull back, to sit somewhere—anywhere—else. But Brianna tightened her grip, nearly crushing Yardley's hand, and tugged her forward.

"It'll be great exposure," Brianna whispered before she made some sobbing elderly gentleman move over so they could sit down.

Mortified, Yardley glanced back at her team, but what could they do? Especially since Yardley felt certain that Brianna would make a scene if given half the chance. Something this family did not need.

So, Yardley sat down and hoped that her fellow Crows were finding out something useful.

Jace walked back into the stairwell of the artist agency that still had Betty's name on the letterhead.

"It's clear at her office, but we'll have to be careful. Some agents are actually working today, but they're holed up in their offices and security is in that back room with all the cameras."

"There are cameras?" Kera asked.

"Not in Betty's office. Mostly on her vault and in her agents' offices because she doesn't trust any of them."

"Why does Betty have a vault?"

"I think that's where she keeps the screaming souls of her past assistants," Erin said. "At least that's what everyone in her office thinks. Personally, I like to pretend it's just a joke."

"Don't worry too much about the cameras," Chloe explained. "Security is made up of shifters and they understand what's important."

"Then why are we sneaking around?"

"The agents. Until we really know what's going on, we don't want them reporting back to Brianna that Betty's friends were hanging around. So be quiet and careful but don't panic."

Erin joked, "So don't start killing people if they happen to see us?"

The others laughed but Kera didn't. "How is that funny?" she snapped.

Staring at her, Erin said, "We *just* had a wonderful, relaxing party barely a few hours ago. How are you already so uptight?"

"*Relaxing* party? How's that eye?"

Erin's non-swollen eye narrowed, but before Jace's two friends could start slapping each other silly, Chloe said, "Jace, Erin, Tessa, Kera, Annalisa, take the office with me. The rest of you, keep everyone else off our back. Nicely."

The team moved and as Jace walked toward Betty's old office, she immediately felt a twinge of nostalgia.

Many good times she'd had here with Betty and some of the Elder Crows.

Jace loved just sitting and listening to them talk. And being chatty bitches, they didn't need Jace to say a word. It had been heaven.

Until now, Jace hadn't thought for a moment that she wouldn't experience those times again. But seeing what had changed in Betty's office . . .

Brianna had clearly made it her own.

There was just so much gold. And mirrors.

Apparently she loved looking at herself.

"It's like a narcissist's wet dream," Annalisa muttered.

"I don't see anything obvious," Kera noted. "Just the office of a tacky woman with an unhealthy love of the color gold."

"We still have to check Betty's private room." Erin pushed open the door to the bathroom, a luxurious space with a shower and a sitting room. She led them inside and, on the farthest end, she pressed her hand against the marble wall.

A latch unhitched and the wall opened to reveal another room.

"Betty used this space for Crow business," Erin explained as they all moved inside. "And sleeping with male actors she thought were hot."

The windowless room was pitch-black, but Erin moved her hand along the wall until she found the switch.

Jace stepped back in surprise at what she saw.

There was no blood. No carnage. But there were nine sacrifices of men and women.

And all suicides from the looks of it.

They'd drunk something and then had lain down to die, their naked torsos draped over the legs of each other until they formed a perfect circle. Their empty wine cups were still gripped in their hands. Smiles on their faces.

Blood anointed their foreheads, chests, and groins. And they'd been tattooed with ancient runes.

They were all young and beautiful.

Standing still, the Crows looked around the room, but

they didn't see any demons. No spirits. Nothing had been called, from what they could see, that would warrant such a sacrifice.

Then the first one moved. A jerk, really. The entire body sort of spasming in death. Because they were dead.

"They're coming back," Annalisa warned.

But Jace didn't think so. "No. They're not coming back. They're a portal."

Chloe pulled out her blades and everyone followed suit. Seconds later a fist punched through the chest of one of the sacrifices. The fist pulled back but was quickly followed by two big arms. Hands slapped against the ground, blood and organs pouring on the floor as a man pulled himself out, blood-soaked leathery wings following.

"Oh fuck," Chloe breathed out, motioning to the others to back away. "Go," she softly ordered. A command Chloe had never given before. A retreat? Crows didn't retreat.

"What?" Tessa asked, as shocked as Jace.

"Go. Now."

Kera turned toward the door but it slammed in her face. "Guys?"

"*Tear it down!*" Chloe screamed at her and Kera turned to her side, angled her shoulder, and ran full-out, slamming her body into the door, ramming it off its hinges.

She and the door landed on the floor.

"Get out!" Chloe yelled, pushing everyone back into the bathroom. "Out!"

Jace looked over her shoulder. More men had torn their way out of the sacrifices. Like full-grown newborns, they were naked but covered in blood and bile and waste.

The Crows all scrambled into the office, Chloe slamming the bathroom door shut and pressing her back against it.

"We have to go!"

"What's happening?" Tessa demanded. "We've fought demons before, Clo."

"These aren't demons." She let out a terrified breath. "They're Hel's Carrion."

The air left Jace's lungs and even Annalisa and Erin showed fear as they backed away and moved toward the front door.

Only Kera seemed confused, looking around at her sisters.

The bathroom door jerked and Chloe shoved back, trying to keep it closed with her body.

"Chloe, run!" Tessa ordered.

But their leader shook her head. "Go! Now!"

Yet Jace knew they wouldn't leave their leader. Not to face the Carrion alone.

"Kera!" Erin barked. And the battle-buddies who rarely got along in everyday life became a mighty team. Understanding each other without more than a word.

Kera dashed forward and grabbed Chloe around the waist, tearing her from the door. Erin took her place in front of it, and flames leaped from her fingers and then her hands. She began to chant and the flames grew until she held two lines of bright orange flame. Like two whips, one wrapped around each arm.

Erin unleashed those whips, slashing through the door. The Carrion roared in rage from the other side and burst through the wood.

They were all big, strapping Vikings of old who hadn't been taken by Odin or Freyja, but Hel herself, goddess of Helheim, land of the dead, and the one Nordic deity who truly did not answer to anyone, even the mighty Odin. Some of the Carrion had been damaged by Erin's flame, parts of them slashed, but already that skin was healing.

Erin spun one of the fire whips above her and when she lashed out, it wrapped around the neck of one of the Carrion.

Erin pulled, trying to remove the head—a move that had worked for her in the past. But not this time.

As one, the Carrion roared again. They had fangs and their eyes were green and black.

Erin released the Carrion's throat and clapped her hands together. When she pulled them apart, a wall of flame spread out from one side of the room to the other.

"Go!" Erin yelled at her sister-Crows. "*Gooooooo!*"

They ran, charging out the door, into the hallway past

shocked agents and security guards, and down the fancy stairs that had won the building's architect important awards.

The Carrion screamed a battle call from the office.

"Move!" Chloe ordered seconds before the entire building shook, all of the Crows tumbling down the massive stairs until they hit the first floor.

Jace was the first to get to her feet. When she looked back at the stairs, she expected to see the Carrion right behind them, but all she saw were the agents and security guards who'd tumbled down the stairs themselves.

The human agents were still too stunned to move, but the shifter security guards were getting to their feet.

One shifter, a woman whose auburn eyes suddenly changed to bright yellow like a dog's, stared past Jace to the front exit. As Jace watched, the woman's lips pulled back over growing fangs, and claws eased out of her hands.

Jace knew what the shifter saw. She knew what scared her.

Jace pointed at the humans. "Get them out of here," she ordered the security team. "Now!"

As the shifters moved, picking up the few agents and running back up the stairs and out another exit, Jace finally turned around and faced what was behind her.

The Carrion blocked the front door—and the Crows' way out.

"Are you frightened, slave?" their leader asked in Old Norse, his voice dark and gravelly. He bent down so that he could look Jace in the eyes. "Because you should be."

"And you should leave, now," she replied, also in Old Norse, surprising the Carrion.

Their leader studied Jace, but before she could convince him, Chloe got to her feet . . . and extended her wings.

"Crow!" one of the Carrion roared.

Weapons were pulled and one of them slashed at Chloe. She reared back, but the blade wouldn't have touched her anyway. Kera's axe—a weapon given to her by Freyja—blocked and held it, the runes on her handle glowing.

As she struggled with the Carrion in front of her, another

came up behind her. Erin tried to step in but was backhanded, sending the redhead spinning across the room and into the wall.

Seeing her sister-Crow harmed, treated like the slave these ancient Vikings believed them to be, had rage rising up in Jace, splintering and racing through her veins.

Jace screamed and charged all the Carrion, no longer caring about their powers, her fear, any of it. She bellowed and ran at the leader. The one she couldn't stop focusing on. The one she automatically hated. She ran at him, launched herself into his arms, and rammed her blade right into his eye.

He cried out in pain. So, she might not be able to kill the Carrion with Crow weapons, but she could hurt him.

She could hurt him! She could hurt him! She could hurt him!

Jace held on, one arm around his neck, the other ramming that blade in again and again and again and again.

Even as she felt her skin burn where it touched the Carrion, she refused to release him, because she wanted him to hurt!

She kept going until hands gripped her waist and Jace was finally yanked from the Carrion.

"*Light him up!*" Kera bellowed.

On her knees, blood pouring from a wound on the side of her head, Erin flung her arm forward. A fireball exploded from her hand and slammed into the Carrion covering the eye Jace had fucked up. Flames covered him and he dropped to the ground, trying to put them out.

Tucking a struggling Jace under one arm, Kera reached down and grabbed Erin by the back of her T-shirt. Chloe and the others ran past them and out the front doors.

"Go!" Chloe ordered and Kera ran out, holding on to Jace, who was snarling and snapping like a wild animal, clawing at Kera's arm with her talons.

Once outside, Kera thought they were going to keep running, but Chloe and Tessa stopped about fifty feet away from the front door.

The men came out, the one who'd been on fire still smoking but seemingly unharmed. So Erin's flame could hurt these men, but not kill them.

Then again, Kera had the feeling these men weren't really alive enough to actually kill. Not in the normal, everyday sense of the word *alive* anyway.

"Why aren't we running?" Kera asked Erin.

"Because of the sun. They can walk around in it, but they're vulnerable. In the dark, they're at their strongest."

"What are they?"

"They're warriors from Helheim. The gods call them Hel's Carrion."

"Why?"

"For they feed on decaying flesh."

"Oh . . . well, that's lovely." Kera gripped a still-struggling Jace tighter. "And I thought the Crows never run from anything."

"We're Crows, Kera. We're smart enough to know *when* to run. And if you ever face a Carrion alone, in the dark . . ." Erin looked at her and said in the most serious tone Kera had ever heard from her, "Then you fucking run."

"Why are you here?" Chloe called out to the men. "Why aren't you in Helheim where you belong?"

The biggest of the men lowered his head and yanked double-edged blades from his belt, but before he had a chance to do anything, Jace started yelling in a language Kera didn't know.

Yelling and struggling and completely losing her goddamn mind. Her friend had gone over the edge.

And yet . . . the Carrion didn't move any closer. They didn't charge.

Then Jace did something Kera had never seen before. She raised her hand and began to chant. She was casting a spell.

At least . . . that's what Kera was guessing because the lead Carrion suddenly made a circling motion with his index finger and the group of nine unleashed their wings and took to the skies.

Once they were gone, Jace lowered her arm . . . and burst into hysterical tears.

"Great," Erin sighed. "Now comes the crying."

"Shut up!" Jace yelled . . . while crying.

"Back to the car," Chloe ordered and they moved, dashing toward the two SUVs parked on the street.

Kera handed Jace off to Erin so she could drive, started the engine, and took off once everyone was inside and the doors closed.

"I don't know what you did," Tessa said to Jace, "but it was amazing. You saved our asses back there."

"I didn't do anything," she sobbed out.

"What are you talking about? You used some spell, right?"

"It was something I read while working at the Protectors. But to be honest . . . I was just saying words." And the "s" in *words* just seemed to go on forever as the crying became worse.

"Well," Kera said while making a wild-ass turn onto Santa Monica Boulevard, "whatever you did was brilliant, Jace."

They all fell silent, the only sounds in the SUV Jace's crying until Erin rested her arm on the back of the passenger seat and asked, "Anyone else feel like we've forgotten something?"

Ski reached down and grabbed the wrists attached to the hands wrapped around Bear's throat and yanked them off.

"What did I do?" Bear demanded.

"You keep talking!" Stieg Engstrom snarled back.

Ski glared over at Rundström. "Are you going to help me?"

Pressing his hands against the wall behind the couch in Brianna's apartment in downtown Los Angeles, trying to find any hidden rooms, Rundström glanced at Ski and replied, "No."

Ski shoved a still-rampaging Engstrom back. "Can we just get through this, please?"

"Then tell him to shut up." Engstrom headed toward one of the woman's many closets.

"I didn't do anything," Bear complained.

"I know." Ski patted Bear's big shoulder. "Don't sweat it. Let's just get this done and get away from them."

"It hurts, Ski . . . so much stupid."

"I know, Bear. I know."

"I don't think there's anything here," Siggy Kaspersen announced, dropping onto one of Brianna's gold couches. The furniture all looked very new, but Ski was surprised she hadn't gotten herself a new house. He couldn't imagine Gullveig staying in what, to her, would seem like such a small space. The living room and dining room weren't even separated.

"Anyone check that walk-in closet yet?" Engstrom called from the other room.

"No," Rundstöm replied just as his phone began to buzz, the sound and vibration irritating Ski's ears. "But get on that so we can get out of . . ."

Rundstöm's words faded away as he gazed down at his cell phone.

Ski watched him a moment before asking, "What's wrong?"

Mouth slightly open, the Raven looked at him. "Hel's Carrion."

At the same time, both of them spun and yelled to Engstrom, "Stieg! Don't go in that—"

Words of warning were cut off by a roar and the sight of Stieg Engstrom being shoved through several thick walls and back into the living room, with one of Hel's Carrion attached to him.

Kaspersen rolled off the couch seconds before his Raven brother and the Carrion slammed into it, knocking it backward.

More Carrion came through the doorway; sharp, jagged blades made from the finest metal of Helheim held in meaty fists.

Rundstöm immediately grabbed the thick, reclaimed-wood dining table and held it in both hands before charging forward.

Ski moved to the floor-to-ceiling windows that covered two walls, and pulled back the thick, light-blocking curtains. The sunlight poured in, but it didn't lessen the netherworld strength all Carrion had.

He pressed his hand against the glass. UV protection. "Bear! Break it!"

Bear, a former college linebacker during his Stanford days,

lowered his shoulder and charged the window that led out onto a balcony. The first hit cracked it. He backed up and charged again, and the window shattered. Unfiltered sunlight poured in and the power of it allowed Engstrom to push away the Carrion who'd been on top of him. But where he'd been touched by the Carrion, his flesh appeared decayed.

Ski started to go over to help him, but he was tackled out onto the balcony. He gripped the Carrion by the neck and flipped him over. He rolled with him so he ended up on top and planted his foot against his chest, pinning him to the ground.

"Eriksen!" Ski looked up in time to snatch the Hel's blade tossed to him by a Raven.

Protectors didn't use weapons . . . but he knew of nothing else that could kill a Carrion.

With a twist of his wrist, he spun the blade around, grasped the grip with both hands, raised it high, and brought it down hard. He aimed right at the Carrion's head, slamming the blade between the eyes.

Ski twisted the blade around to make sure he'd ended the beast, but when he stood, he heard Engstrom yell out, "Eriksen, *move!*"

Ski looked up in time to see the remainder of the Carrion charging toward him. Before he could dash out of the way, they plowed into him like semis, forcing him into and over the balcony gate. As he tumbled backward, about to unleash his wings, a piece of the gate slammed into his head and—

Vig watched the Protector's head collide with that thick metal gate and knew he was out cold, free-falling from the twenty-third-story building. A fall even a Raven wouldn't survive without his wings, much less a much weaker Protector.

Growling—he really hated the Protectors—Vig dove off the edge of the balcony and directly at Eriksen. He caught him in both arms and held him close, unleashing his wings and letting the wind lift him up until he could fly back to Brianna's apartment.

Although now he was pretty sure that they were no longer

dealing with Betty's poor, beleaguered assistant but Gullveig herself who wore Brianna's skin the way Vig's ancestors used to wear bear fur during brutal Swedish winters.

He landed on the balcony and immediately retracted his wings before heading inside the apartment.

"You unleashed your wings during the day," Siggy reminded him.

"I know. I think Odin will forgive that, considering the situation."

"Even though it was a Protector you saved?"

"Hey!" Bear snapped, shoving Siggy by the shoulder. "Shut up."

"What about the Carrion?" Stieg asked.

"They're gone. Hit the ground and took off running. And we need to get out of here. That balcony gate dropped onto some dude's Bugatti and, trust me, he's going to be up here in a few minutes wanting someone to pay for it. And the mood I'm in, I'm liable to beat him to death. Let's avoid that. Kera will just get mad."

They were singing a hymn that Yardley faintly remembered from her Protestant upbringing. All of them facing the—not surprisingly—closed casket of her director.

No matter what she'd felt about the man as a filmmaker, she couldn't deny that his family had loved him. Had she caused this? She hated to think she might have. She never would have said anything if she'd thought for a second that Brianna was actually Gullveig and would take her words so seriously.

Yardley was a Crow, not a monster.

Even when she was dealing with the worst scum on any plane of existence, she didn't fool around with torture or stringing out deaths. She and her team went in, did the job, and got out. That was how most of the Crows operated.

As Yardley sang, she felt her sister-Crows' eyes on her. She glanced over her shoulder. The signal to "get out" was more than clear.

With the hymnbook still in her hand, Yardley simply turned

and walked out of the pew, never looking back. She handed off the book to one of the church workers near the doors and walked outside, her team surrounding her.

"What's going on?" she asked as paparazzi begged her to turn toward them, to pose . . . at a funeral.

"It's bad. The All-Clan meeting's been moved up to tonight. Chloe wants you there with Tessa's team. And Jace's Protector got hurt."

"Eriksen?"

"Yeah."

"Fuck." One of her team opened the limo door for her. She was just stepping in when someone grasped her arm.

She turned, ready to punch the crap out of some paparazzo that she'd have to pay off later when the complaint went to court, but it was Brianna.

The woman's fingers were tight on Yardley's bare arm, her gold rings digging into her skin.

"Where you going, hon?" Brianna asked, all fake Hollywood smiles for the ever-watching cameras.

"Don't feel really well. Gotta get out of here. We'll talk later, okay?"

One of Yardley's team gently tried to separate the two, but Brianna caught hold of two fingers and snapped them back quickly, not only breaking them but leaving them awkwardly bent, so that if it had been anyone but a Crow, the screaming would have had the nearby police there in seconds.

Yardley's sister-Crow, however, simply whimpered and took a step back so that she could attempt to bend her fingers into place while another sister quickly replaced her.

"Now listen to me, slave," Gullveig said, "if you get in my way, even your precious Skuld won't be able to save any of you. When I'm done, you'll be *begging* me to end your lives. So take it as a warning to all Crows, Ravens, and the other worthless human Clans. Don't fuck with me." She took a step back and announced so the paparazzi could hear, "It was *so* good seeing you, sweetie. I'll call you later to check in, okay? Now, you go home and get some rest. Love you!"

Then the bitch winked and walked back to the church in her fifteen-hundred-dollar heels.

The Crows got into the limo and slammed the door. Once they'd pulled out into traffic, Yardley's sister released the cry of pain she'd been holding in.

"Hospital?" one sister asked.

"No," Yardley immediately replied. "Let's get her home." She pulled her wounded sister close and held her tight while another sister grabbed those two brutalized fingers and readied herself to put them back into place as a bottle of forty-year-old Scotch was passed around—especially to the "patient."

"Because," Yardley said softly, desperately trying not to hear the sound of bones being snapped back and the subsequent screams of her sister-Crow, "this is *really* bad."

CHAPTER TWENTY-FOUR

Ski jerked awake, body still ready to fight, but soft hands pressed against his shoulders, and softer lips kissed his forehead.

"Shhh. You're safe."

Knowing it was Jace, he pulled her close, ready to defend her even though his head hurt and he hadn't opened his eyes yet.

"Oh!" she gasped, laughing a little. "Don't worry. We're *both* fine. No need to protect me."

She pulled away and Ski turned toward the voice, blinking, trying to get his eyes to adjust without his glasses. They overcompensated, bringing Jace's image in so close it was like she was right on top of him. He blinked again, but now it was like she was halfway across the room. Ski knew it was because his head hurt. He had the makings of a solid migraine and that always made it tough to quickly adjust his eyesight so that he could see like a human and not someone blessed by a god. But with his brain hurting, it was simply too much work.

Thankfully, Jace put his glasses on his face and he could see her just fine. At least his eyes could move . . . unlike the actual owls Protectors had been based upon. That's why their heads turned so far. Because their eyes didn't move at all. And that's how the Protectors had started out, too. But that made them more vulnerable to attacks by Crows and Ravens, so Tyr eventually fixed the issue . . .

Oh, gods. He was thinking too much. When his brain hurt, it overcompensated by thinking more than usual. It analyzed, debated, constructed . . . anything and everything the brain could do to work through pain.

Like right this second, he was wondering how the ancient Protectors had managed before glasses were invented. Something he really shouldn't be worrying about.

Jace carefully adjusted the frames of his glasses behind his ears and smiled down at him. "Better?"

"Much. Thank you."

She brushed the hair off his forehead. "Are you all right?"

"I have a headache. I dealt with the Carrions well enough . . . didn't see that gate, though, until it collided with my head. To be honest, considering the speed I was going, I'm lucky the damn thing didn't take my head clean off. For instance, if you take the square root of—"

"Okay," Jace cut in. "Let's not square-root anything. Not much of a math girl. It's not my thing. I like words. Are you sure you're all right?"

"I can't stop thinking. Analyzing. My head really hurts. My brain does that when it hurts."

"I'm not surprised it hurts." She winced in empathy. "You have such a knot."

"I'll be fine. I just need to stop thinking."

"Yeah, I've tried that . . . it's impossible for some of us. But good luck!"

That almost made him laugh. "Help me sit up?"

She placed her hand against his back and Ski sat up, legs over the side of the bed, his feet slapping against the floor. He was still dressed, boots and all.

Did it take a long time to make boots? Probably not now, what with all the children in factories putting together the pieces. Child labor . . . morally reprehensible and yet, it was still happening. He should do something about that . . .

"You're doing it again," she warned.

"How can you tell?"

"Because you're staring at me, but I can tell you don't see me. It's like I'm sheer glass. It's strange."

"Sorry."

"Don't apologize. My ex used to accuse me of the same thing." She gave a short chuckle. "Of course, that was because it was easier to pretend he wasn't there or I was somewhere else."

Ski nodded, focusing on the sound of her voice and innocuous rambling. It gave his brain something to concentrate on rather than all the millions of random thoughts in his head at the moment.

He noticed for the first time the bandages on Jace's throat and arms. "What happened?"

Jace shrugged. "Decay and death."

In no mood to ease his way around this conversation the way he usually could, he just asked, "What?"

"I went into a rage." He could tell that. Her eyes were puffy from crying. "Attacked one of the Carrion. His skin touched mine . . . and now I'm permanently disfigured."

Ski put his hands to his forehead. His head *hurt*. He hadn't had a headache like this since he was rammed into a wall by a Giant Killer when he was eighteen. "No, you're not."

"I'm not?"

Ski just reached over and, without looking at her, yanked off one of the bandages.

"Ow!"

"Sorry."

"Hey." Jace scrambled off the bed and went to her dresser mirror. She grinned when she saw her skin back to normal. She removed the other bandages. "Oh, thank God," she finally said. "I don't want to sound vain—"

"You're not vain."

"—but I was worried my skin was going to stay like that. Like part of me was rotting off."

"If you hold on to the Carrions for too long, you'll rot to death. Until there's nothing but bones and dead flesh left for scavenger animals to prey upon."

When Ski's response led to nothing but silence, he looked up to see Jace gawking at him, eyes wide, hands still pressed against her skin.

"Sorry. When my head hurts, I'm like every other Protector you've met."

"Tessa might have something for you."

"Good. I'm assuming the All-Clan meeting has been moved up."

"It's tonight. In two hours."

"I need to be there."

"Okay." She came back to the bed and knelt beside him on the mattress. "There's just one thing, though . . ."

Ski stared at her, waiting for her to tell him what that "just one thing" was. But the longer they looked into each other's eyes, the worse he began to feel.

Finally, realizing what she was asking of him, he barked, "No!"

"He saved your life."

"I don't care!"

"Please. For me."

"No. Absolutely not. Just so we're clear here, Jacinda, your pussy's not worth all that suffering."

Instead of being insulted, she leaned in closer, gaze locked on him, until he had to admit, "All right, it is! But this isn't fair!"

"For me. Please."

"My head hurts."

"For *me*."

He couldn't fight her. He wanted to. He wanted to get up and walk out and never see her again. But he knew that wouldn't happen. He was in too deep.

"Fine."

Grinning, she grabbed his hand and pulled him to his feet and out into the hallway.

"Kera!"

Kera came out of another room, dragging an unhappy Vig Rundstöm behind her.

The two Crows pushed the men together until they faced each other, barely inches apart, neither man willing to look at the other.

By Tyr's missing hand, how had Ski gotten into this?

"Well?" Jace pushed.

"Well what?"

"For me. Please."

"Stop saying that!" Ski let out a very angry but resigned breath. He looked directly at Rundstöm and snarled, "Thank you for saving my life."

The Raven stared at Ski a moment before bellowing, "*Now you owe your soul to me!*"

"Ludvig Rundstöm!" Kera yelled before Ski could punch the bastard in the face. "*You promised!*"

"He does owe his soul to me. It's a blood oath!"

"So you're telling your half-black girlfriend that you're into slavery?"

"*No.* Of course not."

"Then do it right," she bit out between clenched teeth.

It took the Raven a moment, lips in a tight line, unwilling to open to say the next words. But he finally relented under the withering glare of his girlfriend. "You're welcome."

"See?" Kera asked. "That wasn't so hard, now, was it?"

"It's not the way of our people!"

"*Times change!*" she bellowed back. "You're also not allowed to drag me off by my hair and call me your property! It's called progress, Viking!"

The All-Clan meeting took place in a cavern underneath Catalina Island. There were many underwater caves and caverns on Catalina but this one was hidden from non-Clan eyes.

And All-Clan meetings were the only time the Crows didn't have to worry about sea travel. The Claws of Ran would not send the seagulls to attack the Crows so they could be dragged to the ocean floor to drown when they fell from the skies.

Not that any of that kept the Crows from enjoying the ocean when they wanted to, but they did all go into it knowing it might end up a fight to the death.

Once they reached the cave entrance, they walked for about a half hour until they entered the cavern. A circular space with nine sections that jutted out of the rock in rows, creating stone benches. In the center of the nine sections was an empty space. Before each section was the god's rune that represented a particular Clan, and in the center of the room was a circle of all the runes, pulsating with protective power.

The whole cavern reminded Jace of the Coliseum except that no bloodshed was allowed. This was a place of safety and quiet, thoughtful discussion . . .

Kera turned to her. "What's so funny?" she asked, loud enough to be heard over the yelling.

"Just amusing myself."

"So I'm not wrong." Kera threw up her hands. "This is ridiculous!"

No, Kera was not wrong. This was all very ridiculous. The Nine Clans of Southern California had *literally* only been in here for about twelve minutes, but as soon as Josef saw Chloe, the fight was on, and everyone else just happened to join in.

It was funny to watch, too. At least for her. Each Clan stayed in its designated area, behind the correct runes, while they pointed and yelled at each other.

Every once in a while, Jace would look over at Ski and they'd smile at each other. She knew he wouldn't intervene until everything calmed down; then he'd negotiate.

Until then, they sat back and watched the Silent loudly argue with the Isa, who gestured inappropriately at Holde's Maids, who threatened hexes on the Claws of Ran, who spit seawater at the Giant Killers, who sexually harassed the Valkyries, who told the Ravens to kill the Killers, and the Ravens agreed because anything was better than listening to Josef fight with Chloe while the Crows told the Silent that the Isa were planning to kill them.

Jace didn't go to many All-Clan meetings. Not since one of the Killers pushed her out of the way and she tore his ear off, then burst into tears. But Chloe wanted all those involved in today's nightmare at this meeting.

Still, everything was manageable and typical of an All-Clan

meeting—until the Carrion were mentioned. That's when everything sort of fell apart. Mostly because no one knew what to do.

The Carrion had never been part of the Nine and they were rarely on this plane of existence. It was said that once one went to Helheim, Helheim was where one stayed. There was no getting out unless Hel released you, and she didn't release anybody. Even Odin himself couldn't force her to do anything she didn't want, including release the god Baldur, whom the other gods had loved so dearly.

She was, perhaps, the most powerful of the Aesir gods, which was why the idea of Gullveig joining forces with her was definitely terrifying.

And yet . . . here they all were. Arguing. As if that would somehow fix their problem. It wouldn't. It was simply a waste of their time.

Too bad Kera had no tolerance for any of that. She'd been to war-torn countries, fighting to protect others and the United States. So the old Viking ways were not sitting well with the newest Crow.

At least that's what Jace assumed when her friend suddenly stood up and bellowed like the drill sergeant in *Full Metal Jacket*, "That is enough!"

Shocked that someone was interrupting what Erin called the Ritual of Yelling Vikings, the entire cavern fell silent, everyone focusing on the "new girl."

"Do any of you understand what the fuck just happened today?" Kera demanded. "Gullveig is building an army with the Mara and the Carrion. And from what I can tell, the Carrion are the Nordic equivalent of the Red Army during the worst Eastern Front winter. So sitting here, listening to you *bitches* argue over bullshit is not something I'm willing to do."

"Well," the leader of the Silent, Brandt Lindgren, said, his voice dripping with condescension, "what would *you* suggest, since you seem to have such brilliant insight."

"Watch your tone, Lindgren," Vig growled. "Or I'll tear out your tongue."

"No," Kera said, raising her hand at her boyfriend. "I want to answer this, Vig. Because you know what I won't do?" she asked Lindgren. "I won't waste my fucking time with your bullshit."

Erin leaned over and whispered to Jace, "Okay, I kind of love her."

Jace had to agree. Kera was cutting through all the usual ridiculousness and getting right to the heart of the matter. Her Marine sensibilities simply wouldn't let her do anything else.

"We also can't waste our time arguing here. In a cave." Kera looked around at the Clan members. "We need to come up with a plan. We need to stop Gullveig."

"How? Even the gods couldn't."

"They stopped her, they just couldn't kill her."

"And you think that *we* can?"

"I think that everything can be destroyed. You just gotta find what will do the job."

"And you believe that with your eminent brilliance you can figure out what that is?"

Kera glanced back at Jace and Erin, and Erin nodded. "Yeah, sweetie, that was totally an insult."

"Okay. Thanks. I just wanted to check before I snapped."

But Kera didn't have the chance to "snap," because Inka, the leader of Holde's Maids, did it for her. "Oh, shut up, Brandt. At least she's trying to do something."

"And she's not wrong," Ormi added. "Gullveig has to be stopped."

"Then it is up to us," Freida announced, standing and placing the head of her big hammer on her shoulder. "We shall call upon the mighty power of Thor to destroy her!"

"Oh my gawd," Rada, leader of the Claws of Ran barked with a heavy, put-upon sigh. "What part of 'even the gods couldn't destroy her' didn't you understand, Freida? Like, how dumb are you?"

Again, Kera glanced back at Jace and Erin, and Erin whispered, "She's from the Valley circa 1983."

"Ohhh. Okay."

"Our Thor can destroy anything!"

"*Your* Thor grabbed my tits at the Crow party."

"Get over it," Yardley told Rada. "He grabbed everyone's tits at the Crow party. Even the guys'." She glanced at her sister-Crows. "It was *not* pretty."

Kera lifted her hands, palms out. "Okay, let's stay focused. I'm sure if Thor could have gotten rid of her, he would have done so the first time they tried. Three times they killed her. Three times they burned her. She kept coming back."

"Someone's been reading Snorri Sturluson," Erin joked to Jace.

"Except he didn't write the *Poetic Edda*," she told her friend, "which is where Gullveig is mentioned. He wrote the *Prose Edda*."

"Jace, I'm a German Jew," Erin sighed. "I know the *Torah* and I know the *Bible*. That's about it. So stop killing my jokes."

"Except it was incorrect."

"What do you suggest, Crow?" Inka asked Kera. "What do you think we should do?"

Kera's eyes widened a bit. "What do *I* think we should do?"

"You opened your big yap," Erin reminded her.

"Well, I think the first thing we need to do is come up with an action plan," Ski interjected before giving Kera a sweet, encouraging smile. "Don't you think so, Kera?"

"Action plan?" Kera appeared confused for a moment, but her expression cleared quickly. The woman did love active participation. "Yes! An action plan. First we need to list our main goals."

Chloe suddenly reached into her backpack and pulled out a clipboard with a notepad and a rollerball pen. She handed them over to an eager Kera.

"You brought her a clipboard?" Erin demanded, her lip curling in disgust.

"Do you know what makes me a good leader?" she asked Erin.

"Using others to get your work done?"

"Yes. That is it exactly."

"First and main goal," Kera said, writing it down on her pad, "is to destroy Gullveig. But, of course, we can't do that right away. But that's our *main* goal. Our overall objective. Now, all our other goals need to come from this main goal."

Erin looked at her sister-Crows. "I told you guys, and I told you guys. We should *beat* her into submission from the beginning. But nooooo. Couldn't do that! And now look at the situation we're in! *She has a clipboard!*"

Ski had to admit once Kera Watson had her own personal goal—getting everything organized—she was a hell of a wartime general. Of course, she didn't really understand that yet. She didn't understand that not only had Skuld chosen her as a Crow, but it seemed she'd chosen her to lead the human armies of the Nordic gods into battle, but Kera would figure that out soon enough.

Until then, though, Ski had no problem helping her.

He liked her directness. Her no-nonsense attitude. And her intolerance for others' bullshit.

She now stood in the middle of the cavern, with the rest of the Clans staring down at her. She'd passed her clipboard off to Yardley, who, although a movie superstar, was happily taking notes for her sister-Crow.

The plan was simple in design but not exactly in execution. There were lots of moving parts, and a lot of relying on sometimes unreliable people and gods getting things done.

The thing was, Ski knew that Kera would make sure things got done. It was in her nature.

"What about the Carrion?" Lindgren asked. Now that everyone else had begun to take Kera seriously, so had the Silent leader. Not that it made him any less of a dick.

"It'll be up to the Crows and the Ravens to keep them off the Maids' backs."

"And us," Freida called out.

Kera glanced over at Vig, but he could only shrug. If the Giant Killers wanted in, the Ravens and Crows couldn't really stop them. Besides, they needed all the Clans involved in this.

"Of course," Kera finally said, forcing a smile. "That would be"—she cleared her throat—"awesome."

Erin's snort filled the cavern and when everyone turned to look at her, she put her head down and pretended to have a little coughing fit.

"Anything else I might be missing?" Kera asked. When she didn't get an answer, she said, "Okay. Guess that's it."

The meeting broke up, everyone going their separate ways. There was another small skirmish between Chloe and Josef, but that was broken up quickly and the groups headed down available tunnels to reach the ocean.

Ski pushed through the others to get to Jace's side. He slipped his hand into hers and she turned, fist raised. But when she saw who it was, she smiled and put her hand down.

"Hi!"

"What was that?"

"What?"

"You were about to hit me."

"No. Not you."

Still holding hands, they started walking.

"Come home with me?" he asked.

"I'll be back in the morning. We have a list of things we have to research."

"I'm not talking about research, Jacinda."

"I should go home first. I have to feed the dog."

"I can feed him," Kera offered from behind them. She walked with Erin and Yardley, while her Raven boyfriend and the two idiots who traveled with him brought up the rear.

"Maybe you shouldn't listen to my private conversations."

Rundström wrapped his arms around Kera's waist and lifted her off the floor. She squealed and laughed, as Erin pushed past them to say to Jace, "Cut Kera some slack, Jace. She's just trying to get you laid."

Jace abruptly stopped and faced her friend, her hand still in Ski's.

Ski stood there, watching her stare down her smaller friend

until Erin finally asked, "I don't know what you're trying to tell me with this stare."

"She's telling you," Stieg Engstrom explained, "to mind your own business. It's called discretion. You should try it sometime."

Engstrom winked at Jace, but when he looked up at Ski, his expression changed to one of . . . well . . . hhhmm . . . yeah. Hatred. Definite hatred. Then he was gone, down the tunnel and out the exit.

Kera moved past them, now attached to Rundstöm's back. Her arms around his disturbingly thick neck, her legs around his surprisingly narrow waist. She seemed happy, though. Ski couldn't deny that she did seem happy.

"We'll take care of Lev, and we'll touch base tomorrow," Kera said.

"You sure?"

"Of course."

"Okay. Thanks."

"Any time."

As the two Crows chatted amiably, Rundstöm stared at Ski and Ski smiled.

Rundstöm was moving toward him when Kera grabbed a chunk of the Raven's hair and barked, "No!"

"But—"

"No! Just go."

"What did you do?" Jace asked when Kera and the Raven were gone.

"Just smiled pleasantly."

She shook her head as they neared the exit. "Always instigating. You're almost as bad as Erin!"

As they walked down the tunnel, the stragglers passed them and disappeared into the night. Those with wings took to the skies. Claws grabbed their surfboards and went night-surfin'. Those without wings went to their cars, motorcycles, and trucks.

By the time Jace and Ski reached the exit, they were alone and quiet.

Ski hoped that last night hadn't scared her. The excitement one felt right after sex tended to wear off, leaving one feeling . . . regretful? Was that what Jace's silence meant? That she regretted their time together?

He hoped not. But if she did, he'd make it up to her tonight.

He'd take it slow. Maybe make her dinner. They'd discuss philosophers or something. He'd let her know that she meant more to him than just someone new to sleep with.

And he would definitely not jump on her as soon as they walked into the house.

They landed in the Protectors' backyard and Jace shook out her wings before retracting them.

"You hungry?" Ski asked after doing the same.

"Well . . . yeah . . . I guess."

He chuckled. "If you're not hungry yet, Jace, we can do something else. Watch TV. Hit the bookstore down the street. They have cupcakes. Do you like cupcakes? I love cup—"

He loved cupcakes. She didn't know many men who would happily admit that unless they were trying to show exactly how tough they were. "Yeah. I like cupcakes. What about it?" But not Ski. He loved cupcakes. Going to a bookstore was a fun thing to suggest for two people in a romantic relationship.

She didn't know if it was the bookstore or the cupcake talk, but one of them prompted her to stick her tongue down Danski Eriksen's throat.

There was just something about him that made her so crazy. Like hot and cold and itchy. Normally these would be considered signs of an infection. But these weren't unpleasant experiences for her, just something different.

Still kissing him, Jace pushed him against the closest wall, which turned out to be more of a pillar. Their house had pillars? Well, this was LA, so of *course* their house had pillars.

Ski dug his hands into her hair, tilting her head to the side and massaging her scalp with the tips of his fingers, and wow! Did *that* feel good.

For a woman who did not like to be touched—and she really

didn't—she was surprisingly happy to have Ski put his hands all over her. She couldn't think of one place on her body that she didn't want his hands to explore. And his mouth.

That thought had her growling—she wasn't even angry!—and reaching for his jeans. They should do this in his bedroom, but that would have to wait until they got this first one out of the way and—

"There you two are!" Bear said, following a smirking Salka over to them.

And Jace knew that cat was smirking! Evil cat!

Pulling back, Jace unnecessarily adjusted her clothes, but that bit of insecurity didn't last long once Bear shoved a stack of books into her arms.

"Here. Translate these." He looked at Ski. "You'll want to order food in."

Then he walked away. Just like that. Did he not see what he'd walked in on? Did he not care?

Of course he didn't. He was Marbjörn Ingolfsson. The most clueless Bear of them all.

"Is *everyone* here?" Ski asked his Protector brother's back.

"Yep. So get a lot of food. We're hungry."

Ski's head dropped, chin against his chest. "I'm so sorry, Jace."

"It's okay," she told him around the stack of books, making it a little hard to see.

He took more than half the books from her. "Maybe later—" Ski began.

But it was like Bear knew, and he stuck his head out the glass doors to add, "It's going to be a late night. Make sure there's coffee on."

"By Tyr's missing hand!" Ski snarled before walking into the house.

Jace stopped long enough to look down at the cat that was walking beside her.

"I know this was you," she accused. "And you'd better get used to having me around, little miss."

Salka circled her legs, purring and rubbing herself against

Jace for a few seconds before stepping away. That's when Jace saw the cat's tail rise up.

"And don't even *think* of spraying me!"

Jace watched the cat saunter away, tail flicking at her, and she remembered why she was a dog person.

Kera sat down at the counter in Vig's kitchen and poured out two glasses of wine. One for her and one for Vig.

"So, how does it feel?" he asked her from the kitchen, where he was whipping up something delicious, she was sure. He was a great cook, but she couldn't hang with his love of Swedish cooking. French, Italian, Greek . . . fine. But Swedish . . . no. She'd tried, but no.

"How does what feel?"

"Being a war general."

Kera choked on her wine as Vig walked out of the kitchen, a dish towel tossed over his shoulder. He stared at her through all that hair.

"Something I said?" he asked.

"I'm . . . I'm not a war general."

"You are now."

"That's Chloe."

"No. Chloe's the leader of the LA Crows. And she's that leader all the time. But a war general will lead our Clans into battle. *All* our Clans. And when you stepped up tonight, that's what you became. A war general."

He gazed at her for a bit before asking, "You're going to throw up, aren't you?"

Kara shook her head but she guessed he didn't believe her when he stuck the small trash can by the counter under her face.

"I don't have to throw up," she reassured him.

"You sure? When you first got here—"

"I know what I did when I first got here, and no, I don't have to throw up. I just . . . I'm not a war general. I'm logistics. That's what I do. I make things happen."

"For the Clans . . . that's a war general. If we left it up to

everyone else, it would be nothing but fighting and fucking."
He leaned over the basket and kissed her forehead. "You'll be
fine."

"I hope so. Because if I'm not fine, apparently the world will
blow up."

"No. It won't blow up. Just nearly everything and everyone
will be destroyed in a cataclysm of fire, battle, and blood between the gods, the giants, and Jörmungandr the Midgard serpent, who'll wrap himself around our world and crush it."

Kera grabbed the trash can.

"What?" Vig asked her over the heaving. "What did I say?"

His parishioners thought he was being foolish. Coming back
here. But he had to know the truth. He had to know what he
was dealing with.

He made his way onto the property and kept to the bushes,
moving slowly and carefully. It took him ages.

Women sat out in the backyard at tables, talking and laughing. Enjoying themselves while music played. Some danced
with each other. Some drank beer or hard liquor poured
straight from the bottle.

At a rehab center?

And above them all were crows. Hundreds of them, in the
trees. Watching over them.

That was enough for Braddock. He needed to rescue his wife
from this. He needed to bring her back safely into the fold and
away from these whores.

But before he could move, a large pit bull ran over to the
bushes that grew around the house itself and began digging. After a few minutes, she grabbed hold of something and began to
pull. Before long, she pulled out a leg bone.

A leg bone still attached to something that was once human.

He knew who it was. One of his people. The one who'd disappeared while Jacinda's mother was here. Braddock knew this
even though there was no more flesh or skin on the bones.

Placing her front paw against a hip bone, the dog pulled and pulled, head dramatically twisting from side to side, growling as she tried to separate the leg from the rest of the skeleton.

One of the women came over after hearing the noise.

"Brodie? What are you doing, girl?" The woman gasped and Braddock felt a tiny bit of hope. This woman would raise the alarm, wouldn't she? Understand that evil was here.

But that hope was quickly squashed when she told the dog, "No, Brodie. You can't play with that. Bad girl! If your momma sees this, she's going to lose her mind." The woman crouched beside the dog. "Remember? We can't tell your momma what you and the birds did. We can't tell anybody. Right, Brodie? Right?"

The dog seemed to understand her, which was disturbing enough. But then it lowered its top half to the ground, big pit bull ass in the air.

"Brodie Hawaii, don't you dare—"

The dog took off, dragging most of the skeleton with it. The other women saw and screamed. Not in horror, though. There was no horror. Instead, laughing, they chased after the dog. Laughing and chastising all at the same time.

"Brodie Hawaii, you bring that back here!"

"Brodie, stop! Your mom is going to flip out!"

"Brodie! You represent all pit bulls!"

A redhead caught hold of the skeleton's arm. A few of the other women grabbed other parts and that's when the tugging began. The dog dragged the women one way, then another.

"Dammit, Brodie! Give it! Give it now!"

The dog yanked and the skeleton broke apart, but the dog still had the leg bone, hip, and the rib cage. And it trotted around the yard, tossing its head and what was left of the remains in its mouth from side to side.

Disgusted and horrified, Braddock fell back, but he caught himself with his arms. He was still in the bushes, but one of the black birds in the trees looked over. Its head turned to the side, twitched. It saw him . . . and it let out a squawk that the other black birds followed.

Braddock took off running.

Birds slammed into him, pecking at him, tearing at his clothes, his skin, going for his eyes. He swatted at them and kept running until he saw the van.

His men threw the door open and screamed, "Get in!"

Braddock dove headfirst into the vehicle, the door closing shut behind him as it took off. A few of the birds were still attached to him but he pulled them off and crushed them against the van floor or in his hands until there were none left.

When he got his breath back, he looked at the men with him. He knew now there was no saving his ex-wife. She was lost to him and his congregation, which left only one option open to him.

"They all die," he told his men. "Every last one of them."

Erin and the others ran down to the end of their driveway, but the van had already turned the corner.

"Follow them!" she called out to the birds circling above. They flew off and Erin glanced down at the arm bone she had in her hand.

"You want to track him down tonight and kill him?" Alessandra asked.

"We can't."

"But he saw."

"Saw what? A mass of birds attacking him? A skeleton that in about five minutes will no longer exist? Our pure evil? Do you really think cops will take a known crazy cult leader seriously?"

"He may not go to the cops," Annalisa suggested, "but he'll be back."

"We'll deal with him then."

Erin turned back to the house and let out a sigh. "Brodie Hawaii, you get back here with that leg! Damn dog."

CHAPTER TWENTY-FIVE

Ski walked into the library and paused at the entrance, gazing thoughtfully at what he saw.

They all stood at the end of one of the tables, looking at a book. Jace was the closest to the book, her face only inches from the pages, peering through a magnifying glass. Bear, Gundo, Borgsten, Haldo, and Ormi leaned over Jace's back.

"What's happening?" Ski asked.

"We're trying to read this book," Haldo explained. "It's in Latin. Very old. The words are a bit faded."

"A bit?" Bear replied. "The pages are almost white."

Gundo attempted to move in closer. "Maybe there's a way to enhance the lettering."

"Not without damaging the pages." Borgsten pointed at the book. "I've worked with books this old. They are very fragile."

"Gentlemen," Ski said, loudly. They all looked up at him and he sighed. They did all resemble owls, didn't they? Staring at him like that.

Every last one of them—overly intelligent predators.

"Let's work on this tomorrow. It's late, we're all exhausted."

Gundo smirked. "Are you telling us it's bedtime?"

"Long past actually. The sun will be up soon."

"We're not children," Bear complained. "If I want to stay up, I can stay up. You're not my father!"

Ormi's eyes crossed before he asked Ski, "Protection?"

"Holde's Maids have come and gone. The whole house is secure with runes and hexes. The Carrion won't be getting through that any time soon."

"And the other Clans' bases of operation?"

"Handled. Although I do believe your wife got in a fight with Freida."

"Because she thinks the Killers are stupid. And my lovely partner in this world and the next does love saying so to stupid people."

"It's why I get along so well with her."

Ormi laughed. "And the families?"

"Heading up to Yosemite as we speak. The Isa will ensure their safety until after the full moon."

"Excellent. Nicely handled." Ormi looked at the brothers, who'd gone back to gazing over Jace's shoulder at the book. "Gentlemen!"

Like startled birds, the men jumped, but not Jace. She was probably used to that sort of noise level being around so many Crows.

"Bedtime," Ormi ordered.

"There's still research to be done."

"Then bring books with you."

Bear gasped. "Out of the safety of the library? *Have you gone mad?*"

Ormi shrugged at Ski. "I tried."

"I know. And I do appreciate it."

He thought about approaching Jace, but he knew her well enough now to know that she wouldn't take kindly to him interrupting her work.

But as he was heading out, Jace suddenly threw the magnifying glass she held across the room.

"What's wrong?" Ski faced her, but his brothers had backed away like she was on fire. Afraid she'd suddenly attack them in a screaming fit.

This wasn't one of her "rages," though, as the Protectors liked to now call them. She was simply frustrated.

He walked around the table and grabbed her hand.

"I'm not finished," she growled at him.

"You're taking a break." He pulled her toward the glass doors. "Come on. Just a few minutes. A little fresh air. It'll be good for you."

Bear and a few others started to follow, probably thinking a little fresh air sounded like a good idea, but Ski pointed a finger at them. "Get back to work."

"But—"

Ormi grabbed Bear by the back of his hoody and yanked him to the table. "Back to work." He winked at Ski and motioned to the doors with a jerk of his head.

Thank you, Ski mouthed before dragging a pouting Jace out of the house and down the path toward a quiet spot with several benches. He sat her down on one and crouched in front of her.

"Okay, talk to me."

She frowned. "About what?"

"About what's frustrating you."

"Everything."

"Okay. That's a good start. But let's narrow it down a bit."

"I'm not your brothers, you know?"

"I know. You are much cuter and have much smaller shoulders."

She stood and began to pace. "I feel like it's right . . . *there.* But I just can't get it."

"What did you see in that book?"

"Nothing."

Ski sat down on the bench. "What do you mean?"

"I mean, yeah, there was Latin. And it was interesting. But really I was just using it as a palate cleanser."

"A what?"

"Cleansing my brain because . . . something is right . . . there, itching at the back of my skull."

"Now you're starting to worry me."

"I need to figure this out. Me."

"Why you? You've got a whole team of Protectors looking

at those books. The Maids are looking at their own. It'll be a team effort."

"I don't want to fail Kera."

"In what world are you failing Kera?"

"This one. In this world. Right here. Right now. Big, fat failure."

"Are you always this hard on yourself?"

"Yes."

Ski chuckled. "You know, there are psychology studies—"

"Seriously?" she instantly snapped.

"Are you going to let me finish?"

"Fine. Finish. Finish calling me crazy."

"I was not about to call you crazy. I was just going to say that there are studies that say when working on something—for instance, a problem you can't solve—it's a good idea to take breaks."

"I'm taking a break. Right? This is break-taking, isn't it?"

Wow.

"Yes, this is . . . break-taking. But a break where you're actually focusing on something else while you let your brain subconsciously work on your problem. Like laundry or dishes. Something mindless."

"Is this just your way of getting me to do your dishes?"

"No. That's what I have Bear for."

She nodded. "I thought staring at Latin would help."

"Staring at Latin never helps. Unless you're a monk." When she looked at him, he added, "Monks like Latin."

"Okay, so mindless. Do you have any dirty dishes?"

"Nope. I already did them. And I made the guys use paper plates."

"Well, I'm not doing your laundry."

"What's wrong with my laundry?"

"Nothing. But why would I do yours when I hate doing my own?"

"How do you get clean clothes if you don't like doing laundry?"

"I sneak them in with my sister-Crows'."

"That is sad."

"It is. But you forget that for years I had an entire cult doing my laundry because I was the wife of the Great Prophet. And they could really make those whites pop."

"I've only ever seen you in black. Or dark gray."

"Because none of my sisters can get my whites to pop. Except Kera, but I think that's her military training. Oh wait!" She snapped her fingers. "I know what I can do."

"What?"

Then Jace was tackling him off the bench and onto the ground.

Ski pressed his hands against her shoulders and held her off. "Are you trying to use me for sex?" he demanded.

Jace nodded. "Yes."

He surprised her with a smile. "By Tyr, I love your honesty."

"I've been told it's refreshing."

"Definitely."

Ski kissed her then and Jace melted into him. They were out here, in the open; any one of his brothers could walk by at any time, and she didn't care.

Of course, it helped she knew his brothers were obsessive about what they were doing, so chances of their wandering by were slim to none, but that wasn't the point, now, was it?

Jace only felt this free when she was flying at night with her sister-Crows.

She pulled away so she could remove her black tank top, tossing it aside, and unhook her bra. Ski sat up and wrapped his arm around her waist. He kissed her neck, her shoulder.

They weren't as frenzied as they had been the first time. They didn't need to be.

Jace grabbed hold of Ski's hoodie and pulled it over his head. She kissed him, digging her hands into his hair, lifting his chin up so she had complete access to his mouth.

His big hands stroked her back, eased around, and palmed her breasts. She gasped into his mouth, wrapped her arms tight around his shoulders, and rocked against his hips while their kiss went on and on.

When Ski finally pulled back a bit, he said, "I need to be inside you." His voice was low, the sound shooting up her spine, making her toes curl inside her boots.

Using one hand, he reached into the back pocket of his jeans and held up two condoms. Jace snorted and Ski shrugged his shoulders. "A Protector plans for anything, prepares for everything."

Jace slipped off his lap and stood so she could remove her boots and jeans. By the time she had her jeans around her ankles—her boots still on—Ski was already easing a hand up inside her thigh.

His fingers slid inside her, and she knew she was already wet. He leaned in, pressing his face against her. His hand slipped out and his tongue slipped in. She tried to open her legs wide, but she could only go so far with her jeans still on. And he wouldn't stop so that she could get them off.

It was driving her crazy, though. She needed more of him inside her. Jace stepped back and tried to kick her boots off. It wasn't working and, laughing, Ski helped her. He untied the laces and yanked them off. She kicked her jeans away, and threw herself at Ski.

Now they were both laughing, rolling across the ground, playfully nipping at each other, hands exploring.

When Jace was on top again, she reached over to Ski's discarded jeans and grabbed the condoms. She had one on him quickly and, after pushing him flat on his back, she slowly took him inside her pussy.

They both groaned, then grinned at each other.

Jace couldn't really describe how much she enjoyed her time with Ski. It wasn't just the act of having sex, which was unbearably delightful. It was him. The way he looked at her. The way he let her lead or led instead. Without question or complaint.

It suddenly hit her. He liked her. Simply, easily. He liked her and understood her and liked her despite that.

Jace placed Ski's big hands back on her breasts. She loved the way he enjoyed them. Using his entire hand. The fingers, the palms, even the wrists. As if he just liked the feel of them.

She rocked against him, squeezing her muscles as she stared down into his eyes.

He didn't seem to mind that she was taking her time, and she was grateful. It had been a very long while since she'd had what some would consider "regular sex," and he was definitely more than she was used to.

Of course, she liked that he filled her, his cock hitting her in such a way that she thought she might come just from him being inside her.

Their smiles and laughter faded, but their gasps and groans increased. Sweat dampened their skin even in the cool night air.

So Jace wasn't surprised when Ski rolled her over, pinning her down with his body. Yet she didn't feel trapped by him. In fact, the way he was looking at her, she got the feeling he was *more* trapped. By her. Which did shock her but made her feel good, too. Powerful.

Knowing that she wasn't alone in her feelings for him. Knowing that for once, she felt something for a man that wasn't pity or tolerance or fear.

Suddenly Ski stopped, his gaze on her face.

"What?" he asked. "What's wrong?"

Jace cupped his jaw with her hands and replied, "Absolutely nothing."

It wasn't just the words. It was how she said it. The tone of her voice. It touched him on some strange, deep level he wouldn't be able to describe to anyone. Not even himself.

"Kiss me," she ordered, and Ski did.

He kissed her and fucked her and took his time with both.

Jace's fingers dug into his back, stroked his spine, his hair. She lifted her legs, opening herself up as she wrapped them around his waist.

He pressed his palms against the ground and pushed himself up. Angling his hips, he took her with long thrusts, making sure to stroke her clit as he did so.

Her body tensed beneath his, her head falling back, exposing her neck. He licked a line from her collarbone to her ear, then gently bit down on a spot right beneath her chin.

Jace's entire body seemed to clench and she was coming, biting her lip to stop from screaming.

The sight of her fighting her instinct dragged him over the edge, too, and his hips powered into Jace as he seemed to keep coming and coming. Unable to stop, not wanting to, until there was nothing left.

Ski rolled off her, not wanting to trap her under his weight, but he reached out his hand to her and she immediately intertwined her fingers with his. They looked at each other, both grinning . . .

Until Jace's smile faded.

"What?" Ski asked, worried he'd hurt her. "What's wrong?"

"That's it," she said.

"What's it?"

"That! You brilliant, brilliant man!" She kissed him hard before scrambling to her knees and grabbing her clothes. She disappeared down the trail toward the house, but a few seconds later, she shot back, tugging on her clothes as she ran.

Holding her boots, she unleashed her wings and took off.

"Where the hell are you going?" he yelled after her retreating figure.

"I have to see my sisters. I'll be back later!"

"You're driving me crazy, you know!"

"I know!" she yelled back. "I love you, too!"

"Good! But that's not what I meant actually!"

But she was already out of sight and Ski fell back on the grass, laughing. Because that woman entertained him to no end.

Chapter Twenty-six

Erin yawned and went on her toes to reach the cereal on the top shelf.

"Which one of you tall bitches keeps putting the best cereal on the top shelf?" she demanded.

"If it's not easy to get, we won't eat it," one of her actor sister-Crows informed her.

"Deal with your eating disorder on your own time." Erin released her wings and let them carry her up until she could reach the cereal. She grabbed a box, pulled in her wings, and landed on her feet.

That's when Jace ran into the middle of the kitchen and screamed, "*I figured it out!*"

When the Crows just stared at her, she asked, "Aren't you excited?"

Erin yawned. "We don't know what you're talking about."

"Oh. Right!" Then she laughed.

"I warned you guys," Annalisa suddenly announced. "Having a normal sexual relationship with someone was going to push her over the edge."

"No, no," Jace argued. "That's been great. He loves me."

"Did he say that?" Erin asked, worried for her extremely naïve friend.

"He said I drive him crazy."

"Well," Erin said after a brief pause, "for Vikings . . ."

"That is 'I love you,'" the Crows said in unison.

"If you haven't gone over the proverbial edge," Annalisa asked between sips of her morning coffee, "then why are you talking to us? You hate talking to people."

Jace's grin was so wide you'd have thought she'd discovered a sustainable energy source that would make everyone happy and end oil wars.

"I think I know how to send Gullveig out of this plane of existence."

"How?"

"The spell I used to bullshit the Carrion?" Erin nodded since it had just happened a few hours ago. "It's a spell I found in one of those old books the Protectors took from the Russians. In the same book, there were two spells that I *think* will work. The first will allow us to force Gullveig into a contained space surrounded by a protective circle that Gullveig will not be able to get out of. That circle is literally called the God Keeper."

"The second spell?"

"That one will send her out of this world and trap her in another."

"Basically what Odin and the others did to her originally."

"Exactly. Once she's there, we'll have a little time to find a way to destroy her, so when she comes back—because we all know she'll come back—we'll be ready."

"Sounds great."

"Just one problem."

"Of course there is. So what's the problem?"

"It's gonna cost us some favors."

"So? We'll call in some favors."

"Not from any of us," Jace admitted. "Believe it or not, I think only Betty can get us this level of favor in the shortest amount of time."

"Betty—who's still in a coma? That Betty?"

"We've tried everything," Alessandra reminded her. "We can't wake her up."

Jace cringed a little. "I think I know who has enough power to do that."

Erin remembered not being able to speak for a good five minutes. Like someone was pinching her voice box. It was a feeling she had *not* enjoyed.

"I'm already unhappy," Erin complained.

Jace winced in sympathy. "Yeah . . . kinda knew you would be."

Jace watched her grandmother push her way into the Bird House.

Chloe went to greet the elderly woman. "Hello, Mrs. . . . uh . . . what should I call you?"

Nëna looked Chloe over, didn't seem to like what she saw, and turned to Jace. "Where is she?"

Jace didn't bother chastising her grandmother. It was ineffective. So she simply led her up the stairs to Betty's room.

Nëna walked to the bed, carefully placing down her tote bag with "*I heart quilting*" silk-screened on it before putting her hand on Betty's forehead, as if taking her temperature. She closed her eyes and Jace knew her grandmother was exploring, searching for wherever Betty might be.

After about five minutes, Nëna opened her eyes and reached into her tote. The top of the bag held material one might use for a quilt, but she dug under the fabric squares until she found an old wooden box.

Placing the box on the bed, she carefully unlatched the metal lock and lifted the top.

She removed a bottle of oil and opened it. The oil was rose-scented. Rather pleasant.

Nëna anointed Betty's forehead, nose, and chin with the oil and put the stopper back in and returned it to the box. She closed the box, relocked it, and put the box back in the tote, covering it with her quilting material.

She then leaned in and whispered into Betty's ear, chanting something very ancient and powerful.

When Nëna was done, she leaned back and waited.

Betty's eyes snapped open and Jace grinned.

But Betty didn't move. She didn't blink. She just stared at the ceiling. She was still lost.

If Jace's grandmother couldn't wake her, then no one—

"What would you say to wake her up?" Nëna asked the group of Crows hanging outside the room. "Something that would catch her attention."

"Good attention or bad attention?" Jace asked.

"Bad is always better in these cases."

"Oh, I can do that." Yardley slipped into the room, placing her hands on Nëna's shoulders to ease her away.

Nëna's hands went up and her entire body tensed. Jace realized she'd often looked like that when she'd been innocently touched.

"God, I'm just like her," Jace muttered.

Yardley leaned over Betty, gently pushed her hair off her face, and softly smiled. Then she yelled, *Brianna stole your client list! And your Bentley limo!*

Betty's eyes suddenly moved and her hands were around Yardley's throat. She was also already in the middle of screaming, "*Bitchhhhhhhhhh!*"

As the other Crows dove on the bed to get Betty to release Yardley before she killed her, Nëna picked up her tote and walked out of the room. Jace followed.

"Aren't you going to let me thank you?" she asked her grandmother.

"Why?"

"If you didn't want to help me, why did you?"

Nëna faced her. "You called. I helped. We're family."

"Even now?" Jace asked her. "After I took an oath to a god?"

"It was stupid. You have the mind to be like me. That's what I was grooming you for. But you chose. You can never choose. None of them. I told you that."

"I couldn't let him get away with what he'd done to me."

Nëna wagged a finger at her. "Always with the rage, little *inat*. Just like your father. Now you're trapped with these"—her lip curled—"*people*."

"I love these *people*, Nëna."

"They're not family. Not *your* family."

"They are now. They're my family. I love every one of them. Just as much as I love you."

"They're not blood."

"It doesn't matter." Jace shrugged. "They'd all die for me. And I would for them."

"You would, wouldn't you? Stupid girl."

"I don't want to talk about this anymore."

"Good! There is nothing left to say."

Assuming her grandmother would leave, Jace was shocked when Nëna slapped her hand against Jace's jaw, squeezing a bit.

"Owwwww! Stop hitting me, old woman!"

Nëna removed her hand, but where her fingers had touched Jace's skin, she could feel . . . power.

"What did you do to me?" Jace covered the throbbing spot with her hand.

"Do not forget where you come from, ridiculous child! Do not forget who you are. And *never* forget that you're mine. *My* blood. Never forget. I have not forgotten. And protecting you is my only goal. Even when you are so damn stupid!"

Then spinning on her tiny, bright-white Keds, Nëna stormed out.

CHAPTER TWENTY-SEVEN

Kera walked into the overpriced LA gym. She'd tried to get a job at one of the chain's other locations. Everyone had been very nice and seemed more than happy to get her a gym membership—as if she, fresh out of the military, could afford the two-thousand-a-month cost—but she'd had the distinct feeling that the fact her thighs touched meant she'd been too fat for a job there. Even picking up used towels or mopping floors.

She'd never forget walking out with a membership application and passing some guy yelling at sweaty rich people in an attempt to simulate a "boot camp." Kera had actually gone through boot camp and could tell instantly that none of these people would have survived five minutes with a real drill sergeant calling the shots.

At that moment, she'd sworn never to bother going back into a place like this, but desperate times and all that . . .

"Are you sure she's here?" Kera asked Vig.

"That's what my sister told me."

"But why?" She glanced around at all the people trying to desperately stay thin or get abs they weren't genetically meant to have. "She's a god. Would she really need to come to some pretentious gym to get in shape?"

"I don't think she's here to get in shape."

Vig stepped in front of Kera, his brown eyes scanning. A few employees began to walk toward them, but one look at Vig and they all dropped their heads and walked away.

Kera had seen it before and it never failed to entertain her.

Little did they know . . . Vig was the sweetest guy on the planet. He just didn't *look* it.

"This way."

Vig walked off and Kera followed after him. He led her all the way down to the back of the first floor and into a darkly lit room.

And there she was. Freyja—goddess of fertility, commander of the Valkyries, and a god of war because Odin tricked her—leading everyone in the room through an indoor cycling session.

"Come on, everybody!" she shouted above the tech music, colored strobe lights flashing, a giant screen at the front of the room taking them through Icelandic vistas. "Push it! Last hill! You can do it!"

Kera wasn't so sure. There were people falling over their handlebars, slipping off their bikes, vomiting.

"What the hell is she doing?"

"Uh . . ."

Blinking, Kera looked up at Vig. "What kind of answer is that?"

"You're not going to like my answer, so I paused."

"She's killing them, isn't she?"

"I don't think she's using them as actual sacrifices, but . . . more like temporary offerings."

"Oh, my God!"

Freyja, her eyes glowing gold, looked over her shoulder at Kera and grinned.

Kera started to march up there so she could tell the goddess her very pointed thoughts about what was happening here but Vig grabbed her, placed his hand over her mouth, and his other arm around her waist.

"We'll meet you outside," he told Freyja before carrying Kera out of the room.

Polly loved her job. How could she not? She made a lot of money doing exactly what she enjoyed. And every day was new and exciting. She never knew who was going to come walking through their glass front doors. The biggest stars. Important politicians. Billionaires!

The best of the best.

Except when, like now, it was not the best of the best, but people like *her*.

And even worse, this time she'd brought friends.

"Ms. Lieberman. How nice to see you again." And unable to help herself, she added, "How's business?"

Lieberman went for her, nearly clearing the glass counter, but one of the women with her yanked her back.

"And Ms. King, I am *so* happy to see you again," Polly said with real pleasure.

"Hi, Polly."

"So what brings you here today?" Polly asked.

"I need to see Efram," Lieberman barked.

"May I ask what's this is in reference to?"

The woman's brown eyes narrowed on Polly, but before she could say something about "ruining your very existence, perky tits"—as she had said many times before—one of her friends cut between the two.

"It's business," the woman said. "Private."

"Of course. I'll see if Efram's available."

Polly turned her back on Betty Lieberman even when she saw the woman raise her fist, ready to throttle her.

"So what do you want?" Freyja asked. She had a towel around her neck and was drinking heavily from a water bottle.

"Well—" Vig began.

"What were you doing to those people?" Kera demanded, and Vig cringed. Not so much at the question, but at her tone. Freyja wasn't as comfortable being questioned by mortals as Skuld and Odin were. In fact . . . she kind of hated it.

"Giving them the ride of their lives."

"Yeah," Kera muttered back. "I've heard that about you."

Vig quickly stepped in front of the woman he loved with all his heart but was suddenly afraid he was going to lose forever, and said to the god, "We need your help, Freyja."

"*My* help?" She pointed at Kera. "I gave you one of my magnificient weapons and you gave me nothing back. And now you come to me asking for more?"

"Do you want your necklace or not?" Kera snarled.

"Watch how you speak to me, human. I'll rip that haggard soul from your body and turn it into dust."

"Ladies, please," Vig begged, doing his best to keep the pair separated.

The door to the exercise room Freyja had been in opened and the participants began to stumble out. She'd drained most of them very close to death. Probably taking years of their lives just so she could get the high she once got when seasonal sacrifices were all the rage.

Some made it out on their own steam, although they tripped every few feet and some had to stop and lean against the wall, panting desperately. A few, though, had to be helped by others.

One of them, a woman, with her arms around the shoulders of two men, stopped when she neared Freyja. There was such love in her eyes as she gazed at the goddess.

"That session was amazing," she gasped out to Freyja.

"Why, thank you, sweetheart."

"Marry me. I'll give you anything."

"Aren't you just darling?"

Laughing, Freyja waved the woman off before informing Kera and Vig, "If I snapped my fingers, she'd be on her knees in a second . . . and she's not even gay."

"Are you?" Kera asked.

"If you insist on using labels, I prefer flexible."

"I just bet you are."

"Anyway," Vig quickly cut in, "we have a way to get *Brísingamen* back to you." The powerful torc had been stolen from Freyja in order to assist in the return of Gullveig. Freyja had given Kera a rune-covered axe to help in the retrieval of the item, but in the confusion of that day, they'd forgotten about it and now they were sure Gullveig had it.

To Vig's surprise, though, Freyja had not demanded the return of her axe due to Kera's failure to do what she'd promised, and now he understood why. She really wanted that necklace and she wanted the Crows to get it for her. She wasn't about to risk one of her precious Valkyries on such a petty mission, but she'd risk all the Crows in the universe.

The whole thing annoyed Vig, but if they could use Freyja's obsession with that damn torc to get what they needed, then fine. That's what they would do.

"What do you need from me?" Freyja asked.

"Your power."

Freyja gazed at the pair for a moment, then admitted, "Well . . . I *am* incredibly powerful."

"And humble!" Kera barked sarcastically before he managed to cover her mouth with his hand again.

Jace slapped Betty's fist down. "What is wrong with you? You're acting like me just before I snap."

"She was pissing me off," she snarled, eyes locked on Polly's retreating form.

"Everyone is pissing you off," Erin noted. "Calm the fuck down. We're here for a reason."

Leigh looked around the store, her mouth hanging open.

"Nice, huh?" Yardley asked.

Diamonds and rubies and every other kind of rare, expensive gem glittered at them in the perfect lighting of the store.

"This stuff is amazing," Leigh gushed. She randomly pointed at one of the jewels in a stand-alone case in the middle of the floor. "Like, how much does something like this cost?"

"More than you'll ever be able to afford," Erin told her.

Yardley pointed at another beautiful necklace. "I wore this to last year's Oscars."

"I forgot," Annalisa lied, "did you win anything then?"

Jace cringed. Annalisa knew well enough to never ask an actor that question unless one already knew the answer was going to be "yes."

Honestly! The woman never stopped testing the mental health of everyone around her!

"No. But I'm ever hopeful," Yardley replied. A practiced phrase she'd used with reporters who'd asked similar questions.

"You should do one of those movies where you pretend to be unattractive or plain," Erin told her. "That usually wins a hot girl like you lots of awards."

Efram walked out of the back. Unlike Polly, who clearly loathed every breath Betty took, Efram's smile was warm and very real.

"My sweet Betty!" he said, throwing his arms wide. "I am *so* glad to see you!"

The big man hugged Betty tight. "I'd heard such terrible things. I should have known everyone was lying to me."

"Of course they were." Betty pointedly looked at Polly before telling Efram, "We need to talk. Alone."

Seeing Yardley with Betty, Efram gave Polly and the rest of his staff the day off.

Once they were alone, the doors locked, and the windows electronically darkened so no one could look in, Efram returned to Betty.

"What do you need?" he asked.

"We need your store."

"It's yours!" he said, arms thrown wide. "Tell me what you're looking for."

Betty shook her head. "No. We need your store. All of it."

"What are you talking about? For a film?"

"No. To get a god."

Efram stepped back, eyed them all. "Is this about Gullveig?" he finally asked.

Erin's body tensed. "What?"

"Ladies . . . I've been in this business a long time. You think she's the only god who loves her jewelry? I just sold Ares a Breitling watch. You know, something that can take a serious beating." He glanced at Jace and explained, "He is the god of war."

Betty shrugged. "Then I guess we don't have to explain anything else."

Efram raised a finger. "No, no, no. I said I do business with the gods. But I'm not about to let you ladies use *my* store if it involves that psychotic bitch."

"Efram—"

"No, Betty. I love you to death despite the way you terrorize my staff. But there's no—"

"I have an offer."

"There's nothing you can offer me that would make me change my mind. Nothing."

Betty blew out a breath. They'd all hoped not to have to use this, but it seemed there was simply no choice.

"Odin!" Betty called out. "Odin!"

Odin appeared behind Betty. Eye patch and grin in place, dressed in a perfectly tailored Italian blue suit.

"You bellowed, sweet Betty?"

"Odin, this is Efram. Efram, this is the god Odin."

"What am I supposed to do here, Betty? Fall to my knees? I'm Jewish. He doesn't exactly terrify me."

"I'm not trying to terrify you. I have an offer. You give us your business and, no matter what happens, we rebuild and replace."

"Betty—"

"And," she continued on, "you get the next twenty-four hours to hang out with Odin."

"Wait . . . what?"

"You heard me. Twenty-four hours, around the world, Odin-style."

"You're kidding, right?"

Betty glanced back at the god and realized he was now standing with two beautiful, if somewhat used, women.

Betty didn't even bother to hide her disgust. "Ech."

"Valkyries?" Leigh asked Jace, slightly confused. The LA Valkyries, chosen by Freyja herself, were all beautiful girls next door. Like a bunch of sorority girls with lethal weapon skills and winged horses. The ladies Odin chose for the Tri-State Valkyries, however . . .

"From Jersey, I think," Jace whispered back. "So I'm guessing they're all former strippers."

"A whole twenty-four hours of uninhibited, out-of-control, Odin-style entertainment, with the god himself," Betty crooned in that voice Jace was sure she used when trying to get a producer or studio head to do what she wanted because threatening him or her was going to be ineffective.

Efram handed the store keys he held over to Betty.

"Go with God," he told Betty before disappearing with Odin and his hook . . . er . . . Valkyries.

Betty shook her head. "I told you, ladies. I told you. It doesn't matter the race, the religious belief, how they were raised . . . nothing. *All* men are the same."

"You came out of that coma feisty," Erin noted.

"And hungry. Think we can get some pizza before our next move?"

"Nope," Erin replied, suddenly looking at her phone. "Got a text from Kera. It's all a go."

"Are you sure about this?" Jace asked Betty, unable to hide her worry now that she knew her plan was moving forward. "I know this is all my idea, Betty, but our next move—"

"Don't worry, sweetie." Betty placed her hand on Jace's shoulder and grinned at her. "I can't tell you how much I have been looking forward to this."

Gullveig finished bathing in the blood of a virgin—well, actually, in this case, an unemployed screenwriter who thought his idea of a musical version of *Saving Private Ryan* was brilliant, but there wasn't really much of a difference in the big scheme of things—and took a quick shower. She finished dressing and went out into her office and, with a happy sigh, dropped into the chair behind her desk.

She put her hands behind her head and used the tips of her toes to move her office chair back and forth.

Life was good.

"Come in," Gullveig called out when she heard the knock on her office door.

Her assistant, Jenna, walked in. "I got more calls. They're having problems on the set."

"Is he drinking again?"

"Most likely."

Gullveig rolled her eyes and dropped her head back against the chair. "I should have taken his soul when I had the chance."

Jenna's head tipped to the side. She looked like a confused cocker spaniel. "Pardon?"

Before Gullveig could soothe her assistant's concerns—she really should be more careful what she said around the girl—there was yelling and screaming from the hallway.

Her door flew open and Betty Lieberman stormed in, with security right behind her.

Jenna's eyes widened, she lowered her head, and quickly backed away. It was as if she thought she could fade into the wallpaper, like some kind of chameleon.

Amazing that even after all that had happened, Lieberman still managed to instill fear in everyone around her. She'd make a hell of a god if she wasn't a worthless human.

A worthless human but a brilliant agent.

Lieberman stopped in the middle of the office, turned in a circle to look over everything.

"Wow," she stated, voice thick with mocking, "you like mirrors."

"Welcome back, Betty. We've missed you."

Lieberman's head tipped down and she mouthed, *Liar.*

"Awww, Betty. You hurt me."

"I don't think that's possible, sweetie. But nice try."

"So what do you want?" Gullveig asked, putting her feet up on her desk and watching the corners of Lieberman's eyes twitch.

"Jenna, honey." Lieberman turned those sharp eyes on Jenna, who'd been trying to ease her way out of the room. "You've moved up."

"Hi . . . uh . . . Miss . . . uh . . ."

"Why don't you give us a minute, sweetie."

Jenna made some sort of noise with her mouth before dashing from the room.

"That's impressive," Gullveig had to admit. "I'm a god, and I don't get that kind of fear out of her."

"I've been in this industry a long time. Worked my way up from the mail room. And you don't get to where I've gotten by being nice. Or forgiving. Or remotely humane."

"So . . . what? You're here to take me out, Crow? You?" Gullveig laughed. She couldn't help it. The balls on this woman!

"Of course not. Don't be silly."

"Then what? Why are you here?"

"You took from me. I'm here to take from you."

"Take what?" she asked, laughing. "What do you think you can take from me?"

Lieberman laid her hands on Gullveig's desk, leaned in. "Freyja's necklace."

Gullveig's laughter died in her throat. "What are you talking about?"

"*Brísingamen.*"

"I know its name, idiot." Dropping her legs to the floor, Gullveig stood. "And it's my necklace."

"Is it?" Lieberman smirked. "Because according to Freyja, it's hers. And she wants her shit back."

Gullveig started to go over the desk to get to the insolent Crow, but Lieberman pointed at the open office door behind her. "Now, now. Trust me. The entire staff is out there listening, and they're enjoying every second of this. But are you sure you're ready to out yourself as a god?"

Growling, Gullveig went through her bathroom to the small room she'd been using for her sacrifices and to call the Carrion to her. She kept all her jewelry in here but *Brísingamen* had its own special place on a bronze bust of Aphrodite.

But the bust now stood bare.

Screeching, Gullveig spun around, only to be hit in the face by a Crow. She'd wrapped the necklace around her fist and the power of it and her fist shoved Gullveig back until she slammed into the chest with all her jewels.

The Crow ran and, beyond angry, Gullveig tore after her, the walls peeling as she dashed by, her anger ripping away at the thin layer of this world.

She nearly had her hand on the Crow's shoulder when the bitch tossed the necklace to another Crow standing on the far side of her desk.

"Erin!"

A redheaded Crow caught the necklace and Gullveig shifted her attention to her. The redhead ran, sliding under the desk just as Gullveig was going over it.

"*Give it to me!*" Gullveig bellowed, ready to burn the entire state down to get her necklace back.

She lifted the heavy desk and tossed it like so much hay, but the redhead was already near the front door of the office.

Gullveig cut her off there, but the redhead spun around while, at the same time, tossing the necklace.

"Betty!"

Lieberman caught the necklace in one hand and held it up. "This what you want, whore?" she asked. "Then come and get it, bitch!"

Done with this, Gullveig used a mystical doorway simply to go from one side of the room to the other, so she could wrap her hands around Lieberman's throat.

But before she could yank the twat's soul from her body and swallow it whole, talons dug into her from every side, and Gullveig quickly realized that the other Crows were holding on to her.

But why? What the mighty Helheim were they doing? They had to know they couldn't kill her. They had to!

"Go, Jace!" a brown Crow yelled and her curly-haired sister began chanting in very ancient Norse. So ancient, Gullveig was shocked the little bitch even knew it. Almost no one knew that tongue because it was the language of the Vanir gods, not the Aesir.

It was a "call to the gold." A spell so old and misunderstood that the Aesir had banned it from ever being used by their disciples.

What was so misunderstood about it? It was a spell that was often mistakenly used by those looking for wealth or bounty. But it didn't bring anything to you. It brought you to it.

Something most people thought was a fine idea until they ended up at the bottom of the ocean where a long boat had gone down or in the fiery stomach of a gold-eating dragon or trapped behind the locked doors of a king's gold vault with no way to get out.

But this . . . *girl*, she knew the spell. Knew it so well, she was using it to—

CHAPTER TWENTY-EIGHT

They were all standing around in the middle of a Beverly Hills jewelry store, with mounds of gold, diamonds, and rubies placed in piles to create a powerful mystical circle.

They were all at the ready. The Maids that had created the circle, and the Protectors, the Crows, the Ravens, and the Killers.

They all silently waited until . . . they were there. In the center of the circle. Betty having the life strangled out of her by an enraged Brianna and Jace, Kera, and Erin holding on to Betty's god-infused assistant with their talons.

Betty, unable to pull away, held up her hand, *Brísingamen* clutched in her fingers.

Freyja, who'd given Jace enough of her power to have the strength to use the spell that would bring Gullveig here, leaned over the circle and snatched her torc from Betty.

"No!" Gullveig as Brianna, screamed, throwing Betty aside and trying to go after her Vanir sister.

Freyja leaned back and the powerful circle stopped Brianna cold.

"Give it back to me!" Brianna screeched. "It's mine!"

"Oh no, sister," Freyja replied, her voice low. "This is *mine*. And it was your mistake forgetting that."

Then Freyja was gone, leaving a livid god trapped within the circle.

Bear sighed at the loss of Freyja, and Ski had to ask, "Did you really think she was going to help us anymore than she already has?"

"We did get her that stupid necklace back."

"Oh, my friend, gods just don't work that way."

Raging, Brianna began to pace, trapped by the mounds of gold and diamonds that she so favored.

The store was brightly lit inside for its jewelry-buying patrons so she could see all of them waiting.

"What?" she asked. "Do you really think you can kill me? Your gods couldn't kill me! Thor and Odin couldn't kill me!"

"No," Inka calmly told her. "We don't think we can kill you."

The Maids spread out so that they surrounded the circle that Brianna was trapped in, bowed their heads, their white robes covering their faces, and held up their hands. They began the chant that would open a doorway into another world.

A world where they'd send Brianna and the god stuffed inside her.

She quickly realized that, too, eyes growing wide when she recognized what was happening.

"Get ready," Ski told his brothers.

Brianna threw back her head and unleashed a primal scream that radiated out, breaking every glass window and object in the room except for the ceiling above them.

Everyone ducked but the Maids, attempting to protect their faces and vital organs from shattered glass.

Bear lifted his head, turning and tilting it one way, then another. "They're coming!" he warned. "They're coming!"

The Carrion crashed through the tempered glass skylight and flew in through the open windows. The Mara came through the walls as smoke, but quickly turned to their more humanlike forms. Having already faced the Crows, the Mara went after them first while the Carrion targeted the Protectors.

Ski leaned one way, then the other. A Carrion's Hel blade slashed past him. It wasn't just the steel of these blades that worried him, but what the blades were imbued with. Just a touch from that steel would destroy skin and bone on contact.

The Ravens came at the Carrion from behind, moving out

of the shadows so quickly, it was like they'd suddenly just appeared behind them.

Rundstöm came up behind the Carrion fighting Ski and caught hold of his leather wings. While he held the wings, he lifted his leg and rammed his foot against the Carrion's back.

He tore the wings off, ignoring the screams and flying blood as only a Rundstöm could, while Ski grabbed the two Hel blades from the Carrion. He used one blade to cut him across the gut, intestines pouring to the floor, and the other he used to slice the Carrion's throat, nearly taking his head off.

The Carrion dropped forward, and Rundstöm tossed the wings aside.

"Here," Ski said, handing him one of the Hel blades.

Rundstöm took the offered sword. "I thought Protectors didn't fight with weapons."

"We don't," Ski explained seconds before he turned and removed the head of a Carrion who'd landed behind him. When he turned back to Rundstöm, he added, "But that doesn't mean we can't."

The Crows fought off the Mara, the disgusting purveyors of everyone's nightmares. But Jace and Betty were still focused on Gullveig. They couldn't risk the possibility that she'd be able to get herself out of the Maids' protective circle before they opened that door.

So, using their blades, they slashed at Gullveig. Not to kill her. They couldn't kill her. At least not yet. But they could harm her. Especially since the skin she wore was not hers.

It had once belonged to Brianna, and Betty had made it clear when Jace had told her the plan that if there was one thing that must be accomplished during all this, it was the release of Brianna's soul from her captor.

Jace had been a little surprised. Betty seemed to have made it her business to torment Brianna when she'd been her assistant, but Betty clarified that with, "*I* can torture her, but no one else can."

So here they were, tag teaming a god. Betty slashing at Gullveig with her blades while Jace used her talons to strip Brianna's skin off in big swaths and chunks.

When all the skin was removed from Gullveig's chest, Betty stopped long enough to slap her hand between the god's breasts and chant something in Old Norse.

Screaming, Brianna's soul exited her prison of god flesh and dissipated into the air.

Then Betty slashed the god's throat and yanked and spun around Gullveig, reaching up and grabbing her hair. She tore Brianna's face off the god like a Scooby-Doo villain mask.

That's when Gullveig raised her hand and, with a flick of her fingers, sent both Betty and Jace flying across the room.

When Jace landed, she lifted her head in time to see a Hel's blade fashioned as an axe coming down toward her chest. She rolled to one side, and the blade barely missed her, but the Carrions were fast, as well, and this one had pulled the weapon out of the floor and brought it down again before Jace had time to roll to the other side.

She crossed her blades in front of her face, and her rune-empowered weapons managed to prevent the axe from ramming into her head.

Using all her strength, she fought to keep the Carrion from bringing the blade all the way down, which would cleave her skull in two.

She turned her head to the side and saw that several of the Carrion were now inside the circle with Gullveig. They were going to try to get her out, but she didn't think they were strong enough to bypass the Maids' powers.

But then they did something she hadn't seen coming. Inside the circle, they began to open their own doorway. And she knew immediately where they'd take Gullveig.

"Ski!" she screamed. "Stop them! Stop them now!"

Ski charged across the room toward the circle, which held the god trapped but could be entered by the rest of them. Vig and Bear started to follow, but the Mara grabbed hold of them, wrapping themselves around them, using their powers to make them live their nightmares.

That's when the first twitch hit Jace.

Then she saw Ski make it into the circle and slash one Carrion with the Hel blade, then take the head of the other. He grabbed another Carrion. The one who'd picked Gullveig up to carry her into the doorway they'd opened.

The three struggled, but when the Carrion attempted to throw Gullveig into that doorway, Ski reached up, grabbed the goddess by the hair, and tossed her across the circle. She slammed into the other side like she was hitting a brick wall.

Screeching in rage, unwilling to believe anyone had treated her that way, Gullveig forgot about her own safety. She forgot about everything, and instead, she unleashed some spell that caused the doorway the Carrion had opened to start sucking them in.

One Carrion flipped backward, disappearing into it, and the one struggling with Ski tried to turn the Protector so that he'd go next.

That's when the twitch Jace felt unleashed her rage, and everything in the room turned red. No one meant anything to her anymore. No one but Ski.

She shoved the Carrion's weapon away, and rammed her blades into his eyes.

He fell backward, screaming in pain, and Jace got on her feet and went after the Carrion holding on to Ski's throat, his fingers decaying Ski's flesh underneath.

Without thought, only her rage, Jace rammed into the back of the Carrion and all three of them fell into the doorway headfirst.

Kera watched her friend and Danski Eriksen disappear into the pit with one of the Carrion. She charged after them, sliding under one of the Helheim blades that slashed out at her.

But by the time she reached the doorway, she hit a wall. Literally.

The portal was gone and all that remained was a wall. She slammed her fists against it, screaming, "*Jace!*" But she knew her friend was gone.

It took her a second before she realized Erin was right beside her. She'd tried to get to Jace, too. They'd both failed.

Panting, they stared hard at each other. Not in anger. No, they saved that anger for *her.*

Because she wouldn't stop talking.

Brianna's skin lay at Gullveig's feet, ripped so badly it was doubtful the god could repair it. Blood covered her from head to toe but still, her gold skin showed through. Then again, everything on her was gold. Her hair, her eyes, her nails.

"*Did you cunts think you could kill me?*" Gullveig continued to rage at them all from the circle the Maids had trapped her in. "Did you think you could do what even your gods could not? They all tried and they all failed!"

The portal out of this world and into another stood open, but the Maids were weakening now. They could hold the portal open, but they couldn't get the bitch inside it. They were too weak to push her in. And everyone else was busy fighting either the remaining Carrion or the Mara.

Yet Kera didn't care. Her friend was gone, and Kera blamed herself. And she blamed Gullveig.

Getting to her feet, Kera walked toward the god. The Ravens and Protectors kept the Carrion away from her. She didn't run. Instead, she let her anger guide her. Her anger at the loss of Jace.

Jace wasn't the first battle buddy Kera had lost, but she was the one that tore at Kera's soul worse than any of the others. And she let that anger move her through the fight going on around her, working only on instinct and hatred.

As she passed a blood-covered Freida, Kera held out her hand and, without question, the Giant Killer tossed her most sacred weapon to her.

Gullveig was still ranting. "*I will bring Ragnarok down upon all of you! I will bathe in the blood of your kin and laugh in the ashes of your souls!*"

Kera moved up beside her, but before Gullveig could focus on her, Erin moved to the god's other side and lashed out at her with her flame.

Gullveig slapped that flame away easily. "Have you heard nothing I've said, you idiot twat? *Have you heard nothing?*"

Her attention on Erin—who didn't back down in the face of all that hatred and misery—Kera lifted the hammer high and, from the heavens, without her saying one word or asking the gods for anything, lightning slashed down and slammed into the weapon.

Then Kera used all her strength and anger and sense of loss, and swung the hammer right at Gullveig's big, gold head.

It hit the god in the face and the power of it sent her flying back and through the portal.

"Close it!" Vig yelled, because Kera couldn't. Her power had left her as soon as the weapon made contact, and she dropped to her knees.

The Maids quickly finished their chant, commanding the doorway to close. As it slammed shut, the Carrion and the Mara left. The Mara turning to smoke and disappearing back through the walls they'd eased through; the Carrion unleashing their leather wings, and going through the destroyed skylight.

Freida took her weapon back, and Vig was there to lift Kera to her feet, his arms around her waist.

She buried her face against his chest, the tears coming. "I lost her, Vig. I lost her."

Chloe's hands were there, grasping Kera's chin and pulling her around. Her leader looked deep into Kera's eyes. "This isn't done. We'll get her back. I promise you that."

"From Hel?" Erin asked. "The gods couldn't even get Baldur back."

"That was Odin," Chloe was quick to remind her. "We're not Odin. We don't have his rules." She looked at Kera again. "We *will* get her back."

CHAPTER TWENTY-NINE

Ski woke up in a dank cave, with the sound of someone butchering meat turning his stomach. At least that's what it sounded like. But when he looked all he saw was Jace on top of a dead Carrion, stabbing him over and over with his Hel blade.

"Jace?"

Her head snapped around, bloodred eyes locking on him.

Ski slowly propped himself up on his elbows, but then Jace blinked and her eyes were a bright blue again.

"Ski!" She left her Carrion victim and ran to his side, crouching beside him, her hand resting on his cheek. "Are you all right?"

Ski didn't understand. Usually, when Jace's eyes were like that, when she was in a rage, the only thing that got her back to normal was killing and then sobbing or sleeping.

But here she was, back to normal after he knew for a fact she'd snapped.

"I'm fine," he said, taking her hand, kissing her bloody knuckles. "Are you?"

"Yeah. But I'm sorry I got us down here."

"You did what you had to do. I know our brothers and sisters will take care of Gullveig and that's all that matters. I knew the risks."

She pressed her forehead against his, and they stayed like that for several minutes until a voice said, "Hel wants to see you, Crow and Protector."

A small troop of Carrion stood in the entrance of the cavern, staring down at them.

Jace stood and held her hand out to Ski. He took it and got to his feet. Still holding hands, they walked past the Carrion and went to face Hel, daughter of Loki and ruler of the underworld.

Kera sat at the table, her legs pulled onto the chair, her hand constantly wiping tears she hadn't been able to stop for hours.

It wasn't that no one was doing anything.

In fact, everyone was doing *something*.

Even the Giant Killers and the Silent, two groups who cared for no one outside their Clans, were trying to contact their gods, as were the Ravens and the Isa. They were all doing what they could to get Jace and Ski back from Helheim.

Of course, Kera had no doubt that self-concern was part of what motivated all the groups. If Jace and Ski could get trapped alive in Helheim until Ragnarok, what would stop that from happening to any of them?

It was too terrifying for the Clans to think about. Unlike the Crows, they'd spent almost their entire lives becoming the warriors their gods wanted them to be so that one day they would feast in the Halls of Valhalla and join the battle during Ragnarok.

So all the groups rushed back to their bases of operation and began to search for some way, *any way*, they could get a Crow and a Protector back from the underworld.

That had been hours ago, though. It was nearly one in the morning and still nothing.

Yardley put a cup of coffee in front of Kera and sat down at the table near Chloe and Betty.

Brodie rested beside Kera's feet and little Lev was asleep on Brodie's back.

And as soon as Kera thought about Lev, the tears started again.

"Oh sweetie," Betty said, as gently as the hard-ass agent could manage, "you have got to stop crying."

"I know. I know."

Yardley threw up her hands. "Maybe Erin's right! We should all go down there and get her."

"So we can *all* be trapped alive in Helheim?" Betty asked.

"Well, it's better than sitting here, waiting for something to happen."

Brodie's head suddenly went up, ears on alert. Her head turned one way, then another. But when her hackles rose the length of her back, Kera knew something was wrong.

"Brodie, what is it?"

The dog sat up and Lev fell on the ground. Before he could complain too much about the treatment, Brodie grasped the puppy by the back of the neck and trotted off with him in her mouth.

They all sat there watching Kera's dog disappear into the trees surrounding the Bird House. It wasn't that Brodie had suddenly gone off; it was that she took Lev with her.

"What's Brodie doing?" Yardley asked.

"I think she's protecting Lev."

"Why?"

Tears suddenly dried up, Kera admitted, "You know . . . that's kind of what has me worried."

They were led over the Bridge of the Dead and to Hel's hall.

Jace had to admit, this wasn't as bad as she'd thought it would be. She'd honestly expected Helheim to be the worst place ever, but she seemed to be confusing Hel's domain with Satan's.

Instead of pits with fire, it looked like some parts of Iceland. There were mountains and waterfalls and thick forests.

There were also a lot of dead people and, except for the Carrion, none of them seemed to be warriors.

That's why the Vikings didn't want to come here. Not because they thought it would be filled with lakes of fire, but because there'd be no battles. No wild feasts with Odin and Thor. No joking around with Freyja. Or meeting past Clan sisters and brothers who would help prepare them for Ragnarok.

Jace didn't realize until this moment how much going to Asgard had meant to her. She didn't need to go right now, of course. But she'd thought once she'd become a Crow that was where she'd end up on her second death. In Asgard, in battles every day, feasting every night. Maybe sneaking in some reading time here and there.

Hel's hall, which reached high into the dark sky above, was made of white marble and bright silver.

The Carrion brought Jace and Ski into a large room with a big table; Hel was sitting at one end. And on her right sat a remarkably handsome warrior with a warm smile and gold armor.

"Baldur," Ski whispered, shocked at the sight of the famed god who had been killed due to Loki's machinations and was the reason Loki was bound somewhere with poison dripping on him until Ragnarok came.

Hel smiled at them. "Welcome! I have to say I've never had a Crow and a Protector here in my hall before. It's a nice change of pace, isn't it, Baldur?"

"You can't seriously be planning to keep them here, Hel."

"Why not? They came here of their own free will. Who am I to debate that point?"

"Just send them back before Tyr comes here looking for one of his boys. You know how he gets."

"Yes. The lectures. He does like to lecture. But . . . and this is the important part, they've kind of ruined my fun."

"You call Gullveig fun?" Jace had to ask.

"You didn't have fun?"

Jace pressed her head against Ski's arm and muttered, "I'm getting angry."

"I thought," Hel went on, oblivious, "that she was hilarious. Such fun, that one. But you naughty Crows . . . sending her into some random universe. That seems wrong."

Jace had to ask, "Are you planning on bringing her back?"

"It would be cruel to just leave her out there in that netherworld, victim to whatever might be lurking in the darkness. You know, kind of like what you've done to your friends?"

Jace felt a chill spread across the back of her neck, as if Death himself had placed his hand there. "What are you talking about?"

"You. You left your friends to the whim of that man."

"What man?"

"Your ex-husband, I think." She leaned in and loudly whispered, "You should have killed him when you had the chance."

Laughing, she relaxed in her throne-like chair. "Now come. Join me for—"

"Wait," Ski cut in. "What are you saying?"

"He's coming to kill them. Your false prophet and his pathetic followers. I thought he would play a much more important role down the line, but it looks as if he has other plans. To kill your little Crow friends."

Baldur shook his beautiful head. "Oh Hel."

Jace heard the sadness in the god's voice. The chastising. But he wasn't going to do anything, either. No one was going to do anything.

So her rage, it tore up her back and spread out through her body like a vicious sickness, and when she finally screamed—a scream so loud even the two gods in the room jumped—there was nothing, absolutely nothing Ski or anyone else could do to stop her.

Erin had managed to cry alone in a bathroom and then put eyedrops in to clear up the redness so that no one had any idea how much Jace's disappearance was gutting her. There had to be at least one of them who wasn't having an open nervous breakdown about this.

Even Rachel had been in her room crying for the last hour. Strange, since Jace had almost killed her when she'd punched her in the throat.

But if there was one thing Erin was sure about, it was that there was no way they were leaving their favorite antisocial girl to live the remainder of her existence in goddamn Helheim.

Erin came down the stairs, intent on heading back outside to again suggest to Chloe and Kera that they shouldn't be waiting around for the other Clans to come up with something and should just move on this now. All of them. Maybe even Crows in nearby states like Nevada, Arizona, Oregon, and Washington could join them. The whole fucking West Coast Crows if need be!

Erin was stepping into the foyer when she heard the light knock on the front door.

Frowning, she walked over and opened it.

A man she didn't recognize stood there dressed all in black.

"May I—" was the last thing Erin said before the bullet collided with her head.

Knowing they might recognize him—everyone knew who he was these days, and he was sure these vile women were no different—Braddock had sent one of his younger parishioners in first. Once the gun went off, he stepped out of the shadows and into the house.

The red-haired whore who had been shot lay crumpled on the floor. He stepped into the foyer and motioned to his people to get to work.

Armed with freshly purchased automatic weapons and the buried ammo the agents never found, his parishioners charged silently into the house and began the mass cleansing of so much evil.

Ski tried to grab Jace, but she'd already jumped on the table and, still screaming, she charged across it, right at a wide-eyed Hel.

Hel stood and demanded, "What do you think you're—"

Jace tackled the god like she was a linebacker for the NFL, both dropping out of sight on the other side of the table.

Ski ran over and saw that Jace was on top of Hel, punching her again and again. There was no blood, though. No sign that the blows were harming the god in any way.

Hel simply seemed too stunned to actually fight back.

The Carrion reached for Jace, but Ski pushed them back and then held out the Hel blade Jace had dropped when she'd tackled the god. A blade they hadn't bothered to take from her because they'd never thought either of them would dare use it.

He kept the Carrion at bay but mostly because they knew Jace wasn't hurting their god.

She wasn't hurting her . . . until she was.

Jace, in her rage, had grabbed hold of Hel's dwarven-made breastplate and begun pulling at it.

Shocked, Ski and Baldur watched Jace tear the thick metal from Hel's body. And, as it came away, it pulled part of Hel with it.

The goddess screeched in pain, and once Jace had the breastplate off, the stink of decay, disease, and pestilence rose up from the monster Loki had bred all those eons ago.

Ski dry-heaved, Baldur turned his head and put the side of his fist against his nose, and Jace just kept screaming.

Hel crossed her arms over her decaying chest and rolled to her side. That's when Ski realized she was . . . embarrassed.

Embarrassed about what she really was. How she really looked under that beautiful armor. Her true self.

But Jace didn't care. Actual blood began to pour from her red eyes, and her entire body vibrated, she was so lost in her rage.

Baldur grabbed Ski's forearm and yanked him close. "Get her out."

"Where?"

Baldur pressed his thumb against Ski's forehead, and Ski immediately saw the hidden way out of Helheim.

Ski stared up at the god. "If you knew . . . why didn't you . . . ?"

"I made an oath. As a god, I had to keep it. But you're human. What honor do you have?"

Ski opened his mouth to argue, but then said, "Good point. See ya!"

Ski grabbed Jace's hand and yanked her around the table. The Carrion were still there, ready to stop them, but with a wave of his hand, Baldur sent them flying.

"Go!" Baldur called after them. "Never stop running! They'll be coming for you!"

Once outside, Ski looked back, and he saw that Baldur was right—a legion of Carrion poured from Hel's hall to pursue them.

So he ran, with Jace right beside him, and he didn't look back again.

"Those are gunshots," Kera informed Chloe, Betty, and Yardley.

"Here? Are you sure?" Chloe asked.

"I was a Marine. I *know* gunshots when I hear them."

"I've been shot at," Betty tossed in. "A lot. Those are definitely gunshots."

"With me Yardley." Chloe motioned to Betty and Kera before unleashing her wings and heading to the roof entrance of the house.

Kera indicated for Betty to go around the side, and Kera went in through one of the sliding glass doors at the back.

The entire house was dark now. Someone had shut the electricity off.

Reaching down, Kera pulled her blades out of the holster attached to her ankle and eased her way through the furniture of the TV room and out into the hallway.

From the darkness, she watched two strangers meet in the middle of the hallway. One snarled, "I can't find anyone."

"That's impossible," the other said. "They were all—"

Annalisa dropped from above, landing behind one of the strangers. A woman. Annalisa took her blade and yanked it across the woman's neck.

The man raised his weapon and began firing, but Annalisa was already gone, disappearing into the darkness, waiting in the shadows.

A blade flew by Kera's head and slammed into the back of the man's neck. He dropped instantly, and a sister grabbed her blade and vanished.

Without turning around, Kera knew someone was standing behind her. And she knew it wasn't one of her sisters. Or even one of the Clan. She spun and caught the barrel of the machine gun aimed at her. She jerked it to the side, the palm of her hand burning when the bastard fired the weapon, heating up the metal.

Kera buried her blade in the man's neck and quickly yanked it out. She pulled the weapon from his dead hands and threw it at the man who'd just run into the room. It hit him in the face and he went down, bullets tearing across the ceiling.

She ran past him—slashing his throat as she passed—and out into the hallway.

More bullets came at her then, and all Kera had time to do was hit the deck.

Jace didn't realize she still had Hel's breastplate until one of the Carrion got close enough to grab it.

She yanked it from his hand, pulled back, and slapped it into him, knocking him down.

"Jace!" Ski yelled. "Come on!"

She'd followed him deep into some cavern, and she only assumed he knew where he was going.

Even stranger . . . her very rational thoughts. Because she knew she was still in a rage. She would be until she got back to the Bird House and checked in on her girls. Until she knew they were safe, no one else was.

And yet . . . she knew who Ski was. Understood she was trying to escape from Helheim. Knew that Baldur had helped them.

And there was only one explanation for her clear logic while in a rage—her grandmother.

When Nëna had slapped her that last time, she'd done something to her. To protect her, she'd said.

To protect her granddaughter.

Ski pointed to an opening in a crevice high up in the cavern. Extremely high. The pair began to work their way up using their hands and feet—Jace still determined to hold on to Hel's chest plate because, dammit, she'd earned it!—when Ski stopped and stared at her. It took her a moment, then they both rolled their eyes, unleashed their wings, and flew up to the crevice.

Ski looked over Jace's shoulder and suddenly grabbed her. "Think of where you want to be," he barked at her before shoving her inside the opening. She expected it to be a typical mystical doorway that would send her flipping through an unknowable ether into another realm.

That did not happen. Jace had to keep running. And this time she couldn't unleash her wings to fly anywhere, the space was too small.

As she kept going up, she could see loose dirt. That seemed strange because the loose dirt was in the ceiling of a cave, but she had a feeling it was her and Ski's exit.

But just as her fingers grazed the opening, a hand grabbed her ankle and yanked her back.

A hand grabbed hold of the back of Kera's neck and yanked her to her feet. She started to fight, but the pressure of a gun against her forehead kept her a little calmer.

It was a man, and he pushed her toward the double glass doors that led to the backyard.

"Where's Jacinda?" he asked.

"Believe it or not . . . in Hel."

The arm around her throat tightened. "You think that's funny?"

"You asked."

Once outside, he turned in a circle and yelled out, "Jacinda!"

"She's not here," Kera said again.

"Then where is she?"

Kera sighed. "I'm not saying it again."

He leaned in close and swore, "I am going to kill *all* of you."

"Do you realize that you're only alive because of Jace? Otherwise, the rest of us would have killed you a long time ago."

"Shut up!"

A low growl came from the trees, and Kera chuckled. "Oh man. You've done it now."

He turned, still holding on to her.

Brodie stood at the edge of the woods, her head down, teeth bared. He pointed the gun at her.

"I wouldn't draw down on her if I were you," Kera warned.

Before he could even pull the trigger, Brodie charged them.

The bullets hit the ground where she'd been running, but she was flying at them now, her wings unleashed, the metal slamming closed over her muzzle, protecting it.

He raised the weapon, aiming, but Kera grabbed his arm and twisted. Blood splattered across her face, and bone stuck out of his skin.

She took the gun from his limp fingers and stepped away. Brodie had leaped over them and tackled another man coming up from behind. She tore into that man's throat and started to drag him off into the woods.

"Do not drag him anywhere, Brodie Hawaii!" Kera ordered.

Stumbling back from her, the man she assumed was Jace's ex-husband held his destroyed arm against his body. He was now consumed by panic . . . and she knew for a fact that it wouldn't be going away any time soon . . .

The first body dropped from the sky and landed a few feet from Braddock. A few seconds later there was another. And then another.

Horrified, watching the bodies of his followers land on the ground all around him, Braddock started screaming.

"Shut up," Kera snapped; then she growled at Brodie who stood near one of the corpses, "Stop gnawing on that thing!"

The sliding door opened and Erin stomped out, blood pouring from her head and dripping down her nose.

She stormed up to Kera and said between clenched teeth, "If I get shot in the head *one more time!*"

"I'm surprised you're not shot in the head, like, every day." Kera frowned. "If you were shot in the head, shouldn't you be . . . you know . . . dead?"

"How many times do I have to explain this to you? You can't die the same way twice. You won't die if you get another knife to the heart and I can't die from a bullet to the head. Is that really so hard for you to grasp?" she barked, throwing the bullet she held at Braddock.

After the bodies of the cult members stopped hitting the ground, Kera's sister-Crows landed. They left their wings out, moving to surround the man who'd come here to kill them all because his ex-wife didn't want back into their shitty marriage.

He was on his knees and sobbing now. It wasn't pretty. He kept calling on God to help him, but Kera was pretty sure God had better things to do than deal with some needy douche bag.

"So?" Chloe asked as she petted Braddock on the head like a pet. "What do you want to do with him, War General?"

Kera cringed at the title, but she decided to deal with that later.

"Kill him," she finally said, and Chloe grabbed Braddock by the hair, snatching his head back and pressing her blade against his throat.

But before she could make the final stroke, the grass about fifty feet away exploded and Kera pushed past her sisters, Erin and the rest of their Strike Team right by her side. Blades out, they were ready for what might be coming at them next.

And what came first was a piece of metal. It took Kera a few seconds to realize that metal was actually armor. Really, really nice armor that smelled so bad, her eyes watered. Hands shoved the armor out of the hole and Jace quickly followed.

She'd just gotten onto firm ground when she abruptly stopped and kicked her leg back, hitting a Carrion in the face and sending him falling out of sight.

Still on her knees, Jace turned around and reached into the hole. A few seconds later, she was helping Ski out of the same pit, but he was struggling against the hands of several Carrion, the exposed flesh they were grabbing beginning to decay.

Chloe pointed at Rachel and several of her Strike Team. They ran over and helped Jace pull Ski out of the pit. Once he was out, he pushed the other Crows back.

The Carrion attempting to drag the pair back in rushed out of the pit, and Jace and Ski, using Hel blades, tore into them. Lopping off heads, releasing intestines, splitting spines.

Jace cut one Carrion right in half.

Her eyes were that berserker red, but she didn't focus on one victim until she was distracted by another, which was her usual berserker battle style. Instead she logically decimated anything that came near her or Ski until it stopped. And it did eventually stop. For now.

"We need this closed," Jace announced.

Chloe turned to Tessa. "Get the Maids on the phone, tell them about this pit, tell them we need it closed. Now."

"Got it."

Ski pulled Jace to him and kissed her forehead. They looked exhausted but surprisingly healthy. Holding hands, they walked toward the Crows, stopping to hand off their weapons to Rachel and her team, who took over watching the open pit until the Maids could close it down.

As Jace came closer, she blinked a few times, her gaze focusing on her ex-husband. But her rage didn't return, her eyes going back to their normal blue.

Kera didn't know what was going on with her friend, but she was loving it.

Once the pair reached them, Jace shook her head at Chloe. "He lives," she said, still panting.

"Are you nuts?" Erin snapped. "He came here to slaughter us."

"He's a false prophet. That's what Hel called him. A false prophet. She said he'd be of use. I think we're gonna have a use for someone like that. So he lives. For now."

"What are we supposed to do with him until then?"

"I'll take him," Annalisa offered, smiling a little. "He clearly needs proper treatment for his mental illness."

Jace pointed at the bodies of Braddock's followers. "You'll have to get rid of them, though."

"All right."

"And there's something else."

"What?"

"Hel. I think she's going to bring Gullveig back sooner than we were planning."

"And," Ski added, "Hel has *legions* of Carrion. Not just a few."

"That's . . . unfortunate," Chloe sighed.

Jace rested her head against Ski's arm. "We've got to find out how to kill her. But tomorrow."

"Even if Hel brings her back tonight," Ski said, "she'll be too weak to fight anyone for a little while. Once that pit is closed by the Maids, I think we can all get some sleep."

"Go on," Kera told her friend. "We can take care of everything down here."

"You sure?"

"I'm positive."

"Kera's been crying over you," Erin felt the need to add. "And crying. We were embarrassed for her."

"Again," Kera asked Erin, "how do you not get shot in the head every day?"

Jace and Ski headed toward the house. Lev bounded out of the trees and followed them, tripping over his own feet a few times before he made it inside.

"All right," Chloe said, clapping her hands together. "Let's get rid of these bodies first; then we'll call nine-one-one."

"I thought we were just going to bury him in some mental hospital somewhere?" Erin asked.

"The federal prosecutors will notice if he's gone even if they don't care about the cult members so much. Besides, having this idiot under Annalisa's government-sanctioned care means we can get immediate access to him when the time comes. Right, Annalisa?" Annalisa gave a horrifyingly cheery thumbs-up.

Chloe lowered her hands and twitched her fingers forward. "So let's get moving. We've got a lot to do in a little time. And how long do you think before the Maids can close that . . ."

Chloe's voice faded away and she looked at Kera, who turned to Betty, who smiled at Erin, who gave a really cruel laugh.

The Crows immediately got to work bringing bodies over to the Helheim pit so they could toss them in.

Even Brodie helped by dragging over a few.

As Kera bent down to roll one body on top of another so she could carry two at once, she saw Annalisa slowly approach Jace's sobbing ex-husband.

Kera had felt no pity for the man until she watched Annalisa crouch in front of Braddock, gently place two fingers under his chin to lift his head, and purr, "You and I are going to have *such* fun together."

CHAPTER THIRTY

Jace woke up swinging only to realize the only thing stalking her through the dark, winding caverns of Helheim was . . . Bear.

And she wasn't in Helheim. She was in her Bird House bedroom, with a very annoying Bear Ingolfsson silently gazing down at her.

Still exhausted and annoyed at the very sight of him, Jace snarled, "What? What do you want, Bear?"

He reared back a bit—he'd been so close to her when she woke up, she was sure she'd probably hit him with her swinging fists—and replied, "You have work to do."

"What?" She quickly glanced around, now worried she'd ended up in hell itself.

But nope. She was in her bedroom with Ski, safe and sound, both of them still in their battle clothes from the night before. They'd been too tired to do much more than drop facedown on the bed and immediately go to sleep.

So Bear being here? Irritating her at this moment? This was reality. Not a nightmare. A sad, annoying reality.

"To stop Gullveig from returning again," Bear pushed, refusing to be deterred. "The library is waiting for you."

"Do you know where we've been? What we've been through?"

"Yes. And now you're back. So it's time to get to work."

"I'm tired. And I've been through hell . . . and Helheim."

"But you have work to do."

"I'm *tired*."

"I don't think Gullveig will care."

"Go away, Bear," Jace warned him, lying back down and pressing her face against Ski's bicep. "Go away before I *make* you go away."

Jace closed her eyes and tried to go back to sleep, but she didn't hear anything. She didn't hear retreating footsteps or slamming doors. She heard nothing except the calm, steady breathing of a man she was now convinced had obsessive compulsive personality disorder.

She snuggled closer to Ski. "He's not leaving," she growled between clenched teeth.

"He won't," Ski replied into his pillow. "He'll stand there until Ragnarok comes."

"Make him go away."

"If I knew how, I'd have done it a long time ago." Ski paused, then asked, "And what's on my head?"

"The love of my life."

"I thought that was me."

"He was first. He'll be forever. But due to your choice of friends," she added, "I can't actually promise the same about you."

"It's not like I chose him. Clan members are family. You don't choose . . . the gods simply curse you with their presence."

"*Are you two getting up or not?*"

"No!" Jace barked at Bear.

"I can't," Ski muttered. "I'm trapped by a vile beast of undetermined origin."

"Get out!" Jace tried again. "Now!"

The bedroom door swung open and a clear-eyed, freshly showered Kera stood there, taking in the scene.

"What's going on?" she finally asked.

"He won't leave," Jace told her friend. "He's just standing there. Staring at us. Like a psychopath."

"You have work to do," Bear reminded Jace. Needlessly.

Kera quickly sized Bear up and said, "We really need your help downstairs, Bear."

The big Viking sighed. "I'm not stupid. You're not going to distract me."

"It's just that Rachel and her team are pulling the books we have in our library together to send over to the Protectors' house in case Jace needs them."

"So?"

"Sooo . . . Rachel's just tossing those books, willy-nilly into a box. Using her big, ham-hands. She actually said that books are stupid. And asked why we have so many."

Bear faced Kera. "What's wrong with her?"

"Everything. I just think it would be better if you go down there and help—"

The rest of Kera's words were cut off when Bear pushed her into the doorframe on his way out of the room to rescue the books.

"Excuse me," he muttered before disappearing into the hall-way.

Kera rubbed her shoulder. "Ow."

"Sorry about that," Ski mumbled into the pillow.

"No problem. I'll just let you guys get some sleep."

"Thanks." Jace relaxed against Ski and smiled . . .

Until the door opened again and Kera stepped back in. "Just so we're clear, we are on a bit of a time crunch here. I mean, everyone's pretty sure that Gullveig will be back sooner rather than later. So, you know, when you *do* get up, you'll need to jump right in. That's not a problem, right?"

"Nope."

"Great. Great. Thanks, hon."

The door closed, but a few seconds later opened again. "And just so you know . . . once you got home last night—and, man, am I glad you two are home safe and sound, I was so worried— I made a list of things you'll need to accomplish, pretty quickly. In fact, I went ahead and put up hooks in the kitchen down-stairs and placed clipboards on them that have lists of what certain people need to do, and your list is getting a bit long. I'm assuming that'll mean you'll need all the time you can get. Just wanted to give you a heads-up on that."

"Okay."

"Great." The door closed . . . then opened.

"Also, I typed up those lists on my computer, so I can e-mail the lists to you. That way, you'll have them on your phone or tablet or whatever."

"Gotcha."

The door closed. Opened.

"And so you understand where I'm coming from, with all that's happened, you've kind of become the point person on all this research stuff. We really can't get anything underway until you find out some answers in those books. But," she added, "you get some sleep first. Don't worry about anything."

"Excellent."

The door closed and opened.

"If you want—" Kera began, which was when Ski flipped over, and Lev fell back on the bed.

Jace reached out for her dog but Ski grabbed him first and holding Lev out in front of him, shoved the puppy at Kera.

"He's about to pee on me," Ski lied. "Could you take him outside while we get up?"

"Oh. Uh . . . okay. Sure."

"Great. Thanks."

He pushed the pair out of the room and closed the door, then stuck the high back chair from the corner under the knob.

Jace expected that Ski would return to bed, but instead, he opened her closet door and disappeared inside.

She sat up. "What are you doing?"

"I'm throwing some of your clothes into this duffel bag," he explained, haphazardly grabbing some T-shirts and a couple pairs of her jeans. "And I'm going to take them out of here." He went to her chest of drawers and pulled out bras and socks and panties, and quickly shoved them into the bag as well. He didn't even bother properly folding them. That didn't seem like

Ski's way. She sensed he was all about clothes folding, but not at this minute.

Then again, she could sense his desperation. "I will grab Bear and take him out of here," he went on. "You will, as soon as you can manage, meet me at my house. You will be moving in." He stopped and stared at her. "Because I can't do this."

"Do what?"

"Bear was just going to stand there. Quietly. And, every fifteen minutes, on the dot, he would ask, 'Are you up yet?' He's very similar to a snooze alarm and, if things aren't too urgent, I use him in that fashion. But this"—he waved the palm of his hand at the closed door—"this I can't do. If I hadn't shoved that animal into Kera's hands and pushed her out the door, she would have been in here over and over again, every few seconds or minutes, in no real order, with some new thought that had randomly flitted across her mind until—and I hate to say this—I would have been forced to kill her. And I am well aware that such an action would have led to the end of the peace treaty the Protectors have with the Crows and Ravens."

"Plus there would have been some moral issues surrounding her murder," Jace teased.

"Exactly, but it would have been necessary. Because I can't live this way. You can do it and that's admirable, but I can't."

He walked to the door, stopping to yank the high back chair out of the way, and opened it. Erin, who was about to knock from the other side, quickly pulled her fist back.

She smiled in greeting. It was one of her warm, friendly smiles. Not her plotting, evil smile. But the difference didn't seem to matter to Ski. He simply shook his head and said, "No, no, no, no." He looked back at Jace.

"I'll meet you at home," he told her, then picked Erin up by her shoulders, moved her into the room, and walked out.

Erin pointed at the open and empty doorway. "What just happened?"

Jace grinned. "He loves me and wants me to move in with him!"

"Oh." Her friend nodded, smiled. "Okay."

"Erin Amsel!" Chloe screamed from somewhere in the house. "Why is there a goat in my bedroom? *Eating my expensive sheets!*"

Erin's lips briefly twisted before she said, "I forgot about that goat." After a moment, she shrugged. "Still, it was a great party. Totally worth it."

After helping Bear out of an argument with Rachel and her strike team that he was surely going to lose, Ski quickly deduced that there were not a lot of books that they would need to bring back to the house with them. So they'd taken what looked important and got out.

Carrying two small stacks each—and the duffel bag filled with Jace's clothes over his shoulder—they walked into the Protector house and Ski happily sighed in relief.

The quiet. The wonderful, blissful quiet.

"I don't understand why they had so much romantic fiction," Bear complained as he came in behind Ski. "Who reads that stuff?"

"The Crows, apparently. And I saw just as many murder mystery novels as romances. Although I did see several books on Stalin and Genghis Khan." He stopped by the stairs and faced Bear. "I don't know about you, but I found it worrying that the only history books they have in that entire house that didn't involve Chloe as a writer or editor were books on two brutal dictators."

Gundo came down the stairs. "So glad you're back, brother!"

"So am I." Ski looked around. The whole house was busy with activity. The Protectors were working. Preparing for Gullveig's return. But they did it all *quietly*.

"And where's our beautiful Jace?" Gundo asked.

"With the very chatty Crows. She should be here soon."

"What does soon mean?"

Ski sighed at his friend. "Don't you start."

"Don't worry," Bear said, handing the books he held off to one of the younger brothers. "She'll be here."

"Are we sure?" Gundo asked. "Crows can get easily distracted."

Ski, unwilling to have this discussion yet again, began to walk away, until Borgsten came into the house with Jace's puppy in his hand.

"You had Borgsten steal that animal?" Ski demanded of Bear.

"There's no guaranty that she'll follow you here," Bear patiently explained. "But she will follow that dog."

"If the Crows find out you stole her dog—"

"Kera gave him to me herself," Borgsten replied, handing Lev off to Bear, who started to cuddle the little beast, until he realized they were all watching him. "That Marine has a mission now so, yeah—she's going to get annoying."

"True." Ski shrugged. "But she'll get the job done. That's what she does. She'll make a good war general for the Clans."

"You think it'll come to war?" Gundo asked.

"I don't know," Ski answered honestly. "But no matter what happens, our job is to make sure we're all ready. And we will be."

He turned toward the stairs, placed his hand on the banister. "Until then, though, you'd better secure that animal, Bear. Before Salka sees it."

"Too late." Bear walked off, Salka hanging from his ass, her claws dug in deep.

Ski's vindictive cat was not happy about the new presence in her house and she seemed to know exactly whose fault it was.

After a quick shower, Jace changed into jeans and a T-shirt, stuffed her feet into her black Converse sneakers, and ran down the stairs.

She knew she had to get to the Protector house before Bear made Ski's life hell.

She called out to Lev a few times, determined to feed him before she left.

"Borgsten has him and he's gone back to the Protectors' house," Kera said from the kitchen.

Jace met her in the hallway. "Why does Borgsten have my dog?"

"He said Bear knows you'll follow Lev."

"Your working with the Protectors is going to drive me crazy, isn't it?"

"Probably, but it won't last forever. Just until we get the answers we need." Kera took a step back. "What? What's wrong?"

"What if I can't find the answer?" Jace asked. She'd been thinking about that the entire time she was in the shower, panic beginning to sink into her bones. "What if I fail you? What if I fail everybody?"

"You're not in this alone," Kera reminded her. "You've got us. You've got the Protectors who, from what I've seen, adore you. You've got the Ravens. And the Maids are doing their own research. This is a group effort. So you can't fail anyone. Just do your best. I trust you."

Jace glanced down the hall when she heard knocking at the front door, but she knew one of her sisters would get it, so she stayed with the current conversation.

"You're going to make a really good war general, Kera." Her friend cringed and Jace quickly asked, "You're not going to vomit, are you?"

"Everyone needs to stop asking me that," Kera snapped. "I'm not running around, vomiting everywhere."

"Are you sure?"

Kera's eyes narrowed but at least she no longer appeared nauseated. Just then, arguing from the front door caught their attention.

Together they headed down the hall, and that's when Jace saw her, trying to push her way in, and screaming.

Screaming for Jace.

Kera immediately grabbed her arm to hold her back, but Jace shook her friend off and walked up to her mother, catching hold of the sweatshirt she wore and shoving her back out the front door.

"Jace—"

"Leave us!" she ordered her friends.

It took a moment, but they finally closed the door and Jace pushed her mother away from her.

"Go!"

"What did you do to him? *What did you do?*" her mother screamed.

"Your false prophet is no longer here."

"You killed him," she gasped.

"I thought he couldn't die."

Her mother swung at her face with an open hand but Jace easily caught it, held it. Bent the wrist just enough to cause her mother to wince.

"Now listen to me," Jace said softly, but firmly. "Your false prophet is no longer my problem. He's no longer your problem. He's now the government's problem. He's in a facility where he can no longer cause anyone any harm, including himself. You should be grateful. They'll take such good care of him."

"Where are the others?"

Jace gazed at her mother for a long moment before she asked, "What others?"

Her mother shook her head, lips a thin angry line. "You evil, evil child."

"I don't know what you're talking about. He was found on the street last night. Alone. Crazed and out of control. Talking about insane, unfathomable things. He was immediately taken into custody and he's safer now. He won't be hurting anyone ever again." Jace shrugged. "But if the rest of his congregation is missing, I really don't know what to tell you. I have no idea where they could be."

"You'll burn in hell for this. I'll tell—"

"You'll tell who what?" Jace asked. "That they came here to kill me last night? To kill my friends?"

Her mother's mouth slowly closed and she looked down at the ground, proving to Jace that her mother had known all along what Braddock and the others had come to do. To not only kill a group of strangers, but her own daughter.

She'd known, and she'd done absolutely nothing to stop it.

"You should go now," Jace told her, no longer feeling anything for this woman. "My friends don't like you being here. Bothering me."

Her mother lifted her gaze. First to Jace's face and then above her.

Her eyes widened and Jace knew her sister-Crows were perched on the roof, watching out for Jace. Protecting her.

"Go," Jace told her mother again. "And don't come back. I don't ever want to see you again."

Jace turned and walked to the door, but she stopped, and added because she felt she had to, "And just a last word of warning—if my grandmother suddenly comes looking for you, or one of my uncles . . . you better run."

Ski waited on the stairs until Jace came into the Protector house. She took one look at him and sighed.

"Kera called you, didn't she?"

"She was worried. Your mother came to the Bird House and she said you calmly handled it. No red eyes. No berserker rage. The Crows don't know how to deal with the calm you."

"What was there to get angry over?" She stepped in front of him, dropping her backpack at the base of the banister. "She can't touch me anymore. Not emotionally. Besides, she's lost without him. I almost feel bad for her. Almost."

Ski wrapped his arms around her waist, pulling her in close. He pressed his head against her belly and just held her. He felt her body unwind, her fingers stroking his hair.

"I heard from that Claw," he said, talking about Bystrom, the ATF agent and Claw of Ran member who'd been involved in the prosecution of Jace's ex.

"What did he want?"

"That Federal Prosecutor went to the hospital to see Brad-dock. After that, he wanted to come talk to you. Bystrom said he managed to put him off. I didn't ask how. I didn't care."

"That was very nice of Bystrom."

"Well, it was either that or Bystrom would have had to put the poor guy down if he found out too much. It's better he tells him whatever lie will keep him away."

"Agreed. Jennings is a really nice guy. He simply never understood what he was dealing with."

"Well, none of that matters now."

Ski turned his head, looked up at Jace. "I'm glad you're here."

"Me, too."

"And you'll stay?"

"Of course. You told me you loved me and you asked me to move in with you."

"Well, actually what I said was—"

Ski had to stop talking, completely distracted by a silent Bear suddenly walking around Jace, with Lev in his hands. He held the puppy out in front of him and, after moving the dog around Jace's head and face a few times, he began to slowly walk backward, the dog still held out in front of him.

"What . . . what's Bear doing?" Jace asked softly

Ski blew out a breath. "Luring you with your puppy."

"Why?"

"He wants you to get to work."

Jace opened her mouth a few times until she finally shrugged and stated, "Okay."

They walked toward the library together. Her arm around his waist, his around her shoulders.

"Will your brothers mind me living here now?"

"You? Not at all. Kera will also be welcome. Actually, everyone in your strike team will be welcome . . . except Erin. They will *not* be happy if Erin comes here."

"Oh, come on. Erin's not that bad."

"Erin's personal weapon is fire. There is no *way* that Marbjörn Ingolfsson, who comes from a very long line of Viking book lovers, is ever going to willingly allow that woman into our library around our precious books. Just not going to happen."

Jace suddenly slowed down, her gaze locked on a spot across the hall.

"What?" Ski asked. "What is it?"

She cringed. "I *think* I might have an idea. I'll need to research it first. Heavily. But . . . yeah. I might have an idea how we can end Gullveig for good."

"Please tell me it has nothing to do with Erin 'I live to be difficult' Amsel. Please. If you love me . . . *please.*"

"I do love you," Jace said sweetly. "But, sadly, I cannot make that promise."

"Yeah," Ski said as he kissed her on the forehead. "I was afraid of that."

EPILOGUE

The passenger door opened and Jace took Ski's hand. He helped her out of the car and she immediately smoothed down the skirt of her dress. It was a cute dress she'd borrowed from a sister-Crow, but she didn't usually wear clothes like this. But she knew tonight was special, and if she didn't want to get yelled at for "not even trying!" she had to put on the damn dress.

"Breathe," Ski told her.

"I'm breathing."

"Actually, you're growling. And your eyes are getting that red tinge."

He was right, of course, which was why he'd had to drag her here. She'd give anything to be in the Protector library doing her research. That's where she'd been for the last two weeks and she'd been loving it. Every day, she went to the library and immersed herself in books, looking to see if her still shaky—*and possibly ridiculous*—plan could possibly work to kill Gullveig. And every night she went to Danski Eriksen's bed.

It would all be perfect if she had any clue that she was on the right track. But Kera had been right. Jace wasn't in this alone. She had the Protectors and the Maids working right along with her and none of them were about to give up. They wouldn't.

"It'll be fine," Ski promised. "We brought baklava."

Jace laughed and leaned in, kissing him.

"Thank you for coming with me."

"Did you think I would miss this for the world?" He picked up the big box of baklava and headed to the small house.

Seeing it again, after all this time, nearly had Jace exploding into one of her panic attacks, but she fought it. Everything was going to be fine.

"There is one thing," Ski said, stopping in front of her.

"What?"

He winced a little, making Jace think something was horribly wrong until he said, "I love you."

"Oh." Jace nodded. "I know. You told me."

"Actually . . . I didn't."

"You did. I clearly remember you telling me you loved me."

"No. I said you drove me crazy. I meant, at the time, literally that you were driving me crazy."

"Whatever," she said, walking around him, "but that's not how I remember it."

She heard him laugh behind her and knew her face was bright red from embarrassment, but she ignored it and went to the door, ringing the bell.

A few seconds later, the door opened and Jace blinked, looked at a startled Ski, then back at the door.

"Bear? What are you doing here?"

"Your grandmother invited us. She said she wanted to get to know the men who are going to be around her granddaughter. Then she called me annoying and hung up the phone while I was still talking."

Ski sized up his brother Protector. "Did you ask her a lot of questions, Bear?"

"I guess some might say, but I thought they were very pertinent."

"Of course you did."

"She invited you guys," Jace asked, "but not my sister-Crows?"

"She called them whores she didn't want around her other grandchildren."

Jace turned to leave but Ski blocked her with his body.

"Anyway," Bear went on, clueless, "she has Norwegian beer." He held up the bottle, gazed at them both a moment more, then walked away.

Ski blew out a breath. "Why do I do what I do again?" he asked Jace. "Could you remind me?"

"To save the world and dole out Tyr-style justice."

"Right. You're right."

He started to open the screen door, but she caught his leather jacket, tugged. "And you love me?" At the moment, she needed to hear it again. Before she faced Nëna.

Ski smiled, pressed his forehead against hers. "And I love you."

They stood like that for a long time until Jace heard Nëna bark, "Do you two mind not doing whatever disgusting thing you're doing on my front porch so the neighbors don't think I have some whores living here? Thank you!"

Jace growled, and Ski immediately held up the pastry box. "Baklava. We have baklava. Even she can't resist that."

"You *seriously* do not know my grandmother."

Hel, comfortable once again in the new armor created by the dwarves of Asgard, opened the mystical doorway and reached in. She dug around until she felt Gullveig's energy.

She grabbed the god's hand and yanked her into Helheim.

And the snotty bitch was *still* screeching.

"Shut up!"

"*Where the fuck have you been?*"

Hel raised a finger. "We need to make something clear. I don't work for you, heifer. I'm doing you a favor."

"And why is that?"

"Before it was because I was bored. But now it's because the Crows have pissed me off."

"And for that you'll bring Ragnarok down on humanity's head?"

"You're doing it because you're pissed at your sister."

"That's different."

"And what do I care?" Hel asked. "Ragnarok or not, there'll always be a place for the dead and its queen. Now, are you in or out?"

"In." Her hands curled into fists. "*I want my necklace back!*"

"You and that necklace . . ."

Gullveig started to walk away, but her legs gave out and she went down on her knees.

Hel snapped her fingers at one of the Carrion and motioned to Gullveig.

"Go, sister," she soothed, patting her shoulder. "Get some rest. Get your strength back."

The Carrion helped the god up, and she studied Hel. "And then what?"

"And then . . . I think it's time for you to meet my father."

"I did meet your father. He tried to kill me, too!"

Exasperated, Hel snapped, "Okay, dude, you really need to let that go already!"